Stephen McCauley, described by the *New York Times* as 'the secret love child of Edith Wharton and Woody Allen' is the author of *True Enough, The Easy Way Out, The Man of the House* and most recently, *Alternatives to Sex*, all published by Granta Books. He lives in Cambridge, Massachusetts.

Praise for *The Object of My Affection*

'A very funny, exceptionally vivid novel . . . surely one of the best books about what it is like to be young in these crazy times' *New York Times Book Review*

'A wonderful romantic comedy' *New Yorker*

'The characters are vibrant and, ultimately, charming' *Publishers Weekly*

'McCauley has created some of the most appealing characters I've come across in years – quirky, flawed, irresistibly sad and funny . . . I can't think of better company than Stephen McCauley's *The Object of My Affection* . . . A novel that warms like a hug' *San Francisco Chronicle*

THE OBJECT OF
MY AFFECTION

Also by Stephen McCauley

Alternatives to Sex
The Easy Way Out
The Man of the House
True Enough

THE OBJECT OF MY AFFECTION

Stephen McCauley

Granta Books

London

With love
to my mother, Neil and Ken

Granta Publications, 2/3 Hanover Yard, Noel Road, London NI 8BE

First published in Great Britain by Granta Books 2004
This edition published by Granta Books 2006
First published in the US by Simon & Schuster, Inc.

Copyright © 1987 by Stephen McCauley

A CIP catalogue record for this book is available
from the British Library.

ISBN 13: 2-86207-901-4
ISBN 10: 1-86207-901-3

1 3 5 7 9 10 8 6 4 2

Printed and bound in Great Britain by
Bookmarque Ltd, Croydon, Surrey

The Object of My Affection

1

NINA and I had been living together in Brooklyn for over a year when she came home one afternoon, announced she was pregnant, tossed her briefcase to the floor and flopped down on the green vinyl sofa.

"As if I don't have enough problems with my weight already," she said, draping her feet across the worn arm rest.

I was sitting at the makeshift table on the opposite side of the room reading the World War I diaries of Siegfried Sassoon and eating a fried-egg sandwich. I had a Glenn Miller album on the record player, filling the room with bright music that suddenly sounded inappropriate. "String of Pearls," I think it was. Nina's lower lip was thrust out but I couldn't tell from her expression if she was genuinely upset, so I used my standard tactic for dealing with anything unexpected: I changed the subject. I pointed out a water stain on the hem of her dress and passed her half the sandwich.

"We're out of catsup," I apologized.

"I'm out of luck, Georgie," she said, biting into the toast and showering the floor with crumbs.

It was late in the afternoon on a hot, muggy August day, a sweltering day that felt like a concentration of all the fetid air of the summer. I'd pulled down the shades earlier and the apartment was dark, and except for the record player, the persistent sound of a radio blasting on a street corner somewhere, and the upstairs neighbors carrying on their daily dinnertime brawl with their teenage daughter—quiet. The place was no more or less cluttered and disorganized than usual, but somehow the combination of the heat and Nina's announcement made it seem squalid. Her soft blond hair was plastered to her forehead with sweat and her cheeks were flushed a Crayola shade of pink. She looked so young and cherubic, so completely unchanged from the way she always looked, that I, in my general ignorance of pregnancy, felt sure she must have been mistaken about her condition.

She sat up on the sofa and raked her hair off her forehead with her vermilion fingernails. The eight silver bracelets she always wore slid to her elbow with a clank. Perhaps she was suffering from heat exhaustion. The idea that someone who'd spent a good portion of her life crusading for reproductive rights should be unintentionally pregnant sounded crazy to me.

"Maybe I should drag out the air conditioner," I said, glancing toward the closet where it had been stashed since the day I moved in.

"Oh, please, George, let's not go through that routine. I'm not in the mood for it tonight."

I often brought up the subject of the air conditioner when the temperature climbed over eighty, but neither Nina nor I could ever face installing it, especially in the heat. Actually, the air conditioner was only one home improvement we never got around to making; the closet also contained an unassembled bookcase, towel racks for the bathroom, a new light fixture for the hallway, and a couple of extension cords for a twin lamp set we'd never bothered to plug in.

The record player shut off with a loud, springy clunk and the room vacuumed in the noises from every corner of the neighborhood. At least the brawl on the third floor was winding down. I attempted a furtive glance at my watch. My friend Timothy had arranged a blind date for me and I knew it was getting time to change my socks.

Nina caught me rotating my wrist in slow motion.

"Do you have plans for tonight, Georgie?"

"Of course not. When do I ever? Do you want to go out and get something to eat?"

"I don't suppose you feel like going dancing?"

"Dancing? *Dancing?*" I could see Nina in the middle of a dance floor clutching her abdomen in pain while a red strobe light flashed relentlessly on her face. I have a secret passion for tabloid stories of babies born in astrodomes in the middle of rock concerts, but I wasn't interested in being the midwife in attendance. "Maybe we could do something a little more sedentary?"

"I'm not about to go into labor if that's what you mean."

"I'm not that stupid, Nina. Disco or ballroom?" We did both styles, gracelessly.

"Something noisy, I think."

"Hetero or homo?" We alternated, depending on who wanted to be noticed and who wanted to be left alone.

"Homo," she said emphatically. "Definitely homo. We can go to that Mafia-run joint out in Bensonhurst."

She went to the window and lifted the plastic shade and a shaft of bright and hot sunlight cut across the linoleum floor and touched my foot. A strong smell of garlic and burnt coffee wafted in on the closest thing to a breeze I'd felt that day. There was a gentle stirring in the stale air of the room as she stared out past the fire escape to the crisscross of wires and laundry lines that hovered over the gardens and statuary in the backyards — tightly packed rows of tomato plants and lush grapevines, Saint Anthony statues and Virgin Mothers in pastel-blue niches.

At that time, Nina was working for subsistence-level wages at a walk-in women's center in Clinton Hill counseling battered wives and rape victims. She was a psychologist. Or, as she often reminded me, *almost* a psychologist. She'd completed her course work at a clinical psych program out on Long Island and had been attempting to finish her dissertation for over a year. Her subject was the relationship between class background and identification with feminist politics and the perceptions of self-blame in female victims of violent crime. I'm paraphrasing, but that was the gist of it. Among other things, Nina identified herself as a feminist. She was always trying to reconcile her politics with her psychoanalytic training, and I thought the whole conflict was limiting her ability to get anything done in either field. But I've never had faith in politics or psychology so I kept my mouth shut.

She let the shade drop against the sill and folded her arms across her chest as if she were suddenly chilled. "Oh, God," she sighed, "what are we going to do about this baby business?"

I cleared my throat and straightened up on my chair. Nina and I included each other in all of our daily travails, but in this case I was only too eager to assert my complete lack of responsibility. I've never had anything to do with the propagation of the race. "Have you told Howard yet?" I asked.

"Howard?" She started to laugh, a little hysterically, I thought. "Howard? Why on earth would I tell Howard?"

"Well," I said priggishly, "he is the father, isn't he?"

"'The father.' It sounds so serious. Of course he's 'the father,' George. Who else would be 'the father'? You'd know if there was another candidate for 'the father.' But I don't tell him everything. I don't tell him every move I make. I don't report to Howard each time I go shopping at Key Food. There are some things I don't tell *How*ard." She was ranting. "I just found out about this this afternoon and I haven't had time to think. I haven't had time to consider it at all. I certainly don't need Howard confusing the issue. You know how opinionated he is."

"I'd forgotten. Pretend I didn't mention it."

"Anyway," she said looking up shyly, "I wanted to tell you first."

She stood there surrounded by the yellow light leaking in around the edges of the shade and shrugged wearily, and I felt my chest collapse in on my lungs. I got up from behind the arrangement of packing crates and plywood we used as a table, nearly knocking the whole mess on the floor, and put my arms around her. I was obviously the kind of person who could offer a friend in need nothing more substantive than half a fried-egg sandwich.

"I'm sorry, Nina," I said. "I'm a jerk, that's all. You know what a jerk I am."

"Don't get on that track, Georgie."

"It's true. I'm an inconsiderate heel. I just thought of myself first as usual. I didn't even ask you how pregnant you are."

"Seven weeks," she said softly.

I don't know why, but I was cheered by that. It sounded so minor and insignificant. "But that's nothing. Seven weeks isn't bad at all."

"You're right," she said, laying her head on my shoulder, "seven weeks isn't bad at all."

• • •

WHEN I said I'd never had anything to do with the propagation of the race, I didn't mean to imply I'm not interested in children. Most of my waking hours were, in fact, spent with five-year-olds. I was teaching kindergarten at an Episcopalian-affiliated school in Manhattan which catered to the underprivileged children of the Upper East Side's young professional two-income families struggling to get by on a hundred and fifty thousand a year. It was a good teaching job—I was making close to twelve grand—but no one really considers teaching kindergarten a suitable job for a twenty-six-year-old male. People often responded with empathy and concern when I told them what I did for a living, as if they felt sorry for my lack of ambition, as if it weren't by choice that I spent my days mopping up vomit and blowing soap bubbles or whatever it was they imagined I did.

As Nina and I were getting dressed to go out dancing, I recounted the day's events for her. She was always interested in my students and their families due to her fascination with the pathological, and besides, she obviously needed some distraction to take her mind off her pregnancy. I told her that, among minor disasters like the school director testing the boiler at noon when the temperature outside was ninety (an exaggeration, but she loved stories that proved the ineptness of authority figures), Melissa, the woman I co-taught with, had gravely insulted one of our students when he quizzed her on the significance of the Feast of the Assumption.

"Feast of the Assumption?" Nina called from her room. "What kind of a question is that for a five-year-old to ask?"

"Well, his parents are breaking up. The father's Jewish and the mother's Catholic, and I think she's trying to convert the kid before the divorce goes through. He knows the religious holidays inside and out. Anyway, Melissa told him she couldn't keep track of all those martyrs ascending and descending as if they were on an escalator at Macy's. I think Clifford had a *crise de foi*. He was inconsolable. We had to call his mother to come pick him up."

"That's Melissa's fault," Nina shouted to me. "You don't think she's on drugs, do you?"

"Oh, no," I called back. "Melissa's too inconsistent to have a drug habit. Anyway she's usually very considerate of the kids. I think she was done in by the heat."

Nina wandered into my room looking dazed and vigorously beautiful. She was wearing a tight black skirt and an ancient peach-colored blouse made of deteriorating silk. Despite the fact that I'd seen her every day for over fourteen months, I'd never quite gotten over my amazement at how beautiful she was. There was a flawlessness to her features I found captivating at certain times and infuriating at others. I alternated between marveling at her and feeling she'd unfairly received more than her share of good looks. Her efforts at dressing up all her secondhand clothes to look as if they'd been designed expressly for her was another quirk that raised skeptical eyebrows among her political friends.

"What happened when the mother came in?" she asked, toying with a sash she'd tied around her waist.

"Another disaster. I think the woman's losing her mind. She started lecturing Melissa on the breakup of the American family, when she's the one getting divorced. Poor Melissa's not even married. Just because she has red hair she wears in a crew cut, parents think she's immoral. And the mother is in therapy, Nina. She's been in therapy for years now and she just gets crazier."

She ignored me and leaned toward the mirror over my bureau and examined her face. "Do I look like I'm falling apart?"

"Don't be silly," I said. "You look like a cross between a Polish peasant and a Scandinavian film star."

It was the combination of her delicate blond hair, her light blue eyes, her wide cheekbones, her excessive use of eye makeup, and her natural Infant of Prague complexion. Even the extra pounds she carried around looked great on her; they filled her out to a flawless voluptuousness you never see on those pale models who get paid a thousand dollars a day for refusing nourishment.

I put on a turquoise shirt I often tried on but had never had the bad taste or courage to wear out of the house. "Don't you think my face looks grotesquely florid in this color?" I asked.

"You're being ridiculous," she said, fastening and unfastening the top buttons of her blouse.

"Like an alcoholic's face." I took off the shirt and tossed it on the pile beside my bed. "I must have had a fever when I bought that thing."

She pulled the blouse out of her skirt and tied the ends together in a knot at her waist. "I thought you said Joley gave you that shirt."

Joley was the man through whom we'd met, a man I'd lived with for close to a year.

"You're right, Nina, he did. When you're right you're right, and you're right. I must have forgotten."

"I doubt it, George. That's my professional opinion."

I changed into a navy blue jersey with a hole under one arm and a pair of jeans which, like every pair of pants I own, were baggy in the rear end. Generally I look much better in dark colors than loud, cheerful ones; they blend with my coloring and my personality. From my mother I inherited brown eyes, pale skin, and heavy eyebrows that grow close together in the middle. From my father I inherited unmanagable black hair, a long, narrow nose, an absence of buttocks, and a tendency toward maudlin ruminations. I'm no one's idea of handsome, but in the right clothes and the right light I can look stylish in a disheveled, vulnerable sort of way. I think I'm most attractive to towering men with loud voices who like to throw their weight around. Just my type, in other words.

By the time Nina and I had finished dressing, we were overheated and exhausted. The sweat stains under the arms of her peach blouse looked like bruises. I went to the refrigerator and took out an open bottle of beer and a bowl of tomatoes our downstairs neighbor had brought up from her garden.

"Don't start eating or we'll never get out of here," she said as she came into the kitchen. She rummaged around the shelves, filled a bowl with Cheerios and powdered milk and ran it under the tap. "And listen, if Howard calls, tell him I'm not here. Tell him I went to the movies. You better say it was a double feature and I won't be in till late."

"He isn't going to let me off that easily, Nina. He'll quiz me for hours."

"I know, but I can't face talking to him tonight. You don't mind lying for me this once, do you?"

We took our snacks into the living room and spread out on the sofa. I actually don't like tomatoes very much, but, next to popcorn, they're the best excuse around for eating immoderate amounts of salt, which is my favorite food. My technique is to dunk the tomato into a little dish of Morton's and then eat it like an apple. Nina shuddered every time she saw me take a bite—as if her cereal and powdered milk was so appetizing. She was in the middle of a battered Pocket Book edition of a mystery novel from the fifties with a picture of a naked woman wrapped in a Mexican blanket on the front cover. "Four Gorgeous Gals," it promised, "And Each of Them Spelled TROUBLE." This was Nina's kind of book—cheap sexist thrillers people gave away at stoop sales or threw out with the newspaper. As she sat reading she'd occasionally laugh aloud, give a cry of outrage and toss the book across the room in disgust, then hurry to retrieve it and find her place. I went into a stupor against her shoulder, my blood pressure soaring from the salt.

At ten o'clock the phone rang. Nina didn't stir.

"I'll bet school was absolute hell today, George, with all this heat."

It was Howard. Howard never began a phone conversation with anything as mundane as "hello."

"It wasn't the best day," I said, "but at least it ended. How are you doing, Howie?"

"Me? Great, George. Well, not great, but, you know...fine. So school was really okay?" Howard was committed to the idea of men being involved in child care. He saw my job as a profoundly political act, a contribution to the future of American society. I loved him for his misguided faith in me. "Things are really fine?"

"Sure, Howie. You'd know otherwise."

"I guess you're right. Listen, George, I don't want to cut this off, but let me talk to the Butterbean, will you?"

"The Butterbean isn't in. She went out. She went to a movie. I don't think she'll be back for a while."

"Oh? What movie?"

"I don't remember. Something in the neighborhood, something

you've already seen. I'm sure you're the one who suggested she see it, that much I remember." Howard was so competitive he couldn't stand the thought of someone, Nina in particular, seeing a movie or reading a book or eating in a restaurant he himself hadn't experienced. He was happiest accompanying people to movies he'd already seen so he could sit and prod the person next to him and announce "a really great scene" that was about to come on. He was always dragging Nina and me to some restaurant he'd discovered a few days earlier only to despondently inform us the food wasn't as good as the last time he'd been there and the service had gone downhill already. "Listen, Howard, I have to go. I'm making pancakes and I don't want them to burn."

"Well wait, wait a minute. Hold on for just a minute." I heard a rustling of newspaper from the other end of the line and then the receiver banged to the floor. "Sorry, George. Okay, here we are ... wait ... it wasn't that new French movie about the mental institution, was it?"

"I don't think so. You know Nina hates to read subtitles."

"True, true, but maybe it's dubbed. I can call the theater."

"I really have to go, Howard. I can see the pancakes smoking right now. You know how they bubble and dry out and then they start to smoke?"

"Just one more second. Was it that new teenage science-fiction picture about the atomic cow?"

"Atomic cow? I doubt it."

"'Doubt it.' We'll check it off as a maybe. What kind of mood was she in? Maybe we can figure it out that way?"

Howard Lechter was a lawyer at a legal aid office in Manhattan who spent his days huddled over his desk writing criminal appeal briefs for juvenile delinquents. He took out his frustrated urge to badger a witness on the stand by cross-examining his friends in classic television courtroom style.

"I mean, if she was in a gay mood ... I'm sorry, George, I meant happy ... if she was in a happy mood she wouldn't go to that fifteen-hour German thing and if she was depressed ..." He was struck silent by the thought. Howard worshipped Nina. "Was she depressed? I wonder if she was depressed and that's why she went to the movies alone. She did go by herself, didn't she? Don't tell me if she didn't, it's none of my business. Maybe she's angry with me and that's why she's depressed. I wonder what I did this time to get her angry?"

When I finally got off the phone I put on one of Nina's Connie Francis albums and jazzed around on the living-room floor for a while to try and remind her of the reason we'd spent an hour getting dressed. It was useless: Four Gorgeous Gals had her rapt attention. I crumpled on the sofa with a *New Yorker* and read the ten thousandth installment of someone's Third World childhood. An hour later the phone rang again. This time it was my friend Timothy.

"Where the hell have you been, George? I just got a call from Rudy who's been standing in front of the Waverly for the past two hours waiting for you to show up."

"If he was worth meeting, Timothy, he would have met someone else by now. Look," I said, lowering my voice so Nina couldn't hear me, "I had an emergency at home and I couldn't go anywhere, much less to a movie with someone desperate enough to agree to a blind date."

"You're hopeless, George. I just want you to know that. I set up something nice for you, go out of my way to set up something nice for you, and you blow it off. You do everything possible to avoid having a social life."

"I don't have the wardrobe for a social life. It's not my fault."

"I just called to tell you you're hopeless."

AROUND one o'clock, Nina read the last page of her mystery, gave a final cry of indignation and threw the book across the room once and for all.

"I don't know why I bother," she said, remorse wrinkling her forehead. "Did you really have your heart set on dancing?"

"I'll get over it. You're too exhausted to go anywhere, Nina." It might have been my imagination, but her face looked suddenly careworn.

"I feel like a wreck. Motherhood is taking its toll on me already."

Motherhood!

"Just get some sleep and you'll be fine," I said. Someone in the history of the human race must have slept off a pregnancy.

She went off to her room where she'd no doubt collapse on her bed fully clothed until I banged on her door in the morning. Nina had an immunity to alarm clocks; she set hers every night and then slept through the racket in the morning. Fortunately I'm an insomniac, so it worked out all right.

Motherhood. The word had a new, ominously personal meaning that made it sound heavy and alive, a word of power and complexity and several more syllables than I'd realized.

I stretched out on the sofa with a pillow under my head and listened to the train groaning over a bridge two neighborhoods away. A romantic salsa melody poured in from one of the windows across the backyard. I felt myself getting melancholy, as if I'd drunk too much cheap brandy. I gladly would have drunk too much cheap brandy if we'd had any on hand. I shut off the light behind my head and closed my eyes, imagining myself in San Juan in a seedy hotel room with a ceiling fan that didn't work. The hot, humid air was a stew of misleading sounds.

Summer was beginning to linger on too long, making the trees and gardens look unhappily overgrown, even in Brooklyn. I always look forward to autumn and the relief of Eastern Standard Time and, lying on the sofa listening to the sounds of the night, I yearned for a change in the season, an end to the heat. Who knew what could happen in the heat? Who knew what the distant sirens forbode?

HOURS later I jolted awake to the sound of a car alarm blaring in the street. The sky outside the window was a sickly shade of orange, saturated with the city's electric lights and the glow of the approaching dawn. I'd been dreaming of a baby trapped in its crib, crying out for food, wailing in a hideous voice that now sounded suspiciously like the car alarm. My jersey was bunched up under my arms and I was sweating.

Motherhood!

My impulse was to get up and run down the stairs to the street and keep going. But I was too sunk in lassitude to even go to my bedroom. "You're being ridiculous, George," I mumbled aloud. I rummaged around on the floor until I found an unfinished crossword puzzle and a pencil. It's a myth that only organized people can find something when they need it. Joley was the most organized person I've ever met and he could never find a thing when he wanted it, a problem Nina and I never had.

I turned on the light behind me and wrestled with an incomprehensible list of crossword clues, trying to concentrate, trying to block out thoughts of Joley and motherhood and romantic salsas and city-bound trains passing fitfully in the distance, but the car alarm kept wailing in the street, crying out and reminding me of something I wanted to push out of my brain for the moment. There was nothing to do but stare out the window and wait for morning.

2

BEFORE I moved in with Nina fourteen months earlier I'd met her twice and been to Brooklyn only once. I should have thanked Robert Joley for introducing us, no matter how awkward the circumstances of the introduction. No relationship is perfect but the fact that my calamitously imperfect relationship with Joley led directly to Nina's door made up for an abundance of wrongs.

I was twenty-four when I met Joley. I'd just moved to New York to study for a master's in history at Columbia and was living on a loan-padded bank account in a large and filthy apartment in Washington Heights. The first time I saw him across the room at a student-faculty get-together I'm sure I turned away or dropped something; he had exactly the kind of intimidating good looks I found irresistible in my masochistic youth.

I'd like to pretend some powerful intellectual drive propelled me toward graduate school, but the truth is I'd been working for over a year at an inner city day-care center in Boston and was tired of my job and the city, which I'd lived in or around most of my life. I couldn't think of a better way to fund a move than with the assistance of government loans. And New York seemed the likeliest place to go because I was convinced everybody ended up there at some point in life anyway, and I figured I should get it out of the way while I still had the energy.

I went to the Columbia party dressed in a sharkskin suit I'd bought on the street on the Lower East Side, a paisley tie, and a pair of highly polished shoes I'd borrowed from a neighbor. The minute I walked into the plush lounge with its impressive view of Harlem, I realized how off base I was in choosing that outfit, not to mention that course for my life. The room was glutted with a crowd of casually dressed intellectuals devouring each other with condescending smiles. The conversations I overheard in my beeline for the bar revolved around academic journals I'd never read and a cast of celebrity historians the students were apparently on intimate terms with.

When a short, freckled woman standing behind me in the line for the bar asked me what I was studying, I was so intimidated I covered my name tag and quickly told her I wasn't a student. "I'm on the security staff," I said. "I was hired to make sure no one jumps out those windows over there. There's a very high suicide rate in this department."

She pushed her glasses against her freckles and dryly said, "Oh, *really?* That's interesting."

"Yes, it's the constant contact with the tragedy of human history—one mistake following the next and no one learning a damned thing from any of it."

"Well, I'll be sure to call you over if I get the urge to jump."

I quickly made my way to a remote corner with two vodka and tonics and tried to look bored or inconspicuous. I'd finished one drink and was chomping on the ice cubes when I spotted Joley. He was talking to another teacher, gesticulating dramatically and tossing back his head with humorless laughter. He was just tall enough to stand above most of the people in the room without looking towering and mutant. He had thick silky black hair and a carefully shaggy romantic beard. His best features, however, were his emerald-green eyes which, even across the room, blazed with the kind of fierce intensity I usually associate with the eyes of religious fanatics and mass murderers. He caught me staring at him and stared back in an amused, relaxed way. Here, I thought, was a man who knew how to accept a compliment.

Eventually he made his way to my corner, read my name tag and stuck out his hand.

"George Mullen? How do you do? I'm Robert Joley. I'm your adviser this year. I was hoping I'd see you here. You never know who you'll get a chance to meet at these damned things." He said "damned" the way someone would say "nuisance" to describe a five-million-dollar inheritance.

I mumbled a barely audible hello and started on my second vodka and tonic.

"Actually, George, I just finished reading through your transcript this afternoon. Now let me see if I've got this right——" He put a hand to his forehead with staged precision. "You've recently moved here from Boston. Correct?"

"About a month ago," I said.

"Oh, I do love Boston," he said. "It's so much more civilized than New York. I'd move to Boston in a minute if I had the opportunity."

It was the kind of comment I was always hearing from people who'd sooner have a kidney removed than leave Manhattan. I couldn't tell from Joley's accent if he was a born New Yorker. His voice was curiously flat and toneless, as if he'd had speech lessons or was an anchorman on network news.

"Boston's pretty," I said, "but New York is much more exciting." I'd found nothing exciting in the filth and confusion of those parts of the city I'd been able to afford to visit in the past month. The subway, for example.

"Everything's exciting at a certain age," he said magnanimously.

I was curious to know what age that was but I didn't ask. I tugged at my hideous tie and the sleeves of my suit jacket to try and appear a bit more at ease.

"Now, I don't believe I know specifically what it is you'll be studying, George."

As a matter of fact, neither did I. I was interested in history primarily because I enjoy a good story but I hadn't focused on a particular period or topic. I wasn't, however, about to tell this to my adviser and make a bad impression right off. "Lately," I said, "I've been reading a lot on the unreformed public schools of Victorian England." I'd just read a review of a book on Eton in the Sunday *Times*. "I think I'm becoming obsessed with the subject. It has me enthralled."

"Oh, fantastic, George. I happen to know quite a bit about that. Fascinating." He stepped in closer to me and said, in a low voice, "In *Tom Jones*, Fielding calls the public schools 'the nurseries of all vice and immorality.'"

"I didn't know that," I said. He'd quoted mellifluously, and his breath, which smelled faintly of something antiseptic, washed against my neck, but the quote was from *Joseph Andrews*, not *Tom Jones.* "I'll have to look it up."

"Why bother looking it up? I just told you." He smiled at his generosity and said, "I like your tie."

"I like your beard," I said.

The minute the words were out of my mouth I started praying for an earthquake. One of his colleagues called him off to the other side of the room and I rushed for another pair of drinks. After an hour of solitude, riveted to the floor in my desolate corner, I made a contract with myself: I could leave the party if, and only if, I introduced myself to one person. I'd often made contracts with the kids at the day-care center—they could play at the sink if they stopped beating up on their friends, that kind of thing—and the tactic seemed appropriate in this case.

I picked out a man standing by the window dressed in a Lacoste shirt and cordovan loafers who seemed compatible with my sexual preference if nothing else. I went and stood next to him for a minute or two and then said in a drunken, conspiratorial whisper, "So, do you think we're the only two in the room?"

He turned his face toward me so slowly I thought for a minute he might have a neurobiological disorder. "The only two *what*, may I ask?" he said.

"I'm sorry," I said. "I thought you were Irish. It was just a guess, a hunch, if you know what I mean. Great to meet you."

My peers were leaving in small chatty groups, most accompanied by a doddering teacher holding court. I walked out of the lounge thinking I had no choice but to admit defeat and quit school immediately, before the first day began.

IN fact, I stayed for almost six months before I dropped out. I even attended most of my classes. These were a randomly chosen sampling of lectures and seminars taught by professors who seemed bored to their immobile lower jaws from constantly reliving the past. To my own surprise I developed an active interest in the Victorian public schools. I read everything I could uncover on the subject and wrote one brilliant paper on Melly's masterful and misleadingly titled work *The Experiences of a Fag*. Well, I thought it was brilliant anyway.

I also managed to recoup some of the social losses I'd suffered with my fellow students at the get-together party, mostly by limiting my conversation outside of classes to the one subject that threatened no one—third-rate contemporary American movies. Of course, even then I was careful never to mention a film with any historical content lest someone perk up with an analysis of the liberties the director had taken with the material. The neurobiologically disordered person I'd accosted at the party turned out to be as I'd suspected. He was also Irish. For a few weeks we carried on a despairingly pointless affair. Cameron (his chosen, not given, name) had two interests in life: one was to attempt to prove the efficacy of conciliatory politics in social movements throughout American history, and the other was to suppress his homosexual impulses and marry his mother's best friend's daughter back in Chillicothe, Missouri. Unfortunately I couldn't talk him out of either concern.

Although I wasn't miserable, by February I realized I didn't have the intellectual curiosity necessary to sustain years of research and study, and I sank into a feeling of bored purposelessness.

There was also something in the privilege and status of being a student that I feared was eating away at my character. No one who can choose to sleep until noon every day has ever developed a strong moral fiber. I figured I'd be better off working at a paying job than falling asleep in the overheated classrooms and dimly lit libraries of Columbia. I started to read the notices on the billboards around campus, and my attendance at classes lapsed. In other words, I chose to sleep until noon most days.

The problem in finding a job was that I wasn't trained in much of anything besides day-care, I lacked even the most rudimentary office skills, and I wasn't yet desperate enough to sign on with a fast-food chain.

Then, after weeks of fruitless, halfhearted looking, my escape route came unexpectedly while I was studying at a table in the Law School library and was roused from my stupor by two lawyers-to-be with loud, courtroom voices. One woman—a humanities professor going back for the big-money degree, I later found out—was complaining to her friend that on top of exams coming up and her personal life falling apart, a co-teacher at her daughter's kindergarten had just quit his job, giving the director of the school only five days notice.

"Poor Mr. Simmons is frantic," she said. "You can imagine how hard it is to find a decent replacement on such short notice."

Her friend, a young woman with seven gold studs poked through her left ear, said, "What's the big deal? Saint Michael's is a private school. They can get teachers at the drop of a hat, I'm sure."

"Not male kindergarten teachers. You can't find good male kindergarten teachers that easily."

"Yeah, maybe not. I wonder what kind of man would want a job like that?"

The kind of man who was sitting across from them, hanging on every word. In Boston I'd worked with a Rainbow Coalition of kids of unwed mothers in an afternoon program, and technically I hadn't "taught" at all. Still, I figured I could bridge the gaps easily enough if I acted fast.

I called the woman I'd worked for at the day-care center and asked her to write a glowing, vague letter of recommendation. This, along with a beefed-up and equally vague résumé, I sent to Mr. Simmons himself. A few days later his secretary called me to set up an interview.

I went to the school wearing a tweed sport jacket, new blue jeans and a slightly frayed white shirt—clothes I hoped would announce an attention to personal hygiene but a willingness to get dirtied with poster paints.

Mr. Simmons was a tall man in his mid-forties with gray hair and a kindly, confused manner. He had an elongated face, big round eyes, big white teeth, teacup-handle ears, and a shine of hopefulness on his forehead. He offered me a seat as if it were a one-way ticket to eternal youth and then exhausted himself talking about the school and the students and the parents and the salary scale. He acted as if I were interviewing him. By the time he got around to asking me questions he was visibly worn down.

"So, Mr. Mullen, you've been studying education at Columbia."

"Yes, that's right." In a way it was.

"Wonderful school, Columbia. We've had some wonderful teachers come here from Columbia. I taught a few courses there myself,

oh, three or five years ago. Gosh! What a bright bunch. Did you
have many classes with Ellen Gristley?"

"The name's familiar."

"She's a wonderful person. A wonderful person and a real teacher's teacher. And a great lady, too."

"That's what I've heard."

"You've done some interesting work with children, George. I'll
confess I hadn't heard of the school you taught at in Boston, but
I called Miss Ramirez and had a very nice chat with her. Sunshine,
is that her name?"

"Sun*flower*."

"Sun*flower*. I had a little trouble understanding her accent, but
I think I got most of what she said."

Two days later I went back to meet with a panel of four parents.
It was a lunch-hour meeting and all of them sat at the edge of their
seats, turning back the cuffs of their suit jackets to check the time.
What concerned them most was the reputation of the kindergarten,
which would help their kids get into Brown twelve years down the
road, and as the reputation was already well established, they had
very little to ask me.

Mr. Simmons called me the next day to offer me a job.

I didn't tell Joley, or Robert, as I called him then, I was dropping
out until I approached him with a mountain of papers he had to
sign to finalize the move. Aside from our initial, slightly flirtatious
meeting, our relationship was detached and professional and boring. I went to his office once or twice a month and babbled about
my classes, the weather, and the Etonian experiences of Mrs.
Gaskell's son, trying not to stare too longingly into his eyes. Joley
would smile and nod in his handsome and smug way and ask
questions, mostly about his colleagues.

"What about Dr. Peters?" he'd ask. "Isn't he a fantastic lecturer?
I hear he's a fantastic lecturer."

"He certainly has a presence."

"Right, but is he . . . would you say he's exceptional?"

"He's exceptionally fantastic."

I wasn't fully convinced Dr. Peters was still ambulatory let alone capable of delivering a fantastic lecture, but I was eager to agree with anything Joley said. A good deal later I learned his questions were asked in the hopes I'd tell him his colleagues were a bunch of incompetents. I was always too afraid of looking like a groupie to attend any of Joley's classes myself, but the consensus around the department regarding his classroom performance was that he was one of the best lecturers in the school.

"He's incredible," one of my school chums said. "You should see him in front of a room of undergrads—he has them breathing in unison. His lectures are the perfect combination of academics and gossip. From the looks on their faces, you'd think they were watching 'Entertainment Tonight.'"

Joley seemed genuinely upset when he found out I was leaving, as if he himself were to blame. I was really touched by his reaction. He signed all the papers and then said softly, "I don't suppose you'd let me try to talk you into tearing these up, would you?"

"Please don't," I said. "It took me a week to fill them out. Anyway, Robert, I've been thinking this over for some time now. This isn't an impulsive move. I never make impulsive moves."

"You sound resolute."

"I am."

I wasn't. He could have talked me out of it.

He got up from behind his desk and stood in front of a window overlooking Amsterdam Avenue, starting contemplatively at the endless stream of traffic. Of course, he might have been looking at his reflection in the pane. "What will you do now, George?" he said, with a touch of melodrama in his voice.

"I'll be spending my days with five-year-olds. I have a job teaching kindergarten across town."

"Kindergarten?" he said with alarm. "Oh, you did that in Boston, didn't you? I have a good mind for certain details."

"You do. I'm flattered."

"You must be very good with children. I imagine you to be kind and patient."

"The truth is," I said, "I'm a glutton for unqualified affection."

"We won't be seeing much of each other anymore."

"I'll drop by," I said, knowing I never would.

"Is that a promise?"

"Scout's honor."

He stood in the doorway and watched me walk down the corridor. My winter boots squeaked mercilessly on the polished floor and I felt I was walking for miles.

"Hey, George," he called to me. "Don't forget: Scout's honor."

I held up my hand in a mockery of some signal I'd seen a uniformed boy use in a movie, turned the corner and walked down the stairs, fully expecting never to see him again.

I didn't regret dropping out of Columbia, even when the kindergarten was plagued by an epidemic of head lice that lasted almost a month. (The persistence of the problem was later traced to one mother, a celebrity etiquette columnist, who refused to shampoo her child's hair with the necessary chemicals, believing he was too well brought up to contract head lice.) I made the transition from day-care worker to teacher pretty easily. This was partially because I have an abiding respect for kids—the most important qualification for the job in the end—and partially because my co-worker, a woman named Tundra, was pathologically competent and helped smooth over my rough spots. Tundra was a round, bellicose hippie with one of those infamous bedspread wardrobes: long skirts, short dresses, wide floppy pants all cut from the same paisley-on-beige cloth, giving her the appearance of a walking sofa bed. She lashed into me with such fury at every mistake I made that I learned quickly, spurred on by terror. We spent long hours going over curriculum plans, counting rhymes, coordination games and the life cycle of the monarch butterfly. Later she had a nervous breakdown and quit her job without notice, leaving the door open for Melissa, the crew-cut redhead.

SOCIALLY, however, I was far more adrift in Manhattan. Meeting people has never been my forte, and, frankly, I wasn't exactly a stellar attraction in a city with as many aspiring models as failed actors. Several years earlier I'd sought out anonymous encounters at places like the baths where social graces and an expensive wardrobe were entirely beside the point, but by the time I got to

New York the baths were so closely linked in my mind with fatal disease that on the rare occasion I did go, out of loneliness and frustration, I was careful to never do anything with anyone I couldn't as easily have done at home by myself—let alone attempt conversation.

It was at the baths that I met Joley again. It was an early spring night and the place was quiet and relatively uncrowded. In three hours I'd taken two saunas, four showers and watched an educational film on sexual risk reduction in a TV lounge where they'd formerly shown porno tapes. I decided enough was enough, made my usual vow to never return again, and headed for the locker room. I was walking down a dim corridor, my mind on an argument Tundra and I had had earlier in the day over who would bring in storybooks the following week, when I took a bad step in the ridiculous zoris I was wearing and tumbled forward. I reached out my arm to try and get my balance and slammed into the person who was walking in front of me.

He fell like a domino.

"I'm sorry," I said, "I'm really sorry. I tripped over something. My feet, I think. I'm a real oaf. I shouldn't even be allowed out in public."

The person I'd knocked down pushed himself upright and said in a familiar voice, "George Mullen?"

I peered into the darkness. "Oh, Robert, hi," I said in a voice that might have been appropriate for greeting a friend spotted across the lobby during intermission at Carnegie Hall. "I'm a real dope. I was walking along here and I spontaneously . . . tripped. It's these shoes. I got them at one of those eighty-eight-cent stores. . . ."

"I heard all that, George. What are you doing here?"

"Well, nothing really. Just looking. Honestly." I helped him to his feet. He appeared a little dazed. "You didn't get hurt, did you?"

"No, of course not. I'm just surprised to see you. I'm pleased to see you, George. I haven't been here in over a year and I was walking past and I felt an urge to come in, for old times' sake. Well, just to look, as you say. Anyway, I certainly didn't expect to bump into someone I knew from school."

His damp beard shone in the faint light and his eyes were particularly bright. Wrapped in a short white towel he looked considerably less smug and unapproachable than he'd looked behind the desk in his office. He kept shifting his weight from one foot to the other, crossing and uncrossing his arms.

"I'm sorry I haven't dropped by to see you, Robert," I said calmly. My brain had obviously kicked in with some heavy endorphin production. "I keep meaning to drop by but I never get a chance. To drop by."

"You could call. That wouldn't take too much time. You know, for about a month after you left school, I kept hoping you'd call or visit."

"You did?"

"Oh, yes. Then—" he shrugged and folded his arms across his chest—"then I figured you just wanted to forget everything about school."

"Well, almost everything."

"Are you getting lots of unqualified affection at kindergarten?"

"I'm getting some. I can never get enough. I think it's a sign of insecurity."

"George," he interrupted me, "there's something I want to tell you, something I've wanted to tell you for a while."

I clammed up quickly.

"I think you're adorable, George. I've thought you were adorable from the time I met you at that damned party."

"No," I said, "don't be ridiculous."

"I'm not being ridiculous." He unfolded his arms and took a step in toward me and then stopped cold as if he'd suddenly turned shy.

I decided to take a chance. I put my hands on his narrow hips and kissed his mouth hard, and then we walked to the locker room together like old friends and left the place in silence.

THE first time I entered Joley's apartment I was stunned by its cleanliness. I've never been a fan of squalor (although I've lived in it most of my adult life) but I do feel some dirt and clutter is a sign of depth of character. It was inconceivable to me Joley could have accumulated so few unnecessary objects in the ten years he'd been living there. The furniture looked brand-new and was all coordinated as if it had been bought in a single day from an inexpensive department store.

"That's a beautiful sofa," I said, pointing to a low beige piece of furniture I was sure I'd never feel clean enough to sit on.

Joley arranged one of the toss pillows meticulously. "It is nice, isn't it?"

The apartment was a solid two-bedroom off Riverside Drive he'd been renting for ten years, since he moved to New York with his fiancée, a woman he'd met at Berkeley. He was finishing his degree then and trying to come to terms with the fact that he was infatuated with his fiancée's younger brother.

"Bernice and I were seeing the same shrink — separately," he told me over dinner one night. "She'd go in and complain I wouldn't make love to her and I'd chronicle my obsession with her brother. When we finally started talking to each other instead of the shrink, we turned all our anger on him and became great friends."

Joley never discussed his family with me or even mentioned where he was from. In my mind, his past had the same generic flatness as his accent and the furnishings in his apartment. Whenever I asked him about his parents or siblings he gave a vague answer and quickly changed the subject. "Think of me as a New Yorker," he'd say. "Fundamentally I'm a New Yorker. We're all New Yorkers, fundamentally. What happened in kindergarten today?" I later found out, after much prodding and insisting, that he'd grown up in surroundings he considered humiliatingly ordinary: a gray ranch house that looked exactly like hundreds of others in the middle of a middle-middle-class suburban housing project outside of Cleveland called Lawnview Hills. His parents were involved in some sort of pyramid-sales business, pushing cleaning products and vitamins.

He told me he was very close to his family, but the only time I heard him lose his cool completely was the afternoon when I walked into the apartment and found him fighting on the phone with his mother. "I told you I'm fine, Mother," he shouted. "Everything is fine. Fine fine fine. No I'm not dating anyone. Because no one dates in New York, Mother. Maybe people still date in Lawnview, but no one dates in New York."

THE one aspect of the reasonably passionate early days of our relationship which I found unsatisfactory was that we never once spent an entire night sleeping together. Joley always found excuses for getting me out of his apartment by midnight or for leaving mine (on those rare occasions he agreed to visit my Washington Heights hovel) as midnight approached. I had a number of suspicions as to why he didn't want to spend a night with me, most of them revolving around a third person, but I never said anything until one night in June.

We'd spent most of that Friday evening sprawled on Joley's bed and by two-thirty in the morning were sleepily lying in the refuse of our debauchery. As it was long past the midnight curfew, I assumed we'd at last be spending the night together and had drifted into semiconsciousness.

"It's too late for you to take a subway home, George," Joley announced suddenly, rousing me.

"I've done it before," I said, always eager to prove my self-lessness. "I've taken it later than this, too."

"No, it's too late and you're too tired."

"I like the subway, Joley, you know that."

"No subway tonight. I'm calling you a cab."

I propped myself up on my elbows. "A cab?"

"You know, George, those yellow things with the lights on top?"

"Yeah, I know," I said. "I've seen you get into one a few times." I rolled over his body and sat up on the edge of the mattress. "I'd rather take the subway." I pulled on my pants. "Maybe I'll walk home. It's a nice night. Too bad I wasted most of it cooped up in here."

He sat up in bed completely baffled. "What's with you? If you want to take the subway, take the subway. I'm sorry I mentioned the cab."

"Sure," I said under my breath, "I'll take the subway. At two-thirty in the morning I'll take the subway to Washington Heights."

"Then take a cab," he shouted. "I'm paying!"

"You don't have to *pay* me to get out of here, Joley. I'll gladly leave for nothing."

"Well, don't act as if I'm throwing you out, I just offered to call a cab, that's all."

"Look," I said, "maybe it would be more honest if you did throw me out. It comes to the same thing in the end and it's been coming to the same thing in the end for two months now." He was sitting on the bed fumbling with his pants. I saw my chance for an indignant exit. "Thanks for a nice dinner," I said. "I'll drop by your office sometime. Scout's honor."

I stormed out of his room and began to undo the locks on the front door.

"George, wait a minute. You must realize I don't want you to leave."

"I'd have to be a moron not to," I said in a sarcastic tone I'd picked up from my mother. I walked out into the hall and pushed the button for the elevator.

"Please, George," he said from the doorway.

I turned around. He was standing there with a hurt, pathetic look on his face, trying to buckle his belt. It was an expression I hadn't seen before and I gave in to it.

"What is it, Joley?" I asked. "What's the matter? You can tell me."

He put his arm around me and drew me back into the apartment. He carefully arranged the toss pillows on the beige sofa and pulled me down next to him.

He told me that since he'd left his fiancée ten years earlier he'd never slept in the same bed with another person. He'd tried dozens of times, but he had some kind of psychological block.

"It's horrible," he said. "I can't sleep. I start to sweat and get itchy. Sometimes I break out in hives. There's nothing I can do about it."

I was mortified to think Joley would turn into a sweating itchy mess merely by spending a night in the same bed with me.

"I even have trouble sleeping alone," he said. "I have to sleep with the hummer going."

"The hummer?"

We went into his bedroom and he pulled a perforated object the size and shape of a small hatbox from beneath the bed. He plugged it into the wall. "Listen," he said.

The thing started to make a soft, whirring sound.

"Sounds like someone left a vacuum cleaner on in the closet," I said. "That helps you sleep?"

"It neutralizes all the noise in the room. It's very soothing."

From his expression he could have been listening to a symphony. Still, his look was so odd and childlike, I was charmed. I suppose the whole truth is that I was enamored of him and thoroughly convinced that everything he did was correct and intelligent and mature and sophisticated, and I would have accepted anything short of his sleeping in a coffin. I might have accepted that, too, come to think of it.

I spent that night in Joley's extra bedroom, sleeping fitfully. Once I got up and stood outside his door listening to the whirring of the hummer and his snoring. I toyed with the idea of quietly going in and lying beside him, but I decided it would be an unforgivable breach of trust. It was the first of many mistakes I made in the direction of self-restraint.

GRADUALLY my belongings drifted down from Washington Heights to the spare bedroom at Joley's until, after a few months, I hesitantly suggested we rent a van and finish the job off. Joley hesitantly agreed. He supervised the move to make sure I didn't bring too much clutter into his apartment and watched over me like a hawk.

"What are you doing with this old record player?" he asked, referring to the Webcor Holiday I'd been given on my eighth birthday and had been using ever since. "I have a great stereo, George. You don't need this thing. It looks like a suitcase, not a record player."

"I'm used to the way my records sound with this needle," I said.

"While we're on the subject of records, why not dump them, too. They're all scratched and ancient. I've got a great collection at the apartment."

Joley had a huge library of Deutsche Grammophon albums which were arranged on his shelves according to musical period and composer. I refused to go near his stereo. Anyway, our taste in music was widely different. Since my early teens I'd had a passion for big-band arrangements of swing tunes, female singers and vocal groups from the thirties, and the romantic crooners of the forties. I had an almost complete collection of the recordings of Martha, Vet, and Connee Boswell, something rare indeed. Joley was unimpressed.

"Clutter, George," he said as I loaded the last of it into the van. "Just clutter and probably filled with roach eggs, too."

We stuffed it all into the extra bedroom in towering stacks.

To finalize the move to Joley's I bought a change-of-address card and sent it to my mother. Like me, my mother has a passion for receiving mail. When I was a child, the two of us went through all the magazines that came to the house and sent away for every catalog, brochure, and 21-day free-trial product we saw. Usually we ended up tossing the junk out; finding it in the mailbox was the satisfying part. The card I sent her had a picture on the front of three mice loading a truck with dilapidated furniture. I thought it was apt. On the inside I wrote, "Hope you and Dad are fine," and my address and phone number. My mother and I have an unspoken agreement never to discuss the details of my personal life, though a part of me longs to share them with her and I'm sure a part of her wants to know. It was simply easier for both of us to remain discreet, diffident, and unsatisfied.

A week and a half after I sent it off, my mother called me. She sounded breathless. She always sounded breathless on the phone, as if she'd run three miles to pick up the receiver, even if it was she who'd placed the call.

"George? Is George Mullen there?"

"Ma, hi, it's me."

"I didn't recognize your voice, George. You sound different."

"It's just regular old unchanged me, Ma. You sound out of breath."

"I'm exhausted, George. Just the usual around here. Frank has been wearing me to a frazzle."

Frank was my younger brother and only sibling, a nervous, conservative twenty-three-year-old who lived at home with my parents. He and my mother bickered like a married couple who'd been together for twenty years and he and my father spoke exclusively in traded insults as they had identical personalities. He was devoted to both of them. I was crazy about Frank despite our differences. He was amassing a small fortune doing something for a computer software firm no one in the family understood and he didn't have the patience to explain. More than once he'd given a long, detailed description of his job only to have my mother or my father or me say, "Yes, but what do you *do* all day?" at which point he'd throw his hands into the air and leave the room.

"What's up with little Frankie?"

"It's that new girlfriend of his, the one I wrote you about. At your *old* address."

"The one you said was cheap?"

"George! I never said she was cheap. I said she *wasn't* cheap. I'd never say something mean like that about one of my son's girlfriends ... or whatever. Anyway, I'd never say that about Sheree. That's her name. S-H-E-R-E-E. Is that French, dear?"

"I don't think so, Ma." Frank adored women whose names ended in I's and double E's. Sheree, Didi, Loree, Suzi.

"She works for a toy company. She sits in a chair all day every day and tests games. I don't know where Frank met this one unless it was at Schwarz's."

"Well, it sounds like a fun job to me."

"I'm sure some people would think so. Personally, I'd go nuts." My mother had worked at a Catholic Charities office for over ten years; buying her way to heaven was how she viewed it. "I told her jokingly she'd better watch out she didn't get fat sitting around all day playing board games. She has quite a figure." This meant large breasts. A nice figure meant small breasts, and a cute figure was flat-chested. "Of course, she didn't take it as a joke. She got all huffy and upset. At least we know she has feelings." There was a long pause and both of us sighed deeply, readying ourselves for Act II. "Soo ... I got your little card. It was cute. I liked the monkeys."

"They were mice. You liked the card?"

"I just said I thought it was cute."

"Did you like the truck?"

"I don't know if I liked the truck, George. It was a nice card. I didn't rush out and buy a frame." There was more silence, then,

"So...you moved. I thought you told me you liked your other place so much."

"I did. This one is nicer," I said, looking around the sterile apartment. The conversation was inching toward controversy. "My new place is more convenient to work. And...I also have a roommate now."

"Oh? Who's that?"

"What do you mean by 'who'?"

"Well, what does 'who' usually mean, George? I didn't know you were brought up speaking Slavic. I mean is this roommate a man or a woman or a cat or a dog. I mean *who*."

"A man. His name is Joley."

"Joley?" She started to laugh. "What kind of a name is Joley? It sounds like a clown's name."

"That's his last name. His first name is Robert. He's very nice. Very handsome."

"I don't care what he looks like. Is he reliable? This isn't some stranger you moved in with, is it?"

"Of course not. He's very reliable. Steadfast, even."

She laughed softly and to herself. "Joley, Sheree, Didi, Dada, Doodoo? Don't you people know anyone with a nice normal name? Frank isn't going to fall in love until he meets someone with a name like Beatrice, although, believe it or not, he seems to be getting serious about this Sheree. I just don't think she's his type."

"Does he?"

"Well, he must, if he's planning to marry her."

"He's planning to marry her?" We'd all been expecting Frank to announce his marriage plans since he turned seventeen, but his romances always fell apart before he got to the altar. It was my mother's style to keep important news until the end and then state it nonchalantly.

"I didn't say he *was* planning to marry her. I said *if* he's planning to marry her. Don't misquote me, dear, I'm in enough trouble around here already. Your father won three hundred dollars in the numbers last week and Mr. Big Shot hasn't spoken to me since. All he thinks about is the numbers."

"The numbers" was my parents' name for the Massachusetts State Lottery. Since its inception, my father had retreated into a feverish state of anticipation, trying to figure out what number to play the next day and what to do with the money he might win that evening. He sat through meals silently doing computation in his head or counting the number of peas on his plate, looking for inspiration.

My father worked in the personnel department at General Electric. He'd been with the company since I was a child but he very rarely spoke about his job. I'd always imagined he was involved in classified arms-production work which he wasn't at liberty to talk about, but Frank insisted he never mentioned his job because he himself didn't know what he did. He was a quiet, detached man who seemed to have lost his way somewhere in life, probably at the end of the Second World War, when he left the army. Recently he'd set up an apartment for himself in the basement of the house, where he spent most of his time playing solitaire, another source of "numbers" inspiration.

"Tell Dad hello from me, Ma. Tell him we need some light bulbs, if he could send some." My father got an unlimited supply of light bulbs from GE and took great delight in sending them to his friends and relatives.

"I showed him the card you sent. He liked the monkeys. Or mice, or whatever they were. Do you need anything besides light bulbs, George? I could send you some tuna or shaving cream or trash bags. Something easy to send in the mail?"

"Everything's fine, Ma. I don't need anything else."

"I hear about New York all the time on the news. I worry about you. If someone isn't dying from a disease, they're getting murdered by the police. I'm surprised there's anyone left in that city."

"Hey, Ma," I said, "guess who I saw on the street the other day."

"I'm sure I wouldn't know, dear."

I could see her rolling her eyes. Every time my mother called, I told her I'd just seen some famous person on the street so she'd think I lived in a city inhabited by people she knew from television rather than by roving bands of psycho killers. I named an actress who was enjoying an undeserved bit of popularity that month.

"Oh I saw her on one of those makeup commercials the other day. She has gorgeous teeth. A little cheap-looking, though."

"She looks even cheaper in person. She's too thin."

"They're all too thin. They all live on cigarettes. Like this Sheree. She always has a butt hanging out of her mouth. I hope Frank likes kissing an ashtray, not that he'd notice with the amount he smokes. Say hello to this roommate person of yours, whatever his name is."

"I will."

What I hate about some phone calls is hanging up. When someone sends you a letter you can hold onto it and reread it if you like, but with a phone call all you get is silence at the end. "Ma," I said, "I miss you, you know."

"Oh, George, you do not. Don't be ridiculous."

3

JOLEY and I lived together for ten months in varying stages of happiness and discord. True, we slept in separate bedrooms every night we lived together; true, beginning on his thirty-seventh birthday Joley subsisted on a life-extending diet of viscous liquids whirred around in the blender; true, he considered himself a leftist because he read *The New Republic*. We argued long and vehemently over whether my slovenliness or his neatness was more pathological. All true. Still, I loved him—or was childishly infatuated or mindlessly smitten—at first for his good looks and his false air of sophistication and his condescending attitude toward me, and later for all the unglamorous traits that lay beneath the thin fashion-plate veneer. Often, what's most attractive about a person is that part they're trying hardest to conceal, that part they think is least likable. You find out about it and it becomes a secret bond between you, something you never talk about but hold close to your heart and are continually touched by.

So it was with me and Joley's neuroses and his loathing of his own wonderfully dull childhood. I couldn't think of anything more charming than knowing this dashing man had grown up in a boring, characterless suburb with a father who thrilled to the true-life stories in *Reader's Digest*.

Joley eventually revealed to me his insecurities about his teaching and his writing abilities, something he went to great lengths to hide from everyone else. He told me he'd had very little published while at Columbia and was riding on his reputation as a lecturer in his pending tenure case, a reputation he feared he'd earned from his looks rather than any other merits. When I finally did sneak into one of Joley's classes, I was amazed at his skill and magnetism at the front of the classroom. He had a breathless enthusiasm for his subject (the childhood of Queen Victoria, in this case), which he seemed to fill the room with. He paced around with a light, springy step, bouncing off the balls of his feet as he defined the lineage of the Royal Family, dissected the muddle of titles and names as if they were his own ancestors, and tossed in scandalous anecdotes he had me believing he alone was privy to. The students, a bunch of undergrads, each of whom had entered the room with a Walkman attached to his head, looked mesmerized. After class I went to Joley's office to compliment him, and for the first time since we'd met he seemed unsure of himself and embarrassed by the praise. "I really was a little off today, George," he insisted. "You should come back another time when I'm more fired up."

BUT, as winter wearied into a warm and wet spring, the differences in our personalities began to grate. The apartment grew smaller by the day. Joley suddenly became convinced he was growing old and gray and pasty. He made trips to a tanning salon that tinted his skin a flat shade of brown, masking his natural color and giving his body the look of a Miami Beach corpse. He talked more and more about his concern for his career, occasionally ranting about how I should get involved in a training program for international banking, whatever that is. He organized his life in rigid patterns, living by a carefully timed schedule, eating in compliance with complicated food-combining charts and sleeping to the tune of two hummers and a fan and a humidifier. He set little black boxes around the apartment which were supposed to change the charge of the atmospheric ions and reverse the aging process.

I retaliated by living in complete chaos. On Saturdays I'd roam the streets searching for discarded furniture, old books and photographs, orange crates, anything I could stack in my bedroom. When the bedroom was filled, I spilled the junk into the hallway and then the kitchen. It was a nervous twitch, an instinctive reaction. I tried to talk with Joley about the turn our relationship was taking, but he was always too busy pressure-cooking beans or vacuuming the walls. Any discussion had to be fit into his schedule, and that was loaded with activities for months in advance. As much as I cherished the intimacy of knowing his secrets, Joley resented it. I think I made him feel claustrophobic and locked into an identity he couldn't bluff his way out of.

And then May rolled around and we went to a party at his friend Constance's loft and our relationship halted abruptly. It was there that Joley introduced me to Nina.

Joley and I arrived at the party late, and Constance was sitting on the floor in the hallway outside her loft drinking a cup of some foul-smelling tea. She had on a tight green jumpsuit that emphasized her pallor and emaciation, and her permed, moussed, cellophaned hair hung around her protruding ears like wet hay.

"Joley," she said languidly. "I knew you'd come eventually."

Constance was a self-proclaimed artist with a large inherited income and a negligible talent. She made enormous black bug-shaped sculptures out of latex and painted them with streaks of red enamel. The first time I'd seen them hung on the walls of her loft I was reminded of the huge roaches that crawled all over my apartment in Washington Heights.

She stood up from the floor and gave Joley a long embrace. For a minute I thought she'd fallen asleep against his shoulder. She was a tall woman and thin in the extreme way that's considered attractive only in people with money. "I'm glad you came along, too, George," she said limply.

She led us inside hanging on to Joley's arm for dear life and wobbling unsteadily on stiletto heels. The loft was crowded with people with spiky, wet-looking hair sucking on cigarettes and talking frantically. Constance's sculptures had apparently multiplied since the last time I'd been there and they covered the towering white walls. At first I thought someone was banging on the pipes that ran along the ceiling, but it eventually dawned on me the relentless clatter was music, sounding out of speakers so huge she'd probably rented them from Radio City Music Hall.

She brought us over to a long table lined with food. "This is the nonmacro table, George," she whispered to me, still hanging from Joley's arm. "I know not everyone has my taste in food." Constance was on a macrobiotic diet, which, as far as I could tell, did nothing for her except give her a vaguely green complexion and black circles under her eyes. "I'm going to show Joley off, so you just help yourself. Try a Ring Ding, I hear they're fabulous." She let out a laugh that was a cry for help if ever I'd heard one.

The table in front of me was littered with plates of the worst sort of processed food imaginable: dishes of garishly colored chunks of cheese, rolled-up meats, baskets of greasy chips and bright orange cheese puffs. There were frosted doughnuts and cream-filled cupcakes and an array of desserts so drippingly sweet they'd throw any healthy person into a diabetic coma. I grabbed a plate and heaped on as many Twinkies and as much cheese food as I could carry.

Two men were standing at the table, picking up cupcakes and meat chunks and whispering comments to each other that sent them into gales of laughter. They were both striking-looking—sharp and narrow and all right angles—and draped in acrylic sweaters with padded shoulders the width of the East River. Neither of them would deign to put the food anywhere near their mouths but they spent forever playing with it. I was transfixed with contempt. The blonder and handsomer of the two finally stopped talking about the food and got on the compelling subject of his new bedroom set.

"And the *bed*," he said, "is so huge, it practically fills the entire room. I guess that says something about my personality."

"You mean you like to sleep a lot?" I butted in.

"I suppose some people would use it for sleep," he said as if the idea were heretical.

"Some people would sleep anywhere," his companion sneered.

I took my plate of food and found a chair by the door where there was some ventilation and decided to forgo any further attempts at mingling. The music clanged on endlessly and the clouds of smoke soon descended into my corner. The only consolation was the food, which actually began to taste good after the first few bites. Across the room, a group cleared out a two-foot-square space of floor and began moving their bodies spastically, a version of the kind of dayroom shuffling I'd seen Olivia de Havilland doing in *The Snake Pit*.

About an hour later, Constance tottered over to my chair looking more stupefied than ever.

"Georgio," she said, "I've been searching for you. Everywhere."

"Where's Joley these days, Constance?"

"Oh, who can keep track? He's probably with some boy. You know how he can get."

"I've heard."

She grabbed my hand and tried to pull me to my feet. "Get up, George, there's someone I want you to meet." I was trying to stay as firmly rooted in my chair as I could, just to torment her. "Will you please get up? Joley thinks the two of you will hit it off."

As soon as I was on my feet she yanked my arm and pulled me across the room, shoving people out of the way with rude comments. She was a good deal stronger than I would have guessed. I caught a quick glimpse of Joley on the other side of the room talking to the idiot with the oversized bedroom set. Both had wide grins plastered on their faces.

"This way, George," Constance said, dragging me toward the back corner of the room. "You're going to love this woman. She's a shrink. You can tell her your dreams."

We stopped in front of a worn leather sofa where a woman was sitting by herself with her face buried in a champagne glass. "This is Nina Borowski," Constance said. "Nina, George . . . something or other."

She gave me a shove and walked off into the thick of the party. I tried to get a glimpse of Joley, but the mob was blocking him from my view. The woman on the sofa had emerged from behind the glass, and she looked so beautiful and calm sitting there, I took an immediate dislike to her. She was wearing a shapeless black jersey bag of a dress that covered her knees, and one dangling silver hoop earring. The mass of bracelets around her wrist jangled as she set down her glass.

"Hi, I'm George," I said, sitting beside her. She was emanating a faint smell of vetiver I decided was overpowering.

"I just met your friend," she said. "He's very nice."

"He's not my friend, he's my lover. And once you get to know him, he's a real shit."

"Oh, God," she said, "I know the type."

"I'll bet," I said. "I'll bet you shrinks even have a name for them."

"Well, actually, I'm not a shrink yet. I'm still in school. With a little luck, I should be able to..."

"*I* went to a shrink once," I interrupted. "I saw him three times and then I had a dream I used the toilet in his office and it wouldn't flush, and when I asked him to help me with it he said if I didn't know how to fix it, I shouldn't have used it in the first place. I didn't need a doctorate to figure that one out. I called his office the next day and told the answering service I was moving to Nome and wouldn't be in anymore."

She laughed uneasily. "That sounds like the way I end most of my relationships. At least you saved some money."

"I suppose so." Her refusal to play along embarrassed me; I realized I was making a fool of myself. She had character. She also wasn't nearly as calm as I'd thought at first; she was drinking voraciously and tugging at her eyebrows with a nervous yanking motion. She'd slipped off her shoes and I noticed she had wide, clumsy feet. Her outside toes were red and sore-looking, as if they'd been cramped into her shiny shoes—probably cheap plastic. "Are you a friend of Constance?" I asked more gently.

"Not really. I just met her. A friend from school brought me here to meet people. I recently had a bad experience with someone I'd been living with." She tossed down the rest of her champagne with a clank of bracelets. "Frankly, I think this room is full of bad experiences. Anyway, most of these men are out of my league; too handsome to seriously consider talking to."

"That's nonsense," I said, honestly shocked. "You're easily the most beautiful woman here. Everyone else is hiding something. You can tell by their haircuts. Can I get you more champagne?"

"I wouldn't mind. This music is giving me a headache. It reminds of the summer I worked on an assembly line in a shoe factory. Unless I'm hung over already."

I grabbed an open bottle of champagne and a glass for myself and tried to see through the smoke to the other side of the room. It was useless. I sat back down on the sofa and filled our glasses.

"You know, you really shouldn't tug at your eyebrows like that," I said. "You'll pull them all out."

"It's a nervous habit. I always do it at parties."

I couldn't imagine there was any reason she'd feel nervous at a party, but of course I liked her even more for saying it. Alienation loves company.

"Do you know what they originally built these lofts for?" I asked her. "Manufacturing textiles. Can you believe it?"

"Well it's obvious they weren't meant for human habitation. If that's what you'd call this."

We were getting giddy. I could tell if I didn't watch myself I'd start trashing the sculptures.

"So," I said, "you liked my friend."

"He does have nice eyes," she said tentatively. "How long have the two of you known each other?"

"About over a year and a half, I'd guess." A wide man with red suspenders had moved from in front of the sofa and I had a clear view of Joley leaning against an opposite wall, breathing down the neck of the bedroom set.

"Have you been to Brooklyn, George?"

"Never."

"Well, when I told your lover I was looking for a roommate, he said you'd be interested. It's a great place, Brooklyn."

"That's nice." I wasn't listening to what she was saying; I was too busy craning my neck for a better angle on watching Joley move in for the kill.

"My apartment is huge. Of course it's not exactly fancy, but I'm pretty comfortable there. A little lonely right now, to tell you the truth." She shrugged and poured herself more champagne. "Can I refill your glass? If you are interested, we could arrange a time for you to come and see the place."

I turned to her slowly. "Wait a minute, Nina," I said. "Joley told you I was looking for a place to live?"

"Well, yes."

"That man over there," I said, pointing, "told you *I* was looking for a place to live?"

Nina leaned in toward me and looked across the room. Joley

had his hand on the blond's shoulder and was beaming. "That is," she said slowly and then resolutely, "no, no he didn't. I'm a little drunk, that's all, George. You've seen how much of this I've been sopping up. Put a bottle of free champagne in front of me and I've had it."

"He's an asshole," I said. "I mean, really, Nina, we live together. We've never talked about me moving out. Things aren't perfect, I'll admit to that, but we've never discussed me moving out. What kind of a person would do something like this?"

"A narcissist, if you want a name for it. I really am sorry. Look, I'll be honest with you, I don't even know anyone here. That friend who brought me? Well, she isn't really a very close friend at all. The truth is, she used to be a client of mine. I did some counseling at Fordham and she was one of the students I saw. It wasn't as if she was sick or anything, just the usual little family gripes. Anyway, she's the one who thought I needed a night out of Brooklyn."

"Just tell me this," I said. "Am I being small and petty or is that a rotten thing to do to someone?"

"I've heard of more considerate ways to suggest a breakup." She was playing with her bracelets and staring at her lap. "I'm sorry, George. I'm really sorry."

"Don't give it a second thought, Nina. It isn't your fault he's a creep."

"No, I know, but I really hope you believe I had no idea what was going on. I didn't even know you two live together. I just want to make sure you know that, and then I'll head out of here and go sleep it off."

"Of course I know that. I just feel horrible he involved you in this. I'm the one who's sorry."

She looked at me for a moment as if to make sure I was telling her the truth and then took a pencil out of a beaded purse she had stuffed in a corner of the sofa. "Look, take this," she said, writing her phone number on a napkin, "and if you want to chat or anything, just give me a call. I realize I don't know you, but I like you. You're a nice person, George." She stood up with a deprecating cough and walked off, leaving a faint trace of vetiver lingering in the air.

I slumped back down on the sofa, dazed. I could see Joley on the other side of the room making fast and predictable progress with his conquest. As I was about to rouse myself and fight my way out of the loft, a commotion started at the other end of the room. A weirdly sudden hush fell over the crowd. Someone turned down the stereo and people began drifting toward the food table. I heard a loud, razor-thin shriek and then Constance shouting; "You've ruined it! You've ruined it, you *pigs!* I don't care who did it, everyone's to blame. That sculpture was worth thousands of dollars."

I edged my way to the front of the crowd and saw Constance standing over a shapeless mass of black latex. There was an empty space on the wall behind her. Her eyes were wild, and for once there were signs of healthy color in her cheeks. She pushed her abused hair behind her big ears and shouted, "I want everyone out! Right now. *Out!*"

The people near her looked down at their feet contritely and one woman began to giggle uncontrollably. The wide man with the red suspenders who'd been standing in front of the sofa put his hand on Constance's arm.

"It's okay, Connie," he said. "It was an accident. These things happen, they just happen and there's nothing we can do about them. Just try to cool down a little." He turned to the giggling woman and barked, "Get her some Bancha tea, for Christ's sake."

The music was eventually turned back up and half the room lit up cigarettes. I walked to the back of the loft to find Joley but he was nowhere in sight. By the time I'd pushed my way to the front door the party was in as much swing as it had ever been in. Constance was again sitting in the hallway sipping her tea.

"You're not leaving?" she said sweetly. Her eyes were swimming and I doubt she recognized me.

"I'm afraid so," I said. "You haven't seen Joley, have you?"

"Who? Oh, no, no, I haven't. Not for hours."

I sat up in Joley's bed rehearsing the speech I was going to make when he walked in the door. When he finally did come in, it was dawn. He looked pale and tired. His looks, like those of any truly handsome person, only improved with exhaustion or sickness.

He sat down on the foot of the mattress. "I know what you're going to say, George."

"You couldn't possibly, you zero."

He looked at me with a hurt expression in his emerald-green eyes. "I meant to talk it over with you, I really did. I've been meaning to talk it over with you for weeks but there just hasn't been a free minute. Look, we both know this isn't working out the way we wanted it to."

He paused, waiting for agreement.

"Go on," I said.

"Things were great for a while, really wonderful. I love you, George, you know that. But . . . I don't know what it is, but lately it hasn't been . . . so great. Anyway, I had no intention of doing it this way, not talking it over with you first, but that blonde—" he said, waving his hand.

"Nina."

"Whatever her name was . . ."

"Her name is Nina."

"Nina, then. When Nina told me about her apartment, I just mentioned that maybe you might be interested."

"You always were thoughtful, Joley."

"My timing was all screwed up. You know how much I care about you."

"Please, Joley, don't get mawkish."

"I'm so tired. I can't fight with you now. Can't this discussion wait until morning?" He curled up next to me on the pillows. His hair and his clothes smelled of cigarettes and amyl nitrate.

"It *is* morning, Joley."

"I always mess things up for you," he mumbled sleepily. "I'm not worthy of you. I never have been."

"Don't," I said. I hated it when he criticized himself. "You're just exhausted. Anyway, you know you shouldn't be doing poppers."

"It wasn't me, it was that boy. God, what an idiot. I should have been paid for child care."

"*I* get paid for child care," I said. "You never get paid enough for child care. You didn't do anything unhealthy with him, did you? I don't care how young he was."

He didn't respond; he'd passed out. I pulled his clothes off and took a hummer from beneath the bed. The room was growing lighter and the soft, whirring sound was peaceful and soothing. I undressed and stretched out on the bed next to him. He stirred slightly but didn't wake up. I threw my arm across him and we slept together until past noon.

JOLEY crept around the apartment for the next few days, smiling shyly and acting as if it were he who'd been wounded by his thoughtlessness. He was elated about the breakthrough he'd made in sleeping with me, even though, in his case, it was closer to coma than sleep. He told me I'd done for him what no one else had been able to do, broken through his irrational fears of intimacy and so on. After a few days of this, with no attempt at repeating the miracle, I dug out the napkin with Nina's number on it and called her.

I let the phone ring ten times and was about to hang up when someone picked up or knocked over the receiver. I heard a muffled sniffle but no voice.

"Hello?" I said.

"Yeah, hello? Wait a minute." It was Nina. Her voice was tight and thick. I heard her blow her nose. "What is it?"

My luck to catch her in the middle of a nervous breakdown. "Nina? This is George Mullen. I met you at a party a few nights ago?"

"Oh, George, hi. I'm glad you called. How are you?"

"I hope I didn't get you at a bad time."

"No, not at all. I'm sorry I sound like a mess. I've been watching figure-skating championships on TV. I always get weepy watching figure skating. It kills me to see some kid from New Jersey get out there and make good."

I told her I was interested in her place after all, if she was still looking for a roommate. She sounded embarrassed, as if she were responsible for what had happened between me and Joley.

"I'm really sorry," she said.

"It's probably for the best," I told her.

"No, I know, but I really am sorry."

"It's not your fault."

"Of course not, but . . . He does have nice eyes."

"Please. Don't remind me."

"I'm sorry, George, I'm really sorry. I should know better than to say something like that."

We made plans for dinner that Sunday night. She gave me complicated subway directions and told me to bring a loaf of bread.

"But don't let me eat any. I'm desperate to lose weight, as you probably guessed from looking at me."

4

It was raining that Sunday, a cold, heavy rain that grayed the entire city and dripped noisily onto the ledge outside my window. I don't know of any sight more depressing than Riverside Drive in the rain with the old ladies out in their galoshes and clear plastic umbrellas and the cars whizzing by with the windows fogged up. I drew my shade, stacked all of my Boswell Sisters albums on the Webcor Holiday and spent the day slumped in a chair rereading Strachey's *Eminent Victorians,* a book that always lifts my spirits. Late in the afternoon I put on khakis and a faded yellow gabardine shirt and tried to comb my hair into a semblance of order. I walked to the subway stomping through the puddles in the street corners.

The cranky train inched through the tunnels all the way to lower Manhattan, stopping between stops, grinding painfully over the tracks and generally taking so long that by the time they announced the last stop in Manhattan, I thought we must be halfway to Philadelphia.

We pulled out of a tunnel and climbed uphill to the tracks stretching across the Manhattan Bridge. Out one side of the filthy, defaced train I could see the Brooklyn Bridge looming enormous and fragile, like something a child had constructed out of toothpicks. My mother had once mailed me a newspaper clipping about a Japanese tourist who was flicked off the bridge by a snapped cable and sent soaring through the air to the water below. "Just one of the things I've recently read about New York," she'd written in the margin. From the other side of the car I could see a Circle Line boat chugging through the murky water of the East River, slow and lonely in the rain. Streams of daylight flashed through the beams of the bridge as we rocked side to side over the tracks. Finally I caught a glimpse of the Statue of Liberty, and then Manhattan was in the distance looking like a petri dish overgrown with a fungus of steel and concrete.

By the time I got out at Nina's stop, the rain had turned to a soft drizzle. I put up my umbrella, a large black one I'd found abandoned on West End Avenue one windy day, and walked along the outskirts of Prospect Park looking for her street. The rain had brightened all the spring green on the trees and the grass and there was a stillness in the air, a thrum of quiet punctured occasionally by a sharp note from a bird or a car horn in the distance. I could hear the heavy drops of rain falling on my umbrella from the soaked trees.

Nina's street sloped down steeply, perpendicular to the park. It was lined with trees and brownstone buildings with gas lamps beside the stoops, wrought-iron gates in front, and rounded bay windows that shone in the afternoon dimness. It was far more ostentatious than I'd expected.

But as I continued to walk down the steep street away from the park, the neighborhood changed. The brownstones were less elaborately decorated here, narrower and flatter and without the polished look of restoration. Children appeared in the street—unaccompanied and loud in their wet slickers—and the number of trees diminished to almost none. I passed a church advertising a mass in Creole at 5 P.M. and an Italian grocery plastered with signs for fresh ricotta every Wednesday.

Nina's building was in the middle of the block, wedged between two smaller houses. It looked like a poor relation of the brownstones higher up the street—a stridently utilitarian four-story building stripped of all pretense at ornamentation except for the trash barrels chained to the fence in front.

I climbed up the painted cement steps and rang her bell. A window opened on the first floor and a middle-aged woman with thinning brown hair stuck her head and shoulders out.

"Her buzzer don't work," she said and flashed me a nearly toothless grin.

"I'm ringing for Nina," I said.

"That's why I'm telling you her buzzer don't work. She can hear you but she can't let you in. She'll probably come down and open the door for you. What do you think of this weather, awful, isn't it?"

The window directly above flew open and Nina's head poked out.

"George, I'll be right down. The buzzer's broken."

"I already told him, hon," the woman on the first floor called up, sticking her body farther out the sill and looking up. The sleeves of her print housedress were biting into the flesh on her upper arms. "I happened to look out the window and I seen him standing there in the rain and everything. With that broken umbrella."

Mrs. Sarni, Nina's best friend in the neighborhood, as she introduced herself, regarded me up and down and nodded. "You're a friend of hers?"

"Yes," I said. "Well, that is, we just met a couple of nights ago. We're having dinner."

"She's a lovely girl. Very intelligent. She's always got her head buried in some book. How old are you, George?"

"Twenty-five."

"My son's twenty-nine. He has brown eyes like you. Not that I ever see him to know. They could have turned green for all I know."

When Nina stepped out to the stoop she looked sleepy and confused. She held her palm to the sky with disbelief. "How long has it been raining?"

"All day," I said. "At least in town."

"Here, too," Mrs. Sarni said. "She probably had her head in some book all day like usual. Tell him you been reading all day, hon."

"Actually, I've been sleeping most of the day."

She was wearing a pair of threadbare blue jeans and a T-shirt and the same mass of bracelets and the single silver earring she'd had on at Constance's party. Her face looked slightly puffy, as if she'd just woken up, but her eyes were heavily mascaraed.

"You're very casual today," Mrs. Sarni said, eying her disapprovingly. "Mostly she's so dressed up all the time," she said to me. "And I mean nice clothes, too, George, not the usual junk you see. A little old-fashioned, but what's wrong with that? Right? Am I right, George?"

"George might be moving in," Nina said. "He might as well see me at my worst."

"Moving in? Well, that's interesting. That's very interesting. If I knew you needed a roommate, I would have told my son. Not that he'd move back here in a thousand years. You two better get inside before you get soaked and ruin your appetites. She's a good cook, George." She hauled her body inside, shut the window and let the venetian blind drop to the sill with a crash.

"I hope that didn't offend her," I said, "about me moving in. I have a phobia about nosy neighbors trying to plot my eviction."

"Don't worry, she's fine. She doesn't have anyone to talk to, that's all. If you move in she'll have her eye on you for her son. He lives in the Village and owns a neon shop and she's always trying to fix him up with some man in the neighborhood so she'll get to see him more often. You'd be a prime candidate, given the proximity."

We walked up the yellow-and-red linoleum-covered stairs to the second floor. The hallway smelled of cooking—roasting meats and fried onions and burnt coffee. The air was heavy and intoxicating. The walls were paneled with a dark, greasy wood that looked as if it had been absorbing the smells, thriving on them, for decades.

"I should warn you," Nina said as she opened the door, "there's not much in here."

The apartment was, in fact, larger and emptier than I'd expected. Narrow as the building was, it stretched deeply into the yard behind the house. There were six perfectly square rooms, all of them save two completely unfurnished, and each opening off a dark passageway. The floor throughout was covered with the same yellow-and-red linoleum as the stairs in the hallway and the walls were all papered with flowered wallpaper, which, while varying from room to room in floral genus, was consistently faded and grimy. There were fingerprints and seeping, oily stains all over. More than one generation of children had run amok in this place. It was unlike any apartment I'd been inside in Manhattan, and I immediately felt at home.

We walked to her bedroom at the front of the house and she reached up and switched on a bare bulb hanging from the ceiling. The two tall windows were covered from top to bottom with a heavy purple material that was tacked to the frame and blocked out most of the daylight.

"I wanted to clean up in here," she said, "but the thought of dusting and folding and getting plastic trash bags kept me in bed most of the day."

There were only two recognizable pieces of furniture in the room: a huge four-poster pressed against one wall and a mahogany bureau directly opposite. The mirror over the bureau was completely covered with photos and postcards, leaving only a tiny square of reflecting glass. The bedposts were hung with feather necklaces, stray pieces of yellowed lace, terra-cotta bells and wind chimes, and a little girl's straw bonnet with a sky-blue ribbon streaming down from the brim.

The room was in a state of chaos far beyond any mess even I had ever created. The bureau drawers were all open and spilling over with clothes: bright satin and corduroy skirts and frilly blouses and work shirts cascaded down layer after layer. The floor and the bed were strewn with magazines and notebooks and loose papers, dress shoes and sneakers and a pair of red galoshes she must have been given by an old lady on Riverside Drive. Her whole life seemed to be strewn across the floor. There were psychology text-books and paperback mysteries open at the foot of the bed as if they'd been there for months. I counted three vases of dead flowers in various spots and four coffee cups with spoons sticking out and lipstick stains around the rims.

I couldn't imagine how it was possible she'd emerged from this place looking as lovely as she'd looked the night of Constance's party.

On the wall over the bed she'd taped a green-and-white poster of a multiracial group of women with upraised fists shouting "SIS-TERS UNITE, TAKE BACK THE NIGHT."

"Beautiful room, isn't it?" Nina asked.

There was something exotic and unfamiliar about the room, a decidedly "feminine" atmosphere. I couldn't put my finger on any one detail but it all added up to something different from most of the rooms I'd lived or slept in. There was a clay bowl on the bureau filled with tiny tubes of makeup and miniature bottles of oils— sweet almond, vetiver, ambergris. The scents permeated the stuffy air. There was a woven basket with yarn and knitting needles set on the box she was using as a night table. Next to it was an eyedropper bottle labeled "Essence of Mustard—For Depression."

I picked up a small blue-and-silver purse made of mail and felt the strange weight of it in my palm. "If I knew you, Nina, I'm sure I'd think this room was you all over."

She went to the kitchen to heat up a pan of lasagne and make a salad and I sat down on the green vinyl sofa in the living room. Here, at last, was a sofa I could put my feet up on without worry. Through the window I could see the backyard with a Saint Anthony statue at the far end of the garden, dripping in the rain.

"You know what, Nina?" I called out, putting up my feet. "I could easily live here."

She came in from the kitchen with her face flushed pink from the heat of the oven and a towel wrapped around her waist. There were sauce stains splashed on her stretched T-shirt.

"What do you really think, George?"

"I think you look wonderful," I said.

"Oh, well, I meant about the apartment." She yanked off the towel and tossed it behind her carelessly.

"It's great," I said. "It has honest charm."

"I know it's not great, but it's roomy. Don't you think it's roomy? And the rent is a third of what it would be a few blocks from here and about an eighth of what it would be in Manhattan. There isn't a lawyer or an MBA on the block. No one here ever heard of the Land's End catalog. That's where I got these shoes," she said, pointing to her rubber-and-leather moccasins.

WE sat at the unsteady packing-crate table and she cut me a huge piece of lasagne, the center of which was still cold. She filled her own plate with salad, explaining that she was trying to lose five pounds by the end of the week and was therefore living on lettuce. As soon as the words were out of her mouth she started to pick at the cheese and pasta stuck to the bottom of the baking dish.

"It's Mrs. Sarni's recipe. Actually, she brought it up to me the day I got here. It's been in the freezer for a month now; I was afraid I'd polish it off for breakfast one morning if it wasn't frozen."

She told me she'd moved into the apartment in a frenzy a month earlier when the man she'd been living with on Long Island dumped her for a Barnard sophomore he'd met on a trip he and Nina had taken to celebrate the first year of their relationship.

"It was a pathetic situation," she said, scooping shreds of lasagne from the pan. "I stopped some young woman who was walking past on the beach and asked her to take a picture of us. It turns out she was an aspiring photographer. She spent an hour shooting pictures, most of them, I realized afterwards, of Brad alone. Three days later, as I was packing our bags, he came into the room and sat on the bed and told me he was staying an extra week to be with Rhonda."

She went to the bedroom and brought back a stack of photographs. The top one was of herself and a tanned, smiling man standing by the ocean. The colors were beautiful.

"Not a bad picture, is it?" She put a thick piece of stringy cheese into her mouth. "Rhonda. Brad calls and complains to me about her childishness, her wayward soul. He wanted a mouse and he got one, that's all. Lately I've been hanging up on him. His voice grates on me."

"Good for you," I said. "Good for you, Nina." In her situation I would have stayed on the phone for hours, invited the two of them for dinner and planned a reconciliation for weeks.

"It was an easy relationship to give up. Brad's a psychologist, a Rogerian. Don't ever try to live with a Rogerian; it's like living in a big, echoing cave. I'd scream at him for bossing me around and he'd calmly say, 'You're angry at me for telling you to take your shoes off the table.' We could go on like that for hours."

She handed me another photograph, this one of a light-haired man with a well-bred chin, a perfect nose and an appealing, consumptive look. "My ex-husband," she said. "The first love of my life. I met him in a bar when I was seventeen. He was from a big-name Washington family and had just graduated from Yale and was squandering the money he'd started to get from his trust fund. He was easily the most glamorous man I'd ever met. I was wearing miniskirts and white lipstick and he'd had dinner with Robert Kennedy when he was a kid. He'd take me out to his parents' house in Georgetown and harass them for hours. Thomas was making a career of exposing the hypocrisy of his parents' liberal politics even though he had none himself. I think he was interested in me because I was exactly the kind of Polish Catholic girl of no means his family would shudder at the sight of."

Nina had grown up in a brick row house in Baltimore in a working-class Polish neighborhood that sounded a lot like the one she was living in now. Her father was a building inspector for the city, and although they had ample opportunities to move to a bigger house in a better neighborhood, her Grandfather Borowski, who lived in the top-floor apartment with one of her unmarried uncles, threatened to throw himself off the roof if they ever moved out of the house he'd saved his entire life to buy.

"There's a strong streak of melodrama in my family. My mother hated the Borowskis and carried on a feud with my grandfather for years. He was always threatening to throw himself off the roof."

Nina had twin brothers, both of whom took to drinking early in life, married emotional duplicates of their mother, and moved to a two-family house three blocks away from the Borowski estate. Nina was the baby of the family and the only one with a rebellious spirit and signs of brilliance. If she'd been a son she could have been a doctor or a scientist or an astronaut—even an astronaut.

"My father thought I'd stolen my brothers' brains through some mystical female powers. He'd complain at every family gathering. It was his standard joke. I had to learn to play the accordion, and at holiday dinners I'd get up and play polkas and anniversary music dressed in a foolish party dress and he'd say, 'Look at her, if she'd been a boy she could have been an astronaut.' My mother was angry I wasn't thinner so the two of us could go out to Hollywood and get me into the movies. My mother and I are look-alikes."

When she graduated high school she went to work at a factory to prove to her father she didn't intend to go off to college with the brains she'd stolen from her brothers.

"And then Thomas and I eloped and moved out to Arizona. We lived kind of high on the hog for a while, until he got involved in some cult religion and killed my dog in a sacrificial rite."

She handed me a photograph of herself in the desert kneeling beside a lean Irish setter. She was wearing high leather boots and an expensive-looking Indian dress. The dog's red hair was blowing in her face.

"I can't tell you how much I loved that dog, George. I got her when we first moved to Arizona. I probably would have left Thomas after a year if it hadn't been for her. Anyway, when I found out what he'd done, I left all my junk and got on the next plane to Washington. I told Thomas's family what was going on and they blamed me. I was too manipulative and controlling and I'd driven him to it. They had the marriage annulled and gave me thirty thousand dollars to keep my mouth shut. They were convinced Thomas could still have a career in politics after he was deprogrammed. I went back to Baltimore and my parents wouldn't have anything to do with me. As far as they were concerned, I'd blown my only chance at upward mobility because I wasn't strong enough to make Thomas be a good husband. So I said to hell with it and took the thirty thousand and went off to college, figured out I hadn't snatched anyone's brains. I was a natural for psychology, having been around nuts for so long."

By the time she'd finished talking, she'd eaten half the loaf of bread and a portion of lasagne at least equal to the one she'd served me. The salad remained untouched on her plate. Her skin was glowing from the garlicky sauce, and I thought she had one of the most beautiful faces I'd ever seen. When she started to pile the dishes on top of each other, I jumped up and said, "Don't do that. I'll do it, you sit down. You defrosted the meal, I can clean up."

She looked at me curiously. "Until you move in, George, you're the guest."

"That's true, Nina, but at least let me help. I have Southern manners."

We unset the table and I made a pot of instant coffee while she arranged a plateful of fudge she'd bought in case she felt the need to go off her diet. We each wolfed down five pieces, standing at the kitchen counter.

When we were both stricken with nausea, we went for a walk through the neighborhood. The sky had cleared and the stars were far brighter than I'd ever seen them in Manhattan. We walked up the deserted streets to the most prosperous blocks and Nina pointed out her favorite houses, mostly huge old brownstones with odd scraps of landscaping in front.

"I always wanted to live in a suburb when I was a kid," she said, staring at a forsythia bush planted in a sawed-off barrel. "I wanted a yard with some of those trimmed green bushes."

"Yards are horrible. Especially for children. Half my childhood was spent raking leaves and cutting grass and trimming hedges. My brother Frank and I wanted to live in an apartment building surrounded by cement. I'd be a happier person today if I'd grown up with macadam under my feet."

"Does your family know you're gay, George?"

"Oh, sure," I said. "That got taken care of pretty early on. I'd finished my second year at Bowdoin and I was home for the summer and my mother asked me if the person in California I was getting daily letters from was more than my friend."

"I have a feeling he's your lover," my mother had said to me. Her voice was so reasonable and calm, so matter-of-fact, that without thinking I'd said, "Well, as usual, Ma, you're right," as if I was telling her, Yes, I'd love beans with the corned beef. The problem was, I'd never considered my sexuality a problem. I'd never really considered it much at all. I'd always felt on the outside of everything in my life, so I just took it as part of the package when I realized I couldn't care less about going all the way or any of the way with the girls I occasionally took to the movies. I thought I was merely telling my mother the jerk in California was my lover, oblivious to the other implications. At first I figured she was just jealous I was getting more mail than she was.

Two days later, Frank refused to speak to me and my father sheepishly handed me a check for a thousand dollars and told me I had two weeks to get out of the house. My mother had leaked the news to them. I called my pen pal in California and told him what had happened. "I've got a thousand bucks," I said. "I could come out and stay with you for a while. I've never been to California."

"Are you nuts?" he whispered into the receiver. "What would *my* parents think? I've got to count on them for three more years of tuition, you know."

That was the last I heard of him.

I'd called someone I knew in Boston who lived in a huge apartment in an atrocious neighborhood. He was a tall, scrawny black man who wore loosely constructed raw cotton clothes and called himself Ginger. His apartment was kind of an urban commune where people went to crash for a few days or weeks in varying stages of turmoil. There was always someone lying in a corner reading the *Guardian* or coming down from speed or waiting for a political rally to take place. He'd told me I could stay as long as I wanted even though I'm sure he didn't have a clear idea of who I was.

When I'd told my mother I'd found a place to live, she looked at me indignantly and said, "Don't be ridiculous, dear, that's all blown over."

"The crazy thing was," I told Nina, "it had. The four of us were back to our usual insults and sarcasm as if nothing had happened. My father told me to keep the thousand bucks just the same. I gave half of it to Frank, not that he deserved it."

"And that was that?" Nina asked.

"Well, I had five hundred bucks and an excuse to leave home. And I was dying to drop out of Bowdoin anyway since I was as out of place there as I would have been in China. I moved to Ginger's flat later the same week."

Ginger had turned out to be one of those inexplicably well-connected people who knew someone in every walk of life. He'd helped me get a day-care job and saner living quarters in a triple-decker and convinced me to finish my degree at a local state school.

"And then I was struck with the idea of moving to New York," I said. "Stricken, you might say."

"Well, for what it's worth, George, I'm glad you did."

NINA insisted on walking me to the subway even though it seemed ungentlemanly to let her. We didn't mention anything about me moving in; I think we both just assumed I would.

"I'll call you in the next couple of days," I said as I was going down into the subway. "I'll call you tomorrow."

"Great. If I don't hear from you, is it all right if I call? I usually don't answer the phone when I'm at home. I get tired of listening to people talk."

I didn't know if I should hug her or kiss her or shake her hand. I had my closed umbrella in one hand and I gave it a kick with my foot and stuck my free hand into my pocket and walked down the stairs to the train.

5

TWO weeks later I rented a van similar to the one I'd rented to move my junk from Washington Heights, loaded it with the same boxes of the same clothes and records and photographs and books. Aside from being unsettling, I find moving humiliating. I hate riding in a truck weighted down with all of my belongings. I hate knowing my life is so shallowly rooted it can be picked up and loaded into the back of a small van and shipped off to some other temporary lodgings.

Joley came with me, maintaining a high level of forced gaiety. We both acted as if moving had been my idea all along. After the dinner with Nina I was convinced leaving was all for the best, but I still wasn't of such strong moral character that I wouldn't have preferred being the one who ended the relationship rather than the one who'd been told it was time to move on. As we drove across the Manhattan Bridge Joley chattered on about how wonderful it was to be getting out of the city for the day.

"We're going to Brooklyn," I said, "not a farmstead near New Paltz."

Nina was waiting for us on the cement stoop reading a mystery novel while Mrs. Sarni leaned out her window in her print housedress, talking and talking with her arms flailing.

"It's wonderful to see you again, Lila," Joley said, giving Nina a long and practically passionate embrace.

I felt a horrible pang of jealousy as I watched him embrace her; I didn't want Nina to feel partial to him in any way. She was my friend and not his and I wanted her to side with me in this situation, no matter how nice Joley's eyes were.

"He's not moving in, too, is he?" Mrs. Sarni said from her window.

"We used to live together," I said. "He's just helping me with some of my things."

"Oh?" she said. "Isn't that nice. What are friends for, George? Am I right?"

When everything was unloaded and stacked in my bedroom and scattered around the living room and Joley had commented at least five times that the apartment was "admirably bright and roomy," he got into the van and slammed the door shut. He rolled down the window and stuck out his arm.

"That didn't take any time at all," he said brightly. "The place is great, Georgie, really roomy. Great wallpaper, too. I'm just happy you found such a nice place."

"Joley," I said, "give me a call soon. Don't make me be the first one to call."

"It hurts me that you think you need to say that, George."

The minute I heard the practiced indignation in his voice, I knew I was a fool for even mentioning it. I knew I'd be the one to call and try to arrange dinner plans, primarily to keep a semblance of continuity in my life. I reached into the open window and mussed up his hair. "I wish you weren't so good-looking, Joley. I really wish you weren't so handsome."

He laughed, flattered and self-assured. No one could accept a compliment as graciously as Joley. He put the van in first and eased his foot off the clutch and slowly pulled away from the curb. I watched from the sidewalk as he turned the corner, looking at himself in one of the sideview mirrors, combing his hair back into place with his fingers exactly as it had been before I'd mussed it. It was a sunny and balmy spring afternoon. I could go for a walk through the park or take the subway out to Brighton Beach—but I can't handle sunshine when I'm feeling miserable.

"Hey, George," Mrs. Sarni yelled as I walked into the house. "Good riddance. Am I right, George? Good riddance?"

I spent the next week or two angry and sad and surrounded by the boxes I had no interest in unpacking. I read the complete works of Jean Rhys and played Connee Boswell's recording of "Time on My Hands" about a thousand times. Mrs. Sarni called out a cheerful "yoo-hoo" each and every time I walked into the house, and Nina and I, having already told each other our life stories, struggled to find things to talk about. I decided I'd made a foolish, impulsive move to a foreign and not altogether friendly world. Nina's inconsistencies baffled me more and more every day. She was helping to organize a conference on women in psychology and she spent hours on the phone talking to feminists from around the country, lining up workshops and lectures while she brushed Firehouse Red polish on her long nails or smoothed a French Clay mask over her throat. She insisted I accompany her to a nuclear disarmament demonstration and then made us an hour late while she cut the elastic out of the wristbands of a white sweatshirt she'd bought for the event. She drank too much, she spent money she didn't have, she complained about her workload but wasted hours reading valueless mystery novels.

Then one night she came home from work and told me she'd signed us up for dancing lessons at an Arthur Murray school down the street from the apartment. Introductory Ballroom.

"Dancing lessons?" I said. "This is bad news. I've never been able to follow instructions with my feet and I'm not sure I want to."

"You're driving me into a depression with your moping and sulking. This will be good therapy for both of us. It's cheaper than going to a shrink and probably a lot more effective. And I've always wanted to learn how to do ballroom dancing. Maybe we could enter a competition."

Of course I, too, had always wanted to learn ballroom dancing, in keeping with my taste in music, but I didn't want to let on. I was sulking. I went to the first lesson grudgingly.

The dance studio was a ramshackle hall one floor above a florist shop. The walls were a crumbling pastel blue embossed with huge continent-shaped water stains. Exposed pipes ran along the ceiling, and worn and tarnished mirrors covered the front wall, reflecting and magnifying the decay. Our teacher was a neurasthenic cigarette fiend with hennaed red hair and tobacco-stained fingers. She was probably in her mid-fifties, and she reminded me of a distraught, flamboyant librarian. She wore flowing dresses with tight bodices and chiffon scarves either tied around her hair Vera-Ellen style or choking her neck. She always strapped on a pair of black high-heeled shoes studded with rhinestones that had probably been resoled a hundred times. When she stood at the front of the class alone, struck a pose with her sparkling feet firmly planted and her back dramatically arched, and then danced by herself around the room to demonstrate a step, she broke my heart. She was a monument to loneliness. She spoke with a heavy Brooklyn accent, but she always pronounced dance as "dahnse," as Ginger Rogers in jodhpurs might have prounced it.

"Think of every dahnse as a three-minute love affair," she'd say, posed with her eyes shut. Then she'd sail off into a solo demonstration, firmly held by her dream lover.

At the first lesson she explained the school had replaced the record player with a tape machine — even though she, who'd been teaching there for eighteen years, was against the idea. She spent a quarter of every class turning the tapes from side to side, trying to figure out how to work the machine.

Nina and I were the youngest students and the worst dancers. Most of the others were middle-aged couples who wanted a place to go dancing and ignored the lessons entirely, or older singles looking to pair up with someone. We fumbled and flubbed our way through as Miss Reynolds floated around the room keeping time with the music and singing out instructions.

"And *one* two three four, *lift* two three four, *right* leg for ward, *good* job Ni na, *one* two three four ... "

After the first few humiliating classes, the ritual of it began to appeal to me. Nina was rhapsodic. We went to the flea markets on Canal Street one weekend and picked up a bunch of flashy, ill-fitting outfits: puffy strapless prom gowns and open-toed high-heeled shoes for Nina; grossly baggy pleated pants and wide-shouldered sport jackets for me. We didn't dance any better in our new clothes, but we looked wonderful.

One night as we were doing the fox-trot to "How Deep Is the Ocean," Nina looked into the distance over my shoulder, gripped me a little tighter, and started to cry.

"Nina?" I said softly. "Are you all right?"

"I'm fine, George," she said, her throat tight. "I think it's just a combination of things catching up with me. I think it's the music and this dress. I don't know what it is."

"Shall we keep dancing?"

"Please," she said, sobbing.

I held her closer and led us through the crowd of more physically nimble and emotionally stable couples. Miss Reynolds looked at us with horror, lost count, and then went back to the lesson with a trembling voice. After a few minutes, a feeling of melancholy swept over me. My mind wasn't focused on anything in particular, but I could tell I was glazing over. The other couples were swirling around us in a dizzying, graceful blur. I lost track of what my feet were doing, and I, too, burst into quiet tears. I hugged Nina, put my face closer to hers and we slowed to a crawl.

" ... and *one* two three four, *one* two three four, *ten* more minutes, *try* to hang on ... "

At the end of the class I felt a genuine surge of spirit, as if I'd just paid off my entire credit-card bill. Nina wiped her eyes and laughed. On the way home we bought a quart of ice cream and sat up in Nina's bed watching reruns of Mary Tyler Moore. It was a turning point in our relationship and it became a pattern: ten minutes into a lesson one of us would start to cry and then the other would join in and then we'd leave the studio in hysterical laughter. Miss Reynolds abandoned all attempts to correct our dancing. The only time she spoke to us was to tell us how lovely our clothes looked or how nice Nina's hair was done.

"George and Nina," she'd say as we walked in the door. "My best-dressed students." And then she'd suck on a cigarette as if it were oxygen. When our twelve weeks were up she waved us out of the studio with blatant relief.

I sent my mother another change-of-address card with the usual cryptic message and the phone number. She called me to breathlessly wish me well.

"I have a new roommate, Ma," I told her.

"That's nice, George. Who is he and don't ask me what I mean by 'who,' please."

"Her name is Nina. She's very kind, very reliable. She's a psychologist."

"Oh, God, we need one of those around here. A girl, George? Excuse me, I mean—a woman, George?" My mother and I had gone over this ground many times. *My* female friends were women, *Frank's* were girls, Frank and I were *men*, not boys, and *she* (a concession on my part) was a lady. "What does she look like, dear?"

"What difference does it make what she looks like?" I barked.

"Well, don't jump on me, George. I take enough in this house all day without having to pay AT and T to get more from you. All I meant was that maybe she'd be good for Frank, unless you're doing something I would, honestly, be very interested in hearing about."

"Sorry to disappoint you, Ma. Anyway, what happened to Sheree? I thought that was going full steam."

"Oh, that. That's been off for months. I'm sure I wrote you about that. He's been moping around here ever since. Don't ever tell him I told you this—" her voice dropped so low I could barely hear her—"but she dumped him for someone else in his company. Did you hear that, George?"

"I heard. That's too bad."

"He's better off, not that I'd dare suggest it to him. Maybe you could invite him down and do a little matchmaking with this psychiatrist."

"Psychologist. I don't think she's Frank's type." I could see them screaming at each other from opposite sides of a picket line. "She's too old. She's almost thirty."

"Frank needs a new type. He needs someone with more on her mind than cigarettes. Does this Nina eat?"

"No, she doesn't. She lives on air. Of course she eats. What kind of question is that?"

"Well, who knows these days, with everyone starving themselves to death or jumping around on aerobics. I see them on television bouncing around with their behinds sticking out." She sighed so deeply I thought she'd drop the phone. "So I guess it didn't work out living with that Joley friend of yours or whatever he called himself. Just tell me yes or no, George."

"Yes, it didn't work out. Thanks for asking, Ma."

"I'm sorry to hear it. I'm sure you'll find another... whatever. Just be careful what you're doing with all that disease business going on. You know what I mean, dear. I don't know what's wrong with you and your brother, two good-looking young men. Notice I said men, George, not boys. My two adult sons."

"Thank you, Ma."

"I don't understand why you can't meet some decent people. I keep telling Frank he should go on a retreat. I don't dare even mention it to you. And forget about your father. He hasn't had a win in the numbers in about a month and he refuses to talk to me—as if it's my fault."

We gossiped for a few minutes about relatives neither one of us liked. She asked me about Brooklyn and I told her Marilyn Monroe had lived in Brooklyn Heights when she was married to Arthur Miller.

"Well," she said, "there's one person you won't be bumping into on the streets."

"Let's hope not," I said. I told her an ethnic joke to tell my father. "And tell Frankie to straighten himself out." As I was about to hang up, I said, "I miss you, Ma."

"Sure you do, dear, just like you miss the measles."

JOLEY never did call me. After six weeks I broke down and rang him up.

"George," he said. "I was just about to pick up the phone and give you a call."

We made plans to have dinner in one of the eight hundred new restaurants that had opened on Columbus Avenue since I'd moved. Two days later he called back to cancel. "But I have opera tickets I'm not going to use. Maybe you and Lila would like to go?"

"I hate opera," I said, "and *Lila's* afraid of chandeliers."

I occasionally heard about Joley through some of the people we knew in common but it was always the foolish kind of gossip I'd heard about him before I really knew him. And now I couldn't bear to listen to "I think he just up and flew to Rio for the semester break" when I knew Joley wouldn't "up and fly" to Albany unless it had been planned seventeen months in advance.

THERE isn't much to say about my relationship with Nina except that we loved each other and took care of each other and behaved a little like best friends, a little like brother and sister, and a little like very young and very tentative lovers. I suppose the best way to describe our friendship is as a long and unconsummated courtship. between two people with no expectations. Sometimes when we came home late from dancing or a double feature, there was an awkward moment of hesitation as we said good night and each went off to our separate rooms, but that was only sometimes. I think we both valued our friendship too much to make any overtures at exploring the murky and vague desire we felt for each other. I think we were threatened and excited when we were mistaken for a couple by the neighbors who often saw us together on the street or by the checkout people at Key Food who took inventory of our shopping sprees.

On the rare occasion that I brought someone home or went out on a blind date that Timothy had arranged, Nina would get testy and cranky and complain that she'd been woken up in the middle of the night by the front door slamming as we came in or the sound of laughter through the walls. We both knew the charges were absurd, as Nina could have slept through a complete renovation of the apartment, and there was never any laughter coming through the walls on one of my disastrous blind dates. I, on the other hand, felt threatened whenever some man she met through school or work called her up—as they often did—to arrange a date or ask an unnecessary academic question. If I answered the phone, I always put on my most masculine, possessive voice to announce that she wasn't home or, better yet, was in the shower and could I please take a message. What if her boyfriends didn't like me or were homophobes or wanted to sweep her off her feet to some split-level in Westchester County? Stranger things had happened in life.

Nina had met Howard at the Museum of Broadcasting. She'd gone after work to watch an old television documentary on the women's movement and Howard was there killing an evening with a tape of his favorite show from the sixties, *The Defenders*, starring E.G. Marshall. They were seated in booths on either side of the room, and halfway through her film, Nina noticed the man across from her staring alternately at her and her screen.

"He wasn't gawking or leering," she told me that night. "He was just looking and smiling, innocently, really."

When her film was over and she was getting ready to leave, Howard went up to her and introduced himself, first apologizing fiercely for invading her privacy. "I realize I don't have any right to just come up to you and introduce myself," he'd said, "but I happened to notice what tape you were watching."

He proceeded to rattle off every ERA, abortion, and child-care demonstration he'd been to in the past five years. He told her he'd recently discovered a new restaurant in the area and asked if she'd like to go out for dinner.

"What impressed me most," Nina said, "was that he told me beforehand he wouldn't insult me by offering to pay. I figured I didn't have anything to lose even though I was down to my last twenty dollars."

Halfway through the meal they got into a loud argument over the exact date the university was closed in San Salvador, and she left the restaurant in a huff with her meal half eaten and Howard stuck with the check. He called her every day for a week after that and finally she agreed to go to a movie with him. Howard had seen the movie three times and considered it a comic masterpiece. Nina hated it and they had a loud argument outside the theater.

I met Howard for the first time one afternoon when Nina and I went to the Court of Appeals in Brooklyn Heights to hear him give an oral argument. He met us at a coffee shop near the Promenade and nervously wolfed down a huge plate of meat loaf and mashed potatoes while he told me about every gay rights demonstration he'd been to in the past five years and the volunteer work he was doing writing up wills at the Gay Men's Health Crisis.

The case he presented that day was an appeal for an obviously guilty teenager convicted of breaking and entering. What amazed Nina and me and endeared Howard to me forever afterward was that he spoke so softly and shyly in front of the judges, they had to keep asking him to please speak up. He'd clear his throat and say, "I'm sorry, I'm sorry, Your Honors," and then continue in his garbled mumble. He had a huge folder of disorganized papers he almost dropped to the floor at one point, saying, more clearly than he'd said anything else, "Oooooops!"

Afterward he apologized for suggesting we attend such a boring spectacle. "It's a good thing I spend ninety percent of my time behind a desk or I'd be out of a job."

I liked Howard from the first and I felt more threatened by him than by any of Nina's other lovers. I suppose I sensed he was the marrying kind. He was thirty-five and had never been married, which said to me that took the whole idea seriously.

When I finally told Nina I was afraid she'd go off and marry Howard, she reassured me that she wasn't ever going to marry or live with any man who loved her as possessively as Howard loved her or who needed as much care as Howard needed. If she'd wanted to become a nurse, she would have gone to nursing school. "Anyway, George, Howard hates to dance, so there's one thing you and I have together that he and I will never have."

Of course, she was right: a love affair can be wonderful but a courtship is far more enduring. And our courtship endured, right through the love affair, until Nina became pregnant and raised the stakes somehow, tipped the delicate balance of our relationship.

6

THE morning after our fruitless attempt to go dancing, Nina called the women's center and told them she had a fierce summer cold and needed a few days of bed rest. As I was leaving for the kindergarten at 8 A.M., she was sitting on the green vinyl sofa wrapped in a sheet she'd ripped off her bed, eating a half-frozen pan of brownies and reading a celebrity autobiography "with sixteen pages of never-before-released photographs."

"If you don't want to talk with Howard," I advised her, "maybe you should call one of your women friends. Isn't that what sisterhood is all about?"

She didn't look up from her book. "If we had a microwave," she said, "I could have defrosted these brownies."

WHEN I came back from work later that afternoon, she was lying on her bed with the book open in her lap and a bottle of vodka on the floor beside her. Nina loved drinking vodka, especially when she wanted to steep herself in her Polish identity. She gave me a shockingly boozy smirk and said, "No, I didn't call any of the girls today, George, if that's what you were thinking."

"Nina," I said, "you're drunk. I can't believe it. Here it is five in the afternoon and you're in bed, drunk and pregnant."

"I'm sorry, George. I know it's awful. I must look like a wreck. I just need to do some thinking, that's all. Sometimes it's easier to reach a decision in bed."

The hot spell that began the day she told me she was pregnant stretched on unseasonably. Every morning when I woke up, the

stale, putrid air hung over me as I lay in bed, hovering like a
succubus. The tomato plants and grapevines behind the house
looked limp and exhausted and two oval slabs of paint dropped
from the ceiling under the weight of the stifling humidity. The tape
on the bottom of Nina's RZECZ KRAKOWSKA poster pulled off
the wall and the whole thing rolled into a tight, damp scroll.

I used the heat as an excuse for spending too much time and
money going to movies at an air-conditioned theater on the West
Side that was showing a program of classic Westerns. When school
got out, I'd walk across the park, sweating through my clothes,
and collapse in the cool dark until after the sun had gone down.
I saw *Shane, She Wore a Yellow Ribbon,* and three separate showings
of my favorite movie, *Red River.* I think I truly understood the
nature of my erotic fantasies the first time I saw Montgomery Clift
cross the screen astride a frothing horse.

But it wasn't the air-conditioning and Monty that kept me in the
dark eating popcorn dinners; mainly I hated going home and facing
Nina's depression, her drunken television binges that went on day
after day. The sight of her unsettled me. I couldn't understand
what her confusion was all about. As far as I could tell, the only
decision she had to make was choosing the right date for an abortion, and what she needed for that was a calendar, not a half gallon
of vodka. I might not be an expert on pregnancy, but even I knew
the significance of the term "first trimester."

She'd given me strict instructions to tell Howard she was at the
movies whenever he called, and in just a few days I told him she
was at the movies twelve separate times. I felt morally compromised
lying to someone as earnest as Howard, but I saw it as the only
way to protect my own living situation. I never questioned the
sincerity of Howard's pro-choice politics, but in this case his choice
would undoubtedly be a large wedding and a 50 percent share of
the mothering duties, which would leave me a stranded fourth.

"George," he finally said on the thirteenth call, "I just want a
yes or no and then I won't say another word; Is the Bumpkin seeing
someone else?"

"No," I said, "the Bumpkin isn't."

"No? She isn't seeing someone else?"

"No."

"Are you sure?"

"I'm positive."

"But you wouldn't tell me if she were. That's what I admire about the friendship you two have—your loyalty to each other. She's not at the movies, is she, George? You can tell me that much."

"No, she isn't."

"Fine. Is she in the apartment?"

"Yes."

"Alone?"

"Howard, come on, let up on me."

"That must mean she isn't alone."

"It doesn't mean that at all."

"Then she *is* alone."

"Yes. Yes, yes, yes, yes. She's alone. We're all alone, Howard. We're born alone and we die alone and in between we sit in bed alone and watch Mary Tyler Moore reruns."

"I'm sorry, George. I won't say another word about this. It isn't my business anyway. How are the kids? You know, I was telling someone today that if more men would take responsibility for child care, we could balance out the ratio of men and women lawyers in this country."

"I'm not sure I see the relation."

"And isn't this weather horrible? Of course, I don't mind the heat so much, but Nina must be miserable with the way she hates it. Is she miserable, George?"

"Not that I know of."

"Oh? You're not sure? I thought you said she was in the apartment."

"I have to go, Howie. I've got a cramp in my foot and I can't stand much longer."

"Just tell her hello from me. Tell her I think she's an Angel, a Brisket."

SCHOOL hadn't, in fact, been going too smoothly that week. While the kids seemed oblivious to the temperature, the parents came in to drop them off looking battered and ready to kill. Everything

Melissa or I said was interpreted as an attack on them or their children or on the underpinnings of the Family. The divorce rates citywide must have been soaring. One father, a playwright who'd had a successful Broadway show ten years earlier followed by a trio of bombs, absently asked Melissa how she thought his son was getting along. "Well, to be perfectly frank..." she started.

"Frank? Frank? Don't mention that name to me, Melissa. I don't know what he has against me, but he's trying to ruin my life. How can you mention Frank Rich now when you know I've got a play opening in two months?"

"Frank Rich?" she asked.

"Frank Rich!" he shouted. "Why not just tell everyone in the school and get them in on the plot, too."

Mr. Simmons called me into his office at the end of the week to ask how I was holding up in the heat. "Everybody's in a stew, George. You can't tell if people are making rational and reasonable judgments in this weather."

"I suppose not," I said.

"For instance, I received a very strange complaint about Melissa the other day. Do you know anything about her association with the Sulzberger family?"

OVER the weekend, Nina pulled herself together enough to hoist her typewriter to her bed and write up the results of a couple of test batteries she'd given at the women's center earlier in the month. Usually she left a copy of her profiles on my bed before she turned them in; she knew I liked to read the stories behind the confused emotional states of total strangers. I was delighted to see she'd finally done something with her day other than watch the $10,000 Pyramid" but then I started to read.

One woman was described as "a definite borderline personality" with "strong indications of manic delusions" and, very likely, "a tendency toward hysteria." Her treatment would be hindered by her "obvious resistence to authority" and her "apparent inability to express herself as a mature adult." The other women displayed symptoms of "an unresolved Electra conflict" and "melancholic depression." She, too, was an unpromising case for regular treatment thanks to her "refusal to participate in helping herself." I was stunned. Usually Nina's reports were filled with references to the details of people's lives, like their financial backgrounds and family situations. These sounded as if she'd have been content to toss both clients into a state hospital for a few weeks and go on to slaughter the next lambs. As I read through the case histories, I was horrified to see that both women were pregnant and unmarried.

"This is really bad news," I said aloud, tossing the papers to the floor. I stormed into Nina's room, where she was watching television from her cyclone-struck bed. "It's nothing but nonsense," I shouted at her. "A bunch of nonsense."

"What are you talking about, Georgie?"

"Nina, don't take your indecisiveness out on those poor creatures, that's all I'm saying. How can you say someone refuses to act like a mature adult when she's fifteen?"

"George," she said calmly, "if you're just going to insult my judgment, would you mind moving from in front of the TV? Someone's about to score a crucial point on 'Family Feud' and I'd hate to miss it for no real reason."

I snapped off the television and cleared a space on top of her bureau. The smell of ambergris wafted up to me as I sat down next to her clay makeup bowl.

"Those reports say a lot more about you than they do about either of those two girls. You're confused about when to have the abortion, which I can understand, but you can't take it out on other people. I mean, what's an unresolved Electra conflict got to do with a teenager who was raped by her uncle?"

"Excuse me, George, but who appointed you house expert on psychology?"

"I'm sorry. I don't mean to steal your title. I just think you have to talk to someone about this baby business so you can make a rational decision. If you spend any more time in that bed you're going to develop saddle sores. Why don't you pick up the phone and call someone at the women's center?"

"Women's center!" she shouted. "Again the women's center. Do you have any idea how many times you've mentioned the women's

center in the past week? I'd gladly tell you but I've lost count."
She reached over and turned the television back on. "Anyway, I've
already made a decision about the baby."

She sat back on the bed and stared at the screen with uncon-
vincing concentration. The volume was turned up and the room
was filled with the unique garbled noise of a television game show.
I resent television because I wasted so much of my childhood
watching it instead of doing something like reading Dickens. One
of my great ambitions in life is to yank a TV set out of the wall
and throw it through a window in the middle of a heated argument.
At that moment, however, I was happy for the distraction; I didn't
like the tone in Nina's voice, the smugness, as if she were about
to surprise me with something. I picked up a bottle of geranium
oil and carefully opened the cap, recoiling a bit from the acrid
odor.

"George," she said over the blaring TV, "I'm not going to have
an abortion. I've decided I want this baby. I'm going to be a mother,
George."

She kept her eyes glued to the screen as if she'd just made a
mundane pronouncement about not being able to come up with the
rent again. I put a dab of the heavy oil on my fingertip and let out
a long, slow breath. Realistically, I guess I'd always known that
no matter what platitudes about independence Nina was fond of
espousing, one day she'd go off and get married. No matter what
lines she'd fed me about being committed to her career, eventually she'd have a breakdown over her biological clock and want
children.

"When did you decide this?"

"About ten minutes ago. Just before your insight into the test
reports, which was very accurate, by the way. I wish I'd come to
a decision without all of this," she said, sweeping her hand across
the littered bed, "but it doesn't matter much now. I can go over
those reports tomorrow." She looked at me and laughed. "You seem
so crestfallen. This is what they call a joyous event."

"A blessed event," I corrected her.

I had no idea my face was betraying the sinking feeling in the
pit of my stomach. I turned away from her and arranged a vase of
dead marigolds on the corner of her bureau. Mrs. Sarni had brought

them up to us days earlier, and although Nina had carefully stuck them in a narrow carnival-glass vase, she'd forgotten to put in water. They'd probably sit on her bureau until the baby was born.

I looked at her sitting up in bed surrounded by piles of paper, and I became conscious of the same squalor I'd sensed the night she told me she was pregnant. Nina hadn't left the apartment in days, and the thought of all her inactivity exhausted and depressed me. It wasn't uncommon for me to have symptoms of her problems. Once when she was having her wisdom teeth pulled, I'd developed such a severe toothache, I was reduced to sharing her restricted diet of mashed bananas. Now I desperately wanted fresh air and a wide, expansive view. The walls were closing in, lilac print wallpaper and all.

"You know what I'd like to do right now, Nina, before you say another word? I'd like to get out of here. You've been cooped up too long. We could go out to Coney Island and get some fried food and sit on the boardwalk. You could get dressed and we could be out the door before you say another thing. We could go for a ride on the Wonder Wheel."

"Like a celebration?"

"Sure," I said. "A celebration for the blessed event. A baby shower, if you like."

AT sunset we were sitting on the steps leading down to the beach sharing a red-and-white paper tray of greasy fried chicken and shrimp. The sky was a burnt orange, the color of dead marigolds, and the ocean stretched out in front of us dark and smooth as a pond. I felt as if I were sitting in a Cinerama theater with a huge silver screen wrapped around me. The people wading at the edge of the water looked serene and shadowy while the amusement park roared behind us in a neon frenzy. I tossed a shrimp on to the sand and a flock of enormous and filthy seagulls swooped down to fight over it.

"Now look what you've done," Nina said.

As soon as they'd demolished the shrimp, the gulls turned to us and strutted up the sand toward the steps as if they were about to demand we hand over the rest of the food.

"I think we should move away from this spot," I said.

They were the first words Nina and I had exchanged since stepping off the Octopus half an hour earlier, and I was relieved we'd broken the silence. You can never tell what someone's thinking when they give you the silent treatment, and I always assume the worst.

It was on the Octopus, seated in one of the battered green buckets at the end of a rusted metal tentacle spinning frantically, that Nina told me the rest of her plan for the baby. She told me that while she intended to have the baby, she didn't intend to become Howard's wife. She'd been married once and she knew the emotional complications of that racket, and she wasn't interested. And she'd lived with lovers—Brad, the Rogerian, for example—and it boiled down to the same thing in the end. She liked the way her life was going, she liked our living arrangement.

"What I mean, George," she yelled over the roar of the machinery, "is that I want us to keep living together." The tentacle swooped to the ground wildly and my stomach dropped. "I want you to help me raise the baby."

The bucket spun in a three hundred and sixty-degree turn and Nina was slammed against me in the corner of the seat, laughing hysterically. I laughed too, and then I looked her full in the face and said, "Are you out of your mind?"

"Not that I know of," she yelled, sliding off to the other corner.

"You're nuts," I shouted. "The two of us? We can't support ourselves, never mind a baby. Do you have any idea how much a box of Pampers costs?" But then, thinking I was giving the idea too much credence by mentioning things as tangible as money and paper diapers, I said, "Forget that last comment, Nina. The whole thing's too crazy to even think about."

She looked at me, hurt and surprised, as if she hadn't expected me to sound so serious. "Relax, George," she shouted as we were cranked back into the air.

The whole truth was, all during the preceding week I'd spent a fair amount of time fantasizing about helping Nina raise an infant. As I walked in the sweltering heat from the kindergarten to the theater on the West Side, I found myself watching people wheeling babies around in carriages or carrying them on their backs, sitting with them on their laps, bouncing them up and down like big, responsive toys. I went into the Key Food near the apartment and made a thorough tour of the baby aisle, checking out the Pampers display and the rattles and teething toys and the bottles of textureless food with pictures of toothless gnomes on the labels. I'd never realized until that week how many men, and some good-looking men, too, were walking the streets lugging babies, unaccompanied by the mothers. It was all preposterous daydreaming: Nina and me strolling through Prospect Park pushing a stroller, bathing the baby in the kitchen sink, making a cozy bed for it in the top drawer of her bureau. It was harmless nonsense, carried on under the comforting assumption that Nina was about to rouse herself from her bed and announce the date of her abortion. But as we sat on the cruel Octopus, slamming into each other and listening to a group of drugged teenagers howling in the other seats, I was terrified to think my fantasies might become reality.

The ride went on forever, the ground rising and falling beneath us. The junkie operator of the thing was seated in his booth guzzling something from a brown paper bag and fiddling with a radio to get the mood music right. When I'd bought our tickets he'd leered at Nina from the depths of his cage and I was sure he was giving us an especially long ride to impress her with his generosity. When the machine finally slowed to a stop, several of the teenagers screamed "Asshole!" at the operator as they passed by his booth.

"Look at them," I said to Nina. "Do you really want to bring a kid into a world with the likes of them?"

I'd meant it as a joke but she'd walked ahead of me and didn't say a word, not even when I asked her if she wanted corn with the fried shrimp and chicken.

As we walked away from the thuggish gulls, down the boardwalk toward the rotting structure of the old parachute jump, the sun was finally burning its way into the horizon and finishing off the disastrous afternoon. "How is the father going to react to this plan, Bumpkin?" I asked her.

"I don't know. I don't intend to tell him for a while. I don't intend to tell him anything for a while."

My masculine identity was aghast. "Nina! That's lousy! The baby is as much his as yours. You're not being fair to him."

"Life is unfair, Georgie." She dumped the remains of the food into a trash barrel and led me over to a deserted bench. "Look, George," she said calmly, "I can either have the baby or not, that's the first point, and I insist the decision is one hundred percent my own, no matter what. Well, I want to have her. I want a baby. I've had two abortions already and I'm thirty years old, and truthfully, the idea excites me more than anything else has for a long time."

"More than your career, for instance?"

"If I get serious about my work, the timing is perfect. I could get most of the research for my dissertation finished by the time the baby is born and spend the first six months at home breast-feeding and writing. By the time I'm ready to go out and start looking for a job, she'll be ready for day-care."

"And that's where I come in?"

"No, it isn't. As far as Howard goes, since you seem so concerned, I don't want to push the baby on him. He has his own life. If I were having an abortion, I'd take full responsibility for that, and since I'm having the baby I'll take full responsibility for her. And another thing, George, I don't intend to spend the rest of my life battling with Howard over every issue in my child's life from her first step to whether or not she should go to law school."

"But, Nina, you love conflict. Your relationship with Howard is based on conflict. And how do you know the baby will be a girl?" I myself liked the idea of a son.

"I just said 'she,' that's all. I never did plan to spend the rest of my life with Howard. He's a wonderful person and I care about him, but I never planned to spend my life with him. Don't you see that the minute he and I start raising the baby as a couple, our relationship becomes something totally different from what it's been? Our lives would be melded together by the baby, worse than with marriage. Worse than if we bought a co-op together. After all, George, I wouldn't buy a co-op with Howard, so I'm certainly not going to raise a baby with him. It wouldn't be the same with you and me. The commitment would be completely different."

She looked out to the dark beach where a few couples were still splashing through the incoming tide holding their shoes dangling from their fingertips. Her profile was lit by the garish neon of the park. The hollows of her face were filled with queer blues and greens, like a flickering mask of clown's makeup.

"I don't want to give up our friendship," she said quietly, staring off at the water. "I know it started out as a matter of convenience, but it means more to me than that now."

"It means more than convenience to me, too, Nina, but do we have to make it so inconvenient? You have to admit a baby is pretty inconvenient."

"I wouldn't know. That's one of the things that's so exciting about this: it's going to be a completely fresh experience."

"We can ride on the Tornado if you want a fresh experience."

"I'm not proposing marriage."

"I know."

"I just want you to think it over, that's all. We can make this arrangement anything we want. We don't have to worry about getting stuck playing some prescribed roles the way Howard and I would."

I wanted to tell her that a squalling baby at four in the morning is a squalling baby at four in the morning, no matter what role you were playing, but I held back.

After a while we went down to the beach and took off our shoes. The sand was still warm from the sun and the absorbed heat of the day. I put my arm around her waist and then quickly drew it back. Strange fireworks of splitting cells and roiling fluids were going on behind that soft wall of flesh and I wasn't sure I wanted to feel them.

"I'll give it some thought, Nina," I said. "I'll give it serious consideration."

We walked down to the edge of the water, dodging the broken glass and the empty cans and the half-eaten knishes scattered on the sand.

7

THE following day at school I was bored and restless in front of the class, irritable, and unable to maintain control over the kids. I had a policy of not dragging my personal problems into work, but every time I looked at a doughy five-year-old face or a pair of puffy babylike hands, all I could see was a bassinet in the middle of my bedroom floor.

Saint Michael's was, depite the fact that they'd hired me in a pinch, well respected and prestigious. Pregnant women in business suits often wandered through the classrooms on their lunch hours to survey the facilities and fill out applications for their *in utero* offspring. Places in the school were at such a premium, it was difficult to get a child enrolled unless the parents knew someone who could pull strings for them or were of such stature themselves that their presence was an asset at school functions.

The preschool was in the basement of a building which housed grades one through seven of an equally prestigious grammar school. Ten years earlier the grammar school had been famous as an institute of open education where the children were allowed to wander from one room to the next, studying anything or nothing, depending on their mood. Now the educational philosophy was considered progressive because the faculty used disciplinary tactics to encourage underachievers. We in the basement were still more of the old school.

Physically my classroom resembled a spread from *House Beautiful*. The windows were framed with Marimekko drapes and hung with lush plants—trailing, colorful succulents and ominously thick ferns I'd been instructed to leave to the care of the professionals

who came in once a week to water and trim. The children ate at
Danish Modern tables and chairs and napped on all-cotton futons
covered with Marimekko sheets. Every night the room was scoured
clean by the janitorial staff, and more than once an art project I'd
been working on with the kids was thrown into the furnace with
the trash. Mr. Simmons, kind and generous though he was, had
an acute fear of offending the aesthetic tastes of the parents with
one of our amorphous flour-and-water creations.

Melissa and I set up our school day as a series of ten- to fifteen-
minute activities and games and lessons, which we shuffled around
like a deck of cards to keep the kids' attention as focused as
possible. We swapped off the star turn so we'd still be functional
by the end of the day. Ordinarily we'd start off with something
rousing like a song session; we'd do a kindergarten classic such
as "A-way down south in the yankety yank, a bullfrog jumped from
bank to bank..." and then take requests. "Like a Virgin" and
"Tired of Being Blonde" were two favorites. After that we'd go into
the alphabet or a science project, then a story, then snack, more
lessons, then lunch. Afternoons were mainly devoted to projects
that required a lot of physical exertion—hammering and interpre-
tive movement, for example. Most parents liked to pick up an
exhausted child at the end of the day, one incapable of making
too many demands on their free time.

Midway through the morning, as I sat at the front of the room
reading aloud a story about a pig who moves to New York City to
become an actress and ends up waiting tables, I broke out in
uncontrollable yawns before the end of every sentence. Melissa
sat on the floor at the back of the reading area staring off into
space with one of the kids settled on her lap inquisitively running
his hands over her bright red crew cut. Her eyes were glazed over
as if I were boring her, too, into a stupor. By the time I'd read
through half the story, the kids were wrestling and rolling around
on the floor and bopping each other on the head with the Marimekko
pillows scattered around for them to recline on.

"All right, all right," I said, putting aside the book. "You need
to be quiet, right now." It was standard practice throughout the
school to express every disciplinary request as a matter of dire
need. Unfortunately, most of the kids saw through the tactic and

used it on each other. It wasn't uncommon to hear, "You need to give me that book, Bethanne, or I'll kill you," coming from the back of the room.

"You *need* to be quiet," I repeated, more harshly this time.

A little girl with waist-length blond hair and an elfin smile raced to the front of the room, put her hands on her hips, and said in a mocking and sarcastic tone, "You *need* to be quiet, class."

The kids shrieked with laughter and collapsed on each other in hysterics. Rose, the blonde, spun around in wild circles with her arms outstretched and her hair lashing against my chair.

"You need to sit down, Rose," I told her.

"You need a blood transfusion, George."

Rose's father was a prominent surgeon in Manhattan. She had a large medical vocabulary she used to diagnose the real and imagined ills of her classmates. She was a pretty girl who was probably destined for great beauty and success in life providing she wasn't ravaged by adolescent acne and eating disorders.

"Rose, dear," Melissa said, stirring herself from her coma, "this is kindergarten. This is not the Johns Hopkins Medical School, this is kindergarten. Try to keep that in mind."

"My father went to Johns Hopkins," one child intoned from beneath a pillow. "That's in Maryland."

"My mother went to Smith," another screamed.

"My mother *could* have gone to Smith but she went to Radcliffe."

Within seconds the class turned into a shouting match. Parents' academic credentials and professional accomplishments were flying around the room like bullets. I didn't know what to do. For one thing, neither of my parents had gone to college, so I had nothing to contribute. I finally took them outside to the playground, hoping they'd exhaust themselves in the smoggy heat.

I took shelter against the side of the building where there was a patch of cool shade and jammed my hands into the pockets of my jeans. Nina had managed to get herself off to work that morning, but the ban on phone calls from Howard hadn't been lifted. I kept thinking I should call him up and tell him what was going on, now that there was no hope of an abortion, but I wanted to talk it over with someone first.

I looked across the playground and saw Melissa eying me intently as she pushed the tire swing back and forth with one of her scrawny arms. She had on a knee-length white T-shirt with a silver chain belt pinching in her waist and a pair of high black basketball sneakers that were at least one size too big. I could never talk it over with Melissa. Although she was only five years younger than me, she was culturally of a generation I know nothing about; her clothes, her taste in music, her vague political views were all outside my experience and the experience of most of my friends.

Melissa had been hired at the school almost two months earlier, and although we worked together closely, I hadn't shared much of my personal life with her. For one thing, she seemed to have figured it out, to her own satisfaction anyway, and for another, I think I was intimidated by her youth and her haircut. I was too behind the times to feel completely at ease talking to women with punk crew cuts. She'd supposedly had a distinguished academic career at Sarah Lawrence, and I imagined she was intellectually capable of anything despite her flaky demeanor.

In June, shortly after she was hired, she'd invited me to her apartment, ostensibly so she could get to know me better, though, in fact, I said almost nothing for the entire evening. She lived on the twentieth floor of a new glass building in the East Sixties in an apartment her father had bought for her when she was still in college. "He's a very generous man," she said as I walked around the spacious rooms in disbelief, "but let's face it, he knows a good investment when he sees one." She told me she was going to have the entire huge apartment decorated like a 1950s recreation room, with period furniture and appliances, old television sets and radios she'd been collecting since her junior year at Sarah Lawrence. "I want to make it look like one of those family rooms on an old TV series. I was ready to have the whole place paneled, but my father said it would ruin the resale value. Of course, I'm getting my trust fund money now, so I could go ahead and do it if I wanted, but I didn't want to cross him. My father and I are very close, George. We're kindred spirits. I mean, I've idealized him way beyond what's probably there, but there are worse things in life than that. Don't you think?"

I stood behind her in the kitchen as she randomly pulled cans out of a cabinet and lined them up on the counter. "No one ever cooked at home except my grandmother, and I didn't like her well enough to follow her around the kitchen. My parents have a house in West-chester County with a kitchen the size of Gimbel's and no one goes into it. My mother's an alcoholic, so actually it's a blessing she never goes near the stove. She was brought up to never go near a stove. Do you know the kind of woman I'm talking about, George? Golf, lunches, and cocktails, shopping sprees, that's what her life is about. Lately, though, it's all cocktails. I told my father he should threaten to leave her if she doesn't go to AA but he just hangs on and lets her get away with it. Of course, my mother's the one with the inherited money. I'm probably a hypocrite for taking money from her family when I can't stand her, but I figure I've got the rest of my life to have principles. At twenty-two you can be a hypocrite."

She stood back from the counter and took stock of her supplies. "I think I'm going to start buying generic food. I really love those black-and-white cans. It's my generation through and through: characterless. That's why I want this place to look like it came from another era. Not that I know anything about the fifties."

She turned on a television set during dinner and afterward fell asleep on the sofa. I quietly let myself out of the apartment.

As if she were reading my thoughts from across the playground, Melissa let go of the tire swing and came over to where I was standing. She put her hand on my shoulder and stared at me with her usual penetrating gaze. "I want you to know, George, that I'm here for you. I can tell you're not yourself, and if there's anything I can do, I'm here for you."

"I'm really fine," I told her. "I didn't sleep much last night, that's all."

"I'm here for anything. *Anything.*" She uttered the last word with such brutal sincerity, intensified by her deep, raspy voice, I didn't know whether to laugh or shudder or break down and tell her the whole story. "You don't have to worry about me, George. You know what I mean."

"Of course, Melissa," I said, having no idea what she was getting at. "I went to Coney Island last night and spent too much time on the Wonder Wheel. I think I messed up my equilibrium."

"Sickness, problems, depression," she went on rhapsodically, "I'm here for you. I have an uncle out in San Francisco I'm very close with. He tells me everything. I mean, I went through that period at seventeen when I thought there was something intrinsically interesting about gay men, something sexy and sophisticated. But I'm over that, George. Four years at Sarah Lawrence and you would be, too. You don't have to worry about talking to me. I'm a good listener."

"I might be coming down with a cold, an Indian summer cold," I said, thinking an admission of sickness might deflect her. "I should probably stay in bed for a few days."

"*Absolutely*, George. You do that. *Absolutely*."

There didn't seem to be anything more to say on the subject, but she continued to stare at me sympathetically. Even in basketball sneakers she was a good inch taller than me.

"So anyway, Melissa," I said, "what about you? How are you doing?"

"Me? I'm always the same. Nothing ever changes for me. My life is a complete disaster. A shambles."

"I see."

"You know the guy who moved in with me? He's crazy. He's out of his mind. Vince. You know what he cares about in life? All he cares about in life is wine. Wine wine and wine. He gets wine magazines and wine newsletters, he's a member of a wine discussion group. They sit around and talk about wine. I took him out to my folks' house? He fought with my mother about wine. She's a Scotch drinker, George. I said to him, 'Vince, you're twenty-three years old. No one is supposed to care about wine at twenty-three years old.'"

"I suppose not." I was trying to look away but she was boring holes in me with her X-ray eyes.

"One good thing about our relationship and that is all: a great connection in bed. Period. Nothing else."

"I see." I was hoping one of the kids on the playground didn't overhear the conversation and repeat it verbatim over dinner that night. "I should invite you to Brooklyn for dinner sometime, Melissa. I'll show you a real shambles if you want to see one. My apartment, I mean."

"Oh! I'd love to see your apartment, George. I'd love to see where you live. I'd *love* that. I can just picture it."

"Well, good." Her enthusiasm caught me off guard. Again the conversation seemed stalled, but she continued to stare at me. "We'll have to plan it for sometime before the snow flies," I said. She didn't budge. "Next month, maybe."

Fortunately, a child got pushed off the tire swing and I had to rush across the yard to the rescue.

MELISSA was teaching a unit on transportation that week, a subject that elicited a lot of excitement among the kids. They all had competitive stories to tell of BMWs and Volvos and trips abroad on jumbo jets. I was amazed at the amount of traveling most of the kids had done, and, truthfully, I was more than a little envious even though I hate to travel. Much as I'd like to, I can't claim to be above feeling jealous hostility toward a five-year-old, which I suppose was underneath my conflict with Doran Dunne. Later in the afternoon I was looking over Doran's shoulder as he drew with his characteristic concentration. His tongue was drooping out of the corner or his mouth and there was spittle running down his chin.

I had an ongoing love-hate relationship with Doran. He was a teeny, whiny child with a high forehead and a thin-lipped, pinched mouth. There was something neurotically passive about him which I'd disliked from the first, possibly because I saw so much of myself in it. His parents, like many at the school, were both highly paid executives in the middle of divorce proceedings. Doran was shuttled back and forth between the two of them so often, he frequently appeared dizzy and lost. The main issue in the custody battle seemed to be which of the two provided better health care, and, as a result, Doran was constantly being dragged out of school for a doctor's appointment with one or the other parent's pediatricians.

He held a dark blue crayon awkwardly between two fingers and was drawing something that resembled a Celtic harp with wings. Even the limp way he grasped the crayon annoyed me.

"What is that supposed to be, Doran?" I asked, pointing to the picture.

"It's what Melissa said to draw, George. It's a airplane."

"That's not what airplanes look like, Doran," I said with unthinkable pickiness.

"Sure it is," he said. "Me and Theodora took one to Paris in July. She had a business trip."

"I'm sure she did, but the plane didn't look like that, did it, Doran?"

"It did so, George. It was a SST. I got a picture of it from the stewardess after I took my nap. And there was this thing on the wall that said how fast we were going."

"An SST?" I asked incredulously. "You took an SST to Paris in July? Just like that?"

"Sure we did. And then we took it home again."

I quickly reminded myself that neither Doran nor his mother was responsible for the fact that I'd have trouble coughing up the cash for a bus ticket to D.C.

"When Melissa said to draw an airplane, Dorrie, she meant the kind ordinary people fly in. Most ordinary people cannot afford to fly in an SST. Did you know that, Doran? Did Theodora tell you most ordinary people can't afford a bus ticket to D.C.?"

"But everyone on the SST was affording it, George."

"Just draw a regular plane, Doran," I said loudly. "The kind you took to Palm Beach last winter." I reached over his shoulder and crumpled the paper into a ball.

He burst into tears and put his head down on the table. "We *drove* to Palm Beach," he sobbed. "We took a plane *back*."

I felt even more humiliated than I usually do when I treat children badly. If Nina had been there she could have scolded me in the same way I'd scolded her for the inhuman test reports. I looked around the room to make sure no one had seen the shameful display. Melissa was at the water table giving a demonstration of how a submarine works and appeared oblivious. There were two children at the other end of the art table but they were loudly fighting with each other, trying to decide who *needed* to give the red marking pen to whom.

I picked up Doran and held him in my arms. "Hey, Dorrie," I said, "I'm sorry. I didn't mean it."

"I know, George. That's what Daniel always tells me when he yells at me."

"We could get some peanut butter on saltines if you want."

His eyes widened. His parents competed in packing extravagant charcuterie-type pâtés and salads in his lunchbox, but Doran's real passion in life was for peanut butter on saltines; he regarded it as an exotic, forbidden food.

The two of us sat at the table in the teachers' room and carried on polite conversation about his trip. He'd seen the Mona Lisa and been to the top of the Eiffel Tower, taken a boat ride down the Seine and gone to Notre Dame.

"What did you like best, Dorrie?"

"Well, mostly I liked the couscous we ate the second night we were there, even though there was a rabbit in it and I felt bad about eating a rabbit. But mostly even better I liked the boat ride because Theodora came with me instead of that babysitter who didn't speak much English. She had funny-looking hair, George."

"I think all French people do, Dorrie," I said. "It has to do with the weather over there."

He started to laugh at me. "You're crazy, George."

"I know, Doran. I'm so crazy you wouldn't believe how crazy I am. I'm completely gonzo in the head."

"That's what Theodora says about Daniel," he said in amazement, as if he'd found a long-lost uncle.

AT the end of the day, Melissa cornered me in the teachers' room and gazed at me serenely. "I saw you lose your temper with Doran," she said.

"I feel like a rat about that, Melissa."

"Are you kidding, George? All I meant was you have to stay home and take care of that cold or whatever it is. Just take *care* of yourself. And if you want to talk about anything, *any*..."

"I know. I really will. I'm sure I'll be better by tomorrow."

"Don't feel ob*lig*ed to be better by tomorrow. That's the important thing to keep in mind."

"I won't, I promise you. You have a good night."

"Oh, there's no chance of that," she said gaily.

8

NINA had managed to avoid Howard for more than two weeks when he showed up at the apartment unexpectedly. Howard never used his keys to the building when he visited. Instead, he'd knock on Mrs. Sarni's window, have her let him into the building, and then pound on our door yelling, "Open up! It's the police." No matter how many dozens of times he'd pulled this stunt, he always got a laugh out of it, as if he were doing it for the first time. Mrs. Sarni would stand in the hall on the first floor and laugh along with him.

"Where's the Pudding, George?" he asked me, chuckling to himself as I let him in.

"The Pudding's on the fire escape, Howie. We're about to eat."

"Perfect," he said, rubbing his hands together enthusiastically. "I'm famished." He walked toward the living room and tripped over a *New York Review of Books* I'd tossed on the floor. "Right-wing rag," he mumbled as he straightened the collar of his suit.

Howard was a short, small-framed man who carried himself with the posture and aplomb of a football player. He didn't exactly strut, but he entered a room silently announcing he was taking control of things. He had thinning coal-black hair receding from his temples, enormous dark eyes that were usually encircled by dark rings, and a slight, incipient potbelly that added to his stature and was inexplicably flattering. He wasn't as handsome as many of the men I'd seen Nina date, but his features had a sleepy, droopy sensuality—the look of a man who preferred lolling in bed on a weekend surrounded by newspapers and crumbs to dashing off to a forty-eight-hour seminar on mind control and professional advancement.

His only concession to vanity was his wardrobe, which comprised a closetful of designer suits, Italian shoes, tailormade shirts and extravagant silk ties. He wore his immoderate clothes with no fashion sense whatsoever but with the characteristic sloppiness of an upturned collar, a rolled pants leg or a grease stain on a fifty-dollar tie. Altogether his outward appearance was that of a proud and idealistic man who loved taking care of his clients and his friends even though he was incapable of taking care of himself.

Howard was an only child, a fact which Nina claimed explained everything about his personality. He'd taken her to visit his widowed father in Miami early in the spring, and the first thing Howard Senior did when they walked through the door was pat Nina's cheek and say to his son, "She's a Pumpkin, Howie, just like your mother." She'd insisted they return to New York a day ahead of schedule.

Nina was standing out on the fire escape yanking in the laundry line on the squeaky pulley. As she pulled each piece of washing off the frayed rope, she tossed it through the window to the living-room floor. There was a storm of sheets and underwear beneath the sill.

"Look at her, George," Howard said. He held up his hands as if to touch her and then let them drop as if afraid of spoiling her image framed by the window. "Just look at her."

Nina pulled herself through the window feet first. She gave a start when she saw Howard standing in front of her. "Who let you in, Howard?" she asked. She pushed the soft hair off her forehead and smiled. I was relieved to see her dimples light up her face with genuine pleasure. "George was ordered to guard the door."

"I thought it was the police."

"Why have you kept me from you, Pumpkin?" Howard asked. He dumped himself onto the vinyl sofa and sat staring at her like a blissfully overfed kitten. "How come you're so gorgeous, Munchkin? How come?" Nina tossed a towel at him. He picked it up and buried his nose in it. "Who's she been seeing, George? Who's she been standing me up for?"

"Mrs. Sarni's son," I said. "They've been having torrid afternoon meetings at the neon shop."

"That asshole," he said, beaming. "Oh, I'm sorry, George." His voice had turned serious. "You know what I meant."

"No I don't know what you meant," I said to torment him. "I don't expect to have to take that kind of abuse in my own home."

"George, come on, I didn't mean anything by that. I've never even met the man."

"Grow up, Howard," Nina said. She collapsed on the sofa with her head in Howard's lap and smiled up at him. "He's teasing you. You should know that by now. I don't suppose you're hungry. George is making dinner."

"Of course I'm hungry. I'm always hungry. What are you making?"

"A loaf," I said. I'm a terrible cook and the only way I can force myself to prepare a meal is to toss everything into a casserole dish, stick it in the oven, and hope for the best.

"A loaf of what?" he asked skeptically.

"Oh, different things. I read the recipe on the back of a Shredded Wheat carton. I added a few of my own touches."

"I don't know how the two of you survive. If I didn't fix a decent meal every once in a while you'd live on cold cereal."

Howard considered himself a master chef. His schooling in male liberation had included cooking lessons with Peter Kump, and he frequently came to the apartment armed with bags of food and cooking utensils and prepared elaborate feasts for the three of us. He'd spend hours chopping and cutting to perfection, sautéing, basting, and roasting. If Nina or I were within earshot, he'd lovingly describe everything he was doing and give a lesson in techniques for something like clarifying butter or mincing shallots. He followed recipes to the second and shopped meal by meal. The results were always delicious, refined versions of heavy meat-and-potato spreads. They were old-fashioned meals, *masculine* meals, despite Howard's best intentions.

IN the time it had been in the oven, the dinner had taken on the look and smell of cat food. "I told you you shouldn't cook tuna fish," Nina said as I heaped it onto plates.

"Who can trust your word in cooking, Dumpling?" Howard asked.

He pulled his chair up to the packing-crate table, jostling the unsteady top, and tossed his tie over his shoulder. "What are those black things, George?"

"Probably raisins."

"One of your touches, I'll bet." He shoveled a forkful of food into his mouth with one hand while he leafed through the advance sheets of the *New York Law Reports* with the other. "I've offered to teach you how to cook, Georgie. It's a crime more men don't take cooking seriously. Most of the world's great chefs are men. No offense, Angel." Whenever he came to a case in the Law Reports he thought might be of some use, he broke back the binding with a snap and tore out the pages. There were shredded copies of the green-and-red books all over the apartment which he'd forbidden us to throw out. "This tastes terrible," he said through a mouthful of Shredded Wheat, and then launched into an endless description of some legal precedent he'd come across that day. The monologue was as incomprehensible to me as I'm sure it would have been to anyone who hadn't studied for the bar exam. Nina picked at her food distractedly, flaking the chunks of tuna and cereal with her fork.

Howard tore a clump of papers from the Law Reports and then looked up at her suddenly and said, "You're not interested in what I'm saying, are you, Dumpling?"

"I'm fascinated, Howard. I'm enthralled."

He laughed softly. "She couldn't care less what I'm saying, Georgie. I'll bet you couldn't either. I'm so boring I don't know how you put up with me. Why don't you just shut me up, Puddle?" he asked and then immediately described the finer points of an amicus brief being filed by the New York Bar Association in a case involving the operation of nursing homes in upstate New York.

Oddly, I never did find Howard boring even though I understood nothing of what he said. Anyone who spoke with as much passion and enthusiasm as Howard could hold my attention for hours. Not to mention that I was fascinated by his flawlessly white teeth.

"But this new case I'm working on is a killer," he said, laying down his fork and reaching for seconds. "You'll love this, Muffin. You can do a psychological profile of the entire family." He proceeded to relate, in stupefying detail, the history of two generations of his client's family. He gave every bit of information imaginable about each member of the clan short of their social security numbers. The client himself was a twenty-one-year-old psychopath who'd gone on a violent rampage against his family on the afternoon he was fired from his job at Burger King. He went after in-laws and cousins by marriage and smashed most of the dishes and glasses in the house. "And then," Howard said, wound up for the climax, "*after* beating the brother-in-law with a baseball bat, he turned on his wife, who was five, five months pregnant, and went for her." He dropped his voice to a whisper. "In . . . the . . . stomach."

"That's enough," Nina said, paling visibly.

"In the stomach!" he shouted. "And I have to write an appeal for this guy. I think I can get his sentence overturned, too. During the summation of the trial, the judge told the jury. . ."

Nina rose from the table and took her plate to the kitchen. I could hear her scraping food into the wastebasket.

"I guess that was the wrong thing to say," Howard said to me. "I'll bet women are especially sensitive about that kind of thing. I'm sorry, Bumpkin," he shouted into the kitchen. "What's with her, George? She's okay, isn't she? She looks a little beat to me. She hasn't been doing some kind of drug, has she?"

Staring at Howard's worried face across the table, I felt an almost overwhelming urge to reach over, grab the front of his shirt and tell him in a harsh whisper that Nina was pregnant. I was getting dragged deeper and deeper into the mess with every unspoken word.

"She's just tired," I said instead. "You know how she gets in the heat. She'll be fine now that it's passed."

He stood up from the table and straightened his tie contemplatively. "I guess you're right. How about some music to cheer her up?" He went to the Webcor Holiday and put on an old Odetta album he'd brought from home. He turned the volume as high as possible and the sad, deep voice poured from the speakers. Howard couldn't stand my taste in music, or Nina's, and every time he visited he played the same album over and over. His love for Odetta stemmed from the countless political rallies and demonstrations he'd heard her performing at throughout the decades. Recently he and Nina had gone to see her perform at a Manhattan supper club.

They sat inches from the stage and Howard noisily chomped through a steak dinner while she performed to a small, unenthusiastic audience. The incident convinced Howard she was a victim of growing cultural conservatism and had heightened his respect for her.

"You know, George," he said as he hummed to the music, "I wanted to take Ninushka on a trip this summer. To Manitoba. I thought it sounded like the perfect spot—nice and cool. But she refused. Too busy, as usual. Always too busy. She's not seeing someone else, is she? Never mind, you wouldn't tell me if she were. And frankly, I'm happy for that. I really am. She needs a good friend. Everyone does. You know I'm a little jealous of you, don't you? Did I ever tell you that?"

"I don't think so, Howie."

"I am. Sometimes I think she loves you more than she loves me. Different, of course, but more, somehow."

"Well, I'm a little jealous of you, so I suppose we're even."

He looked surprised. "You're jealous of me? But you live with her, George, why would you be jealous? You know, maybe that's the bond between us, now that I think of it, our jealousy."

"Howard, you don't have a jealous hair on your body," Nina said as she came into the living room.

"You look worn down," he said. He grabbed a box of fudge from her hands and took it to the table. "You look exhausted. After two weeks of rest without me I thought you'd be on top of the world."

"It was the heat, Howard. The heat got to me."

"That's what George was telling me. Why don't you sit down and take it easy? Why don't you learn to relax for once in your life, Poodle?" He was furiously poking through the box of fudge, looking for a piece of penuche. "Let me tell you about this union meeting we had today. I swear, we spend half our workday debating the role of the executive committee." He stopped abruptly and looked at me with his head at an angle. "Hey, George—didn't you once tell me you own an air conditioner?"

"Never," I said. "I never told you that."

"Of course you did. Where is it? The two of us can stick it in the window. We're bound to have a couple more days of heat, and there's no point in having Nina faint because you're both too lazy to install it."

"Just sit down and enjoy the fudge, Howie," Nina said. "We'll be freezing in a few weeks anyway."

He put the box on the table and rubbed his hands together furiously. There was nothing like a conflicting opinion to prove to Howard his was correct. I'm sure this wouldn't have been the case if he'd been even one inch taller. "Come on, George. It'll take two minutes to install and then you can use it for the rest of the season."

"There is no rest of the season, Howard."

"What's the point in owning an air conditioner if you aren't going to use it? I wish my apartment was air-conditioned."

"It would be if you installed the machine in your kitchen," Nina said.

"I'm only one person. For me it would be a waste of energy."

I went to the closet where the air conditioner was stashed and cleared off the newspapers and brown bags Nina and I had been piling on top of it all year. "I think it's grown since the last time I saw it," I said. "We'll need a crane to get it out of here."

It was, in fact, an extremely old and heavy thing I'd never once plugged into the wall for fear of blowing every fuse in the city. Still, I couldn't bring myself to throw it out because I doubted I'd ever again find something that weighed so much and cost so little.

"Okay," Howard said. He threw his tie over his shoulder and rolled up his sleeves. He crowded into the closet with me and slipped his hands under one end. "In December you can auction it off as an antique."

We one, two, three picked it up together and squeezed out of the closet. Howard's tie slipped over his shoulder and landed on the dusty top of the machine. "Damn it," he said, despite the fact the tie was already filthy.

Although Howard didn't smoke and rarely drank, he was puffing by the time we were halfway to the window. Exercise and gym memberships were looked down upon as bourgeois vanity in his legal aid office, and Howard was committed to a regime of inactivity.

As we slowly, haltingly inched forward, Howard stepped on one of the bags I'd pitched from the closet and tried to scuff it to the side with his slippery leather-soled wingtips. His foot slid from under him. His upper body was jarred dramatically to the left, contorting him into a painful-looking Elephant Man posture.

Nina jumped up from the sofa and rushed to his side. "I knew that thing was trouble. Just let go of it."

"Oh, God," he groaned, sinking down at the knees but hanging on to his end. "My back, Nina! Take it from me, will you?"

Nina reached under the air conditioner and hoisted it up to her thigh while Howard slipped from under it. I looked at her, shocked and alarmed, as she raised the heavy piece of machinery higher and higher. "Nina!" I gasped. "Are you crazy? You don't lift air conditioners in your condition."

Howard, still bent over in pain, looked at both of us and said, "What condition is that?"

If we'd acted with a shred of composure the whole thing might have blown over and we could have gone out and got ice cream to cure Howard. Instead, both Nina and I let go of the leaden deadweight simultaneously, and it fell to the floor with a thump that shook the walls and sent the needle on the Webcor Holiday skidding across Odetta.

"What condition?" Howard asked again, this time with his voice ominously toneless.

"Heat prostration," Nina said, glaring at me.

"What condition, George?"

"She's tired is what I meant, Howie. She should have gone to Manitoba like you suggested, damn it."

"Nina, I'm in pain and I want an answer from one of you."

There was an urgent rapping at the door and both Nina and I sprang for it. Howard grabbed Nina's arm and held her back. Mrs. Sarni was standing in the hall with her hand pressed to her bosom operatically. "What happened with the noise, George?" she whispered.

"I dropped something," I said. "I'm sorry it disturbed you, Mrs. Sarni. It was nothing important, just a pan. How's your son?"

"Oh, Mother of God," she said, walking past me. "I thought someone died and hit the floor. Did you see that sunset tonight? Gorgeous. Like the whole of Brooklyn was on fire."

She strolled into the living room where Nina was standing with tears in her eyes, trying to get loose from Howard's grasp. The air conditioner was lying on its side with the front panel cracked in two pieces beside it. Nina looked at Mrs. Sarni and smiled faintly. "Hello again, Mrs. Sarni," Howard said, always the gentleman. "Wasn't that a gorgeous sunset?"

She looked at the two of them disapprovingly and then at the casserole dish on the table. "I didn't mean to upset your dinner. It smells lovely." She walked to the door mustering her dignity. "That was some pan you dropped, George."

"I meant to say air conditioner, Mrs. Sarni." I held the door open for her. "Have a nice night. We'll be more quiet. There's nothing else to drop."

"Sure, sure," she said as she trod heavily down the stairs.

I went back into the apartment and leaned against the wall in the hallway biting my nails. If you looked at it the right way, it really was for Nina's good that Howard knew about the baby. And the fact that I'd let the news slip was an accident, no more my fault than Howard's accident with the air conditioner was his. And even if it was my fault, it was Nina's well-being that concerned me. Her well-being and the child's. Nina and Howard's child. I stood with my ear against the wall, listening for some signs of life in the next room, but all I could hear was the upstairs neighbors fighting with their daughter. When I walked back in, both of them were gone. I stood outside Nina's bedroom door and listened to their voices, muffled and tender. I rubbed my hands together vigorously.

The living room was cool and dark. There was a soft breeze blowing in through the window, filling the room with the smell of burnt coffee—caffeine addiction was epidemic in our neighborhood. I put on a Glenn Miller album and polished off the rest of the loaf with gusto.

Whatever disadvantages there are to living my life-style in a bigoted society, the threat of an unwanted pregnancy is not one of them. I didn't expect Nina to share the burden of, for example, having to visit Fire Island once in a lifetime, and I didn't want her to expect me to share the burden of a missed pill or whatever mishap had resulted in her condition. That really didn't seem unreasonable of me when I thought about it, and anyway, it had been an accident.

I went to my room and put on a dark T-shirt and a pair of baggy military pants I usually wear with button-on suspenders. Suspenders are the only jewelry I ever wear, and sometimes I feel a little affected in them, too. But I was feeling elated and reckless so to hell with it.

I hoisted my bicycle to my shoulder and stomped down the stairs to the street. It would take me at least forty-five minutes to pedal out to the disco in Bensonhurst Nina and I had never made it to weeks earlier, and by the time I got there my legs would be too stiff and cramped for dancing, even if I got the opportunity. But I wasn't really interested in meeting anyone; it was the tacky blue lights that lured me out, the smell of stale beer, and mostly just the thought of being with the boys. Where I belonged. After all.

9

THE next morning I woke up at six o'clock to the sound of banging pans and rattling cups. A dish smashed to the kitchen floor and Nina shouted, *"Shit!"* so loudly and shrilly I thought the windows would shatter.

"Just take it easy, Cupcake," Howard said. "Just sit yourself down and take it easy and relax. It's not good for you to get yourself so worked up when you're pregnant."

"Please, Howard, please, please, please, please don't get mid-wifey on me."

Another dish smashed to the floor. "Oh, shit!" she shouted again.

As soon as I heard Howard leave the apartment, I got out of bed and sheepishly made my way into the kitchen. Bits of broken plates were scattered across the floor and two pans of something that looked like dishwater were steaming on the stove. Maybe she'd made pasta for breakfast. The oven was on and the door was open and the room felt like a steambath. I cleaned up the mess as quietly as I could and opened the window.

Nina's bedroom door was ajar. A faint purple light was oozing through the material tacked over her windows. She was standing in front of her mirror, smearing dabs of rust-colored makeup on her cheekbones. I cleared a pile of papers off the foot of the bed and sat down.

"What's the story, Morning Glory?" I said.

She leaned in toward the mirror, peering through the gap in the cards and photos taped to the glass and furiously rubbed her cheeks as if she were trying to get a spot of egg yolk off a tablecloth. Her nails were newly polished and her eyes were heavily lined with kohl—both good signs.

"You're getting ready for work," I said. Sometimes a statement of the obvious is a good conversation opener. "I guess things went well with Howard."

She tossed the tube of makeup into the clay bowl on her bureau and stuffed a stack of papers into her briefcase.

"You're sitting on my folders," she said coolly.

I eagerly reached under my behind and handed them to her. Even a sarcastic thank you would have been better than the silence she gave me.

"Soooo," I said, examining my toes. "You and Howard had a nice talk last night?"

She was rummaging through a pile of clothes spilling out of her closet. She slipped on a white satin blouse, turned up the sleeves, tore it off and threw it back into the closet.

"You talked about the baby?" I said softly.

"What was that?" she shouted. Her head was in the closet. "I can't understand a word you're saying. You're mumbling."

"The baby. The baby. I asked if you and Howard talked about the baby last night."

She stood up straight and swept her hair off her face. "No, George, we didn't. After Mrs. Sarni left we locked ourselves in here for three hours and discussed what to get you for your birthday next year."

"Look, I'm sorry. I just let it slip out. I was afraid you were going to hurt yourself with that air conditioner. I was concerned for your health, Nina. All I can do now is apologize."

"Unfortunately, that *is* all you can do now, and seeing as you've just done it, please shut my door on your way out."

She put on another blouse, turned the collar up and down four times, looked at herself from three different angles, then ripped it off. "Nothing's going to look good on me today. Nothing looks good on you when you wake up nauseated and dropping dishes."

"That did," I lied.

"That didn't and you know it. Your honesty is waning all of a sudden." She yanked on a purple cotton sweater that clashed with

her chartreuse pants, her red fingernails, and her hair, giving her
an altogether rancid look.

"Nina, come on. Do you think Howard wouldn't have found out
anyway? You know he would have. You can't keep something like
this secret forever. It shows after a while."

"That's irrelevant. I was going to tell him when I wanted to tell
him. You had no right to interfere."

She strode out of the room as if the discussion were closed. Nina
had a fierce anger she claimed to have inherited from her mother.
More of her Polish identity. She'd warned me to ignore her when
she got angry, not to let her get away with trying to use her anger
to manipulate me, but I hated to think she might spend the rest
of the day practicing meditative voodoo on an image of my face
while she listened to one of her abused wives.

"I just want to tell you I'm truly, deeply, sincerely sorry," I said
as I followed her into the living room. "It was a mistake."

"There are no mistakes, Georgie," she said with superiority, the
kind of superiority her profession thrives on.

"If you walk out of the house with that sweater on, you'll be
making a mistake."

She looked down at herself despairingly and collapsed on the sofa.
"Everyone's entitled to an off day." Her purple sweater was hideous
against the green vinyl. "You want to know what Howard said about
the baby? Howard said he hoped it would be a girl so there'd be another munchkin like me in the world. Something like 'She'll be a
munchkin, Munchkin.' That's what he said about the baby."

I sat on top of the air conditioner watching her fidget with her
hoop earrings and her bracelets. In this outfit she looked like a
sixties pop singer or a wayward girl eloping to Arizona or a teenager
hanging out on the waterfront in Baltimore—anything but a mental-
health professional about to counsel women in trouble.

"You know, George, when I first told him I was planning to have
the baby, he looked worried. I could be wrong, but I think he
looked very concerned. Just for a second, but I'm sure a kind of
fleeting terror passed over his face."

"Did you say anything about the plan you mentioned to me the
other night?"

"I didn't get into that. I thought I'd wait until I got some sign from you — although I probably got enough of those last night. Where did you go off to, anyway?"

"I went to a lecture at The New School. Something called 'Was Ronald Reagan Really Reelected in 1984?'"

"Well, you missed a phone call." She stared at me accusingly. "Joley called you last night."

"Joley?"

"He left his number, which seemed unnecessary, and then he called me Lila and acted as if we were long-lost pals. He told me he really was sorry we never got a chance to see each other and then he called me Lila."

"Joley called?"

Since moving to Brooklyn I'd seen Joley one time. That was for a hurried brunch I'd treated him to for his birthday the previous January. He was cheery and recklessly optimistic about everything from the weather to the nuclear arms race. He was flattering and talkative in the superficial, meaningless way he was with most of his students. I'd left the brunch feeling as if I'd seen him give an interview on a talk show rather than had a conversation with him. The last time I'd tried to make contact was in March during a late blizzard. Nina and I had bought a bottle of cheap brandy and spent the evening staring out the back windows getting drunk and maudlin. Around midnight Nina passed out on the sofa and I dragged the phone into my bedroom and called Joley, steeped in cheap sentiment. An unfamiliar, pleasant, youthful-sounding voice informed me that Robert was sleeping.

"Are you the answering service?" I asked.

"No, but I'd be happy to take a message." Overly polite, efficient, eager to please, friendly in the face of sarcasm: all signs of an infatuated, unjaded undergraduate with a positive outlook on life and a mind so superficial he probably found Joley "deep" even though he knew nothing about him. "Hang on while I get a pencil."

I hung up.

"I wonder what he wanted?" I asked Nina.

"Who knows? And if I were you, I wouldn't be too eager to find out. He's the kind of man who gives people complexes."

"That's very true, Nina. And we both know I've got enough of those." I got off the air conditioner and stuffed the brown bags and newspapers I'd thrown out of the closet the night before into a pile in a corner.

Joley had called! It didn't seem possible after all that time and with what was going on now.

I grabbed the broom from the corner behind the refrigerator and started to sweep under the sofa. Nina lifted her feet off the floor so I could reach back into the far corners.

"Howard doesn't think you should call either," she said. "He really was concerned that you might."

"I won't call him back, Nina, don't worry. He was nothing but trouble for me all along, even if you and I did meet through him."

"And something else, George: you don't know what he's been up to since you moved out. He's probably a bad health risk at this point."

"He always was a bad risk of one kind or another." Still, I couldn't deny feeling an uplifting kind of curiosity, as if I'd come into a very insignificant but unexpected inheritance. I furiously took the broom to the floor around the packing crates and tried to change the subject. "I meant to tell you I found a shop that sells used maternity clothes."

"I sometimes think there's a streak of masochism in you, George," she said, paying no attention to my remark. "If Joley ever treated you decently, you'd head for the hills."

"I don't like heights, Nina. Anyway, this shop is right near school. I must have passed it a hundred times and never even noticed it. The other day the stork on the sign stuck out like a mole. It's like my friend who had a tooth capped and all of a sudden started to notice every capped tooth he passes on the street."

"What do capped teeth have to do with this?"

I swept off the top and the sides of the air conditioner. "I was making an analogy," I said. "An analogy about becoming sensitive to things you never notice until they touch you directly. Like this friend of mine who had a clump of hair dyed purple and then suddenly started to notice all kinds of people who had purple clumps of hair. People you'd never expect, like bank tellers and meter maids."

"You're babbling, George. You're just trying to avoid the issue here."

"But, Nina, I told you I have no intention of calling him back. Don't put words into my mouth. I'll admit I'm a little curious. Who wouldn't be. But I'm not calling him back."

She tossed it off with her hand as if I were hopeless and she had more important things to think about. "Howard said I'd have to increase my B vitamin intake. He said he'd prepare a big meal for us at least one night a week."

"That sounds great."

"Maybe. But I'm not sure I like knowing he has this plan built into every week. I'm afraid it'll turn into an obligation more than anything."

"For him or for you?"

"For both of us. You know how he gets when he's cooking. He'd be devastated if I canceled one of his meals. I shouldn't have agreed to it. He caught me when my resistance was down."

I stuffed the broom back behind the refrigerator and collapsed on the sofa next to Nina, exhausted. Cleaning never fails to make me feel wretched. I piled her hair into a sort of bun on the top of her head. Inexplicably, the bright sweater looked much less ugly. There was a mangled heap of bobby pins in an ashtray on the armrest and I tried to stick a few into her hair to hold it in place.

When Nina had given herself a final disapproving look in the mirror in the hallway and gone off to work, I settled back into the rumpled sheets on my bed to do my morning exercises. I grabbed the edge of the mattress with my hands, reached my legs as far out to the wall as I could and then went limp against the pillows.

I tried to block out everything connected with Nina's being pregnant and wanting me to help her with the baby. If my life were exactly as it had been three weeks earlier and Joley had called, what would I have done? I rolled over onto my stomach, pushed my upper body off the bed and then, very slowly, lowered myself back down into the sheets with my head turned to one side.

Of course I wouldn't have called him back. I'd decided in March after my unsuccessful phone call that it was time to forget about him and go on with my life, such as it was. If he were sick or in trouble of some kind, that would be a different story, but if that were the case, I'd probably hear about it from someone else before Joley himself told me.

I lifted up my head and pushed a pillow under it.

But, in fact, my life was a lot different than it had been three weeks earlier. Nina *was* pregnant and she *did* want me to help with the baby, and what was I going to do with myself if I didn't want to go along with her plan?

It was only a little past seven and my alarm was still set for seven-fifteen. I rolled my eyes up and down a few times and then shut then tight and fell into a dreamless sleep. When the alarm rang, I jumped out of bed and dialed Joley's number. I got the answering machine: a cool, humorlessly amused Joley announcing the impossibility of making it to the phone. I thought about it for a minute and then, gently, hung up.

10

"Ah, George," my good friend Timothy sighed, "tell me the truth: have you ever once taken my advice?"

"Of course," I said. "I read those Doris Lessing outer space books."

"And?"

"And I didn't like them. I told you that."

"You *will* like them, I promise. It takes a while, but one morning you'll wake up and realize you like them. I don't give bad advice, George. I'm not giving you bad advice now when I tell you to walk away from this whole mess—Nina, Joley, babies and all—get a real job, a decent apartment, and start making a life of your own. You're limiting yourself too much."

I was propped up in the corner of Timothy's bed, leafing through the pages of his autographed copy of *The Golden Notebook*, trying to listen to what he was saying without looking too vulnerable. I always felt vulnerable when I sought his advice. I think I felt obliged to follow it simply because I'd taken up so much of his time in asking for it. In fact, Timothy loved to vent his opinions on every subject, and I almost never acted on any of them. Still, after a couple of weeks of ignoring what was going on between Nina and me, I thought I should talk to someone who spoke with the voice of authority. On everything.

"I've been telling you the same thing for years now and you pay no attention. You're not paying attention now. And please go a little easier on that book or you'll tear one of the pages and I'd never be able to find another signed first edition."

A torn page could easily drive Timothy over the edge, even in a book Doris Lessing hadn't autographed. He was an architect and had all the usual quirks associated with that profession: he was rigid, compulsive, orderly, and fanatically tied to precision and logic. He insisted his life be as neatly organized as a blueprint. Anything that didn't fit into the design he realigned or erased completely.

I'd met Timothy in a sleazy bar in Boston while I was working at the day-care center and he was in graduate school at Harvard. I don't remember who picked up whom, but we left the place together and then, once back at his apartment, discovered a lack of mutual physical attraction. With nothing else to do, we spent the evening talking. He gave me some good advice on a problem I was having at the time, and the pattern for our friendship was established.

I think the real bond between us, though, was our shared fear of being unemployed, unloved, and unappreciated, a fear I flaunted and he hid beneath a mountain of cynicism. I never talked with him about his childhood or adolescence, but I imagined they'd been a nightmare of alienation and rejection. Timothy was as tall and skinny as a basketball player but he lacked any athletic abilities whatsoever. Whenever he got haughty and snide, I saw a towering, gawky fourteen-year-old in baggy gym shorts and size thirteen sneakers exacting his revenge on the world. I suspect he advised so strongly against serious relationships so his own bachelorhood would be less lonely.

He was sitting at a butcher-block table opposite the bed, peeling the skin off a green apple in one long, thin, unbroken strip. If he'd been Asian, Timothy would have made a great sushi chef, but, being of German descent, he'd become an architect instead. "Of course, George, I've always thought Joley was an idiot. There must be some selfish motivation behind his call. Why else would he get in touch with you? He never appreciated you when you lived together, he chucked you out of his apartment, and he insulted me to my face. He wouldn't call just for a friendly chat."

"You never told me he insulted you."

"Well, he did. I've tried to block it out of my mind. Life is hard enough as it is without bringing up every insult tossed your way."

"So what happened?"

"Do you remember the time the three of us went to see that vampire movie at the Ziegfeld?"

"The one you hated?"

"I didn't hate it, I loved it."

"You left five minutes after the opening credits."

"I was offended and I didn't feel like sitting through the rest of the movie beside him as if nothing had happened. The minute we walked into the theater Joley made a big, loud production out of giving me the aisle seat so I'd have enough room for my legs. 'But don't trip anyone coming down the aisle with a box of popcorn,' he shouted. He was purposely trying to embarrass me and make me feel like a lumbering freak."

"I think you took it too much to heart."

"He's an idiot. I don't know what you ever saw in him except his looks, and frankly, that's the last reason I'd chase after someone."

Timothy never chased after anyone. In fact, he spent a substantial amount of time running away from potential romances. Most of the blind dates he was always setting up for me were with men who'd expressed an interest in him, whom he was trying to politely pass on to someone else.

"At least you did the right thing in telling Howard about the baby. You know I like Nina, even though you purposely keep us apart, but the idea of you raising the baby with her is insane. It's bad enough you have to work with children."

"Choose to work with children," I corrected him.

"I was giving you the benefit of the doubt. Anyway, you'd never get out of the house. You'd be stuck there like a servant. I'd have to give your Meet the Moderns ticket to someone else."

Timothy had purchased two subscription tickets to a contemporary composers series at the Brooklyn Academy of Music and given me one of them. Generous as it was, I think I was the recipient mainly because none of his other friends would agree to go off "the island" for any reason at all.

"I always get a headache at those concerts anyway. I hate all that yelling and banging of pans against the floor."

"One morning, George, you'll wake up and you'll love that music, I promise. And just remember who told you so. And if you're going to raise that baby with Nina, you might as well marry her." The knife slipped from his hand and the long strip of apple peel fell to the floor. "You're not thinking of *that*, are you?"

"Of course not," I said. "You know I hate jewelry. I'd never be able to wear a wedding ring."

He picked up the apple peel and carefully placed it in the covered wastebasket under the sink in his kitchenette. With a sponge and towel he wiped up the wet spot and then dried off the floor meticulously. "I'll bet that's what Nina wants. She's in love with you. I knew it as soon as I met her. This is probably her way of bullying you into a proposal."

I never again got together with both Nina and Timothy after the one time the three of us had gone out to a party and they'd ganged up against me. It always happens when you introduce friends to each other; they have nothing in common to discuss except you, so they share amusing perceptions of your faults and bond together. At that party we went to, I left Nina and Timothy alone for five minutes while I got us drinks, and when I returned, Timothy was making jokes about my socks and Nina was laughing hysterically. I blamed myself.

"Did it ever occur to you, Timothy, that I might want to help with the baby?"

"No, it didn't. If you wanted to help her with the baby you wouldn't have leapt to the phone the minute you heard Joley called. You were looking for an out, that's all. And that's fine—I just think you should look for a better out than that jerk."

"But I didn't leave a message when I called Joley back."

"A thin ray of hope. The last shreds of sanity." He bit into the naked apple with a snap.

"I didn't leave a message the first time I called back."

"You called again?"

"If you're not careful, you're going to choke on that apple."

Two days after hanging up on Joley's machine I called back and left a nervous message: "Joley, this is George Mullen. Sorry I missed your call a few days ago. If you need something, give me a buzz." I left the phone number. So far he hadn't called.

"Look, George, I know of a great apartment in the East Village that's about to be vacated. Tell these two dear friends you love them both very much but you just discovered this new thing called your own life."

"I don't have any money, Timothy. 'My own life' costs more than I can afford right now."

"This apartment is cheap. Half the tenants in the building are junkies."

"Great."

"In five years it'll be a palace and you'll be sitting in a very desirable neighborhood with the first option to buy your apartment. You buy for a song and you're on your way."

"I don't want to live in the East Village. I hate green hair, and the thought of syringes makes me queasy."

"Why are you so hostile to this city, George? Why do you continue to live here if you're so determined to shut yourself off from the good things it has to offer? The East Village is the best of New York."

Timothy lived in a studio apartment one block off Sheridan Square on a little side street lined with trees. For all I knew, he'd never been in the East Village. Timothy considerd the Upper West Side suburbia.

He ran his fingers down the bridge of his long, sharp nose. "This conversation is giving me a headache. Let me know when you're ready to meet some decent people and I'll set up another date for you. I just met someone you'd love."

"No more architects, that's all I ask."

He went to the mirror neatly hidden behind his closet door and arranged his clothes into perfect, symmetrical lines. He had to squat down at the knees to look at his face and his hair. He was treating me to dinner at a new Mexican restaurant, and I'm sure he felt he needed to compensate for my slovenliness. I stood behind him comparing our faces in the mirror. Although Timothy was several years older than me, his skin had the kind of unwrinkled freshness I was always noticing on people who live by themselves. I had a great-aunt who'd lived her entire life unmarried and alone and died at the age of eighty-two with the complexion of a twenty-year-old. My mother explained it away by saying all people who lived alone walked around the house day and night with cold cream on their faces, and for years I'd taken this as some kind of crackpot truth. But now, as I looked into the mirror, I thought it was more likely that the strain of cohabitation, of constantly being involved in the emotional disasters of roommates and lovers, was taking its toll on me and etching age into my skin. Timothy was aging more slowly simply because he only had his own crises to deal with. Perhaps the East Village wasn't the absolutely worst place on the face of the earth.

"Do you think I'm looking particularly old and wrinkled right now, Timmy?" I asked him.

He scrutinized me carefully and gently pulled back the skin around my eyes and forehead. "Yes," he said and went back to the collar of his shirt. "You should stop washing your face with soap. Stop using salt. Stop talking to your mother on the phone. Read Proust. Sleep with cold cream around your eyes."

11

ON a clear and bright Friday at the end of the first week in October, Melissa didn't show up at school in the morning and she didn't call in sick. I thought nothing of it at first, being used to her unpredictable behavior, but by ten o'clock I was feeling overworked and much aggrieved. There had been an invigorating touch of autumnal crispness in the air that morning and Mr. Simmons had the furnace turned on for a few hours. The rule of thumb in working with children is: When in doubt, overheat. By ten o'clock my classroom was filled with stale and suffocating air and the kids were cranky and unmanageable. The enormous furnace was separated from my room by only a thin wall, and throughout the winter it belched and roared, occasionally sending a shudder rippling under the floor like some chained beast about to break its bonds and devour us all.

Mr. Simmons stuck his long, hopeful face through the doorway five different times to see if the room was warm enough and to find out if Melissa had shown up yet. Despite his claims that he had absolute faith in her, he sometimes regarded Melissa distrustfully. At eleven o'clock he finally called me into the hall and said, "Darn it, George, I don't think Swithinbank's going to show today. Let me call you a substitute."

"She'll be here, Mr. Simmons," I said. "She would have called in sick otherwise. There was probably a subway delay."

I was beginning to wonder myself whether she would make it, but I wanted to prove my faith in her as well as in my ability to handle the class solo.

The morning reached a low point when I helped Doran Dunne

take a dose of some antibiotic. He'd recently come down with, or at any rate, been diagnosed as having, an ear infection, and was taking two different medications — one prescribed by Theodora's pediatrician and the other by Daniel's. Doran was easily the most overmedicated child I'd ever worked with. I was convinced that he'd be either a junkie or a pharmacist by the time he turned twenty-five. He'd spent most of the morning asking me the exact time so he could coordinate his medications properly. "What time is it *now*, George?" he'd wail as he blew his nose into a large monogrammed handkerchief. At eleven-thirty, exactly, he dragged out a bottle of some viscous pink liquid and a complicated measuring spoon Daniel had picked up for him at a medical-supply store.

"I can't figure out how to work the *spoon*, George," he called to me from across the room.

"Lunch is in a few minutes, Doran. I'll help you during lunch."

"*Noooooo*," he yelled in a piercing vibrato. "Daniel said eleven-thirty."

I slammed down the terrarium lid in the middle of my description of the reproductive cycle of a *Chamaeleo dilepis* and stalked across the room. "Give me the medicine, Dorrie," I said, and grabbed it from him. "You just pour some in the spoon and swallow it. Period." The bottle slipped from my hands as I was trying to undo the top-security cap and fell to the floor with a loud and resounding crack.

"Look what you did, George!"

The medicine glugged out of the smashed glass into a thick pink puddle.

"Don't whine, Dorrie," I said. "It's bad for your adenoids." I bent down and picked up the largest shards of blue glass. "We still have your pills. They should hold you until the end of the day."

"No, George, the pills aren't *strong* enough. Daniel's doctor *said* they weren't strong enough. That's why he gave me this."

"For the next few hours they'll be strong enough, Doran, I guarantee."

He rolled his eyes at my stupidity. "Not for my *throat* they won't be. Daniel's doctor said my throat was *red* after the last time I stayed at Theodora's and now it's going to be red a*gain*."

He put his forehead against the wall and started to mumble something about his throat, which, judging from what I could catch of his monologue, was getting sorer by the second. Rose, the blond junior M.D., was holding forth at the terrarium. She'd lifted the lid and was instructing two other kids to feed the ends of her pigtails to the chameleon.

"You *need* to put that animal down and close up the terrarium," I called. "That animal is tired and needs a nap." I took one of the huge pills Theodora's doctor had prescribed out of Doran's lunchbox and handed it to him with a glass of water. "This will keep you healthy until Daniel comes in to pick you up, Dorrie."

"Theodora's picking me up today!" he screamed. He grabbed the pill and rushed into the bathroom, slamming the door behind him. I was about to hurry to his side with peanut butter and saltines, when Rose dropped the chameleon to the floor. The entire class broke into screams of delight as it lazily crawled into the reading area.

"You need to put that animal back in the terrarium before it drops dead!" I shouted at the top of my lungs.

"He's sick of that stupid terrarium," Rose said, laughing. "He needs to leave the nest, like my older sister did."

At that moment, Melissa calmly walked through the door at the back of the room with a serene glaze over her eyes. She quickly went into the reading area, picked up the chameleon and gently put it back into the terrarium. "Rose, dear," she said tenderly, "that chameleon was very sad to be kicked out of its home and I want you to go apologize."

She was wearing a clinging striped skirt with a slit cup high up her right leg, an assortment of colorful, shredded sweatshirts, lacy white ankle socks, and a pair of ultramarine-blue low-heeled pumps. Her red crew cut was glistening. Her appearance was so astonishing, most of the children fell into a profound silence and regarded her as if she were a kangaroo that had just hopped into the room.

Her pet student, a tall, gaunt boy named Nathan, rushed up to her and threw his arms around her legs. "Where have you been, Melissa? I've been worried all morning."

"I've been trying to get to school, Nathan. I'm sorry."

"Well, George was okay for a while," he said, staring at Melissa's shoes. "Then things kind of fell apart. I really love those shoes, Melissa. They're great."

In addition to being tall for his age, Nathan had a quiet perceptiveness about adult feelings. He'd earned a considerable reputation among the psychologists and administrators on the staff by refusing to do anything at school other than play in the dress-up corner. He didn't know how to hold a pencil and he burst into tears whenever Melissa suggested he try to learn the alphabet. Day after day he wandered around the room in skirts and blouses and tights chosen from the costume box with care and worn with a surprising amount of panache. He loved putting on original plays, his current favorite being a witty comedy called "The King Who Lost His Pants." Melissa was convinced he was destined to become a successful clothing designer and felt compromised each time she tried to focus his attention away from dress-up. She had once confessed to me that some days she dressed to please him. "He has such a fine eye," she'd said.

"They're a nice color, aren't they?" she said, smoothing down his hair and pivoting her shoe on the pointed toe. "I tell you what: If you promise to forgive me for being late, I promise I'll let you wear them this afternoon. How's that for a deal?"

"I'll think about it, Melissa," he said and ran off, almost tripping over the ties of a frilly white apron he had around his waist.

When Rose had finished her insincere apology to the chameleon, Melissa came over to me and apologized violently for being so late.

"Don't worry about it," I said. "As long as you're all right."

"Oh, I'm fine, George. I had a rough night and a worse morning, but everything's going to be okay. At my age, you bounce back quickly from an all-nighter."

"If you want to take a nap or anything, just let me know. I can handle this zoo for a few more hours."

"I wouldn't even think of that, George," she said. "My problems are over now. It's off between Vince and me. It's all off. It took a good twelve-hour battle to get him out of the house, but it's finally over."

"I'm sorry to hear it. Or glad. Whichever."

I wasn't sure I wanted to get too deeply involved in Melissa's life, but she looked downtrodden to me. Maybe it was just the contrast between her complexion and her bright clothes, but her face looked pale and sad. "Do you want to do something after school?" I asked her. "We could get dinner someplace or go on a backstage tour of Radio City Music Hall."

"Why don't you invite me out to your place in Brooklyn?" she said eagerly. "I've been dying to see where you live."

"We could do that, I guess. There's probably not much in the larder, though."

"I don't care about that, George. It just helps to get involved in someone else's life when your own is a mess."

"I suppose." I hoped she realized I'd merely extended a dinner invitation.

One of the kids let out an ear-shattering scream from the back of the room. Rose came dashing up to us with her pigtails flying and grabbed onto my legs.

"Doran's dead in the bathroom!" she shrieked. "He died on the toilet, just like my grandmother!"

Melissa and I ran into the bathroom in time to see Doran, fully clothed and sitting on the toilet, waking up from a nap. I picked him up in my arms and Melissa rubbed his back. "Did you have a nice nap, Dorrie?" she asked.

"George dropped my medicine," he said drowsily. "I'm very sick, Melissa."

We steered him to one of the futons in the nap room and tucked him under a bright pile of covers. Melissa made a plateful of peanut butter on saltines which she put by his bed. Throughout the rest of the afternoon he'd sit up and look around and cautiously sneak a cracker under the blankets with him.

MELISSA talked incessantly on the subway out to Brooklyn in a loud, breathless voice, completely oblivious of the people packed in on either side of us. "It was a lousy relationship, George. I mean really lousy. It stunk, in fact. It was a complete disaster, like every other relationship I've ever had." The car jolted to a stop and she swung out into the aisle, hanging on to her strap. "Not the *sex*," she shouted. "That was fantastic. That was monu-

mental. Vince wasn't good-looking or well built, and he definitely wasn't my type, but we just had a monumental connection in bed. Have you ever had that with a guy, George?"

"Well..."

The woman sitting just beneath us was watching Melissa with a contorted, disgusted look on her face. She was an older woman whose face was twitching with a lifetime of controlled rage. She had a thick paperback in a plastic book cover clutched in one of her hands and she kept looking over the top of it and running her eyes from Melissa's red hair to her bright blue shoes as if she were about to sink her teeth into her neck.

"Of course, even the sex couldn't hide the fact that Vince was insane. Truly insane. You want to know what the fight was all about? Okay, George, get this: he wanted me to invest some of my trust money in a wine store he wants to open in Chelsea. A *wine* store. I said to him, 'Vince, I am not *pay*ing to encourage you in this so-called hobby you're trying to turn into a life-style.' He once told me he wanted to be a dentist when he was a kid so I said, 'If you want to go to dental school I'll pitch in a couple thousand.' Well that did it. We got in a huge row that lasted all night, and then this morning I told him to take his stuff and get out."

"I guess that's why you were late?" I asked. I was talking as softly as I could, hoping she'd follow suit.

She laughed uproariously. "I spent the whole morning riding around the city in the back seat of a cab. Crying. It's what I do whenever I break up with someone. I mean, I've always known I'm the kind of woman you see falling apart in the back seat of a cab. You know the kind you see sobbing and staring off into space when you look into the back seat of a cab that's stopped at a light? So, whenever I feel like falling apart, I just get into a cab and I tell the driver to keep going. Either that or I go to Barney's and buy some pricey men's item like a wallet or a gold tie clasp and then I fall apart at the register. You should try it, George. Of course, I suspect you're the kind of person who knows how to hang on to a man. Isn't that right?"

"Well, that cab therapy sounds a little expensive for me," I said quietly.

"The way I look at it, I have the money, so why pretend I don't.

I think it's insulting to people in your financial situation to have people in my financial situation pretend they don't have money. I have it, so why not support a cab driver for a few hours? Vince told me he'd once been a cab driver. I said, 'Vince, if you want to buy a *cab*, I'll invest in it—anything but a wine store.' Can you imagine someone with an alcoholic mother investing in a wine store?"

The woman beneath us tossed her paperback into a clear plastic tote bag and stood up, pushing Melissa aside with her elbow.

"I'm so sorry," Melissa said, oblivious to the nature of the assault. "You take the seat, George. I've been sitting most of the day."

"Oh, I couldn't do that. You take it, Melissa."

"You look tired, George. You take the seat."

"I can't. Even if I wanted to, I couldn't."

The car pulled into a station and the older woman edged her way to the door. As she was stepping out, she turned to us and hissed, "You two freaks."

"Don't worry about that," Melissa said, unflustered. "It happens all the time with this hair. She probably had a bad day working in some cafeteria, the poor thing."

HOWARD was stationed at the kitchen counter holding the tip of a long knife as he carefully chopped carrots and parsnips. He had on his gray pinstriped suit with the vest still buttoned and a dark blue tie flung over his shoulder, presumedly to keep it from the flashing blade. I was surprised to see him, as he'd already prepared two meals for us that week.

"And who is *this?*" Melissa whispered in my ear cheerfully.

"A friend," I said.

I led her into the kitchen and introduced her to Howard over the rhythmic banging of the knife. The room was littered with white butcher paper, shopping sacks, cellophane bags, and an assortment of tiny spice bottles he'd brought from home.

"I hope you're staying for dinner, Melissa," Howard said without looking up. "I just slid a huge rib roast into the oven. You're not a vegetarian, are you?" Howard considered vegetarianism an eating disorder.

"Certainly not," she said, horrified.

"Oh, good. I marinated this roast for seventeen hours last night. If you don't marinate a rib roast for at least seventeen hours, there's no point in eating it. And it's full of B vitamins."

"I adore rib roast," Melissa said rhapsodically. "There's nothing I adore more than rib roast. And if anyone needs B vitamins, it's me."

Howard looked at her for the first time since we'd walked in. "You're not pregnant, are you?"

"There's no chance of that. One of my former boyfriend's best assets was his infertility. I told him this morning he'd have no trouble getting a new girlfriend to live with if he just mentions they'll never have to worry about using birth control. Now tell me this, Howard, do you do most of the cooking around here or does George?"

"George is a terrible cook, aren't you, George?"

"I have my specialties." (Hot cereal and cake mixes, to mention two.)

"For instance," Howard said, wielding the knife, "George would just take these carrots and parsnips and cut them into chunks and chuck them into the oven. But it's crucial they be cut just right so they cook all the way through without getting mushy. I know it sounds like nothing, Melissa, but it's the little things that make a meal. I for one hate badly cooked vegetables. They can ruin a dinner."

"Oh, I do, too," Melissa said, stepping in toward him. "They're unforgivable. Did you learn to cook from your mother or did you pick it up yourself?"

"I learned to cook from Peter Kump. Have you ever heard of him? The man's a genius. A true genius. My mother was a worker. It wasn't her responsibility to cook any more than it was my father's."

"That's lovely, Howard," she said. She was staring at him intently. "I think it's wonderful when people are able to work out their living arrangements so well. George isn't a great cook, but you love to cook, so it all works out. What is it you do?"

"He's a lawyer," I said. "Legal aid. He's almost as underpaid as we are."

"But he loves his work. I can tell he's a man who loves his work. He's devoted." If Melissa took one step closer to Howard she'd be breathing down his neck. "George is devoted, too, Howard. He's a devoted friend. He could tell I was in a bad way so he invited me out to dinner. And I've told him, I've said, 'If there's ever anything you need, *any*thing, I'm there for you.' I'm sure you feel the same way."

"George and the Dumpling know they can count on me any time."

"The Dumpling?"

Howard opened the oven door and scattered the vegetables on top of the rib roast. He rubbed his hands together vigorously. "Now comes the fun part. Have you ever had spaetzle, Melissa? You're in for a real treat." He set an enormous pot of boiling water on the front burner of the stove with a plateful of thick glutinous batter beside it. As he scraped strips of the batter into the boiling water with the side of a spatula, he told us the history of the dish, the various uses for it, and the exact recipe he was preparing that evening.

"I really am delighted to meet you," Melissa said, ignoring the cooking lesson. "George is one of my dearest friends."

And I had thought we hardly knew each other.

"George is a real sweetheart," Howard said. He glanced at me with a look in his droopy eyes that warmed my heart. "He's the Puddle's best friend."

"The Puddle? Well, anyway, I would say I'm surprised he hasn't mentioned you, but George never tells me anything about his life. He's very discreet. Of course, my memory is so bad he could have told me dozens of times...."

As each of the spaetzle rose to the surface of the boiling water, Howard dredged it out with a slotted spoon and lovingly laid it in a colander. How he managed to get his paraphernalia to the apartment without a forklift was a mystery to me.

"By the way, Howie," I said, "I didn't get any calls while you were here, did I?"

"No, you didn't. Not from anyone. And I hope you weren't expecting any."

"Only from my agent. I'm waiting to hear the results of my screen test." Joley hadn't returned my call yet and I was beginning to feel I'd been had all over again. In some ways I was relieved, but I hated the thought of having to tell Timothy he'd been right.

"How long have you two known each other?" Melissa asked intently. "I'm always curious because most of my relationships crumble after a month or two. Of course, I'm still young, so it doesn't matter that much yet."

Melissa was hovering over Howard so attentively I was afraid she'd start asking him questions about our "connection in bed." Howard was either unaware of the assumptions she was making or refusing to refute them out of deference to my feelings.

"Maybe we should leave the chef to his creation," I said, taking Melissa by the arm. "I'll give you a tour of the rest of the estate."

The apartment was in an even more appalling state of disorder than usual. The broken air conditioner was still beached on the living-room floor along with a scattering of paper cups and white cartons from the take-out food Nina and I usually ate when Howard didn't leave leftovers. The window to the back was open and the shouting of our upstairs neighbors was blowing in on the breeze: "I never said I'd be in by midnight. Never never never *never*. NEVER."

"It's lovely, George," Melissa said without irony. "It really is the way I pictured it."

I didn't know whether to take it as an insult or a compliment. I showed her Nina's room and told her it was where my roommate slept, my woman psychologist roommate. Howard's lover.

She put her hand on my shoulder consolingly. "Then he isn't your lover?"

"Not even sometimes."

"Well, that's a shame, George. He really is a little gem."

THE three of us sat on the green vinyl sofa waiting for Nina to come home, listening to Howard's Odetta album. He lapsed into a detailed description of a brief someone in his office was writing for a client who'd been found rummaging through the glove compartment of a parked car. The car owner had come upon him, chased him for three blocks, wrestled him to the ground and convinced a passerby to call the police. Melissa, who sat between us on the sofa impatiently tapping her blue shoes against the floor, kept interrupting with questions that displayed a surprisingly complex understanding of the law. When Howard was finished with his statement of facts, Melissa said, "Now, *what* was it he was convicted of, Howard?"

"Unauthorized Use is what it's called. What it means is that he was using the car..."

"Well, there's the argument right there," she cut in. "What you described wasn't Unauthorized Use at all. It might have been illegal, but it wasn't Unauthorized Use. Your colleague will have no trouble getting the conviction overturned."

Howard turned to me, silently begging for an explanation.

"Melissa's father is a lawyer," I said.

"He's a partner at Davis Polk." She bent down and pulled up one of her white socks. "Impressive, isn't it? Listen, my father's no dope. Just because he stays married to an alcoholic doesn't mean he's an idiot. Who's this singer we're listening to? I don't think I've ever heard him before."

Howard was wounded. "This isn't a man, Melissa. This is Odetta, the world's greatest folksinger. I'm sure you've heard her before."

"Never. I'd recognize the voice. It's so plaintive, like whale calls from the bottom of the ocean."

Howard got up and put on one of Nina's Connie Francis albums. "Maybe this is more your taste," he said as he lovingly slipped Odetta back into the record jacket.

Melissa had never heard Connie Francis either.

By the time Nina arrived, we'd exhausted most of the record collection without finding one thing Melissa recognized. The apartment was filled with the thick greasy smell of the rib roast. The minute Nina walked into the living room and dumped her briefcase to the floor, Howard sprang up from the sofa and said, "You look tired. Sit down. Take my seat."

"Come on, Howie," Melissa said. "I've never seen this woman before and I can tell she isn't tired; she's radiant."

Nina eyed her shoes and her shredded sweatshirts. "I'll bet you're Melissa," she said. "George has told me a lot about you."

"Then he must know more about me than I know about myself. I couldn't fill three minutes of conversation with personal insights."

Nina looked at me and raised her eyebrows. From what I'd told her, she knew that Melissa had money and suspected that she took a passive role in women's politics—two strikes against her. Also, I think Nina was jealous of any of my women friends. Men were one thing, but female friendship was a territory she'd claimed as her own.

She had on a conservative brown skirt and a tweed jacket, and in contrast to Melissa's hallucinogenic swirl of colors, she looked dowdy. Howard stood behind her and put his arms around her waist. He buried his face in her neck and said to no one in particular, "Isn't she a Daisy? She's a Daisy."

Melissa and I laughed nervously and moved closer on the sofa.

THE meal was a triumph. The roast was dripping with spicy juices, the carrots and parsnips were cooked to perfection, and the spaetzle, drenched in butter and what tasted like a head of garlic, was a masterpiece of indulgence. Howard beamed as he watched Nina eat, occasionally pointing out the nutritional value of some tidbit she was about to put in her mouth. With company present, he kept the Law Reports off the table and in his lap and only once ripped out a wad of papers.

The turning point in the evening came when Melissa asked Nina about her dissertation. Nina hadn't brought up the subject in over three weeks, which I took as a sign she was getting nothing done. Even during her most productive times, she hesitated to talk about it, believing she'd dissipate all her interest verbally, and lately I'd seen her cringe when, passing by, we heard the sound of a clacking typewriter pouring out of an open window. She speared a piece of meat with her fork and said vaguely, "I'm writing about rape."

Howard looked at her incredulously. He never tired of discussing Nina's dissertation. He was as proud of the research she was doing as if it were his own, and Nina once confessed to me he'd given her several good ideas when she was stymied, although she suspected he was mostly trying to assuage his guilt for having written a number of appeals for convicted rapists. "That's not very specific, Nina," he said. "There's a lot more to it than that. She never gives herself credit for her work. You see, Melissa, what she's doing is looking at rape victims, at the ways in which they internalize guilt, the feeling that they are somehow to blame for the crime committed against them. Believe it or not, many women actually believe they are responsible for being raped."

"Of course I believe it," Melissa said. "Some of them probably are."

Both Howard and Nina turned to me. I, after all, was the one responsible for bringing Melissa into the house.

"Well... be that as it may," Howard continued, "the fact is, there's some evidence, or this is what we're examining anyway, what *Nina* is examining, that women strongly identified with feminist politics might tend not to internalize self-blame so readily. Their political convictions might give them a stronger sense of their position in society and make them turn their anger outward rather than inward."

"You mean they might become raving activists?"

Howard shrugged in exasperation. "I wouldn't use the word raving...."

"I take you don't consider yourself a feminist?" Nina asked calmly. Too calmly. The calm-before-the-storm calmly.

"Oh!" Melissa said, as if she'd been accused of being a Nazi. "I don't think many people would anymore. I mean, I suppose lesbians are still involved in that kind of thing."

At the mention of the word "lesbian," Howard looked at me apologetically. "The point is," he said, "getting back to this dissertation..."

"Just a minute, Howard," Nina interrupted. "I'm interested in hearing what Melissa has to say. What is it you find so offensive about feminism?"

"I never said there was anything offensive about it, I just think we're beyond all that. You know, I just don't go in for parading around the streets chanting things. It's fine for the Hare Krishnas, but it just seems undignified for the rest of us."

"In other words, all of your Sarah Lawrence friends got into the business school of their choice, thanks to twenty years of undignified chanting, so what's the point in pushing for minor matters like the ERA? Is that it, more or less?"

Melissa was stunned. She reached over and laid her hand on Nina's arm as if she'd just inadvertently called her mother a slut. "Nina, I'm so sorry. I didn't realize... I mean, I thought you were just *studying* this stuff. You know, I saw Howard and your fingernails and all that, and how was I supposed to guess?"

Nina held out her hand and looked down at her long red nails. "I chipped one today and I almost started to cry."

"So there," Melissa said. "I rest my case." She turned to Howard and grinned.

"Now that's a great idea," I said. All we needed was for someone to mention the word "Apartheid."

"Let me tell you something," Nina said, examining her hands. "The first women's group I was ever in spent three weeks talking about nothing but my fingernails. The only thing everyone could agree on in the course of an entire year was that my fingernails were inappropriate for someone who professed to have politics."

"So," Melissa said, "Why not cut them off and be done with it?"

"Because I like them. And three more reasons: I like them, I like them, and I like them."

"Well, as a matter of fact," Melissa told her earnestly, "I like them, too."

"So do I," Howard said.

I'd never liked Nina's nails so I kept my mouth shut.

AFTER a modest dessert, some kind of inverted apple tart with caramel sauce poured over it, I brought out the newspaper to try and find a movie we could all agree on. Howard looked over my shoulder, running his finger up and down the columns of the timetable. He stopped at one listing and rubbed his hands together wildly.

"I think we just made a decision," Nina said.

It was a film about delinquent teenagers in a reform school which Howard considered one of the great American films of the decade.

In a little under three years he'd seen it twelve times. I think many of the characters resembled his clients in their sociopathic behavior. I'd seen the movie twice, largely for the talents of its attractive teenage cast. Melissa seemed to think it was set in a very different sort of school and said something about the story being of professional interest.

The neighborhood kids who played football in the middle of our street night and day were out in full force, whooping and hollering under the streetlights. Howard led us up toward the park in search of his car. He had his arm tightly wrapped around Nina's waist and the two of them fit together like interlocking cushions. As we neared the outskirts of the park, Howard stopped abruptly and said, "I think we've gone too far. I must have left it on a side street." Howard often misplaced his car in our neighborhood; he always arrived so eager to see Nina he didn't pay attention to where he was parking.

When we finally located his rusting blue Datsun, Nina insisted on sitting in the back seat with me so Howard and Melissa could talk law up front.

"You're going to love this movie, Puddle," Howard said as he pumped and prodded the engine to life. "There's one incredible scene where a kid pours acid over the fence around the school and then pushes through the links. Then, just as you think he's made it out of the place... Well, I won't tell you the rest. I don't want to spoil it for you."

A cloud of smoke boomed from the exhaust pipe and we blasted out of the parking space.

Howard was a wild man behind the wheel. He drove with the fierce aggressiveness he tried, however unsuccessfully, to suppress in other parts of his behavior. As we sped down Ocean Parkway toward Bensonhurst he swerved from lane to lane, ran one red light after the next, and gleefully blew the horn for no reason.

Melissa was tossed back and forth in the front seat, her head swaying from side to side. She had her feet tucked under her on the seat, as there was practically no floor on the passenger side of the car. Still, she seemed oblivious to the jostling as she talked nonstop, giving Howard the details of a recent case her father had worked on. Howard had his eyes concentrated on the road with one hand on the wheel and one hand spinning the knob on the radio.

"I found out the name of a place in our neighborhood that gives natural childbirth classes," Nina said to me softly. She was leaning against me with her head on my shoulder, gently tugging at her eyebrows.

"You're going to do natural childbirth?" I whispered. I've never understood the attraction to painful childbirth, seeing as the end result was essentially the same anyway.

"Of course I am. I've been looking into midwives, too."

"*Mid*wives?" I said, perhaps too loudly, as Melissa turned around and smiled at us. "Midwives," I said more quietly. "You aren't thinking of a home birth, are you?" I could see her lying on the green vinyl sofa writhing in pain, clutching at a dirty dishrag.

"I don't think so. I mainly want to avoid a doctor. You know how I feel about doctors."

"I know, and I feel the same way." I shared her distrust of medical professionals but I overlooked it at the first signs of anything more serious than a cold. "But a midwife? It sounds so archaic. Watch the eyebrows."

"Sorry." She dropped her hand to her mouth and started biting at the skin between her thumb and her index finger. "George, I'd like it if you came to the childbirth classes with me."

"Me?"

"Would you mind keeping your voice down?"

"Nina, that's absurd. I don't know anything about childbirth. Until I was eight I thought people bought babies at hospitals the way you buy a cantaloupe at Key Food."

"You don't have to deliver the baby, I'd just like you there for support."

"What about Howard?"

"What about me, George?" Howard asked, looking at me in the rear view mirror.

"Red light," I said. "You just ran a red light. That's three for three in the past half mile."

"Well, hang on, Georgie, here comes the fourth." He stepped on the gas and laughed demonically.

"I'm terminating with Howard," Nina whispered. "Soon."

I sat up and looked at her as she nervously played with her fingers. The blue streetlights flashed across her face as we raced through the strange neighborhood, and the cold breeze from Howard's open window blew through her hair. There wasn't one feature on her face that could have been improved upon. "Why?" I said.

"It's getting to be too much, the way I thought it would. You see how often he's at the house now, George. Tonight was the fourth dinner he's made this week."

"The third."

"Whatever. In a few months he'll be making noises about moving in."

There was a distracted look in her eyes, as if she was contemplating the dubious future she'd planned for the two of us. I watched in silence as the streetlights flashed over her face like a slow blue strobe.

Howard parked the car on a side street a few blocks from the theater. It was an odd neighborhood, a mixture of dilapidated inner-city-style apartment buildings and suburban homes that easily could have blown in from New Jersey. The main street was lined with Italian pastry shops, butchers, Russian grocers, a stretch of weight-reducing salons, and sandwich shops advertising Kosher Pizza. Melissa insisted we stop three different times to browse. In her slit skirt and blue shoes she looked like a visitor from another country. At one point I had the impression she thought she was in Italy, shopping for presents to bring the folks back home.

The theater itself was an enormous, decaying relic, stifling with the smell of mildew and a gloomy dampness. The lobby was so poorly lit I felt as if we were walking into a dank cavern with decorated pillars and crumbling plaster friezes. I just hoped the wrecking crew wouldn't arrive until the movie had ended. The audience comprised about twenty teenagers who probably thought the movie was a retelling of their life stories.

"Just a little bit closer," Howard kept saying as we walked down the endless, sloping aisle. "There's no point in paying for a movie unless you get right into the action."

We ended up in the third row from the front with the screen looming before us like a skyscraper and at least fifteen hundred empty seats behind us. The film broke twice during the show, leaving the screen black and the audience of reform-school extras enraged. Nina wanted to leave halfway through and once Melissa realized the movie wasn't about kindergarten she fell asleep with her head hanging over the back of her seat. I couldn't enjoy the film. Howard kept reaching across Nina to prod me in the ribs and say, "Oh, George, watch this, watch this, this is a great scene."

"I've seen it *twice*," I told him four times, all to no avail.

Nina's annoucement that she was terminating with Howard kept creeping into my mind. The way she had talked about their relationship as if it were merely another therapy session infuriated me. "I'm terminating with Howard," she'd said. "Soon." If she was a computer programmer she probably would have said she was "signing out" of the relationship. And it wouldn't have sounded any more detached or impersonal.

"I can't believe you dragged us to that movie," Nina said as we crawled up the carpeted aisle to the lobby.

Howard stopped dead. "You didn't like it, Dumpling?"

"I thought it was poorly written, poorly acted, poorly directed, and gratuitously violent. And this theater smells."

"Don't blame me for the theater," Howard said.

"I loved the last scene," Melissa rasped, her voice still heavy with sleep. "Of course, that was the only one I stayed awake through. . . ."

"That was my least favorite," Nina said. "The worst of a stupid lot."

"Anyone for Kosher Pizza?" I asked as we got out to the street.

"Just tell me this, Nina," Howard said. "What was stupid about the movie?" His voice was edging toward his badgering-the-witness tone. "Just name one stupid scene."

"Just one? Okay, the scene in which the girl identifies the rapist."

"What about the scene in which she identifies the rapist?"

"When she looks at the lineup . . ."

"Yeah, yeah . . ." he said, rolling his hands.

"She looks at the lineup and then she turns to the cop . . ."

"Right, she turns to the cop and . . . ?"

"It's what she says to the cop."

"Well, what does she say to the cop?"

"If you'd let me finish, Howard, I could tell you," she shouted.

"I'm sorry, I'm sorry, Mittens. Go ahead."

"She says to the cop, 'I'm positive he's the one,' when, in fact . . ."

"She doesn't say, 'I'm positive,' she says, 'I'm absolutely certain.'"

"Big difference, Howard."

"Well, if you're going to quote the movie, quote the movie. That's all I'm saying, Nina. Be fair and quote the script as it was written if that's what you claim to be doing."

By that time we'd walked the entire length of the street on which Howard had parked his car and were headed into a completely different neighborhood. "I hate to break up the party," I said, "but I think we passed Howard's car."

"We didn't pass the car," Nina snapped. "I've been watching and we didn't pass it."

The four of us turned around and walked back down the street in silence. We came out at the intersection of the main street near the theater. Howard's car wasn't there.

"This must be the wrong street," Howard said. "They all look alike anyway. What was the name of the street, Muffin?"

"This was it."

Melissa put her hand on Howard's shoulder. "I'm very sorry, Howard. Very very sorry. If there's anything I can do, anything, just tell George."

"Let's not jump to conclusions," Howard said. "Let's just retrace our steps."

"We're looking for a car," I said, "not a contact lens."

We walked the length of the street one more time and then back again, carefully eying the cars as if Howard's might be playfully disguising itself and about to come out of hiding.

"It must have been towed," Howard said. "I'll bet I left it in front of a hydrant."

"You didn't," Nina told him. "I'll go get a cop."

"Wait a minute," Howard said. "Let's just think about this for a minute."

"Howard, there's nothing to think about. The car's been stolen and I'm going to get a cop. Right now."

"I'll come with you," Melissa said. "I just love this neighborhood."

Howard and I sat down on the curb and he told me that more than anything else in life he hated inviting the cops into his personal business in any way, shape, or form. It was asking for trouble, no matter how you looked at it. "My apartment got broken into a few years ago and it took me a week before I had the nerve to call them. And you know what happened? They blamed me. They didn't care about anything except trying to prove I was at fault somehow. You watch, George, the same thing is going to happen tonight."

Finally Nina and Melissa pulled up in the back seat of a police cruiser, accompanied by two gargantuan cops who took forever adjusting their belts and assembling their clipboards before they deigned to speak.

"Whose car was it?" the taller of the two asked.

"It was his," Nina said, pointing. "It was parked in this spot here. The license plate number..."

"Let him tell me," the cop said, looking down at Howard and hoisting up the front of his pants. "It was his car, right?"

Howard put his arm around Nina. "She was doing a good job of telling you. You think you can't trust a woman to tell you what kind of a car it was? You think only a man one can describe a car to you?"

"Hey, look, we don't need a lecture here. Just tell me what kind of car it was."

"Well, it was an old beat-up Datsun," Howard said, shrugging. "The floor was rusted out on one side and it had over a hundred thousand miles on it. We drove it to Florida to visit my father last spring. I drove it cross-country when I first got it. Of course, that was years ago. I'm due for a new car, anyway."

The cop turned to Nina in disgust.

"It was a blue Datsun sedan, license plate 2754KBR, extensive rust on the right side, no taillight on the left..."

"How long you been driving without that taillight?" the other cop jumped in.

"Oh, well, why don't you just give me a ticket?" Howard said. "Maybe I was illegally parked, while we're at it."

"No, Howard, it wasn't illegally parked," Melissa said. "We already decided that."

"And it had bumper stickers," Nina said. "'U.S. Out of El

Salvador,' 'I'm Pro-Choice and I Vote,' and 'Bill of Rights — Love It or Lose It.'"

"And 'I Care About Day Care,'" Howard said, smiling at me.

HALF an hour later we piled into the back seat of a car-service station wagon and headed back for the apartment. Melissa was wedged between the door and Howard, which seemed to please her. "I'm so sorry this had to happen to you, Howard," she kept repeating melodramatically.

"All for that lousy movie," Nina said.

"What was lousy about it?" Howard blasted.

"Everything. That ridiculous food-fight scene."

"What was ridiculous about that?"

"I'm tired of food-fight scenes in movies."

"What was the last movie you saw with a food-fight scene in it?"

"I don't remember, Howard."

"Let me get this straight: you're tired of food-fight scenes but you don't remember the last time you saw one? I don't understand. Maybe you could explain it a little better?" he said, rolling his hands.

"I'm not on the witness stand, Howard," she shouted.

The driver, a thin Haitian with a gold band around his two front teeth, turned up the radio to an earsplitting level.

"Now look what you've done," Howard said dejectedly.

We sat in silence during the rest of the ride listening to the thumping music from the radio. I didn't know what to do about Melissa, as it was too late for her to take the subway back to Manhattan alone and the driver had already made it clear he wouldn't take any fares out of Brooklyn at that time of night. I suppose I should have done the chivalrous thing and suggested she spend the night at the apartment, but the next day was Saturday and I dreaded the thought of all the chitchat and coffee that would precede her departure. Once we got out of the car, Nina told Howard he should accompany Melissa back to Manhattan, seeing as he was headed that way and lived in the same neighborhood. She said it in such a way that Howard had to concede, even though he'd obviously intended to spend the night in Brooklyn and didn't, in fact, live anywhere near Melissa.

"Not to mention," I said as we climbed the dark stairs to the apartment, "that Melissa thinks Howard is a little gem."

"Well, that just means they'll have more to talk about on the way home."

I had trouble falling asleep that night. Nina said she felt a sudden burst of inspiration to get work done and stayed up past three typing noisily in her bedroom.

12

THE week after Howard's car was stolen, Joley returned my call. It was mid-morning on a Sunday and I was lying on my bed doing the *Times* crossword puzzle and fighting to stay awake. The night before I'd gone on a blind date with a friend of Timothy's who lived in Brooklyn—another architect.

His name was Thom. As Thom and I were arranging our date he mentioned four times that his name was spelled with an "h" as if this distinction set him above the masses who had names with plebeian orthography. I called Timothy back and told him I didn't think I should go through with it after all.

"You can't spend the rest of your life turning down opportunities for pleasure," he told me. "It's unhealthy. You'll wind up with prostate problems by the time you're thirty-three. Thom is bright and funny and lives within walking distance of your apartment. Just be careful what you do with him and you'll have a great time."

I bought a large bottle of cheap wine and a pair of new socks—both absolute musts for a blind date. Nina helped me pick out something to wear, something that would show an interest in the evening's going well without giving the appearance of desperation.

Thom himself turned out to be a lean American Gothic type with wolf-blue eyes and light hair. His apartment was an advertisement for an organized mind: no dirt, no clutter, no furniture. He met me at the door, took the bottle of wine and tossed it into the refrigerator, and never brought it out again. A feeling of doom settled over me when he walked from the kitchen carrying a plate of raw vegetables and a bottle of cider and said, "I love Fassbinder, don't you? I think he's my favorite director, after Herzog."

By the time we'd finished the cabbage patch he tried to pass off as dinner, my jaw was aching from chewing carrots and keeping a grin plastered on my face. I thought the evening might be salvaged when we headed for his bedroom, but that, too, turned out to be a dead end. He unrolled a futon onto the bare wood floor and dimmed the track lighting to a supposedly romantic setting. Mattresses, box springs, bed frames, and floor lamps have always seemed perfectly functional pieces of furniture to me, and I've never trusted people who feel compelled to replace them with uncomfortable, expensive substitutes. I couldn't contemplate either sex or sleep while lying on the Japanese beach towel. By 3 A.M. I had a stiff neck and lower back pains and a cramp in my left calf. I rolled off the thin sheet of cotton and slipped on my clothes.

"You should cut down on dairy," Thom advised as he let me out. "Dairy keeps some people up at night. You might have a lactose intolerance."

"Thanks," I said. "I've been meaning to eliminate it from my diet. This should give me the extra push."

On the way home I stopped at a twenty-four-hour Grand Union and bought a pint of Fudge Ripple ice cream, which Nina and I consumed a few hours later with toaster waffles, calling it early brunch.

When the phone rang, I called out to ask Nina if she wanted me to answer it. She was sprawled on her bed surrounded by psychology texts doing her own copy of the puzzle.

"Would you mind getting it, George? And if it's for me, I'm not home. I'm at the movies."

"What's a 'dreamy composition?'" I asked. Nina was much better at crosswords than me.

"It begins with an N. That's all I'm telling you. I can't help it if you had too much cider last night."

I picked up the phone in the kitchen without saying anything.

"George?"

"Yeah?"

"George! Finally I catch you in."

I dropped the magazine and sat down on top of the stove. "Joley," I said coolly.

"Do you have any idea how many times I've tried to get in touch with you in the past few weeks? You're never home."

"You know my social life, Joley—one party after the next."

"You should get an answering machine. They're invaluable."

"Nina and I were talking about that when the phone rang. We're thinking of going to Bloomingdale's and buying one next week."

"Well, it doesn't matter. I don't exactly call you every day. I can't expect you to be waiting around for me to call."

"No, you can't."

"You've got a life of your own."

"That's true, now that you mention it."

"I mean, I don't even know if you're involved with someone else, Georgie."

"No, you don't."

"I mean, you could have a new lover for all I know."

"I could," I said. "For all you know."

There was an odd uncertainty in Joley's voice, a tone that was bordering on pleading. In anyone else, I might have relished this sort of self-deprecation, but coming from Joley I found it unsettling. If he'd taken to pleading, what was I supposed to do?

"So what's up, Joley?" I asked after a moment of uncomfortable silence.

"'What's up?' I like that, George. 'What's up?' Nothing's 'up.' I just hadn't heard from you in a long time and I thought I'd give you a call. I want to know how everything is going for you. 'What's up?' I like that."

"Everything's going well. I'm doing fine." I'm broke, sex-starved, and about to become a father. "How are you?"

"Great! No complaints at all. None whatsoever."

"How's school?"

"Couldn't be better."

"Any cute undergrads lurking at your office door?"

"None as cute as you, George. No one's as cute as you."

In addition to leading the conversation nowhere, this comment was alarmingly out of character. Perhaps he'd gone through some sort of religious conversion. I didn't know what to say.

"Hey, George, before we get on to something else, let me just tell you straight out why I called. I hate playing games. You know what I was thinking of a few weeks ago? I was thinking about that weekend we went to Fire Island together. I just couldn't get it out of my mind. Do you remember that weekend?"

"Of course I remember." It was an unforgettable weekend.

"We were happy then, George."

"We were," I said. I had been miserable. It was one of the most miserable three-day periods of my life. Everytime I get a whiff of Bain de Soleil Number Two, I think of my weekend of entrapment on that sandy discothèque. Joley spent the entire time chasing down perfectly tanned and muscled bodies while I carried on a passionless three-day affair with a man without a single redeeming quality. It was a familiar enough pattern in our relationship by then, but the frenzied, drug-induced hysteria in the air over the island made it all the more unbearable. By Monday I was desperate to see a pale, obese body clad in off-the-rack clothing.

"I was obsessing about that weekend the other day, George. I was thinking we should go away again sometime soon."

"You *were?*"

"Of course I was. Don't sound so surprised."

"Well, it's a little out of the blue. You have to admit you haven't called all that often in the past year and a half." Twice, if anyone was keeping count.

"Didn't I admit that in the beginning of this conversation? Don't think I don't know that, George. I've just been so damned busy and preoccupied. I want to try and make it up to you, in some small way."

"Well, that's nice of you, Joley. It's . . . very considerate." Perhaps I'd been wrong about the religious conversion; it was beginning to sound more like a full frontal lobotomy.

"I'm glad you think so because I already made reservations for us."

"Reservations?"

He laughed with a little bit of his old humorless superiority. "Yes, 'reservations.' I read about this inn in Vermont—outside of a small town—that's run by two men who used to own a place in Fort Lauderdale. It just opened up and it sounds great—kind of a pastoral Fire Island atmosphere with mountains."

"I'll pack my hiking boots."

"And we'll be in time for the foliage." He gave me the date of the reservations and told me he sincerely hoped he was giving me enough notice. "After all, you could have plans, for all I know. Oh, and I rented a car so we can drive up. I know how you love to drive."

"It sounds great, Joley. I'll think about it. I really will think about it."

"There's nothing to think about. I made the reservations and I'm paying for everything and we'll have a great time. You can't say no."

While that was probably true, I figured I could at least keep him guessing for a few days. "I'll call and leave a message on your machine."

"George? I miss you, George. I really miss you."

"No," I said, "don't be ridiculous."

I went into Nina's room and stretched out across the bottom of her bed and tickled the soles of her feet.

"You know I'm not ticklish," she said, furiously filling in words on the puzzle. "Who was that?"

"Wrong number."

"Wrong number for ten minutes?"

"They wanted the suicide hotline and I couldn't just hang up on them."

"So . . . what does he want?"

"He?"

She put down the magazine and looked at me critically. "I can tell, George. You have a foolish look on your face, like you're trying to keep from smiling."

"He wants me to go to Vermont with him for a weekend. Some gay inn in Vermont, if you can imagine such a thing. I told him to shove it. I told him he had his nerve to even call here."

"When are you going?"

"Three weeks. Promise me you won't change the locks while I'm gone, Nina."

"I'll give it serious consideration, George."

13

IN the following weeks fall closed in on us. The days grew mercifully shorter and colder and the gardens behind the house began to dry up and die. The trees in Prospect Park changed color slowly and undramatically, with none of the brilliance usually associated with autumn. These trees seemed to be possessed by a creeping brownness, as if they were slowly being choked by the pollution or the city noise or the mere effort of trying to survive.

I was happy to see a definite end to summer with its unnaturally long days and all the forced lighthearted spirits people feel they have to express in warm weather. I pity those who live in a warm climate year-round and never have the chance to seal the windows tightly shut against the cold air and the neighbors or get the opportunity to wear thick socks and heavy sweaters and long coats.

TOWARD the end of October I dredged my fall clothes from the far dusty corners of my closet and weeded out the most ill-fitting and tasteless of the rags I'd picked up in church sales and secondhand shops throughout the years. Aside from carrying out the seasonal purging of my belongings I go through every fall, I felt more in flux than usual, and I thought I should pare down my wardrobe in case I had to beat a hasty retreat to some other corner of the city.

I ended up with a huge stack of bell-bottom sailor pants, wide-wale corduroys, garishly colored flowered shirts, patched jeans, two white satin scarves, thick leather belts, moth-eaten sweaters in a variety of colors, terry-cloth jerseys, two soft hats, and an assortment of foppish bathrobes. Nina insisted on going through the pile to see if there was anything she wanted before I gave it all away.

"George!" she said, pulling out a pair of gray pleated gabardine trousers. "You can't get rid of these. Don't you remember you wore them when we went to Roseland for your birthday?"

"You're right," I said. "I forgot about that." It had been one of my happier birthday celebrations, fox-trotting and trying to rhumba.

She snatched up a long black woolen muffler covered with lint. "And this! You can't throw this out. This is the muffler you have on in that picture of you and Joley skating in Rockefeller Center."

"Standing, not skating. But I do like that picture a lot."

I put the muffler on the bed with the pants.

"Now what's wrong with these?" She held up a pair of overalls. "I don't see any holes anywhere."

"No one wears overalls anymore, Nina. I certainly wouldn't, anyway."

"They're great for bus rides, George, loose and comfortable. With a sweatshirt they're perfect to wear to a demonstration."

I threw them on the bed.

In an hour the bed was littered with clothes from the reject pile which I stuffed back into the closet. The only things left on the floor were two paisley polyester shirts and an electric-blue V-necked acrylic sweater.

"I'll bring these to the free box outside the food co-op," I said.

"Don't bother, George; it would be an insult. Save them for Halloween." She picked up the sweater and examined it against her chest. "Actually, this is a real period piece. I used to drop acid wearing clothes that looked like this. Maybe I'll keep it. I can wear it with cutoffs if I ever get thin."

IT was somewhere in the middle of October that Nina began to withdraw from Howard, to "terminate," as she'd put it. She told him she thought they should spend less time together; she needed more hours to concentrate on her dissertation; pregnancy was exhausting her. Howard complied. He came to prepare dinner less and less frequently and took Nina to fewer movies. He began to make special plans for them—theater tickets purchased far in advance, dinner reservations at a three-star restaurant—as if he needed to have an expensive celebration planned as an excuse for getting together with her. When he did come to the apartment, he acted more sheepish, as if he were on a first date. He limited his discussions of amicus briefs and union meetings and left his Law Report advance sheets on the floor in the hallway. He stopped most of his inventive name-calling, and kept his terms of endearment to Honey and Baby and Ni and Nini, names he'd called her when they were first seeing each other.

One night I walked into the apartment and found Howard standing in the kitchen dressed in his suit and tie, holding a bag of mushrooms and pointing an accusing finger at Nina. She was leaning against the wall with her arms folded tightly across her chest.

"You're talking about repudiating the free speech principles of the First Amendment!" he shouted. "The First Amendment, Nina!"

"Don't talk to me about the First Amendment as if it were the only life-sustaining force on the planet, Howard. I'm tired of pornographers hiding behind the First Amendment while more and more women are suffering. I'm *sick* of it."

"All right, all right. Fine." He sighed out a chestful of rage. "If you're being victimized by pornography, go to Times Square and blow up a peep show. I'll help you make the Molotov cocktail. Just don't legislate against it, that's all I'm asking! Just don't line up with the wrong forces!"

"He has a point there, Pumpkin," I said from the hallway.

"I *want* the government to get involved and take a stand against the misogyny of this society, Howard. That's the whole point."

Howard turned to me with a pleading look. "Don't you agree, George, she's just hiding her basic moral conservatism behind these stupid, half-baked political theories? And if they start legislating against pornography, those feminist tracts about clitoral orgasms crowding her bookshelves will be the first things thrown into the fire."

"Don't talk to George about clitoral orgasms, Howard." She glared at me.

I shrugged sincerely.

"In case you don't know it, Howard," she said slowly, "it is against Nicaraguan law to use women as objects in advertising."

Howard tossed the bag of mushrooms into the sink. This was always the ace in the hole in one of their arguments; the mention of sacred Nicaragua to support a theory. Howard stormed past me in the hall and snatched his woolen coat and briefcase from the floor.

"You'll be sorry, Nina. When your dissertation gets hauled off to some book burning in the middle of Central Park, you'll be sorry. All I can say is, you're lucky I'm not the type to tell you I told you so."

He banged out the door while Nina stood triumphantly in her corner. A moment later he walked back in and stood in the kitchen doorway. "I'm sorry, Nina. I'm sorry I lost my temper. And I apologize for dragging you into this, George."

"That's what innocent bystanders are for," I said.

"Look, Howard," Nina sighed, "I'm not hungry anyway. I'm overtired. I can't seem to get enough sleep. Would you mind if we just skipped dinner tonight? We'll be seeing each other later in the week anyway."

There was a moment of silence in which I saw Howard absorb the blow. He mustered as much dignity as he could in his sagging shoulders and said, "No problem. Fine. I'll leave the food here. The chicken needs another ten minutes. George, if you want to sauté the mushrooms, I'd suggest a squeeze of lemon with the butter. It's up to you. I'll see you later in the week, Nina."

Nina and I stood and listened while he quietly shut the door behind him, walked slowly down the flight of stairs, and then shut the two doors leading to the street. There was a dead space in the room between Nina and me where Howard had been standing a moment earlier.

"Well, I *am* tired," she said. She turned off the oven and put the mushrooms in the refrigerator. "And I'm *not* hungry. And I *will* be seeing him later in the week."

She headed off to her room before I could remind her I hadn't accused her of anything.

ONE afternoon later that week, Howard came to the apartment early, before Nina was home from the clinic. They had plans to hear Michael Manley speak at Brooklyn College and then eat at some Caribbean restaurant in Sunset Park. I was sitting at the makeshift table reading a book on trench warfare during World War I and eating a bowl of popcorn. Howard's clothes were more wrinkled than usual and his nose was running. His eyes were large and sunken, the droopy lids making perfect half-moons of them. He was beginning to lose weight; his paunch had receded from the waist of his trousers and the folds of his unpressed shirt.

"Are you all right, Howard?" I asked, laying aside my book.

"Oh, sure, George, I'm fine." He dropped onto the couch, wiped his nose on his sleeve, and sighed deeply. "You go back to your book. I'm going to try and take a quick nap."

"Can I get make you some coffee?"

"Nothing."

"A drink?"

"No."

"Popcorn?"

"I can't eat, George. I can't eat and I can't sleep and I haven't had a productive day at work in the past two weeks."

"Any word on the car?"

"What do I care about the car? The car is gone for good and it's just as well. It was old and tired, like me. That's what happens when things get old and tired, George, you just plain old kiss them goodbye and get rid of them."

He shut his eyes and started to breathe deeply, as if he were about to go to sleep. I picked up my book. I'd been fascinated by trench warfare since the third grade; Nina had suggested a number of Freudian interpretations to explain my interest in trenches and mud and duck boards, but I was skeptical.

"Is she seeing someone else?" Howard asked suddenly, without opening his eyes. "I think I should know if she's seeing someone else, with this baby and all. At long last I think I have a right to know."

"She isn't seeing someone else, Howard. She'd tell you if she was seeing someone else. You know that."

"I don't know that, George. I thought I knew, but I don't know anymore. All I know is I feel like I'm on trial every time I see her. If I come by once too often or say the wrong thing, it's goodbye. She's cutting me out of her life." He turned his face to the back of the sofa and started to sob.

I reached into the bowl and shoved a fistful of popcorn into my mouth. Liberated as I am, I've never managed to feel at ease around another man in tears. I leafed through my book and studied a picture of the Central London Recruiting Depot.

"I'm being cut out of her life and I don't know why." he turned around and faced me. "Why, George? Tell me, please."

My mouth was so full of popcorn I couldn't speak. I pushed the hair off my forehead and shrugged.

"The funny thing is, I can't get angry with her. All I want is for her to be happy. You don't know how much I love her, George. I adore her. I worship her. She's a Dumpling."

He burst into tears again and curled up on the sofa racked with sobs. I brought a long piece of toilet paper from the bathroom. "Try to pull yourself together, Howie. This isn't going to help anyone." I sat on the floor by the sofa and took hold of his arm. "You don't want Nina to come home and find you in this condition."

He buried his face against my shoulder and I felt his tears rolling down my neck. "What difference does it make now? You don't know the half of it. I can't go on much longer like this. I'd be better off not seeing her at all."

"She loves you, Howard."

"No," he said, blowing his nose in the toilet paper, "she doesn't love me. If she loved me she wouldn't be cutting me out of her life like this. And it's all my own fault. I'm too possessive. I'm too jealous. I'm a hypocrite. What I really want is to marry her and buy an apartment on the Upper West Side with her and raise our baby together. That's what's wrong between us. The first woman I meet who's strong and independent and has an opinion on everything under the sun, who'll always challenge me to a solid argument, who loves a good hearty meal, and what's my first thought? I want to make her my wife. I want to marry her and make her my wife the way my mother was my father's wife. His possession. There's no point in trying to kid myself or her anymore. I want the kind of relationship we're both ideo-logically opposed to. I'd want to get rid of me, too."

"You're being too hard on yourself, Howard. She's confused, that's all. She loves you."

He straightened his jacket and his stained silk tie. "I have to get out of here. If I saw her walk through that door right now, I'd fall apart all over again."

"She won't be here for a while. I'll get you a drink and you can calm down. The two of you can have a nice long talk." You can get on your knees, threaten suicide...

He stood up from the sofa. "No, George, there's no point any-more. Don't even tell her I was here. We'll pretend I stood her up tonight. That way she'll be angry with me and it will be easier on her. She loves being angry."

He left the house quietly and so unceremoniously I was alarmed. I went to the window in Nina's bedroom and pulled aside the material tacked over the frame. The right leg of Howard's trousers was caught in his sock and one side of his collar was turned up. His suit jacket was blowing open in the wind as he forlornly walked up the street. He wasn't dressed warmly enough for the weather.

I'd finished the popcorn and was well into a fried-egg sandwich when Nina breezed into the apartment, apparently on top of the world. I didn't bother to say hello as she sailed through the living room. "How was your day, Georgie?" she asked as she headed for her room.

I didn't answer. I poured a puddle of catsup onto my plate and dunked the sandwich into it.

"I said, 'How was your day, George?'" she called from the hallway.

"It was a pisser," I yelled.

"A what?"

"A pisser. A real pisser!"

"I can't hear a word you're saying."

"Then why don't you come in here where you can hear?" I shouted so loud I thought I'd have a brain hemorrhage.

"What?"

I tossed the sandwich into the catsup and stormed into her room. She was sitting on her bed taking off her shoes. I leaned into the doorway and shouted, "My day was wonderful! Great! Terrific!" and stomped back into the living room. I picked up the sopping sandwich and took a large bite. Nina cautiously came in and sat on the sofa.

"I just asked you how your day was."

"If you wanted to tell me how your day was, you could have told me without asking me how my day was first. We don't have to stand on ceremony around here, remember? It's one of the advantages of our original relationship."

"Don't yell at me. I can't stand being yelled at today."

"Are you getting your period?"

"I'm pregnant, George."

"So?"

"Oh, forget it. Just forget it. If you're angry about something, you could have the decency to tell me instead of bitching at me."

"Is that what I was doing?"

"Yes, it was."

"I'm sorry," I said, softening a bit. One of my greatest problems in life is I'm unable to sustain an emotion for more than five minutes. "Howard was here," I said. "He left in tears a little while ago."

She looked up at me with surprise. "Howard was here and left? We had plans to go out tonight."

"Well he was too upset to go through with your plans. He's hurt, Nina. He's crushed. You don't hold all the cards, you know. He can 'terminate,' too, you know."

"I do know that, George. I just wasn't expecting it to happen so soon."

"You underestimate him."

"I overestimate myself."

She looked around the room despondently, as if she were searching for a lost sock in the midst of the rubble. I could see a kind of panic rising in her eyes, a kind of panic about being in the house for the rest of the evening.

WE went for a walk through Prospect Park with our arms around each other, watching the sun set behind Manhattan and looking over our shoulders for potential muggers. Sections of the park have a wild, deserted look, as if no one has walked there in years. The globes on the lampposts along the walkways are smashed and the manmade ponds and streams are filled with stagnant pools of rainwater and clogged with rotting leaves. I liked to head into those sections of the park where no traces of the city were visible and there was a sense of pending danger.

"You think I'm doing the wrong thing about Howard, don't you?" Nina asked as we knocked against each other.

"Of course I do."

"I'm serious, George. I want your opinion."

"I told you, Nina. I think you're being reckless and foolish. Howard has his faults but he loves you. He'd make a great father for the baby. You're afraid to make a commitment to him, that's all."

"I'm not *afraid* to make a commitment to him, I simply don't *want* to."

"Even though you love him?"

"Who says I love him?"

I was shocked. "Nina, come on."

"Come on what? Come on what, George? What if I don't know? What if I truly do not know? Isn't there such a thing as not knowing?"

"Well, how are you going to find out? When I saw him walk out of the apartment today, I had a horrible feeling I wouldn't see him again." He hadn't slammed the door or pounded down the stairs or run up the street. He left undramatically, quietly defeated. "I'll miss him, Nina. He's a part of my life, too, you know. He's a part of my life I have no control over."

Nina kicked through the leaves scattered across the path in front of us. She was wearing a red beret pulled down over her ears and an orange-and-brown shawl a woman had woven for her earlier that year. Her blond hair was sticking out around the edges of her beret and her mouth was drawn into a pout.

"When are you leaving for Vermont, Georgie?" she asked.

"About a week. It's only for three days."

"I know. It makes me nervous, that's all. No control, to quote you."

"Do you want me to cancel?"

"No, of course not. I hope you have a good time. I just hope you'll... Never mind. I hope you have a good time."

We sat on a grassy hill at the edge of the park. Flatbush Avenue stretched off to infinity on one side of us. It was growing dark quickly and the cars circling the huge war memorial arch in the middle of Grand Army Plaza had their yellow lights turned on. I felt lost, as if I were in a foreign city and the shadows of the evening were closing in on me. I put my arm around Nina's waist and rested my head on her shoulder.

"We could be in Paris," I said, pointing to the towering arch. "That could be the Arc de Triomphe and we could be in Paris."

"That could be the Louvre," she said, looking at the library.

We sat in silence until it was dark and we could see the lights of Manhattan glittering in the distance, bright but unreal. Nina stood up and wrapped her shawl more tightly around her shoulders.

"I signed up for those birth classes," she said, looking toward the city.

"I'm not going with you, Nina."

"You're angry about Howard leaving this afternoon."

"Don't condescend. I'm not the father and it isn't my place."

"It doesn't matter. There's another single woman in the class. It'll be fine if you don't go."

"And don't be so magnanimous." It made me feel worse, unworthy of her once again. "We should get out of here before the drug traffic starts up."

"I don't want to leave yet. I want to stay for a few more minutes."

"Well, come and sit here next to me. It's getting chilly. The lights out there are making me sad."

She grinned at me and then took off her beret and stuffed it into the back pocket of her jeans and ran down the side of the hill into the black, empty field at full speed with the shawl in her hand trailing out behind her.

"Nina!" I called out. "Come on. It's getting late."

I looked into the field but it was dark and all I could see were bare trees and unrecognizable black shapes.

14

JOLEY called me the morning we were to leave for Vermont and told me he'd pick me up in front of school at four o'clock. It was a lost day for me, one in a series of lost days. Doran was out sick, recovering from an attack of asthma, and I abnegated most of my responsibilities to Melissa. She conducted class with her usual high spirits. She'd had her hair clipped even closer to her scalp and had started wearing open-toed shoes despite the fact that it was getting colder every day.

When I told her about my weekend plans she insisted on waiting outside of school with me until Joley showed up. She said she'd rather go homeless than pass up an opportunity to meet someone I'd been involved with, especially unsuccessfully. She and I sat out on the cold cement steps in front of the building for over an hour while she related an involved tale of an aunt who'd been married five times, thrice to the same man and once to his brother. It was a fairly incomprehensible story that seemed completely implausible to begin with. At five o'clock Joley still hadn't shown up and I was beginning to think he wouldn't make it at all.

"Let me ask you this," Melissa said. "If he didn't show, how would you feel?"

"Honestly? I'd feel like taking you to an expensive restaurant for dinner. And then maybe to a show."

"That's a terrible thing to say. You know I wouldn't let you pay. I'd treat."

By the time we'd decided on what show to see, a shiny green Oldsmobile screeched up to the curb and Joley jumped out. He paused on the sidewalk and caught his breath as if he'd just run from White Plains. "George. I'm sorry, George," he said, holding up his hands in apology. "It was the Friday afternoon traffic. What can I say?"

"I have the feeling I'm making a mistake here," I said to Melissa under my breath.

I introduced the two of them and Melissa put her hand on Joley's shoulder and stared into his emerald eyes. "I am truly very pleased to meet you, Dr. Joley."

Joley was wearing a gray flannel shirt and a dark tie with tiny flecks of green that matched his eyes exactly. He had on a huge Japanese raincoat that fell almost to his ankles with sleeves so wide Melissa could have worn either one of them for a dress. There was something noticeably different in his appearance but I couldn't put my finger on exactly what it was. Perhaps he'd finally stopped going to the tanning salon.

"You drive, George," he told me. "I know how you love to drive."

He got into the passenger seat and I tossed my overstuffed canvas sack into the back, next to his leather overnight bag. I went back to the steps and gave Melissa a hug goodbye, calculating in my mind the exact number of hours Joley and I would be together in the next three days.

"I thought you said he had a beard," she breathed into my ear.

"He does."

"Well, *I* certainly can't see it."

I looked back at Joley fiddling with the latch on the glove compartment. "I thought there was something different. He must have shaved it off."

"George," Melissa whispered cautiously, "he has a weak chin."

We both turned and looked at Joley as he studied a road map. Without a beard his neck looked soft and overly fleshy and his chin was sunken in surprisingly close to his lower lip. His face had lost some of its perfect dashing symmetry. Of course, beards are routinely worn to hide a flaw in either facial structure or character, but in Joley's case I'd always suspected the latter.

"Stay out of trouble," I shouted to Melissa as I walked to the car.

"I'm in it up to my teeth. You don't know the half of it." She waved furiously, as if we were disembarking on an ocean liner and then sat back down on the steps.

ONCE I'd successfully navigated the boxy car through several blocks of gridlock, Joley put his hand on my thigh and said, in a gentle tone that caught me off guard, "You look great, Georgie. You look so . . . healthy and fresh."

"Nothing's more insulting than an undeserved compliment, Joley. *You* look great."

"You like me without the beard? I thought it made me look too old so I shaved the damned thing off. I'm creeping toward forty, you know."

"I'd never have known if I didn't know. You'd look twenty-five no matter what you did." Joley had no idea of what it meant to age gracefully, a concept I had the luxury of still believing in while in my twenties. "You look twenty-four without the beard. No, you look twenty-three. Your eyes are more beautiful than ever."

"Thank you, George," he said and fell silent.

I never stopped being amazed at his ability to accept a compliment.

WE said little to each other as I drove through the heavy, slow-moving traffic. Occasionally Joley would turn to me and say something like "It really is great to see you, George," but neither one of us made any attempt at real conversation. At first I told myself we had too much to say to even know where to begin, but gradually I realized there wasn't much of anything at all I did want to tell him. I felt myself getting defensive and self-protective, as if even the most mundane details of my life were too private to discuss with him. And anything he might tell me would probably be so inaccurate and heavily censored, there was no real point in listening. Hopefully he'd had a rough day and would doze off for most of the trip.

Once we got onto the highway I turned on the heater and the

radio and dropped a heavy foot onto the gas pedal. I love driving fast in overheated cars with the radio blasting and, if at all possible, someone in the back seat smoking cigarettes and drinking beer. It's a holdover from my suburban childhood. I'm never more content or feel more in control of my life than when I'm behind a steering wheel. With Joley sitting passively in the seat next to me I felt in control of his life as well, and I was suddenly overcome with a sense of power.

The city thinned out around us as we sped on; the buildings and the bridges and the walls of electric lights lost their grasp on the scenery and gave way to darkening woods and distant, dimly lit houses. It was Joley's turf that was disappearing in bits and pieces, and he was changing in the seat beside me as quickly as the scenery flashing by the window. He was losing his grasp somehow, like the buildings and the bridges. We were an hour past the Connecticut border when his extravagant raincoat ceased to look stylish and began to look merely big.

"YOU know something, George?" he said, his voice sleepy from the heat blasting in his face, "I remember exactly what I said to you the first time we met."

"You do?" If he'd said he remembered what I'd said to him, I could have accused him of lying.

"I do. I guess that makes me a romantic."

"I guess so."

"That was over three years ago. Three years, and I remember everything I said."

"I guess that makes you a romantic."

I didn't know what to say to him. I wasn't used to pandering to his mawkish ruminations and it sounded odd. It reminded me of the time I bumped into a friend from college I hadn't seen in years and he started telling me about the One Godhead. It's the kind of thing you just don't trust. As Joley continued on about our glorious past together, recalling this or that insignificant detail of our lives, I listened with decreasing interest. He was giving me the same bored kind of headache I get when I watch the Macy's parade on TV. It struck me then that beyond escaping Brooklyn for a weekend,

I hadn't given too much thought to what it would be like spending three days with Joley in a place where I knew no one else and probably wouldn't be able to get away from him for more than a bathroom break.

"And do you remember Constance, George? Whenever I see her she asks for you. You're the only one of my boyfriends people always ask about."

"Misery loves company, Joley."

"And my secretary. You remember Elsa, don't you? She's always asking for George Mullen."

At the mention of Elsa's name, a thought crossed my mind and I turned off the radio. "Isn't your tenure case coming up soon, Joley?" I asked.

"She'd love it if you came by for a visit sometime, even if it was just for a couple of minutes."

I opened up the window to let some cool air into the sauna. "Joley? What about your tenure case?"

He turned away from me and looked at his reflection in the blackened window. "It's come up. It's come and gone."

"I'm sorry," I said. "What happened?"

He shrugged. "The usual. The predictable, I suppose. My publishing record is lousy and no one cares what kind of teacher I am. Department politics. A little of everything. The gross injustice of life. You're too young to know about it."

"When did you hear?"

"The last word of the final appeal came in early September. I'll be finishing out the year and then I'm thinking of moving out of the city. I've been reading up on real estate prices and job possibilities in Seattle."

"Seattle?"

"I know a few people who've moved there and they love it. They say it's beautiful."

"Yes. I've heard that too." Joley belonged in Seattle like he belonged in the priesthood, but sometimes the best you can do for a friend is tell him what he wants to hear. He was gravely and sullenly staring into the black pool of the window with the lights of the traffic flashing against the glass, stroking his naked, sunken chin as if it were still covered with a beard.

• • •

JOLEY had a smudged brochure for the inn with a pen and ink sketch of the place on the front and directions on how to get there printed on the back. It was past nine o'clock by the time we pulled off the highway at the prescribed exit and got onto a narrow winding road that seemed to be taking us farther and farther away from civilization. The headlights cut into the darkness a few dusty feet at a time. I kept expecting some disheveled person with blood pouring from his eyes to try and flag us down to tell us that his campsight had just been attacked by Bigfoot.

Finally we passed a trailer park lit up with glaring yellow and red light bulbs and then a row of stately, abandoned Victorian mansions, and then the town itself appeared. The brochure claimed it had once been the major industrial center for southern Vermont but judging from the looks, it had fallen into complete decay and despair. The town was built up along a wide river like some medieval European fortress, and in the faint blue moonlight it looked to have much of the gloom of the Middle Ages. The riverbanks were lined with crumbling, overhanging factories with painted signs eroding off their brick sides and empty windows that looked eerily hungry in the night.

"I guess the inn must be on the other side of town," Joley said peering hopefully out the window. "Out in the country."

I pulled into a gas station to ask for directions. The person operating the pumps, a short teenager with acne scars along his lower jaw and strangely dead eyes, grinned at me. "Thraight up the threet, fellas. At the thoplight." He pointed up the road past a little red diner and let his hand drop limply at the wrist.

"Thanks," I said and got into the car quickly.

"What was that all about?"

"I don't know. I think he has a speech impediment."

"Probably inbreeding. I've heard there's lot of that in these rural areas. A lot of incest."

The street through the center of town was bordered with ramshackle buildings: a Woolworth's and a green-and-orange hardware store and many empty and boarded-up storefronts. There was one dimly lit shop with nothing in it except a circle of gray metal folding chairs. "What do you suppose goes on in there?" Joley asked.

"AA meetings, support groups for abusive parents. That kind of thing." I said.

I parked the car at the stoplight and looked across the street. The only building that could have been the inn was a five-story brick edifice sprouting up from the sidewalk without so much as a window box in front. I'd seen more rural establishments in Queens. There was a throng of about fifteen people parading up and down the sidewalk in front of the place, shouting and making noise. For a minute I thought the building was on fire. I stepped out into the cold air and pulled a woolen cap down over my ears.

"What do you suppose this is?" Joley asked. He wrapped his huge raincoat around his body like a cape.

"I hope it isn't a labor dispute," I said. "I don't care if you've put down a deposit, I don't think we should cross a picket line." There was at least one person wielding a sign.

We got our bags out of the back seat and crossed the street. Midway, Joley froze and pressed his palm into my chest. "George, take a look at that sign."

A tall woman in a red flannel jacket and a hunting cap was holding aloft a cardboard sign with red block letters reading: GO BACK TO SODOM.

We got back into the car and locked the doors. "How did you hear about this place, Joley?"

"I don't remember." He opened up the glove compartment and unfolded a huge map. "We could keep driving. It looks like Montreal is only another two hundred miles or so."

"Forget it," I said. "I'm not up for crossing borders tonight. Anyway, it's our duty to go in there. We can't just crumble to this kind of assault."

"I suppose not," he said peering out the windshield with dread. "Maybe we could go to that diner first and get something to eat."

"Are you nuts? Didn't you get a look at the parking lot of that place? Three pickup trucks, two with gun racks, and a jacked-up Chevy Impala with dice hanging from the rearview. We're better off with religious fanatics. At least they might be pacifists."

We armed ourselves with our luggage and headed across the

street resolutely. As we got closer to the sidewalk a hiss rose up from the mob and continued to get louder until it sounded like a locust attack I'd seen in a movie depicting rural life in America. The faceless crowd closed in on us as we stepped up to the curb, shouting unintelligible things about God and sin and pillars of salt and shoving pamphlets into our hands. The door to the inn swung open and an enormously fat man stepped out and grabbed both Joley and me by the arms. "I've told you people a million times," he shouted, "my guests do *not* give autographs." He yanked both of us inside and swept the door closed behind him, all in one smooth, grand gesture.

"It's our little welcoming committee," he said, grinning pleasantly.

"Are they dangerous?" Joley asked.

"Ah, no, they're fine. There's nothing to do in this town on a Friday night, that's all. Fortunately they go to bed early."

He introduced himself as Grant, one of the owners of the inn. He was almost completely bald and had a broad, friendly face, which, bulbous nose and all, wouldn't have looked out of place on a benevolent, alcoholic Catholic bishop. He had on a green turtleneck jersey that was stretched to near transparency across his massive stomach and shoulders and a silver sunburst medallion hanging against his chest on a silver chain that could easily have been used to lock a bicycle.

We followed him to the front desk, where he shoved aside a stack of papers and reached for the registration cards. The lobby was a monstrosity, a cavernous room stuffed with furniture that seemed to have been dumped carelessly from the back of a truck rather than arranged. High-backed chairs, love seats, round end tables, sofas and floor lamps were scattered around in such haphazard fashion that it would have been impossible to find a chair with ample reading light or a spot where two people could sit facing each other. Joley looked at me and shrugged apologetically as he signed us in. The dominant color in the lobby was red, and whoever had chosen the decor seemed to have a penchant for fuzzy acrylic rugs, the kinds of things someone confined to a bed for twenty years might have made to pass the time.

"The room is all ready for you boys," Grant said. "Right on the front of the house with a nice view of the town and twin beds as requested."

He led us up a grand staircase to a small chilly room on the third floor. There were two narrow metal-framed cots dumped against one wall with a bureau between them. The bureau had been painted brown with a fake antique finish. The walls were the color of a scummy swimming pool. Grant turned on a light by the window and lifted the shade. A shout rose up from the street.

"Oh, for God's sake," he said, lowering the shade. "I have to give myself credit for at least trying with those people. Two weeks ago I went out and asked them for Bibles to put in the rooms. They acted as if I was asking for a four-star rating from Jesus."

He had a bright, infectious grin that reminded me of my students. He looked to be in his mid-fifties, and I'd have guessed it was a rough half-century of living for him.

"I suppose you'd like to hear the activities calendar. Well, there's a bar and disco in the basement that opens in a couple of hours. There's one movie theater in town, but their only show started at seven-thirty. There's a diner at the edge of town you probably passed on the way in. It's open all night but I'd suggest you wait until daylight. Out guests have a way of standing out in this town, if you know what I mean."

"Isn't there someplace we can get dinner?" Joley asked.

Grant looked at his watch. "Brattleboro," he said. "This hour of the night, with no cops out, you could make it in ... an hour. Fifty minutes, maybe. You might find something open there."

"Might? What the hell kind of place is this where you can't get any food at nine-thirty at night? You should have told me when I made the reservations."

"Oh, Christ!" he said. "Just what we need: another live wire!" He laughed raucously and slammed the door behind him.

Joley took off his raincoat and sank despondently into the pit in the center of one of the army cots. "I'm sorry, George. What can I tell you? I heard this place was great. I wanted it to be a nice weekend."

"I know," I said. "It isn't your fault."

"It is my fault. I should have checked it out. I should have known a place like this wouldn't go over in the corn belt."

"We're not in the corn belt."

"I never should have dragged you all the way up here."

"You didn't drag me. I drove, remember? Anyway, you know I hate it when you criticize yourself."

"That's true," he said, smiling. "You especially hate it when I criticize myself for truly reprehensible acts."

"That's right."

"You hated it when I tried to apologize for what I did to you at Constance's party."

"Of course. But that was years ago."

"What I said to that blonde you live with."

"Nina," I told him. "Her name's Nina."

"What I said to Nina. I don't know how I did that, George. It was a rotten thing to have done."

"Please, Joley, just stop." I opened a closet door. "Is there a bathroom in this cell?" The conversation was making me jittery and I was beginning to feel as if someone were wringing my bladder.

"It was rotten. It was the biggest mistake of my life."

I opened two more doors, both of them closets. The room had enough closet space for Diana Ross and her whole Vegas act to stay in, in case they played the lounge in the basement. "There must be a bathroom down the hall."

"Are you listening to me, George?" He got off the bed and walked toward me one step at a time, like in slow motion. "I said it was the biggest mistake of my life."

"Hopefully you've got a good thirty years to try and top it," I said, pulling at the crotch of my pants. "I really do have to find the john."

"I wish I could take it all back. I wish I could turn back the clock."

Whoever had given Joley the crash course in cheap sentiment deserved an award. "It turned out all right in the end," I said. I opened the door to the hallway but Joley reached over my shoulder and shut it. He put his arms around me and stared down at me.

"It didn't turn out all right. It was the biggest mistake of my life. I've been miserable without you."

His platitudes were making me giddy. "Don't say this kind of stuff out loud," I told him, my voice cracking with embarrassment.

"Even if I mean it?"

"No one means it, Joley."

I ran down the hallway to the bathroom, slammed and locked the door behind me and fell on the floor in a fit of convulsive laughter. The absurdity, the ridiculousness of me being in Vermont with Joley hit me like an attack of angina and I couldn't stop myself from laughing. Everything that crossed my mind struck me as hilarious—the ride up, the demonstration, Seattle, Joley's wardrobe. I thought it particularly wildly funny that I had entertained any hopes or expectations, however vague, for a reconciliation, or even a good time, with this man in a Japanese raincoat and a mouth so full of empty platitudes it was a wonder he could find room in it for dinner.

I further indulged myself by thinking about Doran's asthma, Howard's runny nose, an amusing bit of family history my mother had told me when I was twelve. Someone knocked at the bathroom door and told me to open up.

"Get lost," I shouted and kicked at the door so hard a cheap plastic towel rack glued to the wood crashed on the floor.

When I'd finally exhausted myself and had a headache, I got up and took a leak and washed my face in cold water. The person waiting to get into the bathroom was sitting on the floor smoking a cigarette. "It's all yours," I said.

"You mean you were in there *alone?*"

JOLEY was lying on his narrow metal cot reading a copy of *Vermont Life*. He'd unpacked his overnight bag and neatly laid out his clothes in a bureau drawer.

"George," he said, putting down the magazine, "I want you to come to Seattle with me."

"Joley, just be quiet."

"I want you to..."

"Quiet please, Joley." Without thinking about it, I went and knelt on his bed and took off his tie and slowly unbuttoned his shirt.

"We have to talk, George. There are some important things I want to discuss with you."

"Don't say a word." I lifted his arms over his head and pulled off his shirt until his wrists were caught in the cuffs. I wrapped the shirt around the bed frame so he couldn't move his arms.

"I'm serious about this, George."

"You're not allowed to speak."

I opened his trousers and slid them down his legs until they were tangled in his shoes and then gave them a tug for good measure. I turned off the light on the table by the window and took my clothes off.

"What are you doing, George? This isn't what I had in mind for right now."

"Joley, there's no TV in this room, we can't get dinner without driving across the state, we can't get a drink for a couple of hours, I have nothing to say to you, and, honestly, I don't want to hear what you have to say to me, and I'm not interested in that magazine. Our options are limited."

I took the copy of *Vermont Life* and threw it across the room as hard as I could.

15

A couple of hours later I felt an intense craving for a drink. A
chill had entered the room, making it feel more like a cold-storage
closet than ever. Joley was lying under the covers on his narrow
cot complaining of a headache from the long drive north.

"You go downstairs and get a drink," he said, "if you really
have to."

"I don't have to," I said as I got dressed. "I want to."

"You go then, George. Go right ahead."

"I intend to."

I went through the sweater display Joley had neatly laid out in
one of the bureau drawers and put on a thick Missoni pullover that
hung off my body like a nightshirt. I bounced down the four flights
of steps to the basement imitating a tap step I'd seen in a Shirley
Temple movie. Once I almost knocked down a woman trudging up
the staircase wearing a T-shirt with the words ASSUME NOTHING
emblazoned across the front.

The disco itself was a long, narrow room without a window or
any visible signs of ventilation. The air was stuffy with the smell
of stale beer and thick with cigarette smoke even though there was
only a handful of people in the place. The person who'd decorated
the lobby must have had a part in beautifying the basement because
all the walls, the carpeting, and even the ceiling were in various
garish shades of red. There was a string of blue Christmas lights
twinkling against the mirror behind the bar and threads of silver
tinsel hanging from the shelves lined with bottles. The ceiling was
so low I could effortlessly reach up and touch it.

The crowd, if you could call it that, was an even mixture of men and woman of all ages, some of whom looked as if they were dressed for a loft party in Soho and the rest as if they'd spent the day, if not their entire lives, chopping wood in front of a cabin in the mountains. The men were mostly lined up along the bar holding onto drinks, while the women were seated in captain's chairs at tiny square tables pressed tightly against an opposite wall.

I recognized our host standing at the far end of the bar with his arm wrapped around another man, swaying from side to side to the music blaring out a speaker hung precariously over his head. He had changed out of his green pants and turtleneck into an identical outfit in black, with the sunburst medallion still banging against his chest.

"Hey, kid," he called out when he saw me standing in the doorway. "Come over here for a minute. Come over here and meet someone worth meeting."

I crossed the narrow room, choking briefly on the smoke, and shook his sweaty hand. The top of his head was covered with a greasy, pitch-black toupee that drained the color from his face and gave his complexion a jaundiced shine. "I want you to meet Tommy," he said in a drunken slur. "He owns this dump with me." He squeezed the man next to him with one of his massive arms and said, "Tommy's the only person in this state with one single ounce of good sense."

I stuck out my hand to Tommy, but he was so enveloped in Grant's embrace, all he could manage was a wide, tight-lipped smile. He was a short man with a small frame—petit, I suppose—and pastel-blue eyes. His hair was light and fine and he had surprisingly pink skin. I would have guessed him to be in his mid-forties, but he had about him that peculiarly youthful look that clings to men who carry on lifelong relationships with men older than themselves. "It's nice to meet you, dear," he said in a low, throaty voice. "You'd better tell me your name because I'm sure Grant doesn't remember it."

"It's George."

"You can trust me with your last name, George."

"Mullen. George Mullen."

"An Irish boy," Tommy said. "I like the Irish, even though my mother was from that horrible country." He lowered his eyelids slowly. They were so pale and thin they appeared translucent.

"So where's your friend, kid?" Grant bellowed.

"He's sleeping," I said. "The ride was too much for him."

"Well, don't worry, we'll find someone for you, won't we, Tommy?"

Tommy managed another restrained smile.

"Thanks," I said, "but I'm not in the market."

"Oh? I suppose you came down here for the ambiance? I suppose you came down here for the decor? You think that's why he came down here, Tommy? You think he came down here for the decor?" As he spoke his forehead wrinkled into thick folds of flesh while the toupee remained immobile on his head like a Davy Crockett cap. He squeezed Tommy a few more times with his giant's arm.

"Maybe he came down for a drink," Tommy suggested in his Lana Turner voice.

"Well, you should have said so, kid. Have a drink on me. We need some good word of mouth back in New York. Have a drink and forget that big-mouth mannequin you came up here with."

"Actually he's a nice person," I said, out of obligation.

"So's the Pope. What'll you have?"

I ordered bourbon, which seemed to please Grant. He grabbed me with his free arm and squashed me against his sweaty body. When the bartender had poured, I picked up the glass and tossed the drink down in a single shot, really more to impress Grant than for any other reason.

"Good for you," he shouted. "Pour him another one. Now, who are we going to fix this kid up with?"

"Maybe he's not interested," Tommy uttered from the depths of his glass.

"Of course he's interested. Everyone's interested, when you get to the bottom line."

"Well, Randolph came in alone tonight," Tommy said.

Grant looked around the room until his eyes came to rest on a skeleton mummified in black leather lurking in a dark corner. "Randolph," he said, pointing with his chin.

"I don't think so," I said. "I don't trust people dressed in animal skins."

Tommy came up with two other suggestions, both of which Grant vetoed vehemently.

"Well," Tommy said as if he were drawing his wild card, "Paul Schneider sometimes comes in on Friday nights, and I'll bet George would like him."

"Don't talk to me about him!" Grant shouted.

"He's a good person, Grant," Tommy said, independence rising in his voice. It was obvious they'd been through this before.

"He's an asshole!" Grant turned to me. "I could tell you stories about Paul Schneider until you pass out right on the floor in front of me."

"That's okay," I said. "I'm about ready to turn in anyway."

"Believe me, if it wasn't for that goofball, Tommy and I would be sitting on a gold mine right now. When we bought this dump, a ski area was about to open ten miles from the front door. Do you have any idea what that would have done for business?"

I shrugged politely. Obviously the business had only one direction to go.

"I'll tell you! We would have been rich by now. Ski packages, weekend tours, you name it. We had plans, kid. Then that goofball and the twenty-five-cent rag he writes for came along and made so much noise over the fact that they were going to cut down a few half-dead trees for the trails, the whole plan was shitcanned. As if it was any of his business to begin with."

In the time it had taken to deliver his harangue, Grant's face had gone from jaundiced yellow to a high-blood-pressure shade of pink. I was hoping he had a bottle of nitroglycerine tablets in his pocket. He adjusted the toupee on the top of his head as if he were straightening a necktie.

"Paul is a man of principles," Tommy said righteously, "and I admire him for that, even if we did lose out in this case. And if he comes in, George," he said, peering at me from the other side of Grant's girth, "I'd be happy to introduce you. He's from New York so the two of you will probably have a lot to talk about."

"How do you know he's from New York?" Grant asked, smiling broadly. "He knows everything, this guy. I'll bet he could tell you how many hairs Paul has on his ass."

"None."

Grant howled and poured me another shot of Wild Turkey from the bottle the bartender had put down in front of me. "You know something, kid, despite everything else, Tommy is the only person in this entire state with a single ounce of sense. Did I ever tell you that?"

"I think it sounds familiar."

"Well, he is. If it wasn't for him, I'd be in a gutter somewhere at this very minute. It might be in a better town than this one, but I'd be just another drunken bum in the gutter."

He squeezed Tommy so tightly I thought his ribs would crack. A glow was spreading up from my empty stomach, and as I gazed around the disco, the place began to take on a look of grandeur I'd been oblivious to when I first walked in. I sat down on one of the large, clumsy barstools. The tufted red vinyl upholstery let out a whoosh of air.

In the next hour Grant rambled on in a drunken monologue about the town and the inn and his eighteen-year relationship with Tommy. He went into embarrassingly intimate details about their lives together while Tommy smiled faintly and kept his eyes roving over the bar and the few people who straggled in. There was something about the two of them I found appealing, something independent of my inebriated state. I could picture them in bed together lying on a huge mattress with a dust ruffle around the bottom and a wall of mirrors opposite. Under vastly different anatomical circumstances they would have married, bought a tract house in suburbia, and raised a family of functionally neurotic children who chided them for not getting out more often.

"I'll tell you one thing," I said, leaning toward Grant, "and that is that you run a nice operation here. It's friendly. I was at home the minute I walked in the door. Of course, I'm a little smashed right now."

"Oh, really? We thought you were cold sober, didn't we, Tommy?"

I stared at the blinking blue Christmas lights against the mirror and realized they did, in fact, add a note of good cheer to the atmosphere. It crossed my mind that Joley was alone in the pathetic room on the third floor, but for all the closeness I felt toward him, he might as well as have been in Seattle. Slowly I drifted off into a reverie of Nina and me and a bouncing infant living in chaste bliss in Brooklyn, listening to the birds on the fire escape and the traffic in the distance.

"Well, it looks like your lucky day, kid," Grant was suddenly saying, rousing me from my stupor with a flat palm slapped against my back. "Mr. Wonderful just arrived."

I looked into the mirror behind the bar and saw a blurred reflection of a wiry man with scruffy black hair hanging halfway down his neck and a pair of round rimless glasses perched at a ridiculous angle on the bridge of his nose. He had on baggy, rumpled khakis and a yellow sweatshirt that looked as if he'd been wearing it for several days. He was standing frozen in the doorway with his hands shoved deeply into the pockets of his pants and his shoulders hunched up almost to his earlobes.

"He looks harmless enough," I said to Grant.

"Of course he does. His type always does."

Tommy motioned for him to join us and warned Grant that, whatever else he might think of Paul, he was still a customer, a breed already in short supply. I took a last shot of bourbon and looked in the mirror as Paul crossed the room. He had an ambling, self-effacing walk, and as he approached, he gave his hair a distracted push behind his ears. There must have been a wallet or a wad of papers stuffed into the front pocket of his pants that created an off-balance bulge at his right hip and gave his leg a bulky, deformed look. It was the kind of thing I would have fretted over for hours before leaving the house. I immediately decided that far from being a slob, he was one of a small minority of people on the face of the earth lacking vanity.

"Where the hell have you been all night?" Grant asked loudly. "Not out skiing, I'll bet." He gave me a nudge with his elbow that nearly toppled me off the barstool.

"I had trouble getting the truck started." He pointedly addressed Tommy. "I almost gave up and stayed home."

"Well, that would have been a real shame," Grant said, "because this Irishman here has been waiting for your arrival all night."

Paul turned to me and smiled. He had one deep dimple on the right side of his face that lent his countenance an ingenuous sweetness and made me feel like a drunken slug in a six-hundred-dollar pullover. I nodded, embarrassed by my slumped posture, and smiled ineffectually.

"Are you staying at the inn?"

"He is unless he gets a better offer," Grant scoffed.

Tommy laughed into his beer, spilling a trickle down his chin. "We've been keeping George entertained," he said, clearing his throat.

"Free bourbon." I pointed to the bottle in front of me.

"Which he's been drinking way too much of," Grant said. He put the bottle out of my reach behind the bar. "Be a little sociable, George and make some polite conversation. Are you a skier? I'm sure Paul would like to talk about that."

"Why don't you ask Paul how his son is?" Tommy offered.

"You have a son?" I asked, perking up.

"He has one of those imports from the tropics," Grant said.

Tommy laughed into his beer again and chided him with an elbow in the ribs. "Stop it, Grant. Gabriel is from El Salvador. Isn't that right, Paul?" He opened his eyes wide, awaiting verification.

"Of course it's right," Grant shouted. "Tommy knows everything."

Paul looked at me and shrugged. "And he's fine, in case you were going to ask." He smiled, flashing his lopsided dimple.

"You're raising a child?" I asked. "By yourself?"

"Well, friends help out sometimes, but it's mostly just Gabie and me."

He said it tonelessly, as if it were of minimal interest, when, in fact, the mention of a child—from El Salvador, no less—instantly created a romantic aura around him that left me staring at him stunned and smitten. I straightened up on the barstool and tried to pull myself together. "How old is he?" I asked.

"Oh, he's just over five, as near as they can figure. It's hard to know exactly."

I realized then, as I watched him distractedly pulling at the skin around his Adam's apple, that I wouldn't mind a better offer than the narrow bed next to Joley's in the third-floor Frigidaire. I had nothing left to say to Joley, and the idea of spending the night and then the next day together seemed ruefully anticlimactic. Paul ordered a bottle of beer and started to look around the bar uncertainly. I couldn't tell if he was already bored with my company or trying to find something to talk about. "Actually," I said, hoping to keep the conversation going, "I have a child, too."

Paul turned to me with interest.

"Well," I said, "that is, not really."

Tommy shook his head. "Maybe you two would like to dance a little? Clear your head some, George?"

"Nina," I said, "the woman I live with, is pregnant and..."

"And you're the proud father?" Grant asked skeptically.

"And we're going to raise the baby together." I quickly looked into the mirror to make sure this pronouncement hadn't produced any sudden facial ticks. "Sort of."

"That sounds like an easier way of having a child than going through what I went through," Paul said.

"You mean going down there and finding him and all that?" I asked, conjuring up images of him chasing through the jungle and rescuing the kid from a right-wing death squad.

"Well, no," he said, confused. "I mean agencies and paperwork and waiting. All *that*."

"I told you they'd have a lot in common," Tommy said. "George lives in New York, Paul."

"Oh, really? I'm from Brooklyn, George. Have you ever been out there?"

"I live there!" The conversation was really rolling now. I pulled at the body of the sweater and explained that it wasn't mine, that I'd borrowed it from a friend with money.

We carried on ten more minutes of stop-and-go, dead-end conversation interspersed with a lot of leaden silences, until Grant finally asked if we were *sure* we wouldn't like to dance. "This is a fabulous number. What is this, Tommy?"

"Ethel Merman's disco album."

"Perfect. Nice and loud so the two of you don't even have to pretend to talk."

THE dance floor was about the size of a dining-room table, and although there were only four couples frantically gyrating on the polished wood, it was almost impossible to find a place to stand. We shoved our way to the middle of the floor and jostled around some, trying to avoid the flailing arms of the person dancing behind us. Paul kept ducking and smiling, still with his hands shoved into his pockets.

When I'd told him that Nina and I were going to raise the baby together, it had mostly been to make conversation and present myself in a way I thought he might find attractive. It didn't occur to me until later that I could have told him I was a teacher. But once I'd uttered the words, I felt a kind of satisfied lightheartedness come over me as if I'd just made a decision and brought a long period of uncertainty to a close. If I'd been in bed at that moment, I'm sure I would have fallen into a sound, dreamless sleep. Now I looked over at Paul with awe as he banged against me on the crowded dance floor; here was an intelligent, sensible homosexual man, a bit uneasy perhaps, but perfectly sane-looking, and more disarmingly appealing every minute, dancing in a dingy discotheque, doing a creditable job of arranging a one-night stand for himself, and managing to raise a son, an adopted child from El Salvador, all at the same time. I stopped jostling around and stared at him, watching the cords in his neck tighten as he moved from side to side. If Nina had purposely set up a meeting with someone to try and convince me her plan wasn't totally harebrained, she couldn't have picked a better subject.

"Are you all right, George?" he shouted over the music.

"I'm fine," I yelled, still awestruck.

"You're sure?"

I was touched by the concern in his voice. I watched him for another few seconds and then pushed him off the dance floor to a corner of the bar out of Ethel Merman's reach. "The fact is," I said, "I haven't eaten in about ten hours and I had one or two drinks, maybe three, and I was wondering if you'd want to go to that diner outside of town and get something to eat." I was trying to inhale as I spoke so he wouldn't be anesthetized by the smell of bourbon.

He looked at me uncertainly. Probably trying to come up with an excuse, I decided. "Unless you have to go and feed Gabriel or something."

"No, no, he's with friends. It's just that that place is a real dive. Not what you're used to in New York, I'm sure."

Spurred on by a sudden wave of tenderness, I reached out and straightened his glasses. I told him the last place I'd eaten out at in New York was a fried-chicken joint on Flatbush Avenue subsequently closed for health violations. I put my hand on his back and directed him to the exit. At the door I turned and waved to Tommy and Grant. They were standing side by side at the bar swaying in unison to the music. "Good night, boys," Grant bellowed with as much suggestiveness as he could cram into two words.

THE street through the center of town was deserted. The one stoplight was uselessly blinking yellow and red and yellow and red. It would have taken a second ice age to sober me up completely, but in the biting night air I began to feel less saturated by bourbon and smoke than I had in the basement. The town was tranquil now that the protesters had dispersed. Beyond the row of empty storefronts and boarded-up brick buildings, I could see the black outline of the mountains with the moon brightening the sky behind them. I'd avoided going upstairs to get my coat, but I was warm as we walked in silence, swallowed up by Joley's thick sweater.

Paul balanced himself on the edge of the curb occasionally slipping or jumping lightly into the street. If there'd been a stone or a can in the street, I'm sure he'd have been kicking it ahead of him.

"You know ... George," he said after a couple of blocks, his breath visible in the still, cold air, "that diner really is lousy. I wasn't just saying that."

"I don't mind. I don't appreciate good food anyway. I like anything that's canned or greasy and overcooked."

"What I meant," he said, trying to locate my brain beneath the Wild Turkey, "was that we could go back to my house and I could cook something for you. I could overcook something for you."

I thought of Joley lying in the cold swimming-pool room, probably with the hummer going and a bottle of aspirin on the night table, and I thought I should do the considerate thing and go back. Fortunately, the thought passed before I had time to act on it. I told Paul it sounded like a great idea. He pulled his hands out of his pockets and clapped them together. "Good! We can stop and get some canned vegetables, if you insist."

"I never insist on anything," I told him.

His black pickup truck was parked in a lot behind an abandoned Amtrak station on the edge of the river. At least there was no gun rack in the back. We drove out of town across the rusted bridge that spanned the river, past the eerie factories along the banks, and up an unpaved road into the hills. I looked out the rear window as the few twinkling lights of the town disappeared into the darkness.

16

"Who's *he*, Paul?"

I opened my eyes slowly and cautiously and saw a tiny brown child kneeling on the covers at the foot of the bed with his hands pressed down on my shins. He leaned toward me and opened his walnut-colored eyes into huge circles. "What's your *name?*" he shouted.

"Don't yell, Gabriel," Paul said from his side of the bed. "When did you get home?"

"I just brought him over," a new voice said.

I sat up in bed and looked across the sunlit room. A tall woman with waist-length hair was leaning against the dresser running a piece of dental floss through her teeth. She smiled at me warmly. "I'm Annie," she said through the obstruction of her fingers.

"I'm George," I croaked, fighting off a wave of nausea.

"George!" the child shouted. "That begins with a J. My name begins with a G. G—g—g—g—gabriel. You see?"

"George begins with a G, too," I said. I hadn't imagined I'd be back at work so soon or feeling so hung over.

"Like 'gin'?" the dental hygienist suggested from the other side of the room.

"Bourbon," I told her.

"That begins with a B," Gabriel yelped.

Paul reached down and lifted the child over his head. Gabriel laughed hysterically and grabbed a handful of Paul's thick black hair. Without his glasses, Paul's face looked incomplete, as if someone had erased an essential feature.

"Did you have a nice time last night, Gabie?" he asked.

"Gabie had a wonderful time," Annie said. "I was worn down in an hour." The floss was stuck between her teeth and she had her arm twisted into an inverted V to try to dislodge it.

"I helped make dinner," Gabriel screeched. The pitch of the child's voice would have shattered glass, which was exactly what my head felt like. "And this morning," he boasted, "I pooped in her bathroom."

"Good for you," Paul said. "He didn't used to feel comfortable enough in Annie's house to use the toilet."

"I see," I said. Life really is made up of minor victories.

"I can tell George is intrigued," Annie said. She rolled the floss into a ball and tossed it across the room into the wastebasket beside Paul's bed. "I have to get out of here. I have to go fix Jeff's breakfast before he gets out of bed." She looked at me challengingly. "That's right, George, I bring my boyfriend his breakfast in bed. I'm a doting housewife, but I live in Vermont and have long, straight hair so I can get away with calling myself an earth mother." At the door she turned and said, "And if Paul offers to make you pancakes, you should accept. He makes great pancakes. My recipe."

Just hearing the mention of food, my growling stomach sat up and begged to be fed. My head was throbbing, trying to take in not one stranger at seven-thirty in the morning, which was what I'd been expecting, but three, including a five-year-old banshee with an active interest in his intestinal tract and the alphabet.

Gabriel had stationed himself on Paul's chest and was furiously rubbing his hands over his cheeks. "You need to *shave*, Paul!" he screeched.

"Later, Gabie. Maybe you could go play a game or something."

"No games, Paul. You have to shave. Right now."

"Gabriel likes to watch me shave, George. It's his favorite pastime."

"That's because Paul doesn't let me watch enough television," Gabriel explained without malice. "He says it's bad for my eyes."

"Bad for your brain," Paul said, knocking on Gabriel's head. "George is a teacher so he'll agree with me."

"It's bad for your brain, Gabriel," I said. My body was beginning to wake up, and I wouldn't have objected to sitting the kid in front

of a television set for an hour or so while I played barber with the
father.

Paul climbed out of bed with Gabriel clinging to his chest like
a sloth. I watched his behind bounce in his jockey shorts as he
walked to the bathroom. "Stay in bed as long as you like," he
called to me over his shoulder and smiled warmly.

It wouldn't have taken too much coaxing to keep me in bed for
the next twenty-four hours. Paul had a sensible attitude toward
furniture, and his pine bed was a triumph of comfort. There was
a wide picture window beside it, and the sun was pouring in,
warming the top of my head and the portions of my face not buried
beneath the covers. The window looked out to a field of spiky
brown grass surrounded by gentle hills sloping off into haze. I
could see a few patches of bright orange leaves, but most of the
trees were bare—another reminder of the miscalculated excursion
with Joley—Joley, who probably hadn't woken up yet and noticed
the undisturbed bed beside him. I couldn't imagine what his reaction would be, and, lying in the warming sun, it didn't seem to
matter at all. I felt apart from him and impervious.

Paul's house itself was a peculiar little cabin nestled into a grove
of pine trees off the side of a rutted road. Aside from the bedroom,
there was only a large square space sectioned off into living room
and kitchen and study areas. Gabriel slept in a loft connected to
the living room by a ladder. Paul had installed a fireman's pole
for him to slide down, making the place seem even more like a
playhouse.

WHEN I walked through the unlocked front door the night before,
I had been overwhelmed by the sharp smell of wood, as if the
planking on the walls and the ceiling and all the unpainted furniture
were breathing pine freshener into the air. It was inconceivable to
me the smell hadn't come from an aerosol can. I kept glancing
back at the door, which wasn't even fitted with a dead bolt, expecting some crazed mountain man to burst in and start hacking
through all the wood with a buzzing chain saw.

"The place is kind of a mess," Paul had apologized as he turned
on the lights.

Compared to what I was used to, it wasn't a mess at all, but I was put at ease by an the apology. The house was overstuffed with newspapers and toys and stacks of wood and disorganized, overflowing bookcases, but there seemed to be a kind of order to it. There were no clothes thrown around the floor of the kitchen or dirty plates piled on top of Paul's desk. There were magazines and books stacked up in heaps beside the sofa and on the ends of the tables, all within reach of a good reading light.

The one decorative touch I found odd was a large number of free-standing wooden clothes-drying racks set up in the living room and the bathroom. My grandmother had dried her underwear on similar contraptions, but these were designed with a crafted polish that put them in a different class. When I finally asked Paul about them, he told me they'd been left in the house by a man who'd moved out four months earlier.

"He owns a factory that makes these things. We were lovers for a while." He folded one up and put it in a corner and came to sit by me in a window seat. "For two years, actually. I keep meaning to get rid of them, but Gabriel likes them. They remind him of Roger. He and Roger were good pals. You know how kids get attached to people. I was happy to see him go, but Gabie was pretty broken up."

From the dejected tone in his voice, I'd have guessed he had Gabriel confused with himself.

"Well," I said, trying to cheer him up, "if the newspaper folds, you can always take in laundry."

He was unamused and I knew I'd blundered. We were sitting in the window seat, looking out to the field behind the house, with the grass lit blue by the moonlight. I wanted to reach out and touch him and tell him I was sorry, try to cheer him up and get him to show his lopsided dimple, but it seemed presumptuous of me to think I might be able to offer any kind of comfort, knowing him as little as I did.

"What about you, George? Do you have a boyfriend back in New York?"

"Oh, no, of course not," I said.

"Of course not?"

"What I mean is, I'm unlucky in love. In relationships. In love relationships. I do better with friends, like Nina, the person I live with. Our relationship is fairly stable. Most days."

I never did get dinner that night, overcooked or otherwise. While Paul was in the kitchen preparing the fried-egg sandwich I'd requested, I stretched out on his bed with a copy of the newspaper he wrote for. Midway through an article he'd written, "The Psychology of Lying," I passed out, clutching the paper with both hands. When Gabriel woke me up, I was undressed and under the covers, but how I got there was a mystery to me.

THE noise from the bathroom was growing increasingly louder. I could hear Gabriel giggling wildly and water splashing on the floor. I dragged myself out of bed and into the sunny bathroom. Paul and Gabriel were sitting in the tub tossing water at each other. There was a long, narrow window behind the tub with pine needless scraping against the glass. The floor was soaked. The teacher in me wanted to tell them both to quit it and go lie down. Instead, I took a bucket from beneath the sink and filled it with cold water.

"What's that for, George?" Gabriel screeched.

"What do you yell when you see something burning in the woods, Gabie?" I asked.

"Fire! Fire!" he shouted, leaping up.

I hauled back the bucket and doused the two of them. Gabriel let out an ear-shattering yelp and Paul threw an ugly-looking sponge at me.

"Get in here, George," he said.

"I can't. I'll melt."

"You have to," Gabriel shouted. "You're dirty."

"I'm hung over."

The two of them grabbed me by the wrists and dragged me into the tub. Gabriel scooped handfuls of water from beneath his feet while Paul held me under the shower. He was smiling broadly and his black hair was damp and limp, hanging down almost to his shoulders. Gradually, his smile faded and I stopped laughing. I noticed for the first time the way the muscles along the sides of his neck sloped down to his shoulders.

"Hey, Gabriel," he said, "I've got a great idea. Why don't you go to your room and dry off. Doesn't that sound like fun?"

"What's fun about that?" he asked with annoyance. "That's not fun. That's not even anything."

"Well, you could go to your room and, you know, do a puzzle."

"Forget it. I want to play in here." He reached down and started splashing in the water again.

Paul squatted beside him and attempted to bribe him with an entire hour of television.

"Nothing good is on," he said.

"Nothing?" Paul asked incredulously. "Not Mister Rogers or Sesame Street?"

"Phil Donahue?" I suggested.

"Cartoons are on! Can I watch cartoons?"

"They're real educational these days," I assured Paul.

Gabriel jumped out of the tub and bolted for the door. I reached down and drained the soapy water out of the tub and then turned on the faucet until we were covered with clear, warm water.

AN hour later I was contentedly wolfing down a stack of walnut pancakes smothered in butter and syrup. It was one of the most delicious meals I'd ever eaten, possibly because I was on the verge of starvation. Gabriel sat opposite me watching in horror as I shoveled food down my gullet.

"George is a pig," he said to Paul. "I am, too. Annie says so. She says you have good manners."

"He isn't dying of starvation," I said through a mouthful of coffee.

"I'm glad you like the pancakes," Paul said. He'd donned the same outfit he'd had on the night before, with the addition of a few more wrinkles and now grease stains from preparing breakfast. He appeared so unconcerned with the way he looked that in between forkfuls I couldn't take my eyes off him. "Annie taught me a secret for making perfect pancakes when we lived together."

"He and Roger used to live together, too," Gabriel said. "He moved to New Hampshire. He's coming to visit me in one week."

"Two weeks."

"Oh, right, two weeks. He gave me this." He stood up on his chair, hyper-extended his back, and lifted his sweater to reveal a

T-shirt with a picture of a clothes-drying rack printed on the front. "He makes these. In New Hampshire."

"Nice, Gabie," I told him. "Real snazzy." He dashed off to his loft, acrobatically climbing the ladder and making weird fire-engine noises.

As Paul cleared off the table, he told me he and Annie had moved to Vermont together twelve years earlier, just after they'd graduated from Yale. Their plan had been to organize a commune and become subsistence farmers. They gathered a group of twelve friends, mostly Ivy Leaguers with some money and no plans for the future, and bought a piece of land with an old farmhouse on it.

"The commune idea lasted about five years," he said, "before anyone had any desire to settle down. It was always more like a self-contained soap opera than a working farm, with everyone having relationships with everyone else, but it was great, George. I still think it could have evolved into the kind of place Annie and I envisioned if people had been more committed to it." He shrugged it off. "A few people had babies and wanted a private home and a solid income. They built their own houses on the corners of the land we all owned together. I was determined to stick it out in the farmhouse, but one night in the middle of winter, someone over-stocked the fireplace and it burnt to the ground."

He stood at the sink with his back to me, slowly submerging the dishes one by one into a basin of sudsy water.

"After that, everything changed fast. It might have been the times, but I think it had as much to do with getting older as anything else. Everyone got tired all of a sudden. That paper I write for? That used to be considered radical. Revolutionary, even. Now it's mostly an ad supplement for solar-heating panels and wood stoves. I'm so sick of writing about pop psychology issues, I can't bear it sometimes."

"Can't you do something else?"

"I'm not sure what that would be. I'm not about to get into business, I'll tell you that much. And every once in a while I do a story I care about, like the campaign against the ski area, and then I think it's worthwhile. The rest of the time I just tread water."

He had the same dejected look he'd had sitting in the window seat the night before. His face was lined with disappointment. I'm always reassured by morally and emotionally disillusioned people; it was unlikely, for instance, that I could disappoint him more than a decade of social change. Again I wanted to go to him and try to comfort him, but some fear of not knowing him well enough, or perhaps getting to know him too well, held me back.

"What's it like having a kid?" I asked, listening to Gabie roll a truck around the floor of his loft.

"Sometimes it's great, George. Most times it's great. Of course, every once in a while I wonder what I'm doing with a kid, and I forget why I wanted to adopt him in the first place. Usually around three in the afternoon when I'm working at home, my eyes are tired, and I need coffee or a nap. But everything seems wrong at three in the afternoon, and then Gabie comes home and I get caught up in loving and taking care of him and I don't have time to wonder about it anymore. It's easy to love someone who needs you so much. Don't you feel that with your kindergarten kids?"

"Unqualified affection," I said. "You never get it from adults."

IT was mid-afternoon by the time the three of us piled into the front seat of Paul's truck. Gabriel brought along three books which he kept opening and shutting and turning upside down and "reading" aloud. Since the pancakes had absorbed most of my hangover his voice had lost its air-raid-siren quality, and I began to appreciate him.

"What does your family think about all this?" I asked Paul, glancing toward Gabie.

"It's just my mother now. She's not your usual person."

"Molly's funny," Gabriel said, forcing out a laugh he almost choked on.

"Politics runs her life and I don't think she's figured out if my life is politically correct or not. It's a constant irritant to her. She was in the Communist Party until 1968. Mostly what she's concerned about now is that Gabriel learns Spanish. The few words he knew when he came here he forgot right away."

"I don't even have an accent," Gabriel boasted.

· · ·

I gave Paul the phone number and address in Brooklyn, in case
he happened to be in the neighborhood. As soon as I stepped out
of the truck in front of the inn, I wished I'd thanked him more for
the pancakes, had told him I had a nice time, that I thought he
had a comfortable house, had at least patted him on the head when
he'd looked so dejected. I raised my arm to call him back, but he
misunderstood and merely returned the wave. I stood on the sidewalk and watched him drive down the dilapidated street through
town with Gabriel leaping up and down on the seat beside him.

THE lobby of the inn looked even worse in daylight than it had the
night before. All the threadbare rugs and chipped paint and mildew
stains on the wallpaper stuck out hideously. I could hear the whine
of a vacuum coming up from the basement, but otherwise the place
was deserted. I ran up the three flights of stairs two at a time.

The door to Joley's cell was open and the room was empty. There
wasn't a sign of him in the bureau drawers or in the closets. There
was an envelope with my name neatly printed across the front
propped up against the pillow of my untouched bed.

"Dear George," the note inside read, "It is 1 pm and I am going
back to Manhattan. Enclosed you will find a bus ticket and a
schedule. If you've decided to move here permanently, you can
get a refund on the ticket. Keep the sweater if you like. I am
leaving with a clear head and a clear conscience. I hope you can
say the same. Joley. p.s. Don't ever say I didn't try."

The shades were drawn over the windows and the room was filled
with a hazy, poignant light that made me squint from the somber
glow. I suppose I wasn't leaving with an entirely clear conscience,
but I was small enough to be relieved I didn't have to talk to him
face to face. Except for whoever was running the vacuum in the
basement, I could well have been the only person in the entire
decrepit building. I sat on the bed and read the bus schedule and
then, figuring I had an hour and a half to kill, fell into a deep
sleep. I woke up drooling on the bedspread. I took off the sweater
and folded it neatly. Maybe it would fit Tommy.

On the bus back to New York I sat staring out the windows, dazed by the trees flashing by and then by the gathering lights and buildings. I didn't think about much except Nina and what I was going to say when I told her I wanted to stay and help her with the baby. I felt a little as if I were going back to propose. I looked around the smoky insides of the bus and then out the window, and in one sudden break in the trees along the highway, I saw the entire skyline of Manhattan and gasped with a start of surprise.

17

"DON'T interrupt me," Nina said when she heard me slam the door. "I'm on a tear."

"I can see," I said. "It must be all that coffee."

She was lying on the living-room floor surrounded by neat stacks of books and magazines and computer printouts and half a dozen empty ceramic coffee mugs. There was a plate of potatoes on the makeshift table and the Webcor Holiday was playing her favorite Connie Francis album. She had on a gray wool skirt and an angora sweater and a pair of long, dangling silver earrings.

"Are you going someplace?" I asked.

She continued to take notes on an index card as she scanned the page of an open book. "Where would I be going in a gray wool skirt on a Saturday night?" she asked without looking up.

"How would I know? Maybe out to buy more coffee. You know, you shouldn't drink so much coffee when you're pregnant. It can cause birth defects. I read that the other day."

"You're confusing coffee with cigarettes."

"Them, too. But I definitely remember coffee was on the list."

"Well, thanks for the medical advice, George. Just give me five minutes to finish what I'm doing and then I promise I'll ask you how your trip was." She looked up at me. "Okay?"

I was taken aback by the challenge in her eyes. "Okay," I said. I hoisted my duffle bag to my shoulder and headed off to my room. As I passed by Nina's open door, I cast a casual glance inside and stopped dead. I dropped my bag to the floor and walked in.

The room was so neat and clean it seemed to have doubled in size. I stood still in amazement. There were no clothes on the floor or on the bed or dripping out of the bureau drawers. All the drawers, in fact, were shut tight and the top of the bureau was cleared off and polished. There were two small hooked rugs on the floor that seemed to have emerged from beneath the rubble like finds at an archeological dig. The heavy purple material that had been tacked to the window frame was replaced by gauze curtains held back with lacy white ties.

I stretched out on the bed with my head resting on a carefully placed fuchsia toss pillow. I'd never before seen her bed made up, and I was shocked to see she owned a tufted white cotton bedspread with purple heliotrope embroidered around the edges and in a thick clump in the middle. I picked a yellow chrysanthemum from a fresh vaseful on the night table and put it to my chest.

Opposite me the mirror over the bureau reflected the entire room; Nina had removed the scores of photographs and postcards from the glass. The only pictures left were one of Nina and her Irish setter in the Arizona desert and one small black-and-white photograph of her mother.

I wouldn't have been more alarmed and upset if she'd had the entire apartment redone by a decorator from Conran's.

"Nina?" I called out loudly.

I walked into the living room with the chrysanthemum in my hand and turned off the record player. "Nina," I said, "you cleaned your room."

"You're very observant."

"Why?"

"I've taken control of my life, Georgie. Out with the old. I'm master of my fate now."

"But all those clothes and the postcards and the pictures."

"They're gone. Gone to the Goodwill box and the dump."

I sat down at the makeshift table. "You can't do that, Nina. You can't junk all your stuff just like that."

"Well, guess what, George—I already have." She sat up and brushed off the front of her skirt. "Hand me the potatoes, will you?"

As I passed her the plate, my fingers brushed against a piece of waxy gray skin. "They're cold."

"They're potatoes." She picked off a chunk and plopped it into her mouth with her fingers. Her nails were bright red.

"There's no protein in a potato," I said. "You need to get more protein when you're pregnant. You should know that. And you'll never be able to replace those photographs."

"I don't want to. I don't want to spend the rest of my life looking at the faces of a bunch of losers from my past. If you want to, go right ahead. Spend the weekend with them if you want."

I looked at her, stunned by her sarcasm. I'd been trying to believe she'd been giving me the cold shoulder since I walked in the door because she really was immersed in her work.

"Please don't give me that hangdog look, George. I told you I was jealous of Joley before you even left, so you shouldn't expect me to welcome you back with wide-open arms."

"But you haven't even asked me how it went or why I'm back a day early. I wasn't due back until tomorrow."

"I was getting around to it." She stood up and shook out the front of her skirt. "Is there dust on the back of this?"

"A little."

She came over to where I was sitting and I brushed down the back of her skirt with the side of my hand. The wool itched and burned against my skin.

"Do you need a lint brush back there?"

"Lint brush? Since when do we own a lint brush?" The idea alarmed me.

"I meant a record cleaner. It works like a lint brush."

"I don't need it. Anyway, I came back early on purpose. I did some thinking while I was away and there are a few things I want to talk over with you." She didn't say a word. "I've been thinking a lot about the baby, Nina, about the idea of the two of us raising the baby together."

There was a deep and resounding silence in the room. If she had the slightest interest in hearing what I was trying to tell her, she was doing a good job of convincing me otherwise. "If you're not interested, just tell me and I'll shut up."

"I'm interested, George. Go ahead."

She turned around and faced me and I felt like a fool. Her eyes were cold and clear and full of challenge. I had trouble looking at her, let alone rattling off the speech I'd prepared on the five-hour bus ride. "Never mind," I said quietly.

She went to the middle of the room and sat down on a stack of books and slowly unhooked the silver hoops from her earlobes. "I have a few things to tell you, too, George. Do you want me to go first? It might make it easier on you."

"Go ahead," I said. "I can't talk so I might as well listen."

"Well, I did more than clean my room and take notes this weekend. I spent most of Friday night crying, for one thing. When I came home from work yesterday and you weren't here and I thought about you going off to Vermont with Joley, I was hurt. I felt abandoned. I felt like a cuckold. I know that's stupid. . . . And it isn't only you. I felt abandoned by Howard, too. Can you believe that? I'm the one who ended the relationship, I'm the one who's been avoiding his calls for the past month, and *I* felt abandoned." She shrugged, exonerating herself from any blame. "So I curled up on my bed and spent most of the night crying into a pile of dirty clothes. I thought of everything I could to make myself miserable. Do you realize, for instance, that I'm almost thirty years old and I've never had a relationship that's lasted more than a year? I've never even lived in one place for more than two years. Our arrangement is the most stable one I've been in since I skipped out of Baltimore at seventeen." She picked up the potatoes, started to pick at them and then put the plate back down on the floor. "Do you realize that I've spent my whole life worrying about my weight, George? I became a feminist thinking I'd stop caring once and for all, and instead I just became guilty on top of everything because it still mattered to me."

"Nina . . ."

"Anyway, I got up this morning and I started cleaning. I don't know what prompted it. I just tossed things into boxes and bags— the clothes, the dead flowers, the old pictures. The more I cleaned, the better I felt. I polished the furniture, swept the floor. I made my bed with the spread and the toss pillows for the first time in two years. I was so afraid of messing it up, I was planning to sleep in your bed tonight.

"And then I stopped. I stopped and I looked around and I took stock and I said, you know, here I am, pregnant, alone, pushing thirty, almost a psychologist, and somehow, somehow, George, it didn't look so pathetic to me. I took stock, and suddenly it really looked okay. Not great or ideal, but okay. I made myself an eggnog from one of those pregnancy books I bought, and I called my mother and told her about the baby."

"You did?"

"I did. She started to scream something or other and I told her to call me back when she felt calmer and then I hung up the phone. Very gently. How's that for maturity?"

"Pretty good," I said. She was flushed and a little breathless, as if she'd just made a huge confession and was at last free to breathe. I felt myself sinking down on my chair, consumed by jealousy—of her clean room and her call to her mother and her suddenly bright eyes. I picked up the yellow chrysanthemum and started to pull at the petals.

"So, what I mean, George, is that this is my baby and my problem, if it is a problem, and I don't want you to feel bad about not taking care of it with me if that's what you were going to tell me, because it's my life and my decision and if you want to go off and live with Joley, that's fine, too. I have no reason to think that you shouldn't do that or that I have any hold over you. Who knows, maybe the whole idea wasn't so hot to begin with." She smiled at me and went to the record player.

"Nina..."

"What do you want me to put on? How about that Tommy Dorsey album you like so much?"

"Nina, will you please sit down and listen to me and stop being so stalwart?" I'd completely lost control of the situation and I was afraid she was about to go into my room, start packing my bags and show me to the door. I could feel an edge of panic tightening my throat. "Just sit down and listen to me and stop talking about Joley."

She came and sat next to me at the table, looking into my eyes sympathetically. "I'm sorry, George. Did you have a bad weekend?"

"No, not really, but that's not the point." I grabbed both her hands in mine. "Nina, you know how sometimes you see something in a different light, and all of a sudden it looks completely different? For instance, in your case, you might hear a song and just hate it and then two minutes later hear Connie Francis sing it and think it's the world's greatest masterpiece."

"I don't know what you're getting at."

"I'm getting at us. I'm getting at you and me and the baby. All that business you just told me about you not having a lasting relationship or a home or any of that? That's my life story, too. I mean, here I am, almost pushing thirty and"—I looked around the room for inspiration—"and I've never even owned a lint brush. I've never even had any clothes I'd use one on if I did own one." She was looking at me out of the corners of her eyes as if she was expecting me to take a flying leap out the window. "Well, this weekend I thought, maybe it's time to go out and buy one. Buy a real table, a toaster, throw out the air conditioner, fix this place up some."

It was all coming out backwards. I was supposed to be telling her how much she meant to me and instead I was giving her a shopping list. She got up and put on the Tommy Dorsey album as if to drown out my rambling voice. Al Cava's rendition of "Green Eyes" poured out of the speakers and we were under the blue lights at Roseland. I went and put my hands on her shoulders. "I'm talking about the baby," I said. "I'm not talking about a lint brush."

"I figured."

"I want to help you with the baby, Nina. I want to stay here and help you with the baby and settle in for a while."

She tossed her hands into the air and walked away from me. "You're throwing me off course, George."

"I know I know I know," I said frantically, "but I mean it."

"So what happened? What revelation shocked you into this?"

"No revelation, not really. I just saw our lives in a different light. Moonlight in Vermont, I suppose."

"And Joley? What about him? Is he in on this, too?"

"He's moving to Seattle. He wanted me to move to Seattle with him. Can you imagine anything crazier than that?" I went and out my arms around her and tried to move her to the music.

"You mean our situation looks sane by comparison?" she asked, immobile.

"Don't say that, Nina. I know I deserve it, but please don't say it. You know how much I care about you. You haven't just swept me out of your life with all the other clutter, have you?"

"No, of course not," she said, but there was little enthusiasm in her voice.

"It sounded like that a minute ago. You had me worried. This is my house, too, you know. You can't get rid of me that easily. At least tell me you'll think about it."

"Of course I'll think about it, George. It's what I've wanted all along, anyway. It's only that I was finally adjusting to the idea of having it some other way."

"On the Sunny Side of the Street" was on the record player, brassy and hopeful and happy music. "We could go take dancing lessons, like when I first moved in. After we buy a table, we could go sign up for classes. That wouldn't be bad for you, would it?"

"I need the exercise," she said gently but there was a suspicious look in her eyes.

The only time Nina and I had any prolonged physical contact was when we were dancing, and I suspect it was one of the reasons we enjoyed doing it despite the fact we were clumsy and untalented. It was one of the reasons I now wanted to lead her around the living room, through the stacks of books and papers in a vaguely remembered version of the fox-trot. But she was resisting and standing still. We stood there through "Song of India" and "Tangerine" and "Marie" and then the needle on the Webcor lifted off the record and the room was silent. We stayed in the middle of the room with our arms around each other awkwardly. Looking over her shoulder I could see the darkened back window and the drab green vinyl sofa.

"If you really want to do this," Nina said despondently, her chin resting on my shoulder, "it isn't a binding agreement. If it isn't working out or if something changes for either one of us, it isn't a binding agreement. It isn't a marriage, not even one of convenience."

I continued to hug her until it felt too intimate and then we went into the kitchen and ordered a pizza from a place in the neighborhood that delivered twenty-four hours a day. Nina changed out of her dress clothes into a sweatshirt and a pair of jeans, and when the pizza came, we sat on the living-room floor talking about anchovies and laughing at the lunacy of giving a Missoni sweater to a total stranger.

18

I never did hear from Joley again. In the first few weeks after I got back from Vermont I'd occasionally think about calling him and making some apology, finding out if he was getting along all right and had really decided to move to Seattle—but I never picked up the phone. I felt too guilty about leaving him alone that night to apologize without getting defensive. One afternoon Melissa and I went to a movie in his neighborhood, my old neighborhood, and saw him getting into a cab. He was growing his beard back and looked dashing as ever, but I didn't feel a trace of longing or desire, and I knew he was a part of my past.

"I don't like that overcoat on him," Melissa said. "It's always a mistake to get involved with men who don't know how to dress. You think you can teach them, but you never can."

Seeing Joley on the street that day was the first time I'd actually thought about having a history. I began to catalogue the periods of my life and try to put them into some kind of order. I wanted to prove to myself my life was following a logical pattern. Of course, I didn't get very far because logical patterns have never been my forte, and to fit raising a child with a woman into the scheme required certain leaps I didn't know how to orchestrate.

Timothy took the news about Nina and me badly, I thought.

"Enjoy this meal," he said to me over a dish of blackened redfish in a restaurant we'd waited three hours to get into, "because I don't plan to pay for another as long as you're a father."

"At least I'm not going back with Joley," I reminded him. "Give me credit for something."

"At least you're not planning to move in with that muckraker in

Vermont." He burst into laughter. "Commune! It's unbelievable how some people will go out of their way to make themselves unhappy. And with a child. You attract these parents like flies, George."

"You'd probably get along with him. He lives in a house."

"I don't like people who live in houses. Anyone who needs more space than he can get in a studio apartment is just greedy. I'd be ashamed to live in a house."

"He really has nothing to be ashamed of," I said. "I was touched by him, Timothy." I found myself thinking about Paul occasionally, wondering what he and Gabriel might be doing. It surprised me; I hadn't met anyone in a long time who left me wondering about his well-being.

"That's the point of what I've been trying to tell you for years: there's enough in life to be depressed about without being 'touched' by someone else's misery. And speaking of touching, I hope you were careful with him. Just because you're two hundred miles from New York doesn't mean you're beyond the reach of fatal germs."

"I'm cautious by nature," I told him. "I value my insignificant problems too much to risk losing them to a tragic disease."

"Well, I'm glad to hear it. Now just promise me you and Nina won't name the baby after me if it's a boy."

"Howard gets to name the baby if it's a boy—and he and Nina are speaking to each other."

By early November, Nina and I had done a fair amount of work on the apartment. We cleaned the shelves and the closets, stacked our old bills neatly, threw out collected junk, and folded sheets and towels and pillowcases and dishrags with a precision bordering on perverse. Nina brought home a box of household-cleaning products which two months earlier we would have laughed at. As it was, we didn't go to the extreme of polishing pans and washing windows, but at least we had the supplies ready and waiting in case the urge came over us.

The one big purchase we made was a dining-room table to replace the packing crates we'd been eating at for almost two years.

The decision to buy the thing was prompted by our plan to each invite three people out to the house for a Thanksgiving feast. We'd never really had a dinner party, and it seemed like a good time to make the effort, sort of a combination holiday get-together and housewarming. In any case, we agreed we couldn't serve eight at packing crates, so one night after work Nina came into the city and met me at Bloomingdale's. It was the only time I'd been in the place, and from the first minute I felt someone must have hung a sign on my back begging for abuse from the salespeople. Nina fared better because while she obviously wasn't wealthy, she was at least beautiful. The truth is that I'd never before walked into any expensive department store with the intention of actually buying something, and the floors of overpriced goods and shiny mirrors intimidated me.

Ten minutes after entering the store, we settled on a solid maple table with two removable leaves. The saleswoman informed us it was perfect for our needs, even though we weren't given a chance to explain what they were. It was the first thing she showed us, and I was so eager to get out of the store, I would have bought it if it had been a picnic bench. As she was writing up the delivery slip, she told us the top of the table had to be rubbed down with oil at least twice a week for the first three months we owned it.

"You know, kind of like seasoning a wok," she said, madly punching numbers into the cash register.

"Seasoning a wok?" I asked.

Nina looked at me doubtfully. "Maybe we should rethink this. It sounds like an awful lot of work."

"Let's just buy it and get out of here, Nina. We don't ever have to touch it once it's in the house. I'm sure they don't send people out to check on you."

"Don't you have a regular table?" Nina asked the saleswoman. "Something with a linoleum top we can just wipe down?"

The woman looked up and grimaced. "I've got the whole thing written up and ready to go and now you tell me you don't want it? You could have told me sooner, you know, before I spent half my night writing up the delivery slips. It isn't even a very big sale for us."

Nina looked crestfallen, as if she'd accidentally hit the saleswoman on the head with a club. "All I meant..." she started to say.

"Anyway, you can have your husband do it." She was pointing her pencil straight at me. "Pretty soon you won't be in any condition to do it yourself, right?"

"We'll take the table," I said. "We have a cab waiting outside and I don't want to keep him."

As we were getting into the subway, Nina took my arm and said. "That was the first time a stranger noticed I was pregnant."

"That was the first time anyone called me your husband."

"It makes me feel so vulnerable, as if the baby is exposed to the world already."

I put my arm around her. "That woman was crazy anyway. I'm surprised she didn't notice we're not wearing wedding rings." I felt unsettled, vulnerable, like Nina's baby. "Not everyone who has babies is married. You'd think she'd know that. I mean, Bloomingdale's, my God."

"I used to feel like I was carrying around a secret, George. Something nobody but me knew about."

"Look, let's just forget the whole nightmare. I knew we should have gone to some cheap place out on Kings Highway. They know how to treat you out there."

We went back to the Arthur Murray dance studio over the florist shop to sign up for a six-week session of classes. I dragged out one of the old three-piece suits I'd bought on the street and Nina put on a blue strapless prom dress she hadn't thrown out in her cleaning binge.

The place was as grimy as I remembered it and seemed even more poorly lit. The blue pastel paint was crumbling off the walls in huge chunks and there was an exposed pipe on the ceiling leaking into a five-pound coffee can with rust running down the sides. When we walked in, Miss Reynolds was standing behind the reception desk looking gaunt and brittle as ever, wearing a black chiffon dress identical to the one she'd worn for all the other classes. Her hennaed hair was tied up in a thin purple scarf.

"Oh, my," she said when she saw us. "Look who's here. My favorite students." She cracked a weak and troubled smile and pulled a cigarette from a crumpled pack on the desk. "How nice of you two to drop by and say hello."

"Actually," Nina said, "we came by to sign up for lessons."

"Oh?"

"The advanced series," I said.

"Advanced? Well, that is ambitious, isn't it?" She inhaled deeply on the cigarette though not even a wisp of smoke came back out. "But then, why not? I mean, I suppose it doesn't matter much anyway."

She pulled a huge stack of paper from under the desk and flipped through them with her cigarette dangling from her stained fingertips. "And . . . how is everything going for the two of you?"

"Very well," I said.

"Improved," Nina told her.

"She's pregnant," I said.

Miss Reynolds looked up from the desk and smiled at Nina. "Isn't that lovely. Isn't that just *love*ly." She took a long and relieved drag from her cigarette. "You must be very happy, dear. Very happy. You *are* happy, aren't you?"

"I'm thrilled," Nina said.

"Lovely, just lovely. And the father?"

"I wouldn't know," I said.

"Well, anyway, I hope the baby likes to dahnse as much as his parents."

"Oh, the father hates to dance," Nina said. "He's a terrible dancer."

"Nina! George is a lovely dahnser. Very graceful. And such a sharp dresser." She winked at me.

HOWARD called the house one afternoon, before Nina was home from the clinic. I hadn't talked to him in over a month and I was delighted to hear his voice again; I felt as if he might have been away on a long trip and was calling us from another city to check in.

"How is everything, Howard?" I asked him eagerly.

"Fine, fine. Listen, George, have you got a pen there?"

"What's wrong, Howie?" He was talking in a low and rushed

voice as if he were about to divulge some secret relating to the national security.

"Nothing's wrong. I'm sorry I can't chat but I want you to take something down. Have you got a piece of paper?"

"Hold on." I went and tore off a corner of a brown bag. "Okay, I'm ready."

"Good. Now, first you take a head of garlic and peel the outside skin off."

"Howard, what is this?"

"This is a recipe for the most perfect food for Nina I ever heard of. I saw it in a cookbook I was looking through the other day and I knew it was the kind of thing Nina would adore. It's baked heads of garlic. You know how she loves garlic. Just write it down. I don't want her to come home while I'm talking to you."

He gave me the details of a recipe that involved baking an entire head of garlic for over an hour, basting it periodically with olive oil. When it turned soft and mild, the cloves could be mashed onto bread or meat.

"You could mash it into a baked potato for her. That's what I'd do. You know how she loves potatoes. I'd bake the potato, scoop out the inside and mash it with the garlic, then stuff it back in the skin. It would be a great surprise for her. Isn't that perfect?"

"Perfect, Howie." The thought of cooking an entire head of garlic made me slightly queasy, especially since it had turned too cold to keep the windows open.

"Just promise me you won't tell her where you got the recipe, George. You can take the credit for it. I'm not supposed to do things for Nina anymore."

"I'll give her the recipe."

"Maybe you could cook it tonight. You could cook it tonight and surprise her with it and then call me at the office tomorrow when she isn't around and tell me if she liked it."

"Maybe I will," I said. There was a sad, pleading tone in his voice I couldn't refuse.

"You have the garlic there?"

"Of course," I said. "Nina keeps garlic in the house the way most people keep milk."

He chuckled softly. "I remember that. How could I ever forget that? Remember to baste it every once in a while."

"I will."

"George? Is she seeing someone else? No, never mind. Forget I asked. I don't really want to know. I'm miserable enough. Just tell me how she likes the garlic. That's about all I can take right now."

NOVEMBER has never been one of my favorite months, but it passed quickly, almost imperceptibly. There was a bare minimum of the usual rain and depressing cloudiness that settles in in November. The days seemed uniformly bright and sharp. I imagined a kind of permanence in my relationship with Nina, and sometimes, when I was polishing the surface of the new maple table or putting a folded stack of towels into the linen closet, I felt I was doing a reasonably good job of keeping house. I dutifully read through a couple of the baby books Nina loaned me, but frankly, nothing they had to say seemed addressed to me. They were mostly humorless tomes warning parents not to expect their infant to look like a human being for the first few months of life. There wasn't one book available on the role of the roommate of an unwed mother.

At school Melissa was holding up with as much consistent brightness as the weather. She'd planned an elaborate classroom unit on turkeys which she planned to conclude by showing a videotape of a bird's life from the time it was hatched to the final slaughter before Thanksgiving. At home, Nina claimed her dissertation research was moving at an unprecedented rate, despite the fact that she had sworn off coffee at my insistence. Some mornings I woke up before six to hear her portable typewriter clacking away furiously in the living room.

TEN days before Thanksgiving, I got a postcard from Paul with a picture of a ski area on the front.

"Dear George" [he'd written]: "Gabriel and I are coming to Brooklyn at Thanksgiving to visit my mother, and I thought we might be able to get together at some point for coffee, if you aren't too busy. Gabie and I had a nice time when you were here and he's been asking for you. I'll call. Love, Paul Schneider."

The card made me happy. I'd been wondering if he was coming to New York for the holiday. Some afternoons, as I was dragging my body through Prospect Park—jogging, I mean—I'd fantasize about bumping into Paul taking Gabriel for a walk in the park around the holiday. I was surprised he'd signed the note "Love," but I appreciated the self-effacing touch of including his last name.

I carelessly left the card on the dining-room table, and Nina picked it up and read it as we were eating dinner that night. "George," she said indignantly, "you never told me you met someone when you were up in Vermont."

"I didn't?"

"No, you didn't. Who is he?"

"Oh, some guy I met at that dump Joley and I stayed at. I had a drink with him. He writes for a boring New Age newspaper. Just the kind of thing you'd hate."

"Who's Gabriel?"

"That's a kid he adopted from El Salvador."

"George! Is he raising the kid himself? I can't believe you never told me about this. A single man raising a baby and you never told me. And he signed it 'Love.'"

"Let me turn on the grilling lights before you continue the interrogation."

"I'm sorry." She put the card aside and went back to her dinner. "I'm glad we at least cleaned up the house if they're going to be staying here."

"Nina, he's coming to visit his mother for the holiday. If we have a drink together it will be a big deal."

I was hoping that wasn't true. After receiving the postcard I'd made plans to launder my sheets and towels and I didn't like to think the effort would be a complete waste of time.

NINA and I bought an eighteen-pound turkey, two different kinds of squash, ten pounds of sweet potatoes, four bags of cranberries, and enough canned pumpkin to make four pies. Nina went to a maternity shop in Brooklyn Heights and bought herself a dark red dress with a low collar and some sort of elaborate shoulder-pad arrangement. The only preparation neither of us made was getting down to inviting the guests. Every night after dinner I'd collapse with a book and contemplate calling someone up, but I inevitably became too engrossed in what I was reading or just too lazy to pick up the phone. Finally, on the Tuesday before Thanksgiving, I marched into Nina's bedrom and told her I thought we had to do something about invitations. She closed her book and propped herself up on her pillows.

"I suppose you're right," she said yawning.

"Not to mention the cooking."

"And cleaning."

"And we have to buy wine. We forgot to buy wine when we did all that shopping."

"I'll put it on the list of things to do. Where is that list anyway, George? I haven't seen it in days."

"I'm not sure." I sat down on the floor beside the bed and cautiously asked her if she thought our friends would be insulted by such a late invitation. Maybe it was rude not to assume they had other options.

"God, I hope not. I mean, what would we do with all that food if no one could come?"

"I don't know. I suppose we could put the turkey in Mrs. Sarni's freezer if we had to."

"I suppose. But what about the squash?"

"We could give it to the food drive at the Grand Union."

"That's true. And the potatoes will keep."

"The pumpkin's canned anyway."

The ideal arrangement, we concluded, was to put the whole thing off until Christmas. Maybe by then we'd even have a new sofa. We could decorate the apartment and buy a tree. I walked out of her room feeling as if my death sentence had been commuted.

THANKSGIVING Day was warm and sunny and balmy, like a day in the middle of April. I often complained to Nina that I hate holidays, that they make me feel lonely and isolated, but the truth is I usually enjoy them, particularly if I celebrate them by lounging about immersed in heavily plotted fiction with explicit sex scenes. I opened the shades in my room and sat in a shifting patch of sunlight reading a paperback about a fat, unattractive girl who becomes a voluptuous fashion model and marries into a wealthy but tragic family.

It was a quiet day and the only sounds that drifted in through the windows were those of families getting into and out of station wagons on their annual visits to distant relations. When I wasn't dozing or hungrily turning the pages of my book, I kept an ear out for Paul's call. The one time the phone did ring that morning, it was a computer telling me, in a dragged out, slow-motion voice, that I'd won a weekend at a luxury condominium complex in New Hampshire. I didn't even get satisfaction out of banging down the receiver.

In the late afternoon, Nina and I got dressed in several layers of sweaters and took the subway out to Brighton Beach. The train was practically empty, and once we were above ground, Nina dozed off against my shoulder, her hair lightly brushing against my neck. I was lulled into a pleasant state of lassitude by the rocking of the wheels and the flickering light pouring in through the filthy graffiti-sprayed windows.

The shops were dark and boarded up under the shadow of the elevated tracks. In the summertime the streets were always jammed with old people and shoppers, but now they were empty and silent. I felt a sting in my nose as I stepped off the train and inhaled the cool, salty air.

We walked down to the water, past the Brighton Beach Baths with their canvas-covered swimming pools and the shuffleboard courts littered with dry leaves. The boardwalk was lined with old men and women, Russian emigres sitting on webbed folding chairs with their faces turned up to the last rays of the sun. Most of the women were draped in dark cloth coats, with bright kerchiefs tied under their chins, and the men all seemed to be wearing caps, the visors pulled down to their eyebrows. There was a kind of sad nobility to the group, uprooted and huddled as they were, sitting together in the wind and talking in a language that sounded garbled and exotic.

"Where do you think we'll end up at eighty?" I asked Nina, but she wasn't listening. She was staring raptly at a white-haired woman sitting alone, apart from the others, reading a Slavic newspaper with her eyes tightly squinted against the glare of the late afternoon sun. She had a strong, broad face and unkempt hair blowing out from under her kerchief. There was something proud in her posture, in the way she held her head high and erect as she peered at the fluttering pages of the newspaper. She was beautiful, despite her weathered skin and her ancient clothes and her vague look of destitution. Nina was transfixed. "That's me," she said. "That's me in fifty years, George, sitting there by myself. You want to know where I'll be at eighty?"

She pulled a satin scarf out of her pocket and tied it tightly under her chin. We sat on the edge of the seawall and took off our shoes and then walked barefoot to the cold sand.

"The first time I came to New York," she said, "I didn't wear shoes. My boyfriend and I came up from Baltimore in his van and walked around the Village all day, ate on the sidewalk, bought pot from someone on the street, and neither one of us had even brought a pair of shoes with us. It was pure affectation. I was fifteen. I was shocked that everyone in Greenwich Village wasn't running around barefoot. My poor mother."

We stretched out on the beach close to the seawall with one of my sweaters under our heads. I closed my eyes and pretended I was in the dust bowl as the wind coming up from the ocean gently blew sand over us. Soon we'd both be covered, buried beneath a storm of dust and hot wind.

The year before, Nina and Howard and I had spent Thanksgiving Day at the apartment of a woman from Nina's school. She and Nina scarcely knew each other, but Nina was convinced everyone from her program was going to show up and she had an obligation to attend. The apartment turned out to be the first three floors of a town house on Park Avenue. The living-room walls were covered with Renoirs and Chagalls and Modiglianis and works by other artists I didn't recognize. Howard was horrified and Nina was morally offended. The three of us sat on a sofa in a remote corner of the room, ate an impolite amount of the elegantly prepared food and drank ourselves silly on what Howard assured us was very good champagne. We eventually snuck up to the third floor and fell asleep side by side side on a canopy bed that looked as if it had been flown in from Versailles. When we woke up the house was quiet and the windows were dark. A maid was clinking the champagne glasses together as she cleared the tables in the living room. Nina's acquaintance stood at the bottom of the stairs staring at us, mortified, as we walked down the long circular staircase. We thanked her repeatedly for the dinner and slouched out to the street.

"Well, there's one friendship that won't develop," Nina said once we were a block from the house.

"Of course not, Dumpling," Howard said. "What could you possibly have in common with someone who lives with a Renoir?"

I sat up on the beach and wiped the sand out of my eyes. I scratched my scalp and felt the grit beneath my nails. "I miss Howard," I said to Nina.

She rolled her head to the side on my balled-up sweater and squinted at me. "The other day a clue in the crossword was 'hayseed.' The word was 'bumpkin.' My eyes filled up as I wrote it in."

"If that's true, why don't you call him?"

"I miss him, George, that's all I meant. I really didn't expect not to miss him. But it doesn't change anything. The problems are still the same. Whenever I miss him the most and think I should call, I remind myself of why I decided to stop seeing him, and then I know I really can't get involved again."

She drew her hands into the sleeves of her sweater and shivered. "I have a confession," I said. "You remember that baked garlic I made? The recipe came from Howard. He called one afternoon and gave it to me over the phone. He made me promise I wouldn't tell you he called."

"How did he sound?"

"He sounded the same. A little sad, I suppose. He wanted to know if you were seeing someone else."

"I wonder if he's doing all right."

"You could call him and ask, you know."

She gave me a funny look, as if she thought I should know better than to suggest such a lunatic idea.

We got up from the sand and shook ourselves off. The old people along the boardwalk were folding their chairs and moving off in different directions. The sun had gone down and the air was damp and chilly. Nina at eighty, the woman with white hair, had fallen asleep in her chair with her face turned up to the breeze. Her newspaper lay open on her lap, its thin pages rustling in the wind.

MY mother called me later that night. She had just come from dinner at her sister Ida's house and she was noisily struggling out of her holiday outfit as she spoke.

"From the amount of food I ate today, George, you'd think it was good. Did you eat turkey?"

"I had borsht and kasha and boiled beef."

"That doesn't sound very traditional. You're not converting to Judaism behind my back, are you?"

"Nina and I ate in a Russian restaurant out by Brighton Beach."

"Brighton Beach? Who goes to the beach in November, George?"

"How were Aunt Ida's pies, Ma?" Ida had been preparing Thanksgiving dinner for my mother's family for as long as I could remember. My grandmother had shown her appreciation by giving Ida her recipe box before she died, and my mother had been punishing her sister for fifteen years for inspiring the show of favoritism.

"The pies were lousy. She asked me what I thought of them and I told her they were nothing to be ashamed of. I meant it as a compliment and of course she took it the wrong way. She was so upset she'll probably never invite me back—which won't be a major loss to my taste buds." She groaned and dropped the phone to the floor. "I'm sorry, dear. If these clothes were any tighter I could forget about the zippers and just bust out of them."

"Did Dad have a nice time?"

"Who knows? He said three words the entire time we were there. He brought Ida a box of light bulbs, which should keep *him* in her good graces for the next decade. But I have to put Frank on the phone, George. He has some exciting news he's dying to tell you."

She dropped the receiver to the floor. Frank picked up the extension with the same breathless sigh my mother always used on the phone. "How's it going, Georgie? Did you have a turkey dinner today?"

"No, he didn't, Frank," my mother said on the other phone. "And I'm not spending money to discuss menus. Tell him your news."

"Let me guess, Frankie," I said. "You won the *Reader's Digest* Sweepstakes."

"He's getting married, George! In January. Can you imagine it, after all these false alarms? And to a very nice girl, too, believe it or not."

This, of course, was exactly the news I'd been expecting, had been waiting to hear for the past five years, in fact, but listening to my mother's gushing, rhapsodic voice, I felt let down and disappointed, betrayed somehow. "That's great, Frankie," I finally said.

"Well, don't sound so enthusiastic, dear, you might choke."

"I'm enthused," I said. "How did you rope someone into this, Frankie? Is she pregnant?"

"Stop it, George. This is the first nice girl Frank has gone out with. Her name is Caroline. She's an Italian girl but she's very pretty."

"What do you mean, '*but* she's pretty,' Ma?" Frank said. "Why not '*and* she's pretty'?"

"Well, for God's sake, Frank, that's what I meant. Don't pick me up on every and and but. I was just trying to give George an idea of what she's like."

"How about 'a wop with big tits'?"

My mother slammed down her end of the phone. There was a moment of silence during which I suppose I should have made a sincere effort to congratulate Frank, but I couldn't quite bring myself to do it. Instead, I asked him how long he'd known Caroline and why I hadn't heard of her before.

"Well, I've only known her a couple of months, George. I didn't want to introduce her around here until she got to know me a little better. The minute I met her, I knew there was something different about her. She isn't like most of the girls I've been going out with, Georgie; she's a nice kid."

"Nice kid? How old is she?"

"I'm sorry, George. She's a nice 'woman.' Is that better?"

"Much. At least it makes the whole thing sound legal. So why the big rush to the altar? She *isn't* pregnant, is she?"

"No, of course not. You want to know the truth? I'll tell you the truth, Georgie. The truth is, she's the first girl I've gone out with I'm maybe a little afraid of losing. Imagine me being insecure about a thing like this. So, I figure, what the hell, if she wants to marry me, why not do it? I'm not getting any younger sitting around this dump picking up bad ideas on marriage from these two."

"None of us is getting any younger, Frank, but you don't see me going off and getting married."

He laughed, a little too raucously, at what I wasn't sure I'd intended as a joke in the first place. "You getting married, George, we all know better than that, right?"

"So, am I invited to the wedding?"

"No. I'm only inviting Aunt Ida. Of course you're invited. You and that girl you live with, if you want. I hope she's not too beautiful or I'll kick myself for rushing into this. Listen, I'm going to send you some money to buy yourself a nice suit for the wedding. Something to make you look handsome so the bride's family will think we'll have beautiful kids even if they're half Irish."

He wasn't married yet and he was already supplanting my big-brother role. "I'm the one who's supposed to be sending you presents, Frank, not the other way around."

"Hey, I've got more money than you, George, so just forget about presents. I want you to come and look nice and have a great time for yourself. That's all I care about. Screw the presents. Okay?"

My mother picked up the other phone again. "Is it safe for me to get on again? Before you get off, George, *I* have some news for you, too. You have to guess where your father and I are going for Christmas."

"I hate to guess, Ma. I'm lousy at it."

"Florida! We're going down to visit your Uncle Al in Fort Meyers."

"Sarasota," Frank corrected her.

"Stop picking on me, Frank. All those places are the same down there anyway. But, George, the big news is—we're flying!"

"Flying? You hate to fly, mother. You've been afraid of airplanes for the past decade."

It was a fear my mother had picked up on a flight we'd taken to Miami when I was a teenager. The landing-gear light had gone on in the cockpit and the pilot was forced to make an emergency landing in Jacksonville. The stewardesses came around the cabin with big cellophane bags collecting shoes and jewelry and anything that might cause injury during the landing. "I've been trying to get rid of this for years," my mother had said stoically as she handed her wedding ring over; but on the way home she refused to get on another plane, and we ended up on a series of buses and trains that took four days to reach Boston. Her fear of planes was one I shared completely.

"Well, I'm going to have to get over it, that's all. I thought about the alternative of spending three days in the car with your father and I called Delta myself to make the reservations."

I felt betrayed by her sudden bravery. As if it wasn't bad enough my only sibling was going off and getting married, my own mother was taking to the skies gleefully. "When are you leaving?"

"Three days before Christmas. I started saying a novena for good flying weather. And sunshine. I want to have a tan for Frankie's wedding."

19

AT exactly nine o'clock the next morning, as I was standing in the kitchen sleepily spilling coffee onto the floor, Paul Schneider called. There was tremendous amount of noise from his end of the line, shouting and laughter, and I had trouble hearing what he was saying.

"Are you in the subway?" I asked.

"No, no. I'm sorry, George. My mother is trying to teach Gabie Spanish and he gets hysterical every time she opens her mouth. I didn't wake you up, did I?"

"Not at all. I've been up for hours." I figured someone who lived in the country would appreciate an early riser. "How was your holiday?"

"A little crazy. My mother had us serving dinner at three different community centers around town. Gabriel had a great time. Actually my mother has the whole weekend planned for us."

"Oh," I said. "Well, that's too bad." Families are excuses you can't argue with. Still, I was disappointed. "Maybe next time you're in town," I told him. I started to say something about Christmas but then I remembered he was Jewish. I always feel especially shallow mentioning the word Christmas in front of Jews, as if it links me inextricably to all that tinsel.

"Well, the reason I called, George, is because we're going to a demonstration this afternoon that's in Brooklyn, and I was wondering if maybe you and your friend Nina would like to come along."

I was impressed that he remembered Nina's name. You can tell people take you seriously if they remember your friends' names.

"I can ask her," I said. "Nina usually loves demonstrations."

"I know it's not much of an invitation, but we're heading back to Vermont tomorrow. It isn't even much of a demonstration, I'm afraid. My mother's building is scheduled to be torn down and she's organized a tenant's demonstration at the landlord's house out in Sheepshead Bay."

It didn't sound like the torrid afternoon I'd been fantasizing about, but a torrid afternoon's the kind of thing that never seems to work out for me, anyway. I told him I'd ask Nina about the demonstration.

"Great, George, we'll be there around noon."

AT eleven o'clock Nina was in the shower and I was making my bed. The doorbell startled me out of my drudgery. I thought it was probably just another *Watchtower* salesperson buzzing to get into the building and I went to the door with my pillow in my hand to tell them I was a homosexual Moonie.

It was Paul.

He came up the stairs with his gawky walk and his hands jammed into the pockets of his khakis. His round glasses were pushed against his face and, like the first time I'd met him, he had on a sweatshirt that looked slept in.

"I'm sorry we're early," he said. "My mother gets a little crazy when she's going to a demonstration, especially when it's one she organized herself." He pushed his hair behind his ears and smiled shyly.

I grinned back at him and tossed the pillow out of sight. "Don't worry about it," I said. "Nina's in the shower. Maybe you could all come up for a cup of coffee or something?"

"That sounds terrific," he said, but he didn't make a move. He stared at me for a second and said, "So anyway . . . it's great to see you again, George."

"Oh, I know," I said awkwardly, meaning it was nice to see him.

He went down to find a parking space and I rushed into the bathroom. "They just arrived, Nina. You'd better hurry up."

"They're an hour early," she shouted from the shower. "An entire hour!" She shut off the water and pulled back the curtain.

"We're always late," I reminded her, "so what's the difference?"

"The difference is that late is late but early is rude. I'm not even close to ready yet."

"Well what was I supposed to do—tell them to drive around the block until noon?"

"This does not bode well, George. What kind of man shows up an entire hour early? Just remember I warned you. Howard was the kind of man who'd show up an entire hour early."

"I promise you I won't end up pregnant."

A few minutes later, as I was making my third pot of coffee in two hours, Paul, Gabriel, and Molly walked in. Gabriel ran into the kitchen, tripped over the doorjamb, landed on his face and started to scream in a voice I remembered clearly. Paul scooped him off the floor and rubbed his back furiously. "Mother, this is George," he said over the screaming. "George, Molly."

Molly strode over to me and shook my hand firmly. She was a tiny, delicately boned woman, with short white hair and a face so deeply lined with wrinkles it looked as if she'd had them surgically implanted. "Nice to meet you, George," she said, very businesslike and abrupt. "If that coffee you're making is for me, I'd rather not, thank you. There's nothing worse than going to a demonstration with a full bladder."

"Well, I'll have some," Paul said over Gabriel's cries.

"It's fine for you, Paul," his mother said. "You can piss behind a tree. *Cómo estás,* Gabriel?" She pronounced the child's name with a flamboyant roll of the *r*.

At the sound of the Spanish, Gabriel looked up and rubbed his eyes. He dragged his fists down his cheeks, making long brown streaks with his tears. "Look how filthy that child is," Molly said, as if Gabriel couldn't understand English. "I don't care if the two of you do live out in the woods, there's nothing wrong with a little soap and water every once in a while."

"If you hadn't rushed us out of the house so early, Mother, we would have had time to wash up." Paul was nagging—a person's true nature quickly emerges around his mother.

"Would you like something to eat," I asked Molly. "Some eggs, muffins, cookies?" I was nervous in her presence, as I usually am around people with strong political convictions, and all I could think to do was offer food. I was horrified when I realized that, perhaps because she was so small, I'd spoken in a condescending tone, as if I were talking to a child.

"I don't think so, George. I'll just go into the living room and rest for a minute or two while you get ready."

She was telling me to hurry up. I started praying Nina wouldn't take her usual hour to get ready. Molly settled herself on the green vinyl sofa, tugging her shapeless brown cardigan around her shoulders as if to suggest the apartment was too cold. She had on a pair of blue boating sneakers that didn't come anywhere near the floor once she was seated. I made another offer, orange juice this time, which she impatiently refused with a wave of her hand.

Paul walked into the living room with a calmed and beaming Gabriel in his arms. "Do you remember what George's name begins with, Gabie?" he asked.

"He doesn't remember his own language," Molly said, "so I don't know why you expect him to remember how George spells his name."

Gabriel reached out and rubbed my check. "Did you shave this morning, George?" he asked.

"I don't think so," I said.

He got down from Paul's arms and jumped onto the sofa next to Molly. "Cómo estás, Grandma?"

"Bueno, Gabrrrriel. Muy bueno."

THE coffee sizzled and bubbled over on the stove. I rushed back into the kitchen and grabbed it off the burner, spilling about a cup of it onto the floor just as Paul trailed in. "Don't offer to help," I told him. "I'm beyond help." He leaned against the back window and looked out to the laundry lines and telephone wires behind the house.

"You've got a nice view," he said gently.

"It's better at night, when you can see into the neighbors' apartments."

He sat down on the window ledge and looked up at me through

his crooked glasses. A long strand of black hair fell across his face as if it had a life of its own. It was one of those little spontaneous movements that seemed so unintentionally sexy I was completely unhinged. He caught me staring at him and I cleared my throat and launched into an incoherent monologue about a movie I'd seen two weeks earlier and could scarcely remember. "I wish I could think of the title," I said. "Maybe Nina will remember. Of course I'm not sure she saw it with me."

"Gabriel was excited when I told him we were going to see you," he said, ignoring my babbling. "He talks about you a lot."

I was flattered, as I usually am by the attentions of children, and I was about to make some deprecating comment to deflect the compliment when Paul adjusted his glasses and said, "That really isn't true either. He remembers you, but he doesn't talk about you very much. What I meant to say was that I've been thinking about you a lot. I have to stop talking through Gabriel. If you ever hear me do that, point it out to me."

"Well," I said, "I'm not very good at pointing out anyone's faults except my own."

"You have faults, George?"

Fortunately, Nina stormed into the kitchen just then and opened up the refrigerator. Her hair was still damp from the shower. She grabbed a carton of milk and introduced herself to Paul. "You're Paul, I'm Nina," she said brusquely, and then, far too sweetly, said to me, "I thought we were in a big rush, George. I'm surprised you have time to sit around chatting."

"I was waiting for you before I brought out coffee. You know how recklessly polite I am."

"Well, the wait is over."

"She's always like this when her hair is wet," I said to Paul. "Let me show you off to the rest of the family, Nina." As we were walking into the living room I whispered to her, "Don't do this to me, please. You know how I hate scenes."

"Scenes?" she asked loudly.

Somewhere in the room Molly had found a copy of *The Freudian Left* and was curled up on the sofa immersed in it, Gabriel's head in her lap; he was asleep. She looked up at us and held the book in the air as if it were a picket sign. "I suppose this is yours," she said to Nina. "Paul tells me you're a psychologist."

"Almost a psychologist. I still have to finish my dissertation."

"Yes, well, I'm sure it's of no interest to you, my dear, but I don't approve of people wasting their time gossiping with psychologists. There's nothing you can get from a psychologist you can't get from a little political involvement. The whole thing is just a distraction, that's all. I'm sorry, but that's the way I feel." She raised her hands and smiled innocently and benignly as if she were apologizing for something as intrinsic as the color of her eyes.

"Oh, don't apologize to me," Nina said. "Sometimes I feel the same way. I'm hoping to combine politics and psychology, that's all."

"Good luck, dear," Molly said skeptically. "Of course, this book does look like it might be of some interest."

"Anything with the word 'left' in the title interests my mother," Paul said. He sat down next to her on the sofa and gently pulled Gabriel, still dozing, onto his own lap.

"I certainly won't fault her for that," Nina said. She was looking at Molly with rapt attentiveness. I'd mentioned to Nina that Paul's mother had been in the Communist party, so she was intrigued. The old woman's mask of wrinkles, her limpid brown eyes, and her confrontational approach transformed Nina's curiosity into admiration.

As for Molly, I could see her aligning herself with Nina right away by the way she kept her eyes on her. She appeared to be completely indifferent to me at best, and during the next few minutes of conversation she acknowledged me only when absolutely necessary.

"Well, you know," she said, after a complete verbal trashing of the mental health profession as a whole, "when I say I don't approve of psychology, I don't mean that some people might not benefit from it. Paul's father, for instance. Now there was a man who could have used a good shrink."

"Well, then, there goes your whole distraction theory, Mother. Dad was as involved in politics as you."

"Don't even think that," she snapped. "Your father was no friend to the Party. He took the first excuse he could find to leave and he ran with it."

"What excuse was that?" Nina asked. Her desire to have been a Red Diaper baby was becoming more apparent every second.

"The Twenty-Second Communist Conference," Molly said nonchalantly. "Those Khrushchev revelations."

She said the words as if she were mentioning something as insignificant as a canceled television series.

"My mother, on the other hand, took the *second* excuse she could find to leave the Party, and ran with it."

Molly slid herself to the edge of the sofa so her blue boating sneakers were touching the floor, and pointed a steady finger at Paul. "The invasion of Czechoslovakia was not the second 'excuse,' my dear, it was the last straw. Now if you want to say I took the second excuse that came along to divorce your father, I might agree with you. When he left the Party, I said, 'Fine, he's a fool, but I'll give him a second chance.' When he left the Dodgers and started rooting for the Yankees, I took off and brought the baby with me. But Paul never was much interested in baseball, were you, dear?"

"She always tells that story," Paul said, "and it isn't even close to the truth."

Molly broke out into a spasm of high-pitched giggles and slid back on the sofa. "It is the truth, and if your father hadn't died, he'd back me up on it. He might have been a fool, but he was no liar. And George," she said, turning to me for the first time in twenty minutes, "you'd better stop guzzling all that coffee."

"I've told him a hundred times it's stupid to go to a demonstration with a full bladder," Nina said.

PAUL drove his mother's Toyota while she sat on the seat next to him holding a tiny map and giving directions. As we got closer to the landlord's neighborhood, the streets widened out and the yards around the houses turned into rolling, well-tended lawns with trimmed hedges and circular drives in front. It was a section of Brooklyn I'd never seen before and I had trouble imagining it was the same landmass Nina and I lived on. "You think they have fox hunts out here?" I asked Nina.

"The whole idea," Molly said, "is to shake these people up

some, make a lot of noise. If you shame these people in front of their neighbors, it's worse than death to them, even though all the neighbors in an area like this have their fingers in the same pie. Nobody wants to talk about it, that's all. They want to pretend it's just another sensible real estate sale and ignore the fact that one hundred and fifty seniors are going to be left homeless. One hundred and fifty seniors. You think we're going to be able to find a decent place to live at the same rents? You think it's fun to pack your life into boxes and moving vans?"

"We're on your side, Mother!" Paul yelled at her.

Gabriel sat on the back seat with Nina and me and played with Nina's feather earring as if it were an exotic bird that had just landed on her neck. "George took a bath with us," he said to her, stretching out her earlobe.

She looked over at me and smiled. "That's nice, Gabie. What else did he do?"

"I had pancakes," I said. "And don't pump him for information. It's not good practice for being a parent."

When we finally pulled up in front of the landlord's house—a brick fortress with a circular drive and stone pillars on either side of the entry—there was a crowd of elderly people milling around in front, looking lost.

"I'd knew we'd be late," Molly said. She sprang out of the car before Paul had turned off the engine.

I suspect Molly would have been thrilled if there'd been an altercation of some sort that afternoon, but things went smoothly and without incident. Over one hundred people showed up and Molly kept them all organized and positioned, alternating them marching in front of the house and resting in one of the cars parked along the side of the street. Paul and I took Gabriel for a walk down the wide, tree-lined streets, looking for a place for Gabriel to pee, and when we returned, a photographer was snapping a picture of Molly with a bullhorn to her mouth and Nina standing off to the side looking wistfully at the old woman's face.

In the early afternoon, Molly rounded everyone up and announced it was time to "get the hell out of this horrible neighborhood." Paul and I drove the Toyota back to the apartment while Nina went off with Molly and Gabie to a lunch at the threatened building which Molly had arranged.

"Your mother doesn't like me," I said to Paul later in the day. We were lying on my bed eating popcorn from a huge bowl between us.

"She doesn't have anything against you, George. It's just that she doesn't see any purpose in befriending you so she isn't going to make the effort. My mother's very practical in her choice of friends, very purposeful. She's that way about everything."

"What about Nina?"

"She's charmed by Nina. I could tell that right away. When my mother gets confrontational with people the way she got with Nina, it usually means she's interested enough to test them. My mother likes to have protégés, George. She likes to take people on, take them under her wing. But I'm glad you care what she thinks of you; that must mean you care what I think of you."

"I care what everyone thinks of me. It's one of my great weaknesses."

"You want me to tell you what I think of you?"

He was smiling shyly, his mouth turned up on the right side and his dimple dug into his cheek. He'd taken off his glasses and his face had the same vulnerable, incomplete look I'd noticed when I woke up beside him in his bed in Vermont. We were both undressed. His rib cage looked narrow and fragile through the pale stretch of his skin. There was a thin line of hair running up from his belly button which half an hour earlier I'd marveled at and now was inexplicably saddened by.

"No, I don't," I said in answer to his question, because once someone tells you they care for you, you have a greater responsibility for them, which, at that moment, I wasn't ready for.

I heard the front door to the apartment open and Nina called out an inquisitive, cautious hello. I jumped out of bed and reached for my pants. I tossed Paul his shirt as I pulled on my socks. The sleeve landed in the bowl of popcorn.

"She called hello, George, she didn't cry for help," Paul said. He tossed the shirt back at me.

I stuck my head into the hallway. "Nina? Is that you?"

"No, George, it's the Aga Khan."

"We're in my room," I said. "Come on in." I was buttoning up my shirt as fast as I could. Paul was still lying on top of the covers brazenly eating popcorn. "At least get under the blankets," I said.

"I'm not cold."

I tossed a sheet over the lower half of his body. "How was the lunch?" I asked Nina as she walked past my room.

"Wonderful. Your mother's terrific, Paul," she called out.

"You can go in and tell him," I said.

"I want to lie down. I'm tired.

"Do you want some popcorn?" I asked her, holding open the door.

"Stop acting so weird," she whispered to me. "I just want to get off my feet."

"Weird? Who's acting weird? I'm not acting weird."

"Yes, you are," Paul said.

"Thank you, Paul," Nina called out, confirming my belief friends should never be introduced to each other.

Nina went off to her room and Paul sat up in bed staring at me with annoyance. "Nina does know we're not old college roommates, doesn't she?"

"Of course," I said.

"Then what was that routine all about?"

"Nothing," I said. I listened for the sound of her bedroom door closing and then I took off my shirt and sat next to him on the bed, feeling distant and eager for him to leave. "I just don't want her to feel left out, that's all. She lives here, after all."

"Right. And I'm visiting for the afternoon. So what's the problem?"

"There's no problem," I said, but I still felt uneasy.

LATER in the afternoon we went for a walk around the neighborhood and then up to the edges of Prospect Park and Grand Army Plaza. I wanted to point things out to him, my favorite houses and certain trees I especially liked, but I held myself back. We sat on a park bench looking at the traffic endlessly circling the War Memorial arch in the cold gray twilight. Paul put his arm around my shoulders in a friendly, familiar way. "Doesn't that remind you of the Arc de Triomphe, George?"

"I don't know," I said. "I've never been to Paris."

"Well, don't you think it looks like pictures you've seen of the Arc de Triomphe with cars going around it and the lights shining up on the stone?"

"I hate to travel," I told him. He looked over at me with dismay, and I felt a kind of panic race through me. I was out of control and acting like a jerk. What if he got up then and just walked away into the Parisian twilight? "But it reminds me of the pictures I've seen of Paris, Paul. I tell that to Nina all the time." I reached over and pushed his glasses up to the bridge of his nose.

20

In early December Timothy took me to the Brooklyn Academy of Music to hear a singer he described as the new Callas. Of course I'd never heard the old Callas perform, but I couldn't imagine there was much of a resemblance unless it had something to do with a tapeworm. This woman appeared on stage in a red Mylar gown and stood fellating a microphone and screeching at the top of her lungs for a full forty-five minutes. Somewhere in the middle of the performance I became intensely paranoid that I was losing my mind. Why else would I sit through this? I felt as if someone were running a piece of dental floss through one ear and out the other.

"What you don't realize," Timothy told me later, "is this woman is working within an entirely different musical framework. She's a fearless chronicler of our times, George, and the old musical styles are inadequate for conveying her message."

"Come on, Timothy. Where did you read that? She's the victim of deinstitutionalization like most of the other nuts ranting on the subway who think they have a message. Just because someone propped her up on stage with a microphone in her hand doesn't mean she's an artist. She needs help. She needs compassion."

He looked at me with a sad, empathetic shake of his head. "Sometimes it strikes me as almost pitiful the way I really do want you to open up and expand your horizons. The only thing that keeps me dragging you to these concerts is the thought that one day you'll wake up and realize you understand the music, and then you'll remember the attempts your friend made on your behalf."

"Face it, Timothy, none of your other buddies will come out to Brooklyn. That's what keeps you doing this for me."

I talked him into going to a Cuban restaurant near the theater which Howard had once described as superb though he qualified the recommendation by saying it had probably gone downhill since his last meal. The inside of the place was decorated with a bizarre hodgepodge of clashing colors and odd bits of atmosphere, like a fisherman's net hung over the ceiling with little plastic cows stuck in it. Timothy took one look around and insisted we leave.

"Haven't you noticed there's no one else in here? Doesn't that tell you something?"

"Only that the service will be great. I like this place. There's not one thing on the menu over four ninety-five. Cubans eat late, that's why no one's here," I explained, even though it was past eleven-thirty.

We were seated on either side of an enormous round table in the center of the restaurant and then abandoned for a full fifteen minutes while I told Timothy about the Thanksgiving weekend. The entire staff seemed to be on a break, lolling at a table at the rear of the room and smoking fat cigarettes that smelled like body odor. "I get the feeling Paul likes me," I said, trying to distract Timothy. I was afraid he'd suggest we get up and leave, which is something I find torturous to do in restaurants, no matter how bad the service. "It worries me. You know the way people get when they like you; they start to think you owe them your life."

"And we both know your life is already promised to Nina, isn't that right?"

"It's not promised to Nina. It's different between the two of us. We don't have those kinds of obligations."

"Then why did you panic the minute she walked in the door and caught you in bed with someone?" He leaned into the middle of the huge table, so he didn't have to shout. "I'll tell you why: because you felt you were betraying her."

"Betraying her?"

"Betraying her. And why? I'll tell you: because you've taken on an obligation you're not willing to admit to. Simple as that, George. I hope Nina is half as good a psychologist as I am. And if someone doesn't come over to this table in thirty seconds, we're leaving."

"We can't leave," I said. "I already drank the water and unfolded the napkin." Timothy motioned to a waiter for the fifth time and the crew at the back table looked at us in bafflement. "Someone just put out a cigarette back there. I think it's a good sign."

"Let's hope so. As for that demonstration, the mother is entirely right. It's outrageous the way they tear down these old buildings. I'm sure the place needs some rehabbing, but that's no reason to demolish it. It's too bad she hates you."

"She doesn't hate me," I said. It was a point I was sensitive on because I feared she did hate me. "She just wasn't overly friendly, that's all."

"Well, I'd steer clear of her. If you have any hopes of carrying on this affair with the muckraker, steer clear of the commie. That's my advice, which I realize you don't want."

"Of course I want it," I said. "I always want your advice. For instance, Paul invited me to Vermont over Christmas. What do you think I should do?"

"Go to Florida with your mother. At least there are some buildings to look at down there, even if they are all hideous. How do I know what you should do? How do you feel about this character?"

I was hoping he'd come around to asking me so I could try out the sounds of a few different answers. "I like him," I said. "I was excited to see him again and I had a good time with him. I just wish he didn't seem so interested in me."

Timothy threw up his hands in dismay. "You're a very confused man, George." A waiter came over to our table and looked down at us silently. "We'd like to order now," Timothy said, suddenly very polite.

"Order?" the waiter asked.

"Order. Our dinner?"

"We're closed. We close at midnight."

"But we got here half an hour ago," I said. "We've been sitting at this huge table in the middle of the room for half an hour trying to get someone to come over and take our order."

The waiter shrugged and looked at me with profound sympathy in his eyes. "What can I tell you, señor? I'm so sorry for you. The cook leaves at midnight. I'd go in there and cook it with my own hands but the freezer's locked tight."

"Couldn't you have told us this when we came in?" I asked.

"George," Timothy said pushing his chair back from the table, "he can't do anything, that's all. Let's not make a scene."

"A scene? Timothy . . ."

He stood up looking wretchedly humiliated and dropped a hand-full of bills and coins on the vinyl tablecloth.

"Anyway," he said once we were out on the street, "you already know what I think you should do, George: get a nice studio in the East Village, go back to that diploma mill you were at and finish your degree, find an easy academic job and start enjoying the city. By the time you're thirty-two you could be a happy man."

"We just want different things out of life, that's all. And why did you crumble in there? If we'd made a big enough stink they probably would have given us something."

"Let me tell you a little secret, George: six-foot-five people who weigh a hundred and forty pounds don't need to draw attention to themselves by making 'stinks' in restaurants run by brawny Latins."

"I'm sorry," I said.

"Forget it. Life is hard enough without dwelling on things like this. You don't know what you want out of life. That's your problem."

"Well, maybe," I said, "but this way I'm at least not so wide open for disappointment. And besides, I already told Paul I'd go up to Vermont for Christmas."

"Great. You're afraid he's getting too attached to you so you're going to spend the holidays with him in the woods. Makes perfect sense to me."

"I want to see Gabriel. I like him. There's nothing wrong with wanting to see a five-year-old, is there?"

"If there were, George, do you think I'd ever spend time with you?"

The truth was, as fearful as I was that Paul was taking too much of a liking to me, I was more afraid he might forget me altogether if I didn't see him again within a month. And if I did go to Vermont, at least Nina and I would have another excuse for not having a big dinner party.

21

ONE morning in the second week in December, Melissa and I were standing in the teachers' room arranging rémoulade and celery sticks on plastic plates for the kids' midmorning snack. Melissa was afraid of getting rémoulade on her black stretch pants so she'd wrapped a white sheet around the lower half of her body. It was a cold morning and the boiler in the next room was sputtering and belching. The sound reminded me of the singer Timothy and I had gone to hear. As I was describing the performance to Melissa, she offhandedly interrupted me saying, "Oh, George, you'll never guess what happened the other day. Howard's car was found!"

"You're kidding! That's great." I hadn't thought of Howard's lost car in weeks and the news cheered me. Howard was due for some good luck. "Where'd they find it?"

"Red Brook? Someplace like that. Someplace out in Brooklyn."

"Red Hook," I said. "Dylan mentions it in a song. 'Born in Red Hook Brooklyn in the year of who knows when.' It's a song about a gangster."

"I never listen to Bob Dylan," she said. "Those songs go on forever. If I want a Russian novel, I'll read one. But the car was a complete mess. The back was filled with clothes and rotten food. Someone was living in it. Can you imagine? It was uncomfortable enough to ride in, as I remember."

"Howard must have been thrilled. He loves that car." I took a handful of digestive biscuits from the stash reserved for the kids and put one into my mouth. "You want some, Melissa?"

"Always. Howard's going to have the thing fixed up, get the body repainted, have the floor rewelded." She dipped a cracker into the rémoulade and then slammed the cover back on the plastic tub. "I told him, I said, 'Howard, you should buy a new car. It isn't as if you're poor. You just think you're making a contribution to society by pretending you are.'"

"He'll hang on to that car forever. That's his style."

"I'm finding that out." She took off the sheet and lifted the tray to her shoulder. At the door she turned to me with her mouth open.

"What's wrong?"

"Nothing, George. Nothing at all."

It was another hour before I realized what "Nothing at all" amounted to. I was reading a story aloud to the class. I dropped the book to the floor in the middle of a sentence and sat staring at Melissa nervously puttering around at the back of the room.

"Oh, brother," Rose said when she saw my eyes glazing over. "George is having a petit mal." She got up and opened the book to the correct page. "Read, George. 'And the funny little woman . . .'"

"'And the funny little woman . . .'"

"'Brought the sheep into the house . . .'"

"'Brought the sheep into the house . . .'"

I was still dazed when I brought the children outside to burn off the last of their energy before their parents came to pick them up. It was windy and gray and I stood huddled against the school building in a long overcoat with my woolen cap pulled on my head thinking about the last time I'd seen Howard walking up the street in Brooklyn with his pants leg caught up in his sock and his collar askance. I'd been duped, taken in by his tearful goodbye on the green vinyl sofa, by his devoted find of the baked garlic recipe. The wind whistled through the rusted pipes of the fire escape with a damp suggestion of snow. On top of everything else, winter was approaching rapidly.

"George! George!"

I snapped out of my trance and saw Doran's mother standing in front of me nervously looking around the playground. "Where's Dorrie, George?"

I was sure she expected to see him hanging from a tree by his neck. "I didn't see you come in, Theodora. You're early today."

"I'm in a very big rush today, George."

Theodora was always in a very big rush. She was an officious woman with a booming voice and a slightly mannish demeanor. She did consulting work for an advertising firm and was reportedly out-earning her estranged husband by one digit. Whether or not this was the main problem in their relationship I didn't know, but she and Daniel were fond of making ugly scenes in front of people to prove how much they detested each other. Once, in the presence of Melissa, Mr. Simmons, and me, Daniel had accused her of breastfeeding Doran long past the age at which he should have been weaned. She countered by calling him a "pale, flaccid flop" and storming out of the room. I was terrified of her.

"Doran's probably under the tire," I said. "It's his favorite spot these days."

"Probably? You have to keep a better eye on him, George. He's a very unpredictable child. Very impulsive."

A ridiculous charge if ever I'd heard one. Doran didn't have an impulsive organ in his body.

"I'm running very late today, George, so if you'll get him from wherever, I'll go collect his things from inside."

She walked toward the basement door and I instinctively looked down at the sheet of paper that listed each child's name and which parent, babysitter, father's girlfriend, mother's secretary, uncle, or household servant was going to pick him up. Next to Doran's name was DANIEL, printed in block letters.

"Oh, I'm sorry, Theodora," I said, "but isn't Daniel supposed to be picking up Doran today?"

She turned around and adjusted her heavy for coat into a more comfortable position on her shoulders. "Obviously, George, there's been a change of plans."

"Well, obviously," I said, running my hand up and down the list. "It's just that Daniel didn't mention anything about it this morning when he dropped Dorrie off."

"The fact that Daniel is absentminded is the least of the reasons I'm divorcing him."

I reminded her there was a rule against allowing a child to go home with anyone other than the person on the list unless both parents had sent a written request. She reminded me that she was

Doran's mother and had no intention of letting him be held captive in school against her wishes, and then called for him in her booming, authoritative voice.

Doran came crawling out from under the sawed-off truck tire buried in the sandbox and ran over to us with his coat flying open in the winter air. I felt a chilling blast of the wind myself and pulled my hat farther down over my ears.

"Honestly, George, I don't wonder Doran is sick all the time with the way you let him run around." She bent down and buttoned up the child's calf-length camel's-hair coat. "Frankly, I thought we paid for better attention than that."

"I'll just quickly call Daniel while you two are getting ready."

"Oh, please, George, don't get carried away with your petty authority here. It isn't as if I'm a stranger in a clown suit trying to lure the child into a truck with a bag of juju bears. Doran, go get your lunchbox and make it fast. We have early reservations at Lutèce." He ran into the building while Theodora smiled at me with a calm and surprisingly pleasant grin. "Lutèce is his favorite restaurant. You're looking admirably thin today, George. Do you eat bran?"

"Bran?"

Melissa came out of the school surrounded by a devoted group of students she'd been teaching to play jacks. She looked at me nervously and slowly walked off to the sandbox like a naughty child. She had on a flimsy cloth jacket and I was surprised she wasn't freezing. Sometimes Melissa seemed curiously inured to the effects of the elements. I motioned for her to come over and she stood contritely in front of me with her eyes on the ground. "I'm sorry. I kept meaning to tell you, but I never could find a good time to do it."

"We can talk about it later," I said.

"It's only been going on for a month now. Or a month and a half. Not very long. And, George, please don't forget Nina's the one who dumped Howard. At least don't forget that fact. At least I didn't break them up."

Doran flew out of the school basement with his lunchbox clutched under his arm. Miraculously, his coat was wide open again.

"We don't have time for that, Doran," Theodora said as he started fumbling with the buttons.

"I think it was the dinner he cooked the first time I came out to Brooklyn, George."

I looked at Theodora furiously buttoning up Doran's coat and handed the list of names to Melissa. I pointed to Doran's. Melissa quickly turned around and asked Theodora where Daniel was.

"I wouldn't know, dear. In one month I won't be his wife and I've never been his keeper."

"Well, the list we have here..."

"George and I have already discussed your inaccurate lists, Melissa."

"Well, I'd like to call Daniel so we can discuss them with him, if you don't mind."

"I don't discuss anything with Daniel—my lawyer does." She took Doran by the hand and airily said, "See you tomorrow, children," and walked around the building and out of sight.

"What a bitch," Melissa said. "If that kid doesn't turn out queer, no one will."

"Melissa!"

"I'm sorry, George. Let's not get overly sensitive here."

It occurred to me I should go in and call Daniel, but my curiosity on one point got the better of me. "Just tell me something, Melissa," I said. "Did Howard mention to you about Nina?"

"What about Nina? And if you tell me she's pregnant, I'll never speak to you again."

I told her Nina was pregnant.

She rushed up to me and threw her arms around my shoulders and started to sob loudly into my ear. "No wonder Howard is such a fanatic about birth control."

Not only am I not much good at consoling a man in tears, but I'm not much good at consoling a woman in tears either. And I wasn't sure I wanted to console Melissa anyway. I felt as if I were betraying my friendship with Nina merely by keeping my arms around her. I felt a tug at the leg of my pants and looked down to see Nathan staring up at me with concerned eyes.

"Is Melissa all right?" he asked. His adult tone of voice contrasted weirdly with the Dutch dairymaid's outfit he was wearing.

"She's just a little upset, Nathan."

"Yes, I can see that. Would you like me to get you a drink of water, Melissa?"

She reached down and rested her hand on his hair. "No. No, thank you, Nathan. But do you have something I could use to wipe my eyes?"

"Of course," he said. He pulled a lacy handkerchief out of the pocket of his apron and said, "You can keep it."

She picked him up in her arms and kissed him on both cheeks. "You're a Dumpling, Nathan. Did you know that?"

"Is that what Howard calls you?" I asked indignantly.

"It isn't. It's what he used to call me until I told him I couldn't stand being referred to as a boiled lump of dough." She blew her nose into the handkerchief. "It's over, George. It's all over. I'll call him up the minute school is out and put a lid on the whole disaster. I knew I shouldn't mess around with men in their thirties."

"Don't go and do anything rash," I said.

I was actually beginning to pity Howard. Being rejected by Nina had probably been such a shock to his system he didn't know what he was doing. Not that he was blameless, but he didn't need another blow less than two months later. If I should be angry at anyone, it was Nina.

I stood under the fire escape with Melissa, safe from the howling wind, and watched the children run around in mad circles until gradually the adults came and carted them off to a babysitter or a day-care center with an extended afternoon or to some corporate play group. Sometimes I was amazed at how exhausting their privileged lives seemed, dragging from one place to the next all day as if they, along with both their parents, were carrying the burden of a full-time job. There were only three children left in the playground when I glanced up and saw Daniel coming around the building. He had an unmistakable walk, a self-conscious swagger of exaggerated confidence he probably practiced at home, and the second I saw him, I felt my stomach tighten into a knot. He had on a fur coat identical to the one Theodora had worn. Presents to each other in happier times, no doubt.

I nudged Melissa.

She gave a start of horror. "Oh, God. I hope he's under sedation today. You'd better let me handle this, George. His type is terrified of women."

She grinned at him flirtatiously and said, "Well, look who's here. Aren't you looking fit this afternoon, Daniel."

"Thank you, Melissa," he said in his one-minute-manager's tone. "I do try. Between the gym and jogging and all the rest, I'm surprised I have time to make money. But, at my age, men have to watch themselves, right, George?" He gave me a pathetic wink. "How was my boy today?"

Daniel and I were on the best of man-to-man terms, a state of affairs that made me avoid him at every possible turn. "The fact is," I said hesitantly, "Doran is..."

"Under the tire, I suppose. He told me it's the only place at school quiet enough for him to think. You know, I worry about him under there with the ground getting cold. Especially since his mother takes him to a quack pediatrician who wouldn't know a cold from a bee sting."

"Speaking of his mother..." Melissa said.

"I'd rather not, Melissa. My lawyer talks to her and my analyst talks about her." Melissa laughed a little too loudly and for a second too long. I hoped she wasn't on the verge of hysteria. "It's true," Daniel went on, encouraged. "Theodora wouldn't know a brain tumor from a sore throat. And she expects to get custody of Doran. Do you know that she breastfed Doran until he was almost four years old?"

"Daniel," I said, foolishly trying to snap him back to reality, "the fact is, Theodora just came by and picked up Doran. She told us you'd rearranged your plans. We were surprised to see you walk into the yard right now, weren't we, Melissa?"

"We were very surprised, Daniel. Maybe you just forgot Theodora was coming by? My father happens to be forgetful, too. I think it's a very manly trait."

"What did you just say, George?" he asked, ignoring Melissa completely.

"I said—"

"I *thought* you said that Theodora came in and picked up Doran this afternoon."

"Well, that's about it. They have early reservations at Lutèce," I said. At least he'd want to know she wasn't planning to starve him to death. "Doran's favorite restaurant."

"Lutèce is *not* Doran's favorite restaurant, George. He likes Le Cirque much more. *Much* more. And today is *Tues*day, George. *I* pick up Doran on Tuesdays. I've been picking up Doran every Tuesday for the past few months without a hitch and you're trying to tell me that Theodora just waltzed in here and waltzed out with my son?"

"Well, after all," I said, trying to recoup, "it isn't as if she's some juju bear trying to lure him into a truck with a clown suit."

"George is right," Melissa said.

"You stay out of this, Melinda. This is between George and me."

I'd always known I'd have to pay for our man-to-man terms some day. "I'm sure there's nothing to worry about," I said even though I could feed a trickle of cold sweat sliding down from my armpit.

"How can you two idiots stand there so calmly? Don't you realize she could be over the state line in an hour? My God, she could be in Spain by morning."

"Not Spain," Melissa said. "She was wearing a fur coat."

There was no point in trying to defend myself any further because Daniel had the unfair advantage of being in the right. If, as usual, I hadn't been so preoccupied with someone else's life, I wouldn't have let Theodora take Doran home. What's more, Daniel looked so pathetic standing impotently in the cold in his fur coat and his expensive leather shoes, I began to feel deeply sorry for him. We went into the school and called Lutèce. There were no reservations under Theodora's name. Daniel immediately called his lawyer and told him what had happened, then dialed another number and left a message with Dr. someone-or-other's answering service.

WHEN all the other children had been picked up, Melissa and I went to a bakery on Madison Avenue and stuffed ourselves with sweet buttery pastries. Melissa unraveled her croissants into long shreds and chewed without any sign of tasting them. Our miniature table was jammed into a corner, and all the patrons sitting around us at equally doll-sized tables seemed to be speaking French.

"That's what I hate about this city," Melissa said to me dejectedly. "No one speaks English here. I feel like I'm living in a Truffaut movie without the subtitles. Why are all these French people here, George? What do they want in this city that they couldn't as easily find in Paris?"

"I don't know, Melissa. Why don't you ask them?"

She turned around and excused herself and in rapid French asked one of the older matrons behind us what she was looking for in New York. The woman eyed her red crew cut suspiciously, pulled her mouth into a Gallic pout and started to whisper to her companion.

"You see, George, they don't even know themselves."

"Just answer me one thing," I said after another palmier. "Are you in love with Howard? It doesn't matter to me, but I think I ought to know."

"Listen, George," she said slowly, "do you remember that cookie you just wolfed down? Did you love that cookie, George?"

"Melissa..."

"No, you didn't love that cookie but you ate it. You ate it because it was there and it had the appeal of a foreign name."

"Howard does not have a foreign name."

"You're forgetting I'm from Westchester. Oh, all right, I don't love Howard. I don't *love* Howard and I don't think he *loves* me either. I don't know what exactly, but there's something about him I like. Liked. I was lonely, all right? He called me up one night and asked if I wanted to have a drink. I remembered what a good cook he is, I thought I could teach him how to dress. I felt sorry for him, George. What do I know? It always happens this way with me; I step into the middle of some disastrous relationship and make enemies with a woman over a man I don't really love, a man who doesn't even know how to dress. Do you know how many women friends I have? I have two women friends and I don't really like either one of them." She looked around the restaurant. "At least they both speak English. Would you mind telling that woman over there her chapeau is blocking my view?"

I think the sugar from the pastries had finally reached my brain. I had an urge to laugh or cry hysterically over the whole miserable afternoon and the nagging fear that I'd never see Doran again and would be out of a job. I wanted to cross the restaurant and knock the floppy fur hat off the woman's head. As much as I felt Howard was betraying Nina, I felt he had somehow abandoned me by giving up on her, left me holding the baby.

"Let's get out of here," I said pushing the toy table away from me. "Nina and I have a dancing lesson tonight and I'm already late."

"Dancing lesson? In her condition? I guess women do everything when they're pregnant these days. You see them out shopping all the time."

As we walked down Madison Avenue, she pulled on a pair of red-and-black leather gloves with a line of silver studs running down the seam. "I want you to remember that whatever happens with Doran, George, we're in this together. I'm as responsible as you are. They aren't going to dump two staff people over something like this. One maybe, but never two."

"You're a comfort, Melissa," I said as I kissed her goodbye at the subway.

At the bottom of the urine-stinking staircase I looked up to the street and saw her helping a ragged old woman down the steps. She had one gloved hand on the woman's arm and one hand clutched to her chest in horror.

I was ten minutes late for the lesson. Nina was leaning against the wall in the reception area nervously pulling at her eyebrows. She had on one of her strapless dresses, with the pinched waistline let out, and she looked like a parody of a pregnant teen-ager going to a school prom. The music was pouring out of the next room mixed in with Miss Reynolds's singsong instructions.

"Where have you been?" Nina asked, taking my arm. "I was getting worried about you."

"I was out eating pastry. I'm sorry I didn't get a chance to change." I still had on my work boots and a sweatshirt splattered with poster paints.

"I don't care about that, George." She led me out to the dance floor and smiled at Miss Reynolds. "Are you sure you're all right? You look a little harried."

"... and *one* two three four, *look* who made it, *left* two three four, *glad* to see you..."

"I'm fine," I said. I put my hand against the middle of Nina's back and started to drag my feet to the music. I had no enthusiasm for dancing or listening to brassy music. I'm sure I was as thrilling a partner as a broomstick.

"... and *look* a live George, *lift* those feet four, *lift* two three four, LIFT two three four..."

I gave Miss Reynolds a sneering look as she fluttered past us with her rhinestone shoes sparkling and told Nina what had happened at school with Doran's parents, stressing the fact that it was a major gaffe, one I was probably going to have to pay for dearly. "I could easily lose my job over a thing like this," I said morosely.

"You aren't going to lose your job, George. You're a good teacher and they like you."

"There are limits to their affection."

"I don't see what the big deal is. You let a child leave the school with his mother. That isn't the kind of thing people get fired for. Just try to relax and enjoy the music."

"You don't understand, Nina."

She shook her bangs out of her eyes. "You think I don't understand because you just want to dramatize and feel sorry for yourself."

"I don't feel sorry for *myself*." I was paying no attention to my feet at all. Twice I stomped on Nina's toes and once I backed us up against the mirror at the front of the room with a shuddering crash. Nina was enjoying my clumsiness. She thought it was hilarious. I couldn't stand to see her laughing so raucously when, at least from my point of view, her world was falling in. "There's something else you should know," I said.

"It sounds very very serious."

"They found Howard's car."

"Oh?"

"Howard didn't tell me they found his car; Melissa did. Melissa told me."

She missed one beat of the music, one single step, and then she said, "Well, I'm glad they found it. Howard must be ecstatic."

I stopped dancing altogether and stared at her. "Nina, Melissa knew about the car because she and Howard have been seeing each other. For over a month now."

"I figured that out already."

A couple who'd been taking lessons for over a year came dancing past us wrapped in each other's arms like newlyweds. Their name was Protano, and they'd once treated Nina and me to coffee after class and proceeded to tell us the story of their marriage as if it were an example for us to follow. Mrs. Protano had on a beaded sweater with a corsage pinned over her breast.

"Smile, dears," she said gaily. "This is our thirty-fourth anniversary. Isn't that marvelous?"

Mr. Protano swung her around. His chin was resting contentedly on the top of her head. "Lighten up, Georgie. After thirty-four years you just get numb."

"Isn't he awful?" Mrs. Protano said as they glided away from us.

"Is that all you have to say about it?" I asked Nina in disbelief. "Don't you care?"

"Of course I *care*, but in case you've forgotten, I'm the one who ended my relationship with Howard. You don't think I expected him to stay celibate the rest of his life, do you?"

"I don't know what you expected." I wanted her to tell me she was still in love with Howard. I wanted her to give me the chance to console her. I don't know what I wanted.

She glared at me for a few seconds and then took my arm and started to lead me around the dance floor. "Just because you had a bad day, you don't have to try and ruin mine."

"You're leading," I said.

"Someone has to."

"I'm supposed to be the one leading."

"Since when, Georgie?"

We'd raised our voices above the usual hushed tones. Several couples were eying us warily. Miss Reynolds was looking everywhere in the room but at us.

"Since always, as far as I can tell," I whispered loudly. "You're such a very independent woman you dumped Howard as soon as you got the results of the pregnancy test. You couldn't wait to raise the baby on your own, but you dragged me into the scheme pretty quickly."

"*Dragged* you?" she shouted. "Who the *fuck* dragged you into the 'scheme'? You're the one who came running back to me, begging to help with the baby as soon as you figured out exactly what Joley was worth to you. Dragged you! That's lovely, George."

Miss Reynolds floated over to the tape player and fumbled with the volume until she'd jacked it up several decibels. Nina dug her fingernails into my side as she gripped me around the waist.

"That's not the reason I decided to help you with the baby and you know it."

"Well, what was the reason? You wanted to impress the journalist with the Salvadoran kid? And while we're on the subject, why is he being dragged into this?"

"No one's dragging Paul anywhere."

"Thanksgiving, Christmas, why don't you just invite him to move in with us?"

"You're jealous again, Nina."

"You're right I'm jealous again. You've got a boyfriend and I don't. Even though I'm pregnant I wouldn't mind having sex every once in a while."

" ... a *lit* tle sof ter, *keep* it sof ter ... "

"It's not so fabulous that you have to jealous about it."

"I'm not interested in the quality of your sex life, believe me, George."

"I wanted to help you with the baby because I love you." I held her tightly by the shoulders, away from me at arm's length. "I love you, Nina."

She pried herself loose and ran across the front of the studio with her heels clicking on the wooden floor. She let the door to the street bang loudly behind her. "You just get numb, George," Mr. Protano called out. I slowly walked across the room, trying to appear as composed as possible. As I was leaving, I saw Miss Reynolds lean against the wall by the tape player lighting a cigarette with trembling hands.

• • •

SHE was standing on the sidewalk with her coat draped over her shoulders and the ruffled skirt of her dress sticking out from under the bottom of it. It had started to snow, and under the blue glow of the streetlamp I could see a fine white powder gathering on her blond hair. I went up behind her and softly kissed the top of her head. She shuddered at my touch. "Don't, George."

"I'm sorry," I said, kissing her again.

"Please don't do that." She walked away from me a few steps. "I've always accepted our relationship for what it is, but it's hard on me sometimes."

"I know, Nina." I went to her and tried to take her hand.

"Don't. Just . . . don't." She stuck her hand into the pocket of her coat and walked off down the street. I was immobilized. I didn't know whether to follow her or not. I stood under the humming streetlamp and watched the snow falling down, sticking to the shoulders of my jacket. "Can I walk with you?" I finally called out when she was a block away.

"Of course you can walk with me." She stood with her back to me while I caught up to her. She was smiling and there were tears in her eyes. "Don't ask me if you can walk with me, George. Don't ask that dumb kind of question. All I meant was this relationship is hard for me sometimes. But all relationships seem to be hard for me." She took my hand and started to cry silently.

"I'm sorry," I said after we'd walked a block. "I'm so sorry, Nina."

"What for, George? Really, what for?"

"I don't know," I shrugged. "For disappointing you. I don't know. Sometimes . . ."

"George—" she cut me off. "You don't disappoint me. And I didn't say I wanted to change anything. I didn't say it and I didn't mean it. I just wanted to say what I said and that's it."

. . . Sometimes, sometimes when we were sitting together in the living room late at night or sprawled in our respective rooms doing crossword puzzles and calling out questions to each other, I wanted to go to her and make love to her, make love to her in front of a fireplace or on an empty beach or in a canopy bed, in a dozen foolishly romantic and artificial settings. I wanted to make love to her with sweet words and tender looks and all the packaged images that have never in my life had anything to do with the genuine lustful passion I've felt. I wanted to feel closer to Nina than I sometimes did, to bring down what often felt like an enormous and invisible wall separating us. And still, I knew that if we ever did make love, it would be the act to consummate the end of our relationship and not the beginning of it. If we ever did make love, we'd be unable to go on with our dancing lessons and our cluttered life together, our safe, celibate relationship. It wasn't really what either one of us wanted, and the fact that it never came up was one of the things that held us together. I was glad she'd stopped me from finishing the sentence and making a fool of myself. I was glad we could still walk down the street holding hands with the snow falling around us.

"In thirty-four years we'll just be numb," I said.

"In thirty-four years I'll probably be a grandparent with a face that looks like Molly's."

"You're infatuated with Molly."

"I love knowing such a tiny person can take up so much space in the world."

ON the way home we stopped at a magazine store owned by two lesbians from Montana. They were tranquil women who'd inherited a brownstone in the neighborhood from the maiden aunt of the younger. I sometimes went out for drinks with them at a bar down the street. The larger and shyer of the two had a crush on Nina her lover was forever teasing her about. For months, Nina had unsuccessfully been trying to persuade them to stop selling *Penthouse*. We bought four candy bars and a book of crossword puzzles and spent the rest of the evening in front of the television watching a figure-skating championship, eating the chocolates, and mindlessly filling in the words on the puzzles.

22

THEODORA didn't bring Doran back to school on Tuesday or on Wednesday or on Thursday. Daniel was in daily telephone contact with the head of the school, and every time Mr. Simmons passed me in the hallway or came to observe on the playground, he gave me a hostile glare. Melissa assured me I was merely being paranoid, but I was convinced parents were arriving to pick up their kids more promptly than usual, as if to make sure Melissa and I didn't ship them off to Madrid on the night flight.

"You just have to get over your guilt," she advised. "When Doran's face shows up on a milk carton, *then* we can all start to worry."

Along with fretting about the fate of my job, I found myself missing Doran in class. At the lunch table I felt a nostalgic longing for his pale face and red, runny nose, and the sound of his voice telling me it was time for some new medication.

On Friday morning word filtered back to Melissa and me that there was a meeting between the parents and the school administrators and teachers scheduled for that afternoon—a meeting neither one of us had been invited to attend. At the end of the day I stayed in the teachers' room nervously pacing back and forth. Melissa was sitting at the table in the middle of the room running her hands through her red crew-cut hair. She was looking pale and drawn, and I assumed the incident was taking its toll on her as well.

"You know what they're discussing in there right now, don't you?" I said.

"Yes, George," she said wearily. Her raspy voice sounded more depleted than usual. "All those people in there are discussing *you*."

"Well, answer me this, Melissa: When was the last time we weren't included in one of those meetings?"

"Oh, I don't know," she said. She wrapped her bright red kimono tightly around her body. "I can't start worrying about all that, too. I'm a betrayed woman. I've been had."

She sounded so genuinely crestfallen I forgot myself for a minute. "What is it, Melissa? Do you want to go somewhere and talk?"

"We could take a cab out to La Guardia and I could fall apart in the back seat. Or we could go to Barney's and I could buy a five-hundred-dollar briefcase and collapse in your arms while they get an approval code for my credit card."

"Howard," I said.

"I'm a betrayed woman. I had dinner with him last night. We did a nice barbecued chicken in the oven and Howard made cornbread, some wonderful three-layered concoction with a custard in the middle."

I was silently praying she wasn't going to give me the recipe.

"Anyway, afterwards we were sitting on the living-room sofa and he was tearing out cases from the New York Law Reports, and I, just very casually, said, 'By the way, Howard, I found out Nina is pregnant. George told me.' He paused for a second. 'I told him about us,' I said. Well, he sat there, George, and he kept tearing out pages and then he looked past me, not at me, and he said, 'I suppose Nina knows now, too.' And then he went back to his damned Law Reports and waited for me to serve him coffee."

She stared at me for a moment with wide, incredulous eyes.

"So I said, 'Is that all you have to say for yourself?' and he looked up at me and smiled and said, 'You're a Bumpkin, Melissa, did you know that?'"

I couldn't tell if I was shocked or not. On one hand, it was hard to imagine Howard would be so insensitive to Melissa, but on the other, it made more sense that he'd pursued her to incite Nina's jealousy than to try and get over her. Howard didn't accept defeat easily.

"So did you throw him out of the house?"

"No, I did not," she said righteously. "I sat there and I looked at him and I said, 'Well, I have some news for you, Howard: I'm pregnant, too.' I let him sit in shock for a few minutes and *then* I threw him out." She sighed and slumped back in her chair. "Poor Howard, I suppose I should call him back. I'd never forgive myself if he went out and had a vasectomy or left town or something."

Poor Howard, Father of the Year.

"You know what, though? I really didn't get much pleasure out of it. I don't *love* him, but there is something about him. . . . Now I suppose Nina hates me, too. Another woman who hates me over some ridiculous man who doesn't know how to dress. Just don't tell her about this. I don't want to look like a complete fool in her eyes."

"I promise I won't mention a word."

"If I didn't have my damned trust fund, it wouldn't be so bad. I just hate the idea of being the poor little rich girl."

We sat around the teachers' room, each absorbed in our own woes, until the janitor came in to empty the trash barrels and mumbled something about the two of us being the last people in the building.

"The big shots are having a meeting," I said. "They'll probably be here for hours."

"That meeting broke up at five o'clock," he said as he lined the wastebasket with a plastic bag. "Once the coffee ran out, they all left the building."

I looked up at the clock. It was past six. Melissa hoisted herself up from the table and gathered her things together. "Let me point out," she told me, "that as far as I can tell, we're both still employed. I'm a betrayed woman, but at least I have a job. Nothing looks worse than a betrayed rich girl without a job."

"I can't believe Howard would stoop that low," Nina said when I reported what Melissa had told me. "She's just a kid. He never should have involved her. I really feel sorry for her, even if she does have money."

"That's nothing compared to what Howard would do for you, Nina. He's in love. He's obsessed."

"He's a jerk. I should call him up and scream at him."

I couldn't imagine there was much that would give Howard more pleasure than the sound of Nina's voice, even if she was screaming at him. I could picture him holding the receiver away from his ear and beaming.

PAUL called me on Saturday. I dragged the telephone into my bedroom to guard against the possibility of Nina's overhearing and going through another cycle of jealousy.

"Why are you talking so softly?" he asked me. "I can hardly hear you."

"It must be the connection. Maybe someone is listening in on the other end of your party line."

"I don't have a party line, George. Not everyone who lives in Vermont has a party line. I don't know anyone who has one, in fact. Are you still planning on coming up here for Christmas?"

I'd sent him a postcard telling him I was "probably" going to Vermont for the holiday, providing the weather didn't deter me.

"Well, sure," I said. "But it's still two weeks away." Plenty of time for me to change my mind. "I mean, if there's an earthquake or something, I couldn't very well come."

"I'm getting things ready at this end. I have been for days." His voice was sleepy and heavy, as if he were being manipulated by a masseur. "If I were coming to visit you, I'd be packed already."

"I don't want to rumple my wardrobe. My Armani suits don't travel well."

"You'd look good in anything. What are you wearing right now?"

From the sound of his voice, the conversation was about to turn into a heavy breathing session. "My usual," I said. "A leather jockstrap and gladiator boots."

"Tell me."

"My uniform from the high school wrestling team."

"Tell me, George."

Gradually he wore down my resistance to new experiences. I was glad he didn't have a party line and that he was paying for the call. When the conversation had returned to more ordinary subjects, he told me he was eager for me to meet a friend of his who was setting up a school on the other side of town. "He's a little lost about the kindergarten and I thought you might be able to give him some advice about setting up the room."

"I don't know anything about setting up rooms. You saw my apartment."

"I just mean the kinds of spaces kids need for different activities." He forced out a laugh. "He might even offer you a job."

"I have a job," I snapped. "Did someone tell you I don't have a job? As far as I know, I have a job."

On Monday morning Doran calmly walked into school holding Daniel's hand. He had a new lunchbox and was wearing a miniature pair of expensive-looking leather boots. I was totally bewildered, but they both looked so serene and unflustered I acted as if it were just another Monday morning. Daniel was smiling like a great sloppy bear.

"We're all ready to start school again after our little vacation," he said to me over Doran's head, winking moronically.

"I see," I said. I'm a firm believer in never turning down a free meal, and I wasn't about to start asking questions.

"Now listen, George, we have this new medication that Doran is to take at eleven o'clock sharp." He opened up the lunchbox and took out a thermos-sized bottle.

"I *hate* those pills," Doran said, rolling his eyes.

"I know you do, Dorrie," he said. He patted him on the back sympathetically. "Theo and I took him to a new doctor over the weekend and he gave us this extraordinary prescription. We threw out all the other antibiotics. He really is one of the finest doctors in the city. He said if this doesn't help, he'll set up an appointment with a hypnotist in Kingston. But we're confident that won't be necessary. Aren't we, Dorrie?"

"We are," Doran agreed earnestly. "We're very confident, George."

"I see," I said again. "So this trip to the doctor was a kind of joint venture?"

"You're a smart guy, George." Daniel gave me a firm slap on the back. I was obviously back in his manly confidence. "I'll bet you could get into a field where you can make some money, if you wanted to."

When he'd left the building, Melissa came over and swung Doran up into the air. "Where have you been, you snotnose?"

"Spain," he said calmly.

Doran was remarkably alert for the rest of the day. The finest doctor in the city had probably prescibed sugar pills that finally lifted Doran out of the drugged stupor he'd been in for most of his parents' separation. I went to him while he was sitting at the drawing table bent over a piece of paper with a crayon limply clasped in one hand and his tongue poking out from between his lips. I put my chin on the table and looked up at him.

"I missed you while you were away, Dorrie."

"Well, George, I was very busy so I didn't get a chance to miss you too much."

"I don't mind," I said. "I'm glad you're back, that's all."

He held up his drawing of a huge, square building. "This is the Prado, George. There's paintings inside here."

I celebrated Doran's return later that afternoon by purchasing a Christmas tree for the apartment. It was a pathetic-looking thing bought from an equally pathetic derelict on a street corner. It amounted to about three sparse branches that had probably been chopped off the top of a larger tree, but I was in a festive mood and I managed to bargain the price down to eighteen bucks. The minute I got it in the door of the apartment, I realized I didn't have a stand. I propped it up between two chairs and set the scrawny trunk in a bucket of water. After I put on a Doris Day Christmas album, I went into the kitchen and took a bag of cranberries out of the freezer and popped a huge bowl of popcorn. I'd once seen a TV show on natural, holistic Christmas ornaments and strung popcorn and cranberries were the featured specialty. What they hadn't mentioned was that you need the patience of a soybean to run a needle and thread through nine hundred pieces of delicate popped corn and the impenetrable skins of cranberries.

By the time Nina came home I'd abandoned the project, eaten

most of the popcorn, and was guzzling a bottle of diet soda. I did, however, have a Mormon Tabernacle Choir record on the Webcor Holiday. She took one look at the tree propped up between the chairs with a three-inch piece of decorated string flung on it and burst into tears.

"I'm sorry," I said, following her as she ran into her bedroom. "If you don't like the tree, we can just throw it out the window. It'll fit."

"How could you do this to me, Georgie?"

"Do what?"

"It's bad enough you're leaving me here for the holidays, but to add to it by bringing that sad thing into the house is really too much."

"I'll go pitch it out right now."

"No!" she screamed. "Don't you dare. I want to leave it there to remind me of what a lonely holiday I'm going to have."

"Look," I said. "You know how I hate to stand up for myself, but I told you I was going away weeks ago. You could have made plans."

"That's beside the point." She composed herself and said, "Anyway, I already have made plans!"

"What plans? You never told me you made plans."

"You didn't ask. You said I should make some plans and I'm telling you I already have. Molly invited me to do some community work with her. I wouldn't call dinner in a women's shelter a festive occasion, but it should be rewarding."

"So you and Molly are in contact?" I felt threatened at the mention of the woman's name.

"We talk on the phone sometimes. I've had coffee a couple of times with her and a few of her friends."

"Why didn't I know all this? At least I'm honest about what's going on in my life, Nina." Honesty is the easiest and weakest virtue to have to fall back on, but any port in a storm.

"I thought you'd be upset, knowing how she feels about you and all."

"Then she really doesn't like me?"

"Grow up, George. She resents your relationship with her son, that's all. She'd be much happier if I was going to Vermont to visit

Paul. Then she would have invited *you* to the shelter for dinner."

You can't argue with a Ph.D., and when she put it that way, it seemed to me I was getting the better end of the deal so I kept my mouth shut.

THE day before the Christmas vacation, Mr. Simmons called me into his office and generously offered me a seat. He'd tried to dress up his tweed suit with a red-and-green bowtie in the shape of a sprig of holly, but all it did was draw attention to his ears jutting out from his head a few inches above it. He sat down behind his cluttered desk and started to play with a toy truck he kept in his drawer. I took it as a bad sign right off that he was carefully avoiding looking at me.

"Soooo, George," he said, with what seemed like all his concentration focused on the toy, "are you looking forward to your vacation?"

"I think so, Mr. Simmons," I said. "I'm not a big fan of Christmas, but otherwise it should be nice."

"Well, that's good to hear," he said thoughtfully. "That's very good to hear. All of my daughters are coming home for the holidays so Mrs. Simmons and I are stocking up for a full house. I like a full house."

"Especially in poker," I said, but he didn't respond.

"In any case, I hope the news I'm going to give you won't spoil your holiday. I truly mean that, George."

As uncomfortable as I'd felt from the start, at the sound of these words, I pictured myself slowly being lowered into a pool of something slimy. "Oh, I'm sure it won't," I said.

"Good, then I won't beat around the bush."

"Or the Christmas tree," I said, grinning moronically.

"Yes, well . . ." Not even an attempt to crack a smile or look me in the eyes. "The fact is, the administrative board has decided to suspend you for the spring term. We came to the decision after meeting with the parents a couple of weeks ago and then deliberating independently for many long hours. And just for the record, it was not a unanimous decision."

I was staring at a picture over his desk one of his daughters had drawn when she was seven years old. It was a weird black bird with thick red crayon strokes encircling it. If one of our students had drawn it they'd immediately have been taken for psychological testing. "I don't understand," I said after a long silence. "I mean, the business with Doran turned out all right. His parents are even back together. I should be promoted to marriage counselor."

He cleared his throat politely at my joke. At least he was showing signs of life. "I thought you were calling me in for a raise," I said, and then started to laugh loudly to make sure he knew I was only kidding.

"The whole incident raised so many concerns among the parents, we have to make a gesture to show them we're not letting this kind of thing go unreprimanded. I'm glad Daniel and Theodora are back together, but I'm sure you'll agree that has nothing to do with the basic problem." He tugged at the ridiculous bowtie as if it were strangling him. "If you think you're being scapegoated, you're probably right, but keep in mind the initial error was your own."

A hard fact to dispute, seeing as it was true. Still, I felt I was up to my neck in the pool of slime and was about to go under. I saw myself standing behind a counter at Nedick's grilling hot dogs in a funny-looking hat. "I've been a good teacher here for two years, Mr. Simmons. The parents have been pleased and the kids love me. I'd think you'd give me another chance before you fire me."

"Oh, I never said anything about firing, George. Please don't exaggerate. I said 'sus-*pend*'." He said the word as if he were giving me a lesson in phonetics. "There's quite a difference." He took off the tie and opened up his collar. He seemed tremendously relieved now that he'd broken the news. "If you want to know the truth, I've never liked Christmas very much either. But I don't tell that to too many people."

Being taken into his confidence on his opinion of the birth of Jesus seemed like paltry consolation for having to face putting together another résumé. I had a strong urge to reach across the desk and yank on his Dumbo ears. I was amazed I'd been oblivious to his ugliness for two whole years. Judging from the picture on the wall behind him, he was probably a sadistic father, too. He hadn't said where all the daughters were coming home *from*, but now that I thought about it, it was probably Creedmore.

"Anyway, we'll reconsider hiring you again in the fall."

"Fall? What about summer?"

"Well, once you're on unemployment, you might as well stay on until the fall. It's all the same thing."

"Look," I said. "There has to be some other gesture you can make to the parents. Maybe you could hire a security guard or something."

"Like a department store! That's a very funny idea." He stood up from behind his desk, announcing that our little chat was over. "So what are you planning to do for the holidays, George?" he asked brightly.

"I was planning to go to Vermont for a few days, but now I suppose I should stick around and try to get a job as a Santa Claus at Macy's."

He laughed heartily and patted me on the shoulder as he ushered me out. "I don't think you're round enough for that. I'd say an elf was more in your line."

I left the school in a daze. I didn't feel up to facing Melissa so I snuck out of the building without saying goodbye to her and headed down Madison Avenue, pushing my way through the crowds of shoppers. It was a cold night and the few patches of sky I could see between the buildings were colorless and joyless. I'd never been fired from a job before, and I felt humiliated and ashamed. Surely every one of the well-dressed jet-setters I bumped into could tell I was incompetent and unemployed, incapable of holding down even the lowly job of kindergarten teacher.

I kept walking south on Madison into thicker and thicker crowds of people. It was close to five o'clock, and the offices were beginning to dump their victims out into the streets. By now the subway would be too jammed to find a seat and the bookstores would be too mobbed to browse. Every step I took I bumped into another employed person, in front of me or in back of me or on either side of me. I looked up for relief, but the buildings seemed to be curving in over the sidewalks, sealing off the sky. Down the avenue the traffic was clogged for miles.

When I was nine years old, my parents took Frank and me to New York for a long weekend. We stayed at a small dilapidated hotel in Times Square my mother, the travel agent for the trip, had read about in a book called *New York on Five Dollars a Day*. We all slept in one room, and my father put his money, my mother's purse, and the watch I'd been given for my seventh birthday in his pillowcase the first night. After one day of struggling through lines at every major tourist site in the city, it was decided New York was too big and too noisy and too dangerous to venture forth in. We spent the rest of the weekend in the ugly hotel room on the sixteenth floor looking out the tiny windows at the traffic-jammed streets below. That was my first impression of New York, and now, struggling down Madison Avenue, it came back to me vividly.

I fought my way to the end of a line at the nearest phone booth and prayed someone in front of me would collapse from exhaustion. When I finally made it to the phone, I dropped the first two quarters I took out of my pocket. The receiver stunk like expensive cheese.

Nina wasn't home.

A blast of sharp wind swirled down the tunnel of buildings and hit me on the head like a brick. I took out my woolen cap and yanked it over my ears.

"Hey, are you making a call or doing a costume change?" someone in the line called out.

Timothy's line was busy. Quickly, before the mob behind me attacked, I made a collect call to Paul.

"George?" he asked with concern. "Are you all right?"

"Listen," I said, "I'm wearing a pair of worn jeans and a peacoat and a black watch cap. Ha ha, only kidding."

"Are you in a phone booth?"

"I'm in the lobby of the Plaza. I was having high tea and I thought I'd just give you a call."

"Have you been drinking, George?"

First impressions are impossible to live down. "Calm down, will you? I was stuck in a crowd of people and I needed to hear a familiar voice. You don't mind, do you?"

"Of course not. But you sound a little frantic. Did something happen?"

"Nothing happened. I just needed to hear a familiar voice, that's all."

"I'm glad you thought of me."

"You were the first person to cross my mind."

"You're still coming up tomorrow, aren't you?"

"I'll be in at four."

"We'll pick you up. I have great plans for the week, George. Gabie can't wait for you to get here."

"I can't wait to see him."

The second I hung up the receiver, someone leaped on it as if it were the last drop of water in the city. I walked along the uncrowded edge of the curbstone a little calmed. I tried to relax every muscle in my body to stop my teeth from chattering, but it didn't work. I walked along the curb all the way to where the back of Saint Patrick's was lit up and looming like a huge melting candle. Eventually I stepped out into the street and hailed a cab. I counted the money in my wallet and gave the driver the Brooklyn address. Then I fell apart against the cold, cracked Naugahyde seat.

23

PAUL and Gabriel were standing under the roof of the drugstore when my bus pulled in the next afternoon. The town was quiet and dusky. It was snowing lightly, the fat flakes dropping lazily into the street, slowly and silently burying the whole town. The streets looked softer than when I'd seen them in the fall. I stepped off the bus and sucked the cold air into my lungs, as if to freeze some part of me. Gabriel came dashing out from under the roof and I picked him up and squeezed him in my arms, flattening out the puff of his down jacket.

"I was afraid you weren't going to make it," Paul called out. "After that frantic phone call I was afraid you were having second thoughts about coming."

He was standing under the overhang of the roof with his hands stuck, monklike, into the sleeve of his jacket and his neck wrapped in an electric-blue muffler.

"I was panicked by shoppers," I said. "Too many people and not enough sidewalk."

"Well—welcome to Vermont, George," he said and swept an arm toward the nearly empty street.

I wanted to embrace him, feel the warmth of him through my jacket and cry on his shoulder about the loss of my job, but I noticed there was a salesperson in the window of the drugstore, a demented-looking man wearing a pastel-green lab coat, and it seemed like the wrong moment. We flung my duffle bag into the back of the truck and drove across the bridge and onto the wooded roads up to his house.

The peaks of the mountains to the north were covered in deep shadows the color of lilacs. From behind there was a bright yellow glow of the sun as it set, but there was no warmth in the light. It was a lull in the afternoon, a sudden icing that happens at four o'clock on certain sharp winter days. I rolled down my window and stuck my head out and let the winter air wash over me. In the time it had taken to get to Vermont, I'd forgotten what Manhattan looked like. I knew then I wouldn't get around to telling Paul about losing my job. I didn't want to spoil the time we had together, and it didn't matter here. Here it was easy for me to pretend there wasn't an unemployment line waiting for me back in Brooklyn. I let out a loud shout of relief and watched the truck plow through the snow, sending up a powdery white spray.

THE week with Paul and Gabriel passed quietly and peacefully. The three of us spent most of our time aimlessly wandering around the house, preparing huge meals and watching movies on Paul's video machine. It snowed almost every day and the temperature never got above freezing, but I remember the week as one of constant warmth—the sun streaming in through the windows, the wood stove filling the house with scented heat, Paul's body against mine under his down comforter. I slept immoderate amounts that week. I'm an insomniac by nature, and it's only when I'm with someone who puts me at ease that I feel relaxed enough to sleep long hours instead of staying awake gnashing my teeth, trying to figure out what to do next to impress him.

Afternoons I'd sit in the window seat overlooking the snowy field and read until I dozed off, waking up after the sun had set and the pane had turned cold. At night, when Gabriel had fallen asleep, Paul and I walked along the paths through the woods watching the stars in the crowded, speckled sky and the yellow lights of lone houses glowing in the distance. I liked walking beside him, banging into him and telling him stories to make him laugh. Mostly I told him tales that exaggerated the disasters of my youth. I didn't care that he believed less than half of what I said; I just liked to hear him laugh.

"You're making it all up, George," he'd say. "I can tell you're just making it up so you'll sound ridiculous."

But I'd look over at him and he'd be smiling. Sometimes he looked so adorable walking beside me I couldn't resist crashing against him and knocking him down into the snow.

MOST of Paul's friends turned out to be escapees from Manhattan or New Jersey or Boston—stolid, urbane types who read *The New York Times* religiously and kept copies of *Interview* and *Vanity Fair* in their bathrooms beside the organic no-flush toilets. The long, straight hair on the women and the straggly Lytton Strachey beards on the men notwithstanding, I felt like a hick in their midst. Their accents were refined and their words well chosen whether they were talking about a gallery opening on Madison Avenue or a load of damp maple delivered to their woodpile the week before. As a group they reminded me of a large, diverse family. They'd been together for so long and had shared so much they took their closeness for granted and seemed vaguely bored by one another.

On Christmas Day we went to a potluck dinner at a renovated old farmhouse miles into the woods. The house smelled of pine needles and spiced wine. The bathroom was the size of my Brooklyn apartment and had a hot tub built into the floor. An eight-foot Christmas tree lit with dripping white candles glowed in the center of the vast living room. It all looked and smelled like my fantasy of a Victorian Christmas feast, even though the business with the tree seemed like a dangerous affectation.

Given the commune history of most of Paul's friends, I'd expected a relaxed, casual party, but most of the women were dressed in elaborate long dresses—chic secondhand things with sequins and shoulder pads and rhinestoned belts—and the men all had on dark suits and starched white shirts. It looked like a grand costume party. After listening in on a few conversations I realized that most everyone there was relieved to be finally spared the burdens of youth and nonconformity. They felt liberated by their three-piece suits and velvet skirts.

As far as I could see, most of them had replaced nonconformity with children as the major distractions in their lives. There were handfuls of squalling babies, screaming four- and five-year olds and a couple of uncomfortable eleven-year-olds hovering on the edge of puberty. All did their best to try and make me feel a part of the group by pointedly including me in conversations and asking questions about this or that upcoming New York event, which I, of course, knew nothing about.

What surprised me most was the zeal with which they were all pursuing their entrepreneurial business endeavors: the Rolfing practice, the solar-panel installation company, the soybean-processing plant, the Saab dealership. They were far more concerned with making money than I thought anyone living in the country should be, even if their means of doing so were unusual. Paul seemed apart from them, more careworn than most and more disillusioned. They'd all actively changed their lives, updated their images, cast off their ideals happily, while his life had been changed for him by the times. Maybe Gabriel was his attempt to keep up with his friends, with their marriages and their families, but if so, the effort had failed. Gabriel was treated with the special love and attention always lavished on outsiders, minorities, and visitors from New York.

"We think it's wonderful Paul's seeing someone from the city," one woman said to me, speaking for what cross section of the group I couldn't tell. "He's so serious sometimes."

I suppose she meant depressed. She'd cornered me against one end of the dessert table and was distractedly eating soft butter cookies as she spoke. She told me Paul was very fond of me and then waited for me to respond while she ate another cookie. I looked across the room at Paul in his sweatshirt as he listened to a man in a bow tie and smiled at me. I had the impression this woman was telling me Paul's friends were behind him and I'd better not let him down. I unconsciously reached up and started to tug at my eyebrows. "Well," I said uncomfortably, "I'm fond of him, too." "Good," she said. "Good. That's good. I'm glad to hear it. Why don't you try these cookies, George, they're wonderful."

Of course I immediately wanted to flee from the room, firetrap that it was. It's one thing when someone has designs on you, but when his friends get in the act, the pressure becomes stupefying. I started to count up in my head the number of affectionate pushes into the snow I'd given Paul in the past few days and wondered if they could be considered misleadingly intimate.

Later in the week I met the man who was setting up a school and spent the better part of a day surveying the grounds with him. He was a sincere and friendly person who struck me as oddly detached from education. He saw the school strictly as a business venture. He was putting up the money and converting an old farmhouse and the adjacent barn into classroom space; the teachers he hired would collectively make the school policies as they went along. The students would come from the families of former hippies from miles around who wanted to provide their kids with a better education than the local public schools offered and a more liberal one than they'd get at the church-affiliated private schools. Among the more salient advice I gave him for setting up the preschool was not to bother getting Marimekko pillows for the kindergarten.

"Oh, of course not," he said, laughing. "Jill, the weaver you met the other night, already has a contract for handsewn pillows and quilts, all made out of pure cotton and naturally dyed with flowers and organic vegetable roots."

Before he dropped me off at Paul's house, he told me that he hadn't yet hired a preschool teacher. "You should send me a résumé. You'd have a lot of say in the way the school runs. Except for the pillows."

I told him I'd never had a say in anything of importance and reminded him it was a five-hour commute from New York.

"So, what did you think of the school?" Paul asked me when I got in.

"I wouldn't call it a school yet. It's still a barn."

After he'd pumped me for my impressions for the next ten minutes, he came out and asked if Samuel had said anything about a job.

"A job?" I asked as if I'd never heard the word before. "I already have a job—you know I have a job."

"I know, but I meant at his school. He told me he was going to mention he was looking for a preschool teacher."

"Well, he did that," I said. "But it's not exactly a convenient commute for me, and anyway, I already have a job, don't forget that. I can't just go back and quit."

Toward the end of the week, a tense silence developed between Paul and me. Neither one of us was willing to talk about our relationship and it seemed inappropriate to talk about anything else. I didn't know what to say to him. I hated the thought of leaving, of going back to New York and saying goodbye to him and to Gabriel, but I couldn't bring myself to admit it aloud. Once you talk about something like that, you're done for. You sink into a swamp of responsibility you can never get out of. At least, if you don't mention your feelings, you can claim a misunderstanding later on when the demands start to hit the fan. And besides, there's no cold shower more effective than a long, serious discussion of love. Or whatever it was I felt for him.

When we walked through the woods on my last night, we kept our hands in our pockets and our eyes on the trees. Whenever I did look at Paul, I'd smile to myself, amused that he and I were the same height. In the past I'd look at a boyfriend standing beside me and see a shoulder or an armpit and it was nice to see a face for a change. I kept meaning to tell him, but even that much stuck in my throat.

ON the day I was leaving, Paul and I finally had our serious talk, which, like most of the serious talks I've had, occurred as I was walking out the door. He was driving me to the bus stop and it had taken me longer than I'd expected to get ready, probably because I was stalling. By the time I had my bag packed and was standing by the door, Gabriel had fallen behind. He was up in his loft scurrying around, trying to find his coat.

"Hurry up, Gabie!" Paul shouted in a harsh tone that unsettled me. "You're going to make George late. Hurry up, damn it."

"Listen," I said, "it doesn't matter. If I miss this bus I can wait around for a few hours and take the next one out."

Paul merely frowned at me and yelled up to the loft again. With his coat in his hand, Gabriel slid down the pole from his room and landed feet first on top of the plastic fireman's hat I'd brought him for a present. The thing made a sickening crunch and caved in like a cracked skull.

Gabriel let out a terrified screech, as if it were his own head that had cracked. He sat on the floor and hammered his fists into the collapsed hat.

"I'm sorry, Gabriel," I said. "I'll get you another one and mail it to you. You'll probably have it in less than a week."

He was too far gone for consolation. Paul picked him up and rubbed his back with a gloved hand. "It isn't the hat he's crying about. He's upset you're leaving."

"I'll be back, Gabie."

"When?" Paul barked.

"I don't know. I'm sure I'll see you both again. I hope so, anyway."

"I'm glad you hope you'll see us both again," Paul said sarcastically. "When do you think you might bless us with your presence, Mr. Mullen?"

"I don't know," I said. "Maybe the next time I get an invitation."

"George, how the hell am I supposed to know if it's okay to invite you back or not invite you back or anything else? Every time I say something nice to you, I see you cringe. It's like you've got a lover back in Brooklyn and I'm being some kind of home-wrecker. I don't know how I'm supposed to treat this relationship or arrangement or whatever it is that you have with Nina."

I took off my coat. Fighting with someone in a wood-heated house wearing a calf-length woolen coat is not something I'd recommend.

"Oh," he snapped. "Now you're staying?"

I put the coat back on.

"Well, you could at least wait until Gabie has calmed down before you rush us out of the house."

"You're bonkers," I said. I slumped down on the bench beside the door and took off my hat. "Why didn't you let out some of this rage before I practically had one foot on the bus?"

"I didn't want to spoil the few days we had together." He put Gabriel on the floor and he scurried up the ladder to his loft with the hat clutched in his hand. "So while we're on the subject, George, what is your arrangement with Nina?"

"You know what it is," I said. I was hoping he did, because I was incapable of discussing it intelligently.

"No, I don't. Why don't the two of you just get married and make it legal?"

"Listen," I said, "if anyone should talk about marriage, it's you.

You're the one who has all these married friends with their kids. Don't force me to the altar just because you want to keep up with them."

"Oh? And who are you keeping up with, George? Who's this marriage of yours pleasing? At least I'm looking for a relationship that makes some kind of sense, that isn't some celibate romantic fantasy. How long do you think you're going to be satisfied with that?"

He was standing in front of me with his hands jammed into the pockets of his pants. He had on jeans that made his hips look especially narrow and work boots with a two-inch heel. I was crumpled on the bench with my feet splayed out in front of me and my pants pinching me in the crotch. His hair was a little dirty and greasy and his eyes were lined with exhaustion, and I just stopped listening to what he was saying and concentrated on how attractive he looked at that moment—not handsome or flawlessly featured, but attractive; sexy and slightly bloated from a week of too much food and sleep, and completely unconcerned about the way he looked.

"I'm sorry, Paul," I finally said. "I have trouble thinking about long-term plans, that's all."

"You have trouble thinking about a lot of things, George, that's obvious. For example, you haven't given a second of thought to how Gabriel feels. You just callously befriend him and then move on. You remind me of Roger sometimes."

I knew I was in trouble when he started comparing me to an old lover. "Don't compare me to someone I've never met, or I'll take it as a compliment."

Gabriel stuck his head over the edge of the loft. "I think we can fix this hat," he said calmly.

"You see," I said. "It wasn't me, it was the hat."

Paul glared at me. "It wasn't the hat. It was you. He loves you. He loves you."

"Look..."

"I'm not talking about him, George, and you know it. I'm talking about me. *I* love you."

The proclamation was made in the most disgruntled voice imaginable. "I'll cherish that," I said.

"And I'm getting a little tired of your constant sarcasm, too, if you want to know the truth."

"I had a bad week in New York. I'm sorry. I probably shouldn't have come up here at all."

"What happened before you came up here? Why did you make that frantic call?"

I took off my coat and settled myself comfortably on the bench. I told him about Doran and his parents, about Howard and Melissa, about the aborted dancing lesson with Nina. I started talking and I just rambled on. I couldn't shut myself up. I didn't care if I was boring him or not, if he had any interest in what I was saying on not. When I'd finally finished, I felt more relieved than I would have imagined. I felt satisfied. I looked up at him expecting him to console me.

"Do you mean all of this has been going on and you didn't tell me?" he asked.

"I didn't want to spoil the time we had together." The sentence sounded vaguely familiar.

"Well, I guess I know now how important I am to you. You lose your job and all this other shit is going on and you don't even say a word about any of it to me. I'm glad to know you have so much confidence in me. I'm thrilled to find out we're on such intimate terms."

I'd expected him to come over and comfort me, offer some tenderness. I'd even arranged myself so he wouldn't trip over my feet when he rushed across the room. This response was entirely motivated by self-interest. I felt ridiculous. "Don't you think you're being a little selfish?" I asked.

"Of course I'm being selfish, George. I'm in love."

I stormed out of the house and across the front yard, sinking into snow up to my knees. The bottom half of my coat was white when I slumped into the front seat of his truck. At least there was some satisfaction in knowing I wasn't entirely off my rocker in knowing once and for all that nothing motivates selfishness, lack of consideration, and mean words more quickly or completely than love. At least Nina and I understood the limits of our relationship. At least we knew what we could expect from one another, which, even if it wasn't much, was more than endless selfish devotion.

Paul drove into town wildly and silently. Gabriel sat between us laughing hysterically as we bounced over the narrow, bumpy road. The bus was loading as we pulled in front of the drugstore. I kissed Gabriel goodbye, jumped out of the truck, and handed the driver my ticket as they were slamming the luggage compartments shut. From my window seat I watched Paul drive the black pickup out of town in a cloud of snow. I was infuriated that he hadn't at least waited for the bus to pull out of town.

24

"WHY didn't you tell me this before you left for Vermont?"

"Don't start on me, Nina. I'll only admit to a certain number of errors in judgment." Actually, the number was infinite but I wasn't in the mood for self-deprecation.

She advised calling a legal clinic to see if there was some breach-of-contract complaint I could file against the school, but it wasn't the kind of thing I'd ever do because, one, I was resigned to my guilt in the affair, and, two, it would be too humiliating to go to the courts begging for a job.

"It's better than begging in the streets," she said.

"I didn't have that in mind either. There's always unemployment insurance."

She looked at me doubtfully. She was sewing a Spandex panel into the front of a pair of ugly stretch pants to accommodate her new bulk. In the week I'd been in Vermont, her stomach had blossomed to the proportions of a prize pumpkin. She looked as if a spring inside her had sprung, as if the baby had kicked its way into a larger home. Her face had a new shine, a glow under the skin that lit up her cheeks and her eyes. She claimed it had nothing to do with the baby; it was related to the amounts of work she was getting done on her dissertation.

Molly had given her the name of a doctor in the neighborhood whom she considered to be reliable, and Nina had made an appointment to see her. I was relieved someone had talked her out of seeing a midwife, but I would have been happier if it had been me instead of Molly, my pint-sized nemesis, whom she'd turned to for advice.

"You don't trust doctors," I reminded her. "They make even more than shrinks and once they're covered by malpractice insurance, they don't care what they do."

"Molly trusts this woman, George, and I trust her."

"She's probably an old buddy of Stalin."

"You should have told me this sooner, George. I could have been working on finding you a job while you were lost in the woods."

"I don't need a job, Timothy," I lied. "I can get unemployment."

"You can't live on unemployment. Besides, this situation is setting you up for becoming a househusband and I refuse to let that happen."

We were sitting in Madison Square Garden at a benefit performance of Ringling Brothers Circus and Timothy was in a bad mood. He hated the circus almost as much as he hated the thought of walking into Madison Square Garden, but the money was going for AIDS research and he was committed to the cause. I myself wasn't a big circus fan either. I could barely see what was going on miles below, and judging from all the noise and confusion, it didn't seem like anything I'd care for anyway.

"Frankly, George, this might turn out to be the best thing for you. Maybe now you'll be forced to get a real job instead of playing school all day."

"What would you suggest I look for? I can't use the school as a reference and I can't say I was in a coma for the past two years."

The person behind us tapped Timothy on the shoulder and asked him if he could slouch down in his seat a little lower so he could see the show.

"There's nothing to see," Timothy told him. "A bunch of people doing things with animals. Believe me, you don't want to see. Anyway, George, in New York they won't even notice a gap of two years. Time passes differently here. As for this Paul person, I'm happy he showed his true colors. When are you going to start listening to me and stop chasing after romantic impossibilities? Everyone is out for himself. Period. And if you don't play along, you've had it."

"Paul's called four times in the past four days."

"Wonderful. Is your steamer trunk packed and ready to be shipped north?"

"I don't talk to him."

Nina had strict instructions to tell both Paul and Melissa I was out at the movies whenever they called. I couldn't face Melissa's sympathies or Paul's apologies or arguments. As it stood now, I could make a clean, unemotional break with him and spare myself a few tears. The only clear notion I had in my head of what I wanted to do for the next several months was to lie in bed reading long Victorian novels and eating roasted peanuts. It wouldn't help pay the rent, but at least it would keep my mind off the various disasters falling in my path.

Down below us, someone came rocketing out of a cannon and landed in a net.

"George!" Timothy grabbed my wrist. "I have the perfect job for you. Just to fill in for a little while." For a minute I thought he'd been overcome with excitement at the performance.

"If it's grilling hot dogs at Nedick's I'm not interested."

"Nedick's? What are you talking about? Listen; I have a friend..."

The man behind us tapped Timothy on the shoulder again and asked him if we'd mind keeping our mouths shut so he could hear.

"They're doing *Hamlet* in the middle ring," Timothy whispered to me and then continued on softly. "Anyway, this friend of mine owns a marketing company. She sets up demonstrations of products in stores around the city. She pays under the table. All you do is call the office every morning and see if she has any work for you that day. It's like substitute teaching except you're not risking your life."

"Demonstrations? Picketing and like that?"

"Please. You pass out samples of things, cheese, candy, show people how some toy works, tell them it's wonderful, and try to get them to buy. You've seen people doing it in stores. It's a little like modeling."

"Modeling? Since when do people model cheese?"

"If you have the right attitude, anything can be modeling."

He wrote down the woman's number and promised me that if he called her first, I could be on the payroll by Monday morning. We left the circus as some woman in a tutu was torturing a dog with fire. Timothy said the terrier reminded him of one he'd had as a child and he couldn't stand to watch.

THE invitation to Frank's wedding arrived in an envelope bulging with papers and addressed to both me and Nina. Inside, Frank had included a check for four hundred dollars and a note that read: "Buy yourself a nice suit, Georgie. If there's any money left, get Nina some flowers."

Inside the same envelope there was also a postcard of a desolate beach with one lone palm tree off to the side and the word SARASOTA splashed across the bottom in bright red letters. My mother never mailed anything while she was away because she only trusted the postal service in Boston.

"Dear George," she wrote. "Had a lovely flight down including a nice baked chicken and a piece of apple pie that would put your Aunt Ida's to shame. Rain so far every day and I've never seen more bugs. I should have brought calamine lotion instead of suntan oil."

On the very bottom, in a tiny scrawl, she'd written, "Don't be a fool! If Frank sends money — *take it.*"

THE demonstration job turned out to be one of the more humiliating experiences of my life. Timothy's friend was a brassy business-woman who told me I could have the job if I agreed to do something about my messy hair. "People hold to a certain standard of hygiene even when they're taking something for nothing," she informed me.

My first day of employment I spent in the basement of Macy's making peanut butter in a souped-up three-hundred-dollar blender. The idea was to try and convince the passersby that this one culinary feat alone would save them enough money to make the machine an economical purchase. "If you sell fifty of them," my new boss informed me, "you get one for yourself."

I fared a little better at Barney's the next day, wandering around the first floor offering to spray shoppers with some designer's latest cologne creation "for the Sensitive Man," a breed which Barney's specialized in.

Wednesday was a home computer even a child could operate, a claim I'm sure I could have proven if I'd managed to figure out how to turn the thing on.

By Thursday I was praying the bottom would fall out of the economy and I'd be spared another modeling session.

"We have cheese for you today," Timothy's friend told me brightly over the phone. "The Red Apple on One Hundred and Third and Broadway. Should be an easy one—there are plenty of hungry people in that neighborhood."

The "cheese" was a nacho-flavored plastic that shot out of a tube and could be arranged in decorative patterns on crackers and vegetables "for a real Mexican treat." It was a dismal day. My index finger developed a severe cramp from aiming the nozzle on the tube, and my best dancing shoes were practically ruined by the sawdust on the floor.

Around six o'clock, as I was getting ready to close down the cantina, I turned around and felt my throat tighten as I spotted a familiar figure pushing a wobbling shopping cart down the aisle in front of me. Tired and worn down as he looked, it was unmistakably Howard. The suit he had on was hanging limply off his shoulders and the collar of his shirt was loose. His shopping cart was filled with paper products and frozen dinners and two copies of the advance sheets of the *New York Law Reports*. I called out to him, but he seemed to be in a trance. He turned his cart around with difficulty and headed down the aisle.

"Howard! Over here, Howard!"

He turned around slowly and squinted down the length of the aisle. "George!" He gave the cart a shove away from him and came over to the display table. "What are you doing in this neighborhood?"

"Care to try some nacho cheese spray?"

"Why are you doing this? Is something the matter? Do you and Nina need money?"

"Everything's fine. It's one of those long stories."

I was so delighted to see him, I dropped an open box of crackers onto the floor and crushed them under my foot. "I've got a great idea, Howie," I said as I picked up the mess. "Why don't you take me out to dinner and we can talk."

"I'd love that, George," he said with sincerity. "I've missed you, you know. I was afraid to call and even say hello after all that... well, Melissa, for one." He grabbed the *Law Report* sheets out of his cart and walked away from the rest of what was in there. "I don't need that other crap anyway. I just didn't feel like going straight home after work. Can you believe I've sunk to the level of TV dinners? Me with my training, my five million cooking utensils and three million spice bottles and two million cookbooks. I don't even own a TV."

"It doesn't look like you're eating much of anything. You're getting pretty slim."

"Am I? I hadn't noticed. I don't notice that kind of thing anymore, George."

We walked out of the supermarket with our arms around each other and went to a rib restaurant on Ninety-third Street. Howard ate slowly and with none of his usual enthusiasm. He didn't bother to toss his tie over his shoulder, and twice he splattered it with barbecue sauce.

"So what's been going on with you?" I finally asked him, after blabbing about myself through a plate of baby backs. "You don't seem your old self."

"You know what's going on, George. You know the whole rotten story. You know all about Howard Lechter, the lousy louse. I don't sleep, I have no appetite." He picked up a rib between two fingers. "See? It does nothing for me. And I'll tell you the most tragic part: I have only myself to blame. I screwed up with Nina and then I went out and I made things worse with Melissa. The whole foundation just caved in under me. All these years I've been thinking myself so superior to the other miserable men out there, and it turns out underneath it all I'm just a prick like the rest of them." He looked up apologetically. "I'm sorry, George. I mean a shit, a real shit. Every day I deal with men who beat up their wives and their girlfriends, and you know what the difference is between them and me? I know how to make spaetzle and they don't. What difference does it make if I cook dinner for Nina when I still drive her crazy with my obnoxious personality? And I used Melissa like a towel. Like a towel. I'm an asshole. I'm sorry, George, I mean a creep. A rotten creep."

"Don't you think you're being a little hard on yourself, Howie? You loved Nina. I know that."

"Loved her? *Loved?* I love her still. I adore her. I worship her. I cherish her. She's a Dumpling."

The old Howard was rising from his loose clothing like a phoenix. I looked up from his stained tie to his enormous dark eyes filled with tears.

"Call her," I said.

He gave me a shocked look, as if the thought had never occurred to him. "And antagonize her more? I can't do that."

"Just call."

"I'll think about it, George."

"Don't think, Howard. Call. She misses you."

His lower jaw dropped down loosely. "She does? She misses me?"

"Of course she does." If Nina knew I was having this conversation with him she'd probably have decapitated me, but I couldn't resist the temptation to try and make Howard feel better. After all, Nina had admitted she thought about him. I wasn't making anything up. "I know she does, Howie."

"She really misses me?" He seemed to be fighting with his facial muscles, contorting his mouth into odd twisted shapes, but eventually his lips parted in a real smile. He opened one of the *Law Reports* and started to flip through the cases to distract himself from his joy. "I never thought she might miss me. I thought that was too much to hope for." He looked up. "Not that I hoped she'd be unhappy, but, well..." He opened a greasy napkin and blew his nose. "The spicy food," he explained.

Out on Amsterdam Avenue he made me promise I wouldn't tell Nina we'd had dinner together. He offered his legal services to help me get my job back, but I told him I was content with my new profession.

• • •

"YOU'LL never guess who I just talked to for over an hour," Nina said when I walked in the door later that night.

"Abba Eban?"

"Melissa. You have to call her, George. She's been trying to get in touch with you for weeks now."

"I'll call," I said and wearily dragged out the polish for the top of the table. I'd been hoping Howard had jumped to the phone while I was riding the subway back to Brooklyn.

"She quit her job. As soon as she found out you got fired, she quit her job. Now that's what I call having principles. Anyone can talk a big game, but when someone gives up their job for someone else's sake, that's what I call principles. I underestimated her."

I put down the polishing rag and sat at the table, stunned. I'd never done anything for Melissa that warranted such a show of devotion. I was fated to forever feel unworthy of my friends. "What's she going to do now?"

"Well, she says she's always harbored a secret desire to go to law school and she's going to spend the next month preparing for the boards."

"Law school?" Somehow I couldn't picture Melissa in a business suit standing in front of a courtroom.

"She'll be brilliant, George. She really does have her head on her shoulders, after all. I mean, there's a woman with principles. We need more lawyers like her. I'm glad to see Howard had a good influence on her, if he had anything to do with this. You know, I really feel like calling him up and telling him. Not that I intend to."

I took part of the four hundred dollars Frank had given me and bought a cheap suit at a department store off King's Highway. It was blue pinstripe in some highly flammable manmade material. I looked remarkably ordinary in it. Anyone who claims clothes don't make the man probably has a closet full of designer suits. Tax included, this rag cost $93.00, so yard for yard, it was a great value.

With the remaining cash I went down to the Village and bought

Nina a pair of enormous silver hoop earrings and a bracelet to match. I had them wrapped in fancy silver-and-white paper and gave them to her, telling her they were "wedding presents."

THE next week my modeling career came to an abrupt halt. My Monday assignment was to demonstrate lamb's-wool bicycle seats at Macy's. There was a tandem bike set up in the sporting-goods department with seats covered in matted-looking wool. I had to sit on the front end and pedal for eight hours and try to convince the passing shoppers to get on the back end and treat their behinds to a soft ride. I didn't thrill to the idea of this forced entry into the Tour de France, but I got on and started to pump. After less than an hour, I'd sweated through my shirt and felt as if I were about to pass out. Dedicated worker that I am, I would have kept at it for at least another hour if I hadn't noticed the seats were manufactured in South Africa. Politics had never seemed so important. I jumped off the bike as if it were headed for Niagara Falls and rushed to the nearest line behind a phone booth.

"How's it going?" Timothy's friend asked me.

"It isn't going," I told her. "Why didn't you tell me those seat covers are made in South Africa?"

"I didn't know and I don't see what difference it makes to you."

I told her I had no strong objections to hemorrhoids, but I wasn't interested in bringing them on prematurely just so the government of South Africa could ship another few thousand blacks off to the homelands. "Don't you have any Danish cheese I could pass out?"

"We have lamb's-wool bicycle seats and the clients have already paid me. Get back on that tandem, George."

"I'm sorry. I claim conscientious objector status."

"Fine. You can claim unemployment while you're at it."

I was becoming a pro at getting fired; this time I was overjoyed. I gave a momentary thought to how disappointed with me Timothy would be, and then I went downstairs and bought a grilled hot dog at the Nedick's on the corner.

25

IT was snowing the morning Nina and I were to go to Boston for Frank's wedding. The minute I woke up and saw a drift piled in the corner of the window, I panicked. As much as I hate flying in any weather, the thought of flying in a snowstorm instantly gave me morning sickness. For two days I'd been trying to talk Nina into taking the train, but I never told her the real reason, as fear of flying seems like such an unsophisticated phobia.

I dragged myself out of bed and randomly stuffed as many clothes as I could into my duffle bag. I put on my new suit and slicked back my hair with an expensive French fixative I'd bought for the occasion. By the time Nina came into the living room in blue jeans and a billowy peasant blouse, I was playing with a plate of cold fried eggs. She was carrying her suitcase in front of her with both hands. Her outlined belly looked huge.

"Are you going like that?" I asked, admittedly concerned.

"My dress is in the suitcase."

"What about the plane?"

"What *about* the plane, George?" She sat down opposite me and began to pick at my English muffin.

"Nothing," I said. I was brought up to believe you never get on an airplane in anything less than Sunday best, to show respect for the miracle of flight and to make sure you don't disgrace the family name when they scrape your body off the runway. "I just thought you might want to look a little spiffier, that's all."

"We're taking the shuttle to Boston, not embarking on the *Queen Elizabeth*. You're going to wrinkle that suit and get the shirt all sweaty."

She spoke in such a gentle tone of voice, I immediately felt like an overdressed horse's ass. I took the plate of food and dumped it into the garbage in the kitchen. "All right," I shouted. "If you want to know the truth, I'm afraid of airplanes."

She came into the kitchen and put her arms tightly around my shoulders. "You're nervous about the wedding."

"I'm not nervous about the wedding; the wedding is on the ground."

"You haven't seen your parents in over a year."

"I haven't been on a plane since I was fifteen."

"Your relatives are going to ask when you're getting married, if there are any girls waiting in the wings. And we should have told your mother I'm pregnant." She ran her fingers through the stiff hair I'd combed behind my ears. "I like you better with your hair mussed. I can't recognize you when your hair's not a mess." She stood back and examined my face. "I'm glad you have no idea how handsome you are, Georgie."

"Don't be ridiculous," I said. "I'm overdressed, and Frank got all the looks in my family."

IN the end I wore a pair of woolen pants, two layers of casual but clean sweaters, and three scarves my mother had given me for birthday presents wound together into a thick cord around my neck. The flights had been delayed due to weather, and by the time we took off the sky was a bright, cold blue and the snow along the sides of the runway was sparkling in the afternoon sun. Nina squeezed my hand as the plane shuddered down the tarmac. I looked out the window and watched the entire vast city fall off into the distance in a few insignificant seconds.

Once the plane had leveled out, I found the hum of the jet engines surprisingly soothing. The air in the cabin was thin and dry and still, and with my seat reclined and my eyes lightly closed, I drifted into a reverie of Frank standing at the altar in a tuxedo with a lit cigarette dangling from his fingers. I've never enjoyed weddings, and the more I thought about this one, the more angry I became. I was jealous, admittedly, of all the attention and enthusiasm and gifts and forced gaiety about to be lavished on my brother for marrying some woman he'd known for a few months, while my relationships were a trial to have acknowledged, let alone celebrated. The fact that my relationships were a trial even for me to endure was completely beside the point.

I suppose I also felt abandoned by Frank in a curious way. There was a point in our childhood when we were best friends, when we spent hours together wandering around the suburbs, drinking beer and sneaking into movies and generally making my mother's life miserable, and even though I had no illusions about reliving my youth, this wedding seemed to be putting an end to it with a finality that bothered me. When the pilot announced we were about to land, I was disappointed; I wanted more time to stew in my bile.

"I'm not ready to arrive," I told Nina as a sound like a death rattle emerged from the bottom of the plane.

"What about me?" she asked. She was flipping through a magazine without looking at a single page. "I'm pregnant and I have to make a good first impression. You've got it easy."

FRANK was standing in the airport lounge with a cigarette in one hand and a steaming Styrofoam cup clutched in the other. He was leaning against a wall anxiously tapping his feet and shaking his legs. To me, Frank has always had the looks of a big-band singer from the forties: nervous, scrawny, sexy looks that convey insolence, self-absorption, and tenderness all at once. Women generally find Frank irresistible; they want to protect him, they want to calm him down and feed him a good meal. I think it has something to do with the way his pants always bag and wrinkle at the knees.

"He looks older than you," Nina whispered to me.

"That's because he makes more money than I do," I said.

When he spotted us, he waved and dropped a woolen hat he'd had clamped under his arm. Frank was always dropping things. It was such a persistent trait, I sometimes wondered if he didn't do it on purpose. He tossed his cigarette into the coffee cup and swaggered over to us, his long coat hanging unevenly off his shoulders. "Well it's about time," he said and hugged me awkwardly.

"I thought you'd never get here. I thought Georgie probably led you onto the wrong plane," he said to Nina. "I figured you were probably in Tucson by now."

"Be nice or we'll make a scene at the wedding," I said. Frank's hair and clothes smelled of coffee and cigarettes and a suffocating, rooty aftershave he'd been wearing since he was fourteen and had got it in his head he had a problem with body odor. It was a warm, familiar smell, and as soon I hugged him I felt myself molting off about sixteen years of life experience and remembering the time Frank and I locked horns over ownership of a stray cat my mother later threw out of the house. "Frankie," I said, "this is my roommate, Nina."

"I knew she wasn't your sister, Georgie." He flashed her a suave smile and shook her hand graciously. "You're too good-looking to be part of this family."

"I hope you haven't been waiting long," Nina said softly.

"He doesn't mind," I said. "If he wasn't here drinking coffee he's be at home drinking coffee."

"We would have called but we didn't know when the plane would actually take off."

The explanation seemed unnecessary. I could tell she was being taken in by the baggy knees.

"Nervous about tomorrow, Frankie?" I asked, putting my arm around Nina's shoulder.

"Of course I'm nervous. I'm always nervous. I'm especially nervous about tomorrow." He gave Nina another of his charm-school smiles. "It's forever, isn't that what they say? But, hey, I can't wait to introduce you to Cici. She's dying to meet the two of you. She's anxious to find out the rest of what she's marrying into."

"Cici?" I said. "I thought her name was Caroline."

"Cici's my name for her. Those are her initials. At least until tomorrow, right?"

"Then she's taking your name?" Nina asked.

Frank was completely baffled. "Well, who else's name would she take? Richard Gere's?" He looked at me and laughed. "Right?"

"Some women do keep their own names when they get married," Nina told him.

"Well, some people get married in a barn, Nina, but that's not my style. I mean, if she didn't want to take my name, why would she marry me? Right, Georgie?"

"I think you'd look good in a barn, Frank, now that you mention it."

He led us through the airport, walking so quickly he had to stop twice and wait for us to catch up. I was weighted down with the two heavy bags and the burden of my sweaters and the scarves. There was never any point in trying to keep up with Frank, since he regularly drank at least nine cups of coffee before lunch.

"Has he always been this nervous?" Nina asked as we waited on the curb for him to bring the car around.

"It started at puberty," I said. "I think his hormones went wild then. I remember him as a pretty slothful child."

"He's cute, George. There's something sexy about him."

"You only think that because you know he's unavailable. If he was seriously making eyes at you it would be a different story. And he has those pants specially tailored so they'll bag like that. Don't be fooled by the knees."

After a solid twenty minutes of standing in the cold, Frank pulled up in a powder-blue luxury liner with dark leather upholstery and a white vinyl top. The car wasn't new, but it was in shining, perfect condition. Frank was a fanatic about keeping the car washed and having the oil changed and the engine tuned; it was one of the more useful things he did with his nervous energy. He'd probably kept us waiting to make sure the car was properly warmed up before daring to pull out of the parking space.

I stretched out across the wide back seat with my head on the armrest and inhaled the smell of Frank's cigarettes. The heat was on high and the radio was turned to an easy listening station, and I felt as if I'd just stepped into a comfortable cocktail lounge. Jealousy and sibling rivalry and all the rest aside, I was happy to see Frank. I find my brother charming in a way that sometimes mystifies me. I think it has to do with the fact that he embodies all the values I was brought up with and fatuously claim to have rejected. I'm drawn to Frank for the same reasons I can't help but say "Good afternoon, Sister" each time I pass a nun on the street.

As we sped along the highway, he told Nina stories about this or that adventure from our childhood which put me in a surprisingly and undeservedly good light.

"He's making it all up," I finally told Nina. "You can't believe a word he says because he was too young to remember any of it."

"I was never younger than George. He was taller, that's all."

"I was never taller than him," I said. "I wore orthopedic shoes and I had bad posture."

"I wore orthopedic shoes," he shouted. "You wore a retainer at night. And he was never older than me, Nina."

THE house I grew up in was given to my parents for their wedding present by every member of the immediate family on both sides. My mother often said she would have preferred to start off her marriage in a small apartment where she didn't feel obliged to fill the empty bedrooms right away. As it was, I think certain relatives felt their present had been unappreciated when my mother produced only two kids. It wasn't a large house, but it was divided up into an incomprehensible number of small rooms on several disjointed levels. From the outside it looked like any other characterless suburban ranch house, but overnight guests had been known to lose their bearings on a 3 A.M. trip to the bathroom, wandering up and down the various tiny staircases.

When Frank and I were kids, there was a small, buggy swamp behind the house and a shallow woods across the street, making the neighborhood look almost secluded and rural. But in recent years the neighborhood had changed so completely it was barely recognizable; the woods had been cleared and the land covered with a development of poorly constructed houses inhabited by, in my mother's words, "cheap families," and the swamp where Frank and I skated in the winter had been filled in and was now the site of a massive industrial park. At night the purple lights from the parking lots of the chemical plants and testing labs bathed the house in a weird ultraviolet glow.

As Frank pulled into my parents' driveway, I sat up in the back seat and began combing my hair. I always comb my hair before I enter my parents' house. It's an instinctual response. My mother was standing in the window, but as I waved to her, she withdrew discreetly.

"She doesn't want you to know she's been waiting there for the past two hours imagining a plane crash over Providence," Frank said.

Nina gripped my arm as I took the bags out of the trunk. "George," she said, panic-stricken, "I suddenly feel as if I should have worn a dress."

"It's the driveway. You're not used to visiting people who live in houses with driveways. You're making assumptions about my parents based on their driveway."

The three of us stood on the doorstep while Frank buzzed the hell out of the doorbell. When my mother finally opened up, she looked at us with amazement and said, "Well, I didn't expect you this early, George. What a nice surprise."

"We're three hours late," Frank said. "And we saw you standing at the window." As he walked past her on his way to the kitchen he slapped her behind affectionately.

I have a picture of my mother my father took when I was ten years old and the whole family went ice-skating at a pond in the next town. She's on skates in the picture, with her ankles turned in and her muffler blowing out behind her. She has brassy blond hair and bright red lips and her arms are thrown open for balance. She's smiling. I always expect her to look as young and happy and flushed with activity as she does in that photo, and I'm always surprised to see that she's aged, that she's let her hair go back to its natural gray-and-brown, and has put on weight. She was now in her mid-fifties and still had a healthy, youthful glow in her eyes, though lately her shoulders had begun to take on that hunched, slightly curved look Irish women are prone to in later life, particularly if they're devout in their Catholicism.

She was wearing a green sweater I'd given her for her birthday and her graying hair was sprayed into a starched updo, obviously in preparation for the wedding. The sweater didn't fit and the color wasn't flattering. She was wearing it for my sake.

"I hope you didn't come on the plane dressed like that," she whispered to me as I hugged her.

"It was only the shuttle, Ma."

"Even so, it wasn't the bus." She kissed Nina on the cheek awkwardly. Everyone in my family is a little awkward with physical affection. "I'm so happy to meet you, dear. George talks about you all the time."

"He talks about you too, Mrs. Mullen." She smiled girlishly. Nina was beginning to slip into a fifteen-year-old stance. It was the driveway.

"I'm sure he does, but I meant he says nice things about you. Anyway, you must be exhausted after the trip. At least you were on a plane and not on the highway."

Frank came strolling out of the kitchen holding a white ceramic mug with his name printed on it filled to the brim with coffee. "If we don't watch out," he said, "Ma's going to apply for a stewardess job with TWA." He put down the mug and helped Nina off with her coat. "All she talks about these days is flying. Everytime a plane goes over the house her eyes glaze over."

"Oh, I had the best time on that plane, Nina," my mother said. "It's the first time I've felt like anyone was really waiting on me, trying to make me feel comfortable. You can imagine no one around here does that."

As soon as Nina had struggled out of her coat, both my mother and Frank zeroed in on her stomach as if it were lit with neon. They looked at each other and then turned to me.

"Where's Dad?" I said.

"Excuse me, George?" Frank said, clearing his throat.

"I asked where Dad is hiding out."

"Oh, he's probably in the basement," my mother said, looking at me out of the corner of her eyes. "That's where he spends most of his time these days. He has his own apartment down there, Nina. He usually emerges for meals. Why don't you go see if he's still alive, Frank? Tell him George just got in. I'll bet you two are starving. I can fix you a nice sandwich, Nina. We've got chopped egg or cream cheese or turkey loaf."

"Ma," I said, "give us a chance to get in the door." Since Nina had taken off her coat, my mother was talking so fast I could barely understand her.

"I'd love a glass of juice, Mrs. Mullen," Nina said.

"You see there, George, the poor girl is dying of thirst. Don't pay any attention to him, Nina. We've got cranberry or orange or pineapple or root beer. You don't smoke, do you? I'm so glad. When I found out Caroline doesn't smoke I told Frank to marry her with my blessings. Why don't you get rid of those bags, George, while Nina and I fix a snack?"

"I think she figured out about the baby," Nina said as my mother opened the refrigerator door with a bang of bottles. "I knew I'd feel like this. I just feel like such an unwed mother."

"Well, that's what you are, and it never bothered you before, so just forget about it."

I hoisted up the suitcases and took them to my old bedroom. It was dark and quiet with only the faintest traces of afternoon sunlight coming in through the curtains. The twin bookcase-backed beds looked tiny and lost in the gloom. Eight years had passed since I'd moved out of the room, and nothing in it had changed. I closed the door and turned on the light behind my bed. The room had a nautical decor, with lamps on the walls that looked like ships' lanterns and wallpaper printed with bowsprits and compasses. I reached into the bookcase behind me and pulled out my copy of *Johnny Tremain*. It had been my favorite book as a child and I reread it whenever I went to visit my parents. The pages were yellowed and grease-stained. Inside the front cover my mother had inscribed, "Happy Tenth Birthday, Georgie. Keep up the good work in school. I hope this is the book you asked for. Love always, Mom and Dad. p.s. This doesn't mean I approve of the amount of time you spend reading."

As I was leafing through the book, Frank came in and slammed the door behind him. He inhaled deeply on the cigarette butt hanging out of his mouth, blew the smoke through his nostrils, and stared at me with his eyes bugged out.

"Calm down, Frankie," I said. I stretched out on the bed with my feet up. "In twenty-four hours it'll all be over and everything will be fine. And legal. You get too nervous about everything."

He lit a fresh cigarette off the one in his mouth, opened the window, and tossed the butt out to the snow. "She's pregnant," he spit out at me.

Stupidly, I took this to be a confession, though I couldn't imagine why he was confiding in me. "Well," I said after a moment, "you're doing the right thing, Frankie — you're marrying her. What more can you do?" What more could I say? I held up the copy of *Johnny Tremain*. "You know, I never forgave you for not reading this book. I kept telling you you should read it and you never would."

"Put that book down." He came over and grabbed it out of my hands. "I'm not talking about Cici, I'm talking about Nina. Nina, the one who looks like she's got a beachball under that shroud she's wearing. The one you'd have to dress in a refrigerator box to hide the fact she's pregnant."

"I don't think Nina wants to hide the fact she's pregnant. At least she hasn't for the past seven months."

"You're a real beaut, George. Every time you show up here it's something else, some new disaster we all have to suffer through. A pregnant girlfriend is the last thing I expected from you." He looked down at the book in his hand. "I read this thing. Who cares about some cripple?"

"Frank, first of all, Nina isn't my girlfriend and the baby isn't mine, and secondly, it's not your business, so I don't see what you're so upset about."

"I realize the baby isn't yours, George."

"So what's the big problem?"

"The problem is figuring out what I'm supposed to tell Cici and her whole goddamned family. I already told them the two of you aren't married."

"You told them she was my girlfriend?"

"That's right. I implied it, anyway." He looked at me self-righteously. "Well, for Christ's sake, George, I wasn't about to tell them the truth. Not before we get married."

"Why not?"

"Oh, come on. Your friends might be a bunch of open-minded liberals who don't see anything odd in your life-style, but believe me, it wouldn't make for a romantic evening for me to uncork a bottle of wine and tell Cici my brother's a homosexual. She's a sweet kid. She's the kind of girl who probably wouldn't understand what the word means."

"I hope I'll have time at the reception to explain it to her."

"You could at least do the right thing, as you yourself just said, and marry the poor girl."

"Frank, you're talking crazy. Why would I marry her?"

"For appearances, George. Did you ever hear of them?"

My mother nonchalantly strolled into the room holding a pastel-blue dress against her body. "What do you think, George? For the mother of the groom? Nina loves the color."

"Shut the door, Ma," Frank said. "We've got problems here."

"What now, Frank? You're not getting cold feet, I hope. This dress cost a fortune."

"The problem is Nina's stomach. Unless maybe you didn't notice. Unless maybe they took your eyes out on that famous plane ride."

My mother smiled. "I thought she looked a little heavy for a girl her age." She looked at me hopefully. "Well? You're not the father, are you, George?"

"Of course he's not the father," Frank said.

"I almost got excited there for a minute. So what's the problem, Frank?"

"What the hell are we going to say when these two show up at the wedding tomorrow?"

"That they're married," she said without a pause. "What else would we say?"

Frank opened a fresh pack of cigarettes and shook one out. "I already told Cici they're not married."

"So we'll say they got married in secret. It really isn't so complicated, Frank. Honestly."

I was lying on the bed in a mild state of shock listening to the two of them bickering back and forth about exactly how they planned to rearrange my life. Apparently it hadn't occurred to either one of them that I was still in the room. "Excuse me, folks," I said, "but before you close the lid, this corpse is still breathing. Nina and I are not married and we're not telling anyone we are."

My mother looked at Frank silently and then back at me. "Caroline's family is very religious, George, unlike this bunch of heathens. One of her aunts is a nun. Pretty girl, too. We can't just say you came to the wedding with a pregnant girlfriend. It would put you in a bad light."

"Well, tell them she isn't my girlfriend and the baby isn't mine, if they're all so hungry for information."

My mother and Frank laughed in perfect unison. "Be realistic, dear. Who else's baby would it be?"

"The father's?" I suggested.

"It's very simple," my mother said. "We'll tell them the two of you were married in secret. It's the kind of thing you'd do, George. You always did like to have secrets. Of course, they'll still think you got married because you had to, but they'll just have to accept the fact that you did the right thing by her in the end. People are more open-minded nowadays."

I looked at Frank nervously pacing back and forth on the worn brown carpet. He didn't look like a sexy band singer to me anymore—he looked like a weasel. His eyes were squinted from the smoke pouring out of his nostrils. I had the feeling the two of them had me locked in a cell and were reprogramming me. I took the copy of *Johnny Tremain* and put it back in the bookcase. "Listen," I said, "the whole thing is crazy and insulting. Nina and I aren't married and it doesn't bother me and it doesn't bother her and that's that. We came up here for your wedding, Frank, not ours. Everyone just relax."

"Frank's never been relaxed a day in his life," my mother said. "I don't know why you expect him to be relaxed now."

"All right," Frank said, sitting down on the bed opposite me. "As long as everything is settled. Okay, George?"

"Okay," I said. "I'm not married, Nina's not married, and if we have to be married to attend the wedding, we'll stay home."

He threw his hands in the air. "Oh, that would look great. My own brother not at my wedding.'

"Have it your way, Frankie."

"How about this?" Frank said. "Nina could stay home tomorrow."

"Well, why don't you go out and tell her it was nice meeting her but you'd like her to stay here and watch game shows all day tomorrow so she doesn't offend any of your in-laws."

My mother went to the mirror and held the dress against her chest. It was a fairly hideous, flouncy floor-length thing she'd probably been intimidated into buying by some overbearing salesperson. "I'm not sure this color really does suit me. Nina was just being polite. She's very polite, George. And all this chiffon is going to make me look fat. I never should have bought it."

Frank looked around for an ashtray in exasperation. "Ma, will you please put that rag down so we can come to a decision here? What am I going to tell Cici?"

"How do I know what you're going to tell her?" my mother shouted. "And will you please stop calling her Cici. Her name is Caroline. *Caroline*. She's the first nice girl you've gone out with and you have to give her some cheap-sounding name like Cici! Now go out there and entertain Nina. I want to talk with George. And get your father out of that goddamned basement. Maybe Nina can do therapy on him while the chicken is roasting."

ONCE Frank had closed the door behind him, my mother let out a long sigh and shook her head from side to side. She looked at me disapprovingly, her eyes narrowed. Then, very gently, she said, "Do you like this sweater, George?"

"I gave it to you for your birthday."

"I know that, dear, I just wanted to make sure you remembered. I've been wearing it all winter. They decided to keep the heat down in my office as some sort of political statement. Just my luck." She pushed at the mass of her hair as if it were separate from her body. "I'm sorry you have to see me for the first time in over a year with this bird's nest on my head. I've done everything wrong for this wedding—wrong hair, wrong dress, I didn't lose any weight."

"Don't put yourself down, Ma. Sometimes it really bothers me."

"Caroline's mother is gorgeous. She's one of those dark Italian beauties with a perfect olive complexion. She has quite a figure, too."

"You'll look fine tomorrow."

"Of course I'll look fine. I'll look fine and Caroline's mother will look gorgeous. There's a difference, you know."

Like me, my mother sustained herself on self-criticism. Most times she did it on automatic, only half seriously or half aware of what she was saying, but now as I looked at her slouched shoulders and the traces of weariness in the wrinkles around her eyes, I sensed she truly did believe she wasn't pretty or gracious enough to carry out her role tomorrow. I wanted to reach out and take hold of her hand, but I knew it would make us both uncomfortable.

"I'm sorry about all this," I said. "I didn't mean to turn this into another battle."

"It's not a tragedy, George. Frank just read three biographies of the Kennedys, and he thinks all family relations have to be melodramatic. It's only a wedding, it's not a presidential campaign. Anyway, this family doesn't have enough money to be truly tragic."

"You do understand, don't you?" I always wanted her to understand me, to at least acknowledge that much common ground between us. "You see my point, don't you, Ma?"

"Of course I see your point, and if I were in your shoes I'd probably feel the same way." She looked at her hairdo in the mirror one last time and then turned to me with a sternness that caught me off guard. "But I'm *not* in your shoes, George, and I don't feel the same way. Let me point out that you're the one who lives with Nina and you're the one who brought her to this wedding. I can't tell you how delighted I was when I found out you were bringing her. I assumed we'd quietly pass her off as your girlfriend. All I'd have to say is, 'They're roommates,' and shrug, and everyone would just chalk it up to living in the big city and I'd look like a good liberal parent to boot. When I saw she was pregnant I was even more thrilled. I figured there'd be no question about telling Caroline's family the two of you were married."

"Well, you figured the wrong thing, Ma, that's all."

"Does the father of the baby live with you?"

I shook my head.

"So it's just the two of you? I really don't understand. And don't tell me about it, because I'm not sure I want to. You know, dear, you could have brought . . . well . . . you could have brought someone else to this wedding if you wanted to. It seems to me Frank and I aren't suggesting anything so far from the truth. You and Nina are probably as intimate as your father and me."

"The whole thing makes more of a difference than you think, Ma," I said, feeling my life outside this room was very fragile.

A familiar loneliness and despondency were settling over me. The sun was going down and the room was getting darker and chillier. All the afternoons I'd spent here throughout my adolescence, staring at the ceiling, waiting for dinner, imagining a world beyond the suburbs, were sailing out of the nautical wallpaper, called forth by the sound of the radiator pipes banging as the heat came up. I wanted to pick up my bags and make a run for it.

"I can't settle your future for you, George, and I'm not trying to interfere. If you want to be honest, you have to admit I've never interfered in your life very much. Not that I haven't wanted to; I'm too unsure of myself to try, that's all. But right now I'm concerned with getting through tomorrow without turning this wedding into an Irish wake." She came and sat next to me on the bed and combed my hair to one side with her fingers. I was suddenly six years old and going to school for the first time, and completely dependent upon her. "Sometimes I dream you're a baby again, George. I dream you're crying out for me somewhere in the house but I can't find you. Isn't that ridiculous? I have your phone number and your address. I do know where you live. Even so... there's so much distance between us now. I wonder when it really happened that all this distance came between us."

I could have told her the exact moment I thought it happened, but she looked too sad and tired.

"It doesn't look to me like you're going to get married in my lifetime, and I have to at least pretend this is Frank's only wedding. I want it to be something nice for me to remember. You don't have to tell anyone you and Nina are married. Let Frank and me tell them. Just don't contradict us."

"What is Dad going to think about all this?"

She broke into peals of laughter. "You don't think we're going to drag him into this, do you? He wouldn't notice if I were pregnant, let alone Nina."

"Give me few hours to think about it," I said. "I'll talk it over with Nina."

She went to the door trailing the dress behind her. "If you don't go to the wedding, George, there won't be anyone for me to dance with tomorrow."

I sat on the bed looking at nothing in particular for fear of being swept beyond rational thinking by some remnant from my past. The lights in the parking lot behind the house had gone on and the bedroom was flooded with purple fluorescence. I felt like a plant under a grow light.

As usual, my mother was right; on the surface, the lie she and Frank had improvised wasn't such a long way from the life Nina and I were living. They were suggesting we play house for a few hours, which was exactly what we'd been doing for a year and a half. As usual, I was adrift in my own uncertainty and my resolute inability to consider anything beyond my next unemployment check. For weeks I'd been carefully pushing down any thoughts of Paul that crept into my mind for fear of having to face the fact I missed him and longed to see him again. For months I'd been ignoring the fact that in a very short time Nina's delicate condition would result in another living human being, whom I was accepting some degree of responsibility for. What, really, was any more ludicrous about Nina and me dancing across the floor of some suburban function hall with our arms around each other than the two of us dancing across the floor at Miss Reynolds's classes? The difference seemed suddenly insignificant.

I stood up and turned out the light behind my bed. The room was still bright from the glow of the industrial park next door.

NINA and my father were seated on the living-room sofa, pressed uncomfortably into opposite corners as if each were afraid of catching something from the other. My father was telling her about playing the numbers, speculating as to how many times in the past five years he'd bought a lottery ticket. She was listening with her head propped up in her hand and a dim fog over her eyeballs.

"So you figure," my father was saying, "at least two plays every week for, what, fifty-two weeks times five years. And when I say two plays, I'm underestimating for easy figuring."

Nina looked at me hopefully as I walked into the room.

"George!" my father said. "It's good to see you, son." He stood and shook my hand with the familial awkwardness. "We haven't seen you in a while, have we, son?"

"Son" was what my father called me for the first three minutes we were together and kept up the pretense of having something to say to each other. I always felt sad when he called me that. His father, whom he'd worshipped, had called him son until the day he died, and I couldn't help but think the term made him realize what a sham our relationship was compared to his with his father. I was a little shocked by his appearance. He was much thinner than the last time I'd seen him and his complexion was oddly cadaverous, as if he had indeed spent the past fourteen months in the basement. His eyes had the sad, far-off look of someone retreating from the world a step at a time.

"You look a little pale, Dad," I said, holding his hand longer than necessary. "You look tired."

He took his hand from me and sat back down in his corner of the sofa. "I'm tired of losing, son. I haven't had a good win in years now."

The numbers. If anything else ever passed through his mind, it was a mystery to me what it might have been. I sometimes wondered if he had any plans for the money if he did have a big win. Perhaps he'd leave the house in the middle of the night and head for a warmer climate. He might have had his bags packed for the past twenty-five years, for all I knew.

"Why don't we talk about something besides the numbers, Dad?" I said. "Nina's not interested in that."

"George," she said, "please. I am interested. I don't know anything about the lottery."

"He doesn't either," Frank said standing in the doorway from the kitchen. "That's why he keeps losing."

He had his FRANK ceramic mug held in his right hand at an awkward angle. Coffee was spilling onto the floor in little splashes.

"You're dripping, Frankie," I said.

"He doesn't care," my father said. "He's leaving this place tomorrow. He wouldn't care if he burned a hole in the floor."

"He wouldn't notice if I did," Frank said to Nina. "Unless he was down in his apartment and the ceiling fell in on his head."

"At least I didn't lose my head over some girl like he did, right, Nina?"

Nina opened her mouth to say something but my mother came in and cut her off. "He did that thirty years ago and look what it got him." She sat between them on the sofa and patted my father's knee.

"I got what I deserved," my father said. He winked at Nina.

"He got me and Frank," I said.

Nina looked a little battered from the conversation bouncing off her. She was fingering her earring nervously and smiling, but I could tell from the way she was glaring at me, she wanted out of the group therapy session. I tried to think of something to say that wouldn't incite controversy but I kept drawing blanks. Finally Nina resettled herself in her corner and said to my mother, "This is a wonderful sofa, Mrs. Mullen. It's very comfortable."

"Oh, don't say that in front of him—" she pointed to my father— "or he'll never agree to get a new one. And we've had this thing since Kennedy was shot."

"I don't see any reason for a new sofa," my father said. "Do you, Nina?"

"Well, really, I . . ."

"You don't have to answer that, dear," my mother said. "He doesn't know when he's putting someone in an awkward position."

MY mother had set the dining-room table with her best dishes and with silverware I'd never seen before. I really was touched that she'd made such an effort to please Nina even if it was only because she wanted to pretend she was her daughter-in-law. The dining room faced the back of the house and, like my bedroom, was exposed to the hideous parking-lot lights from the industrial complex. Even with the good china, we all looked as if we were eating under the fluorescent tubes at a cafeteria. My parents were seated side by side at one end of the table. There was something in the way they were sitting, separated from the rest of us by the table and linked together by their age and the position of their chairs, that made them appear, for the first time in a long time, oddly compatible and somehow in control of the family.

"Did you tell Mr. Mullen you're a psychiatrist, dear?" my mother asked Nina.

"Technically," I said, "she's not called a psychiatrist."

"Don't be so negative, George, of course she is. Aren't you, Nina?"

"Well, technically, I'm a psychologist," Nina said.

"Oh, well, no one here knows the difference, so why bother to mention it? I'm sure one's as good as the other anyway."

"Well, whatever you are," my father said, "you could probably be kept in business for the rest of your life if you stuck around here."

Nina smiled at him graciously and passed him a bowl of green beans. Frank intercepted. "He doesn't like beans, Nina. No one in the family likes beans except George. Every time George comes home we have to suffer through beans."

"Isn't he terribly abused," my mother said. "I just hope he finds a more attentive servant in Caroline. Of course he won't. Girls today won't let themselves become slaves the way they did in my day. Isn't that right, Nina?"

"Well, I suppose some women still do. It's never appealed to me much. But neither has marriage, to tell you the truth."

There was utter silence. My mother and Frank exchanged glances.

"How's the chicken, Nina?" my mother asked. "Lousy, isn't it? I really overcooked it, as usual."

"The dinner's delicious," she said, even though she hadn't had a chance to eat a forkful.

Of course no one brought up the subject of Nina's pregnancy, and the wedding was mentioned only once when my father asked me what Nina and I were planning to do the next day. "The wedding," Frank said and rolled his eyes.

After dinner my mother set up her Scrabble board at the kitchen table and snared Nina and my father into playing with her. She was an expert at Scrabble and easily beat everyone in the family. Her method was to spend as long as possible staring at the board and then plop down one letter that made three different words and earned her several double- or triple-point scores. She was also a thoroughly convincing bluff when it came to inventing odd-looking three-letter words with no vowels.

Frank and I drove to the discount drugstore near the house to get film for his Polaroid. He cruised up and down the aisles picking up one of virtually every trial-size product in the place. "I need this stuff for the honeymoon," he told me, brandishing the shopping basket in his hand. "Where are you going to find a one-ounce bottle of. . . . What is this? . . . Dex-a-Diet in Barbados? And this is just the kind of thing you want on a trip." He also picked up two cartons of Luckies for his carry-on bag in case the plane was hijacked en route. As we were driving back to the house, he suggested we stop in at Cici's parents' house for a few minutes. "The whole extended family will there, George. It'll be a good trial run for the reception."

I was panic-stricken by the thought.

"I don't think I'm up for that, Frankie," I told him. "It's been a long day."

"Long day, hell, Georgie. You talk like an eighty-year-old."

"It's not fair to leave Nina home alone with the folks."

"Hey, George, you left me alone with them in that house for six years, so she can put up with it for an hour or two."

"I'm not going, Frank. Period." I wasn't about to get hooked into any of his plans before the wedding even began. And the thought of barging in on a crowd of strangers getting their daughter ready to be married off to my brother was more than I could stand. "Plus it's bad luck to see the bride the night before the wedding. It makes the groom impotent for the next nine years."

Fortunately I was behind the wheel so after a few more attempts to convince me foiled, there was nothing Frank could do but sit back and adjust the vent so the heater was blasting in his face. As I drove us through the indistinguishable maze of suburban streets that led to the house, I told him I was worried about our father, about the sunken look that seemed to have taken hold of him. "He's in a fog," I said.

"So, what's new about that?"

"Well, don't you think it's odd?"

"Of course it's odd. He's odd. So are you and so am I. So's Ma, for that matter. Just a bunch of oddballs, that's all. He's no different than he ever was, only more so. Do you ever remember him being very involved in anything other than the numbers? No. So now he lives down in the cellar, that's all. In a lot of ways it's the best place for him."

"Well, don't you think we should do something about it? Try to get him a little more . . . alert?"

"Alert for what? To figure out how unhappy he is? I'll tell you something, George: he and Ma don't see each other enough to really have a bad marriage. You want to upset that balance? I'll give you the whole problem in one word. The word is bachelor. Our father's a bachelor. He never should have married at all because he's a bachelor by nature. God," he said, shuddering, "what if *I* am?" He lit a cigarette from the lighter on the dash. "Cigarettes never taste as good when you light them with one of these things. A match is the only thing to light a cigarette with. Of course, in his day, there was no such thing as a bachelor, just like there was no such thing as divorce. Well, not really, anyway. But our father was a genuine single man. He never should have left the army. He was somebody when he was in the army, and now he's not. He's a just a bachelor with a wife and a family he never knew what to do with. A real duck out of water. It's sad."

He put his feet up on the dashboard and blew a full lung of smoke against the windshield. "What do you think?" he asked me, "You think I'm a bachelor? Maybe this kind of thing is inherited."

I thought about it for a moment and as I was pulling the car into the driveway, I told him that I didn't know. Though it seemed to me he was a lot like my father. He had the same kind of detachment and independence of spirit, and he, too, would probably never be fully involved in raising a family when there were other things on his mind—not the numbers, but cigarettes and coffee and whatever it was he did with computers.

"Never mind," he said, "it probably isn't an inherited trait. You probably have to idolize your father to pick it up. You're not a bachelor, George. I can tell. That's why I think you should just go ahead and get married."

"There are all kinds of marriages," I said, but I doubted he'd know what I was talking about, and I wasn't so sure I did.

BY the time Nina and I had closed the door to my bedroom, she looked as if she'd been doing heavy physical labor for eight hours. She lowered herself onto one of the twin beds, took off a shoe and threw it across the room at me. I ducked and it hit the wall. The ship's lantern lamp shook.

"Do you have any idea what the past several hours have been like for me, George? Every comment has been passed through me or bounced off me or skimmed over me. It's a shame no one in your family ever thought to address anyone else directly. You'd all be amazed at the amount of time you'd save. There are names for this kind of thing, you know."

"I know," I said. "It's awful, isn't it?"

"And don't try to pretend you don't play the same game, because you're as much to blame as everyone else. And that father of yours, Georgie. Now there's a sad case."

"He's all right," I said. "He's just a bachelor, that's all."

She clumsily hoisted one leg over the other and untied her other shoe. She let it drop to the floor with a thud. I pulled down the shade over the window to try and cut out some of the purple fluorescence. "As bad as you think it is, Nina," I said, "you still don't know the half of it."

"The half of what?"

"Frank. Frank doesn't want us to go to the wedding tomorrow."

"What?"

I told her again.

"George, he invited us and sent us money. Of course he wants us to go." As she swung her legs onto the bed, she looked down at herself and sat staring at her belly. Quietly she said, "I did think everyone was being awfully discreet about that. I was beginning to get afraid they thought I was this fat naturally."

I told her what had happened in the first half hour after we'd walked into the house. I told her everything Frank had said and everything my mother had said. I didn't mention what I'd been feeling in the aftermath. She sat listening with her elbow on the top of her stomach and her head held in her hand. "Unwed mother. I knew there'd be trouble," she finally said. She brushed her hair off her forehead. "I knew we should have said something before we got here."

"It's not the unwed mother, it's the homosexual sibling."

"It's probably the combination. So what's the plan?"

"I'm still trying to figure that out."

"Look, I brought some books along and I'm tired anyway and if it will make things easier on everyone, I'll stay home and eat pickles all day."

"Out of the question, Dumpling. It's too insulting to you. And the idea of us going as man and wife is out as well. That's an insult to me."

"The idea of us being a couple?"

"Well, the kind of couple they want us to be, yes. Don't you think so?"

She shrugged and settled back on the pillows. She had on two pairs of thick socks and her feet looked hugely wide. I remembered the first time I'd met her and how impressed I'd been by her clumsy feet. "If you think it's insulting, then it's insulting. I don't know what their intentions are, but if you feel insulted, then that's all that counts. If you decide not to go, then we'll stay home. Or go home. Whatever. It's your family."

It was becoming less and less clear to me who was insulting whom. She turned out the light over her head, got undressed and slipped under the covers. "It's so odd, George, but every time I'm in a house like this, this kind of suburban split-level house, I feel like my entire life and every choice I've made in it is wrong. I feel like I'm some sort of wanton woman. I should warn you I snore. I don't usually admit to it, but I do. Howard used to say it put him to sleep at night."

When she'd fallen soundly asleep I went into Frank's room and confiscated a pack of cigarettes. I never have any desire to smoke except when I'm at my parents' house and prey to high anxiety. If there had been a television in the room I'm sure I would have been glued to the screen all night. I sat up reading *Johnny Tremain* and smoking Luckies. By 3 A.M. I could barely breathe and my eyes felt as if they were about to drop onto the bedspread. I turned out the light and undressed and pulled the crisp sheets up to my nose, listening to Nina's snoring.

It occurred to me then that we could easily be Ozzie and Harriet chastely lying in our separate beds while the kids dozed next door dreaming of the Big Game tomorrow. My lungs were badly bruised from all the tobacco. There was one spot on my left shoulder that itched with a burning, insistent sting. I took the pillow from behind my head and threw it across the room.

It was irrelevant to me whether I went to Frank's wedding or not. As I've mentioned, I don't particularly like weddings, and this one promised nothing more spectacular than the usual necking for applause and gaudy cake-cutting ritual. I really didn't want to go disguised as Frank's perfectly acceptable married older brother about to become a happy father. I'd be hard pressed to come up with a list of accomplishments, deeds, or facts of my life I'm actively proud of, but there's nothing about myself I've ever been ashamed of either. I saw no reason for making excuses now to all my relatives as well as the people I hardly knew whom Cici was bringing along with her into the family. I wasn't even thrilled at the idea of telling the troops that Nina and I were roommates and leaving them to assume what they wanted.

I will admit there have been times when I've felt proud to walk down the street with my arm around Nina, times when I've felt attractive and desirable thanks to her attentions, times when I've glared hostilely at passing men who turn around to admire her from another angle, as if I had some claim on her. But there is a side to our relationship I've always considered fundamentally audacious. And it's this audacious side which, publicly anyway, has always pleased me the most. This fake marriage arrangement we were expected to make was draining the audacity out of our relationship in quarts and replacing it with a respectability I've never strived for or wanted. And somehow, the respectability made the whole relationship seem wrong. "Who's this marriage of yours pleasing?" Paul had asked. Had I thought to invite him to the wedding instead of making a career of avoiding his calls, I might have been able to make a stand for myself and avoid the impending disaster.

Nina rolled over in bed and said, "Stop tossing and try to get some sleep," and then immediately started to snore in a softer pitch.

I got it in my head that Paul was at that very moment lying under his quilt curled against another warm body, probably that of the New Hampshire clothes dryer. All it takes is one sudden rejection to drive a person back into the arms of a former lover. My name had probably been torn from his address book and thrown into the wood stove along with yesterday's newspaper and a bundle of damp kindling. The soft acrylic blanket began to itch me through the clean sheets. I was suffocating from lack of oxygen and unable to consider sleep with all the racket Nina was making in then next bed. I chucked back the covers and wrapped myself in the nautical bedspread and padded down the maze of stairs to the kitchen.

I let Paul's phone ring four times and then I hung up. It was too late at night to call him. It was too late, period. I took a leak and washed my face. I walked to my bedroom, made sure Nina was sleeping soundly and hurried back to the kitchen.

On the ninth ring, Paul picked up.

"I know you're busy right now," I said before he got a chance to say hello, "and you've scratched me off your list anyway, but I just wanted to tell you I'm sorry for being a jerk for the past month and not calling you."

"Busy?" he croaked. "Who the fuck is busy at four in the morning in Vermont unless they're milking cows, George?"

"Thanks for remembering my name," I said. "I don't want to keep you up, Paul—I just wanted to tell you I'm sorry."

"Are you drunk? What are you doing calling me at this hour?" I could tell from the sound of his voice he was waking up quickly. I heard him open up the front of the wood stove and rattle the coals around. "And where have you been for the past month? One argument, one lousy argument, and you do a disappearing act. You can't treat people like that."

"Listen," I said, "you shouldn't get yourself so worked up at this hour or you'll never get back to sleep."

"Who says I want to?"

"I'm sorry. I just wanted to apologize. I was wondering if maybe I could call you in a couple of days and talk a few things over with you?"

"Like what things?"

"I can't get into it now. I just mean a few things. Like the fact that I should have invited you to the wedding after all."

"What wedding? What are you talking about? And don't hang up the phone, I haven't finished yet, and since you're paying for the call I'll gladly stay awake."

He rambled on for the next ten minutes telling me what an inconsiderate person I was and how immature I was being about our relationship and how much Gabriel missed me.

"I miss you, too, Paul. I've missed you since about two days before I left Vermont. I know you probably don't believe that, but it's true."

"Of course I believe it. I want to believe it, so there's no reason I wouldn't." He moved the receiver to his other ear and changed the tone of his voice. "Hey, George," he said, "what are you wearing right now?"

"A bedspread. You wouldn't happen to know if that friend of yours hired a kindergarten teacher yet, would you?"

"No, he hasn't. But he's about to. Why do you ask?"

"Do you think I could call him on Monday?"

"You could call him right now if you wanted to. Just pretend you're calling from another time zone. Tell him you're calling from London."

A few minutes later I was under the blankets on my bed sleeping soundly and probably snoring as loudly as Nina.

26

I woke up three hours later feeling as if I'd just closed my eyes. A suffocating smell of frying bacon was wafting in from the kitchen and a radio was blasting out a weather report that called for snow and sleet and freezing rain. "It's a bad omen," Frank shouted over the noise of the meteorologist.

"It doesn't mean a thing," my mother said. "Your father and I were married on the most beautiful day of summer, so you can never tell."

I could hear the wind moaning as it circled around the buildings in the industrial park behind the house. Nina was still sleeping soundly. Her hair was scattered across her pillow and her eyes were moving back and forth beneath the lids. I wanted to crawl into bed with her, wrap my arms around her stomach and curl against her body. I'd betrayed her a few hours earlier and I expected that once she woke up she'd instinctively know something was amiss. I knelt on the floor by the bed and kissed her cheek. She groaned and turned away from me. I shook her gently until she opened her eyes.

"I can smell breakfast if you're hungry."

"Did you get any sleep, George?"

I told her I'd dropped off like a rock sometime around four-thirty and left it at that.

THE kitchen was in a state of chaos. My mother was standing at the counter trying to stuff everything in the house into the dishwasher. She had on a light blue robe that looked oddly like the dress she'd bought for the wedding. Judging from the stiffness of her hair, she'd probably spent the night sitting up in a chair.

"Leave the dishes," I said. "We can do them for you. You should be getting dressed."

"It's my job to do the dishes and I'll do them," she said. Her voice was on the verge of cracking.

Frank and my mother and father were leaving for the church early to make sure the alcoholic priest wasn't preparing for a funeral instead of a marriage. My mother gave me the keys to her car and told me we had to be at the church by eleven-thirty. She was so caught up in the details of getting ready she seemed to have completely forgotten the controversy of yesterday afternoon. "Now please please please make sure you get there on time," she said. "You know how you love to be late. Make sure he gets you there on time, Nina. Will you promise me that?"

After breakfast, Frank cornered me in the living room. He had on a black tuxedo with a red carnation in the buttonhole and a cigarette dangling from his lips. He looked exactly as I'd imagined he'd look in my airplane fantasy of the wedding. His hair was slicked down flat against his scalp like a shower cap.

"You look great, Frankie," I told him.

He grabbed me by the shoulders with terror in his eyes. "Forget what I said yesterday, George," he gasped, blowing smoke in my face. "I was all keyed up and I didn't know what I was saying. You're my brother and I don't care what they think. You're my only brother and I don't care whether Cici's family approves of you or not. To hell with them. Blood is blood, right? I don't care. It doesn't matter one stinking bit to me."

This sort of emotional outburst was so unexpected, so out of character for Frank, that, coming on top of everything else that had happened in the previous twenty-four hours, I broke down. I threw my arms around him and squeezed him as hard as I could. "Frankie, I hope this is great for you. I hope you have a beautiful marriage and lots of kids and everything else you want."

"I don't want lots of kids, but thanks. It's going to be fine. And if there's ever anything you need, money or help or anything, you know you can count on me. Family's what counts. That's all that counts."

The two of us stood there in the middle of the living room with the wind blowing sharp crystals of sleet against the picture window, filling the room with soft pinging sounds. I felt as if one of us was going off to war and we were saying goodbye, maybe forever. Once we'd pulled ourselves together, Frank lit a cigarette and yanked a handkerchief out of an inside pocket. "So," he said, blowing his nose, "Nina knows what to say today, about the baby and the two of you and everything?"

I looked at him in disbelief. There wasn't a trace of irony in his eyes. Not only had I been duped into believing Frank was becoming a human being, I'd also wasted five minutes of a sort of emotional outburst that came to me all too rarely. "Don't worry about a thing," I said. "I've told her the whole story." And then, as he was walking out of the room, up one of the miniature staircases to the bedrooms, calm and collected, every strand of his hair in place, I said, both because I wanted to hurt him and because it was true, "You know what you look like in that outfit, Frankie? You look like a bachelor. You look like a lifetime bachelor going to his best friend's wedding."

As Frank and my mother and father were leaving the house I took a picture of them with the Polaroid. The three of them are standing on the back walk huddled against each other in the cold wind with their clothes blowing around them. My mother is smiling, hopeful and uneasy, with one hand on the top of her hairdo, looking as if she's afraid it will blow away. Next to her, Frank is yelling at me to hurry up and snap the picture before they all freeze, while my father stands calmly and obliviously staring into the distance as if he's watching an accident in the street. I kept the picture and put it in a plastic frame. It's the only photo I have of Frank's first wedding day.

I sat in the living room in my bathrobe and listened to the wind. Through the picture window I could see the cheap families across the street beginning their Saturdays with their fat, snowsuit-clad kids and their nondescript dogs and their gas-guzzling station wagons. Another pale, discontented weekend just beginning. More gnawing desperate longing for a different life—a lottery ticket and a case of beer and a carton of cigarettes. This was the life Frank and I had been brought up to believe was noble and praiseworthy, moral and blessed. A few years of this earthly misery and then eternal forgiveness and bliss would be ours. I couldn't help but think this was the life Frank was headed for in his marriage, headed for with a blind reckless panic as if he'd be lost and unhappy without at least trying for it. In some ways, in my own way, I suppose I'd been attempting a version of the same thing.

Around ten-thirty Nina came into the living room in the dark red dress she'd bought for our intended Thanksgiving feast. Her hair was pulled back from her face with an intricate network of tiny gray combs and one of the silver earrings I'd bought for her was dangling from her left ear. I gave my usual start of surprise when I saw how lovely she looked, and then, as I sat on the sofa staring at her, I became ineffably sad and tired. I had trouble facing her or thinking about the rest of the day. The confusion of the past several years of my life was catching up with me. I was experiencing one of those moments in which aging catches up with you and overtakes you in a swoop.

"Why do you always wear only one earring?" I asked her, taking her hands in mine.

"Because," she said slowly and suspiciously, "people notice one earring more than they notice two. And why aren't you dressed?"

"I hate weddings," I said. "I hate all that cake and nonsense. It won't matter a bit in the end. When my mother realizes we aren't going to show, she'll make a big to-do over the fact that the woman I came with got sick at the last minute and I unselfishly gave up the honor of attending to take care of my friend. She'll tell everyone how we braved the snowstorm to come to the wedding and were struck down by tragedy in the end. It's my mother's kind of story."

"We came all this way for nothing?"

"It's never for nothing."

She walked away from me and sat in the center of the living room floor with her feet tucked uncomfortably beneath her. "You still think it's an insult for the two of to go as man and wife?"

"Yes."

"I suppose I should, too. I suppose it is, in a way. But why do you think it makes me unhappy to hear you say it?"

"I'm sorry," I said. "I didn't mean to upset you."

"George, you apologize too much. It is just a wedding we're talking about, I suppose. And it's your family, it's your choice."

"These storms blow over quickly in my family." She looked small and childlike in the middle of the rug and I felt a sad responsibility for her. I lay down on the rug and put my head on her thigh. "We've got my mother's car," I said. "I could take you around the town and show you where I grew up." I didn't have any friends from high school I was still in touch with and I had never shared my childhood with any of the people I knew as an adult. "We could go out to the mall and have lunch and then we could catch an afternoon train back to New York, before they come home from the reception."

I put on the hideous suit I'd bought for the wedding and the two of us drove around town leaning against each other in the front seat of my mother's oversized Buick. I took her to the brick monstrosity where I'd suffered through four years of high school, past the house of my best friend in grammar school, to the corner where I'd been in my first car crash. I kept one arm around her shoulder and turned the floating power-steering wheel with the other hand. We went to the shopping mall where I'd spent the better part of my adolescence. It was, as I knew it would be, completely unchanged from the way I remembered it. The artificial lighting, the air temperature, the fake trees in their perpetual springtime bloom were all exactly as they'd been for the past fifteen years. I bought hamburgers and ice-cream sundaes and we ate on a park bench beneath the branches of a plastic weeping willow.

"Do you realize," I said, "this is probably the only place on the face of the earth I'll ever feel a real sense of belonging? It's the only place I'll ever feel at peace with my childhood and my past."

She laughed as if I were joking.

"It's true," I insisted. "I don't really feel at home in the house I grew up in, or in Boston or New York or Brooklyn."

"What about Vermont, George?"

"Not Vermont either," I said, but I wished she hadn't asked in such a cautious tone of voice. "This is the only place."

It was three o'clock by the time we got back to the house and the afternoon was beginning to turn cold. I stealthily packed my copy of *Johnny Tremain* into my duffle bag, as if I were stealing a family treasure. While the cab was honking for us from the street, I scratched a quick note to my mother and taped it to the refrigerator.

"Dear Mom," I wrote, "I'm sorry we missed the ceremony but Nina began to feel sick after breakfast and we thought it would be best to get back to New York so she'd be closer to her doctor. I wish we could have been there. Maybe next time. I hope you got to dance."

We got to the station just as the train was about to leave. I helped Nina up the narrow steps and we sat down and curled against each other with the armrest between us. The heater was broken in our car and the temperature alternated between stifling and frigid, and even though most of the rest of the train was deserted, neither one of us made any effort to get up and move. Nina had a mystery novel and a psychology text with her, but she didn't open either one. We sat in shared silence, lulled and riveted by the dark scenery out the window.

New York seemed days away to me. I wished it was days away. I wasn't ready to get back to the apartment in Brooklyn, to the flowered wallpaper and the smell of burnt coffee, to the clutter and chaos of our life together. I wasn't ready to tell Nina I was moving out after the baby was born. I wasn't ready to tell her I was abandoning our life together. Not abandoning her, but us and the idea of our relationship. I could tell from her silence and the suspicious and sad way she looked at me she could feel me drifting away from her. In Providence we saw the sunset reflected in the windows of the Biltmore Hotel, bright and orange and ominous and sad. When I told Nina I was leaving, I wanted it to be with a note of finality and assurance, but I wanted it to be tender and loving, too.

When the conductor announced a stop in Westerly in three minutes, I grabbed Nina's hand and pulled her to her feet. I yanked our bags down from the rack over our seat and pushed them to the end of the car.

"What are you doing?" she called out.

"Come on, Nina," I said. "I want to get off here. I have this urge to spend the night by the ocean."

"In Westerly?"

"Florence Nightingale's cap is in a museum here. In a glass case. We can make a pilgrimage tomorrow."

"I don't want to do this," she yelled to me. "I have a bad feeling about this."

"Please, Nina. We can get a room in an inn overlooking the water. We're not due back in the city until tomorrow. It'll be our secret stopover."

I chucked the bags out to the ground the second the train stopped, before she had a chance to say no and before I had time to think about what we were doing. We got into a cab and I told the driver to take us to an inn overlooking the water. Someplace where they had central heating and took credit cards.

We got out in front of a big white guest house with the black ocean stretched out behind it like a cold, dark inkwell. The owner of the place was eating dinner in front of a television set in the living room. She had on knee-high woolen stockings and a thick gray cardigan. Grudgingly, it seemed to me, she took us to a chilly room at the back of the house. She pulled open the drapes and turned on a small space heater by the window. "In the summertime," she said, "when you can leave the window open, you can hear the ocean. And if you hit the season right, you can smell roses all night long."

I told her we'd have to plan a return trip for sometime in the summer.

"We don't allow children," she said firmly. "Especially babies."

Once she'd left, the room was filled with silence. The one large bed had a quilted magenta spread and several fluffy white pillows tossed against the headboard. Nina sat in an overstuffed chair by the window and pulled her coat around her shoulders. She put her feet up on the top of the space heater and look at me sadly, wearily.

"What are we doing here, George?" she asked.

I sat on the floor beside her chair and held her hand in silence for a long time. I could hear the ocean through the sealed windows. It still wasn't clear to me what half-baked plan was in the back of my mind when I'd dragged her off the train, and I was growing more and more confused in this sad, cold room.

"We have to talk," I said finally. "There are some things I want to tell you."

"We could have talked on the train."

"I didn't want to tell you on the train. It didn't seem like the right way to talk about this."

"We don't have to talk about it. I know what you want to tell me. I didn't think we came here to see Florence Nightingale's cap. I've probably known all along. I'm glad we tried it for a while." She looked out the window but there was no moon and there was nothing to see. "I guess, in the end, this isn't really what I wanted either. I love you, George. Maybe I love you because I know I can't have you. But maybe I just love you." She smiled at me and I read forgiveness into her look even though it might not have been there. "I'd like you to stay until the baby's born but you know you don't have to. That's part of the agreement."

"I want to, Nina."

She leaned over the side of her chair and kissed me on the lips and her feet fell off the top of the space heater. I pulled her face closer to mine. I put my hands around the back of her neck. Gently I slid the gray combs out of her hair and let it fall down around my fingers.

I took her hands and led her across the room. We stood beside the bed staring at each other cautiously, touching tentatively, knowing that in the morning when we got up everything would have changed between us and we would be farther apart than ever before.

27

On a warm Sunday morning at the end of August I woke with a start before dawn when the bedroom was still fuzzy with gray light and the woods outside the open windows were filled with the thudding sounds of a passing rainstorm soaking the trees. Paul was snoring lightly beside me, his back expanding and sinking beneath the sheets. I'd woken as if a pain had jolted me out of sleep, and even though I did a quick all-systems check and knew my body was in one piece, I was gripped by a vague uneasiness. I quietly rolled out of bed and slipped on a pair of cutoffs and a T-shirt and made myself a cup of instant coffee. I went out to the cement steps at the back of the house and sat just out of reach of the warm drizzle watching the sun come up over the back of the field, sending a thin steaming fog rising from the grass. The field and the woods were overgrown now, unhappily overgrown, burying themselves under the weight of their own lushness. Summer was lingering on too long and exhausting every growing thing. It's the time of year I like the least, the time of year most filled with uncertain expectations and sweltering heat, and there is nothing to do but wait, hopefully, for fall.

I went back into the house to make a pot of real coffee and a couple of fried eggs, and as I opened the refrigerator door sluggishly, I was seized by a violent fit of loneliness. It was the same feeling that had woken me earlier—it hit me with the same jolt, anyway—but now I was alert enough to realize what it was. I missed Nina. The rainstorm had passed and the thudding in the woods had changed to a gentle, insistent drip. It was only a little after six-thirty. The day in front of me seemed endless. I tossed

all my breakfast preparations into the sink and dashed into the
bedroom. The keys to Paul's truck were resting on top of a dish
of loose change. I lifted them up slowly so I wouldn't wake him
and scratched off a note on the inside cover of the book he was
reading. "Paul—I borrowed the truck, hope you don't mind. Just
a ride to get out for a while. I'll be back before midnight. xxx G."
I grabbed a handful of cassette tapes for the drive and filled a
thermos with instant coffee and tap water. On my way out of the
house, Gabriel stuck his head over the edge of his loft. "Where
you going, George?" he asked sleepily.

"I'm going to Brooklyn, Gabie," I said. "Just for a couple of
hours. Don't wait up for me, okay?"

ONCE I got to the highway I put on a pair of round sunglasses and
slipped a Boswell Sisters tape into the cassette player. It was going
to be a bright, hot day. I adjusted the side vent so a steady stream
of air was blowing in against my stomach and my chest. I had the
happy feeling I was playing hookey from my life and my job. I
deserved a break from both.

The school I was helping organize was due to open in September,
but everything there was still unfinished and up in the air. The
spring had been unusually wet and muddy and the main building
was still under construction. Most of us on the staff spent ten and
twelve hours a day at the school helping to pound nails and unload
furniture and cartons of supplies. In between, we met at each
other's houses and argued about the philosophy of the school and
the disciplinary ground rules and the amount of freedom the kids
would be given in choosing what to study. I hadn't taken a day off
since the end of March, but I didn't mind. It was an exciting job,
in many ways more exciting than anything I'd ever done. For the
first time in my life I felt as if I were taking an active part in
creating something of substance. I was an equal among the others
on the staff and not a mere employee. I'd written Nina that my
responsibilities were forcing me to look at the world with less of
an outsider's eyes. She'd written back that I was probably just
getting older and shedding some of the passivity of youth.

I hadn't seen Nina since I moved out in March, three weeks

after Emily was born. I'd left them in a dazed kind of hurry, not really regretting what I was doing, but wanting the deed to be done and completed with a minimum of disturbance and emotional upheaval. Paul had come down in his truck to help me move my pared-down belongings and Nina and I had kissed each other goodbye on the steps outside of the house. I told her I'd call her that night, as soon as I got to Vermont, but I never did. I knew I'd have said "I miss you," which would have sounded too obvious a thing to say to be sincere, and then I'd have asked how Emily was, to which she could have responded "What do you care?" though I knew she wouldn't. Later in the week I wrote her a letter telling her about the mud in Vermont and she'd written back telling me about one of her clients. I wrote her about the school, about the snow melting in the mountains and she'd written about Emily's eating habits and an ERA demonstration she'd taken her to. I wrote her a long, exaggerated letter about the horrors of sharing a bed with someone on a regular basis, even someone I cared for, and she wrote to tell me Howard had started to come by the apartment, at her invitation, sometimes just to cook dinner and spend time with Emily and sometimes to stay over. We wrote each other at least twice a month, but neither one of us called. There were days I longed to hear her voice, but I was always afraid to pick up the phone and dial our old number. I don't know why. I wrote her I'd come down for a visit as soon as I had a break and she promised that she and Howard would bring Emily up one day before the end of summer. Neither of us made any plans. Now as I sped down the highway I realized I never would have made any plans; I'm no good at plans. Only an attack of loneliness and melancholy could get me out of the house.

FOUR hours later I drove onto the Brooklyn-Queens Expressway, a nervous wreck. I was terrified I'd forget the street we'd lived on or I wouldn't recognize the house. I had a paranoid fantasy Emily would take one look at me and start to scream. Maybe I was afraid Nina would do the same thing. As I turned off the highway, I looked at the strange jungle of buildings in amazement; it didn't seem possible I'd ever really lived here.

• • •

OUR street was crowded with noisy teenagers tossing a ball around and blasting their radios. I walked past the house once and then I turned around and walked past more slowly, scrutinizing it from a different angle. The windows on the second story were open and a white curtain was blowing out. The air had a dusty, sulfurous hue I'd never noticed, a polluted yellow tint that made the bricks of the house glow with a rusty sepia light. Resolutely I went up the stoop and rang Nina's bell three times, my heart thumping against my ribs as if I'd just downed a quart of espresso.

A screen slid open next to me and Mrs. Sarni awkwardly stuck her hefty body out the window frame. "You'd better ring again. She probably can't hear you with the baby crying and everything."

I smiled at her and said hello. She peered at me through narrowed eyes. "Come on, Mrs. Sarni," I said. "It's me. It's George." I took off my John Lennon sunglasses.

"Mother of God, George, how do you like that? I didn't even recognize you standing there. You look like a regular hippie."

"My hair's getting a little long," I told her.

"Well, that's the opposite of my son. The last time I saw him he looked like Yul Brynner. Before he died, I mean. By now he could have hair to his knees, for all I know."

I heard someone run down the stairs and fumble with the locks and then the door swung open into the dark, cool hallway. I shoved my hands into my pockets and stepped back. She just stood there silently in the shadowy hall clutching a book in her hands, staring at me uncomprehendingly. She didn't shriek. She had on a pair of jeans and a man's white dress shirt and one of the silver earrings I'd given her. She was thinner than when I'd last seen her and she looked older somehow, as if the shape of her face had changed.

"Well, aren't you two going to say hello?" Mrs. Sarni asked me.

"We will," I said looking at Nina. "Just give us a chance."

Nina came out to the stoop and took my arm and we walked up the dark linoleum-covered staircase. I inhaled the familiar odors of garlic and burnt coffee deep into my lungs, realizing I'd been craving the smell for months.

The living-room windows were open and a noisy, warm breeze

was blowing in, rustling the heavy drapes. I sat down on the cranberry-colored, crushed-velvet sofa and looked around the strange room. The worn furniture and the framed photographs and pictures on the walls looked as if they'd been there for years, even though I myself had helped move them in five months earlier. The new maple table was the only piece of furniture I'd ever used and I was saddened at the sight of it—my only contribution to the place, the only tangible reminder I'd ever lived there.

On the same day that Paul had come to Brooklyn to move my things to Vermont, we'd made five trips to Molly's building to transport her lifetime of belongings to Nina's apartment. The Thanksgiving demonstration had been a failure after all, and her building was being demolished. She needed a place to live and Nina needed a roommate. Nina wanted a mentor and Molly had found a protégée. Emily needed a grandmother.

"Do you like the way the place looks?" Nina asked me apprehensively.

"I'd never recognize it," I said.

"I sold most of the other furniture. I made a grand total of about twenty bucks." She sat down at the table and started to fidget with her bracelets. "It's pretty comfortable, George. I know it must look a lot different to you now."

"Do you use the table much?" I asked her.

She smiled and nodded with what seemed a strange politeness. I shifted my weight on the sofa and sank into the puffy, overstuffed cushions.

We sat and stared at each other silently as the drapes blew in and a slow Spanish song filled the air outside the window. There were sheets on the laundry line, billowing and snapping in the gentle breeze.

"George!" she said finally, smiling at me, "what are you doing here, just showing up like this? Why didn't you call?"

"I wanted to surprise you. I just came down for the afternoon to see Emily and to take you to the beach."

"Take me to the beach?"

"Is Emily asleep?"

"We'd know if she was awake. She's a loud baby. Molly says I should drink more beer while I'm nursing to keep her quiet. She has a lot of competition for attention in this apartment."

"Can we go see her?" I asked.

Howard was sitting against the headboard of Nina's bed tenderly cradling Emily against his chest. He looked up at me as we came into the room and voicelessly shouted out my name, grinning radiantly. He tilted Emily toward me so I could get a better look at her face. He had on an old fashioned sleeveless T-shirt and a pair of dress pants and he was flushed, whether from the heat or from happiness, I couldn't tell.

Nina had written me that Howard and Molly had taken a strong dislike to each other the moment they met. They disagreed on everything and often woke up Emily in the middle of one of their shouting political debates. Nina claimed her relationship with Howard had become more distant and more passionate, like lovers who lived in different cities and saw each other on weekends. Of course he was a self-educated expert on infant care, and Nina often called him for advice when Emily woke up screaming in the middle of the night or refused to eat.

"Howie," I said, laughing quietly, "you look like a real father sitting there holding her."

He shushed me and pointed to the bundle of flesh in his arms. "Isn't she gorgeous, Georgie?" he whispered. "She has all Nina's features, thank God. She's a Munchkin baby. She's a Munchkin!"

He was overcome with tenderness, and he squeezed her against his body in a bear hug. She woke with a little scream.

ON the drive out to Coney Island I stopped and bought a six-pack of dark, heavy beer. The windows in the truck were wide open and Nina's blond hair was blowing across her face as we roared down Ocean Parkway. I played a Glenn Miller tape, and after one slug of beer I felt lightheaded and giddy and comfortable for the first time since I rang Nina's bell. "So," I said raising my bottle, "here's to a quiet baby. Drink up, Nina."

"Aren't we going to say hello to each other first?" she asked me.

I shook my head and laughed at her. "We don't have to. We're beyond all that." I stepped on the gas and ran a red light in honor of the father.

"You should see Howard driving with Emily in the car," Nina said as I carelessly swerved into the right lane. "He drives twenty miles an hour and he swears at every person who has the nerve to pass us."

"Does he still have the Datsun?"

"He had it all fixed up and painted. But he says it still makes him nervous to drive Emily around in an unsturdy Japanese import. He's thinking about getting an old Volvo."

"For the three of you?"

She smiled at me and shrugged. "I'm happy with the way things are right now, George, believe it or not. I'm not sure what's going to happen, but right now I'm content." She pulled her hair off her face and tied a kerchief around her head. "Howard and I don't talk about the future much. I suppose we're both afraid to. I'm afraid he's going to start talking about moving in or getting married, and I imagine he's afraid I'm going to pull back again. Anyway, since Emily was born and you moved out, I haven't really wanted to make many plans. There'll be a showdown someday, I know. There always is."

IN the late afternoon we walked along the beach with our feet in the water and our arms around each other. We were both a little drunk and exhausted from the heat. I had a headache from the long drive.

"Have you met any of your students?" Nina asked me as we sunk our feet into the mud.

"I've met some. They'll probably be the same as the kids at Saint Michael's. I used to think they'd be different, less neurotic, but that was because I thought the parents would be less neurotic."

"And now?"

"And now I've met the parents. Now I know better."

Nina told me her dissertation was almost completed and her adviser had shown it to a publisher who was interested in having her rewrite it for a book. "I don't know, George. I'm not even finished and they want me to rewrite it. Molly thinks it sounds like a good idea. She's all for me becoming a big shot in my field."

"I thought she didn't like psychologists."

"She doesn't, but she likes me. She encourages me when she thinks I really want something even if it offends her politics."

We walked up the boardwalk to where Steeplechase Park had been and where the crumbling remains of the old roller coaster still stood. There were surprisingly few people around and most of the workers in the food stands were leaning against their counters sullenly staring out to the water. It was the end of a hot day at the end of summer and most people were too sick of the sun to bother trudging out to the beach for another layer of sunburn. Fall was coming just in time. Nina put on a huge pair of sunglasses that hid her eyes and her eyebrows and half of her cheeks.

"Do you know what we were doing one year ago at this time?" I asked her.

"One year ago was a long time ago, George."

"You'd just found out you were pregnant. And now Emily's a real person already." She didn't say anything but she looked at me suspiciously.

"I'm so happy to see you again," I said.

"George," she said softly, looking away from me, toward the park. "Are you happy up there in Vermont? I can't be sure from your letters."

She sounded so serious that completely out of the blue I started to laugh. "My mother keeps telling me my biggest problem in life is that I believe I have to find happiness in life to be happy."

"I'm not sure that's an answer."

"I know, Doctor."

I told her I was living quietly and contentedly in Vermont, I was learning a little Spanish, learning to cook, learning something about the stars, I enjoyed waking up next to Paul in the morning and I was watching Gabriel grow. The summer was almost behind up now and the fall would be cool and bright. Did that add up to happiness? I didn't know. Something stuck in my throat when I tried to answer.

"Are you in love, George?"

"In love?" I asked her as if I'd never heard the expression. "I suppose so. But sometimes I think I really don't know. Isn't it possible not to know?" I looked out to the flat bleached sand and beyond into the hazy distance. Huge jets made their approach into JFK in the shimmering heat waves, returning from places I couldn't imagine and would probably never see. "I miss you, Nina," I blurted out, overcome by the sudden silence of the place and the dreamy sight of the planes landing in the distance. "I'm happy and everything's fine, and I can't say I regret moving, and I probably do love Paul, but I miss you."

She took my hand and we walked into the park together.

"Do you think we'll ever be strangers to each other?" I asked her. "Do you think someday I'll come down here to visit you or you'll come up to Vermont and we'll look at each other and we'll be total strangers?"

As we walked to the truck we passed the Octopus, the creeking, twisting green-and-white structure we'd been on months earlier when Nina told me she wanted the two of us to raise the baby together. The flashing neon lights were blinking on and off and the arms were swirling wildly through the air, but there was no one riding on it. The operator was sitting in his booth fiddling with a radio and sucking on a grubby cigarette butt, looking lost and bored. Nina took off her sunglasses and turned to me, and I felt a fleeting moment of our old companionship and an almost painful stab of my affection for her. I knew that we would keep in touch over the years and send each other letters and make visits; I would mail birthday presents to Emily and I'd follow Nina's career; there'd be other days when I'd drive to Brooklyn on a whim, out of the need to see her and go off to the beach with her or to a park or sit in the apartment with her and laugh; and still, we'd grow apart; we would grow older and our faces would change and one day we would be strangers to each other. And there was nothing to do about it.

We walked up to the booth and I took out my wallet and told the operator I wanted two tickets. He eyed Nina up and down with a sunken leer and told us he was having a special that day: free for as long as we could take it.

We got into one of the buckets and slammed the gate shut. Very slowly, the arms lifted up and started to turn, gradually picking up speed and frenzy. The entire amusement park was beneath us in a shadowy, warm blur of colors and smells and indistinct shouts and screams. We hovered above it for an instant and then went swooping down to the ground dangerously. We must have stayed on the thing for twenty minutes, spinning in circles, getting tossed into the air, thrown against each other in a corner of the slick seat by some centrifugal force as inevitable as death and much stronger than love.

ACKNOWLEDGMENT

I'd like to thank Jill Charles, John Nassivera and Gene Sirotof at the Dorset Colony House in Vermont for their generous hospitality, and Stephen Koch for his advice and assistance.

Also by Stephen McCauley and available from Granta Books
www.granta.com

TRUE ENOUGH

Jane Cody keeps lists. After all, how else would she keep track of her life? – her job producing a Boston TV show; her amiable but frankly dull second husband; and her precocious six-year-old son who 'doesn't do small talk' but loves to bake. And as if that weren't enough she has an acid-tongued mother-in-law living in her barn, an arthritic malamute lodger to walk, and a dangerously seductive ex-husband on the scene . . .

'His style reads as if Anne Tyler had been drafted on to the writing team of *Sex and the City*' *Guardian*

'McCauley is a snappy, acerbic, self-conscious satirist. Characters are clearly conceived, captured economically with a single mannerism or phrase. There are deft descriptive touches, a stream of noirish one-liners and a *millefeuille* of snarling East Coast irony' *Observer*

THE EASY WAY OUT

Patrick O'Neill is a travel agent who never goes anywhere. His closest confidante Sharon is chain-smoking her way to singles hell, passing up man after man. His parents, proprietors of a suburban men's store, can't help fighting about how best to interfere in their three sons' lives. And his lover Arthur, whom Patrick can't quite commit to, wants to cement their relationship by buying a house.

Then a call comes in the middle of another sleepless night. Tony, Patrick's straight-as-an-arrow younger brother, has fallen in love with a beautiful lawyer . . . unfortunately, she's not the woman he's already pledged to marry. Tony's life is a mess. Finally, the brothers have something in common.

'Superb' *New York Times Book Review*

'*The Easy Way Out* weaves its way deftly through the tangled web of modern allegiances, heaping irony upon irony, yet never once losing its remarkable generosity of spirit. The people we meet here are as exasperatingly human as our own friends and families. No one tells of the heart quite like Stephen McCauley'
Armistead Maupin